AGGRESSOR

Dean Crawford

Dean Crawford

Also by Dean Crawford:

The Ethan Warner Series
Covenant
Immortal
Apocalypse
The Chimera Secret
The Eternity Project

Atlantia Series
Survivor
Retaliator
Aggressor
Endeavour

Independent novels
Eden
Holo Sapiens
Soul Seekers

Want to receive notification of new releases? Just sign up to Dean Crawford's newsletter via: www.deancrawfordbooks.com

We should have known better.

We know that there are few survivors, few of our kind still clinging to life.

They say that when the end came some embraced it willingly, shrugged off their lives like old skins and allowed the Legion to infiltrate their minds and their bodies and become one with the machine. Most, however, did not. Most fought, and died, trying only to remain who they were.

The Legion, the instrument of the Word, our governing law, took life across all of the colonies. Worlds fell; Ethera, Caneeron, Titas; the mining settlements and the outlying systems and the uncharted clouds of asteroids and meteors beyond consumed by the monstrous and insatiable thirst for knowledge and power that is the currency of the Word. The greatest creation and achievement of our human race turned vengeful deity, the destroyer of worlds.

We now know that there are several forces at work within the Legion, an immeasurable swarm of mechanical devices ranging in size from as big as insects to as small as biological cells. There are the Infectors, the smallest and most dangerous, for it is their mission to infiltrate the optical nerves, the brain stem and the spinal cord of human beings, turning them into mere instruments dancing to the macabre hymn of the Word's destructive passion. Then there are the Swarms, the clouds of tiny but voracious feeders who break down all and any materials into the raw ingredients for more of their kind: metals, plastics, even human tissue, consumed en masse and regurgitated into further countless devices, all of which evolve with startling rapidity as though time were running for them at breakneck speed. Finally, there are the Hunters: bigger than the rest and with only a single purpose – to find and to kill intelligent biological life wherever it is found in the cosmos.

We are the last of our kind, and despite the horrors that we witnessed when we fled the only star system we could call home, we now know that we must return. There is nowhere else to run to, nowhere else to hide, for if we do not make our stand now then we condemn our children or their children after them to face what we could not. We must fight back and step by step, system by system, we must take from the Word that which was ours and liberate ourselves from the living hell that we have created and endured.

The Atlantia, a former fleet frigate turned prison ship, is the last home we have. Our crew is comprised of terrified civilians, dangerous former convicts and a small but fiercely patriotic force of soldiers and fighter pilots for whom there is no further purpose in life other than to fight for every last inch of space between here and home.

Our lives may become the last that will ever be lived, and thus we tell our story in the hope that one day others will read of it and remember our names.

Captain Idris Sansin

Atlantia

1

Dean Crawford

I

'They're coming back again!'

Ishira Morle glanced down at a small monitor embedded in the control panel before her and her skin crawled as she saw something moving against a sprawling backdrop of countless stars, a massive shadowy bulk that loomed ever larger to fill the screen. The cockpit of the freighter was a galaxy of glowing coloured lights and deep shadows that mirrored the endless expanses of space outside.

'Can we outrun them?'

Ishira shook her head as she looked down at her young daughter perched upon the seat next to her, and tried to keep the grinding fear she felt out of her voice as she replied.

'No, we can't honey. We're already at full power.'

The sound of distant alarms echoed into the cockpit from the depths of the ship behind them, wailing through lonely corridors and distant holds devoid of stores. Vapour hissed from damaged pipework where the environmental systems were losing control of the vessel's internal atmosphere, lights from the corridor beyond the cockpit enshrouded in a misty gloom.

The barrage had come from nowhere, an overwhelming salvo of plasma blasts crashing into the ship as it fled through the lonely blackness of deep space.

'What's going to happen to us?'

Ishira gripped the controls tightly in her slim hands, her deeply tanned skin stretched taut across her bones. She was starving, as was her daughter Erin, and the entire ship's compliment were also suffering from malnutrition and dehydration. Disease was beginning to rear its ugly head throughout the ship, a severe shortage of medical supplies compounding the spread of infections.

The deep, inky blackness of space ahead through the viewing panel of the merchant vessel *Valiant* was pierced by the flare of a star unlike any other that Ishira had ever seen. The ship's computer identified the star as a yellow-spectral type of unremarkable mass, but it was the star's metallic content that interested Ishira. The build-up of heavy metals inside the star and of elements like helium and oxygen told her that it was nearing the end of its life, a fact vividly illustrated by the violent halo of ejecta radiating from the star in kaleidoscopic halos of bright blue, green, orange and yellow.

The star was dying and would soon swallow all of its orbiting planets in a fiery oblivion from which there would be no escape. Ishira stared into the star's distant fiery depths, the brilliant flare dimmed by photo-receptive sheilding in the viewing panel, and she knew that her destination lay ahead.

'I know what I'm *not* going to let happen to us,' she replied. 'We're not going to be captured.'

Erin was nine years old, her long straight brown hair parted in the centre and framing an angelic face and big, wide brown eyes that reflected the twinkling lights of the cockpit. Erin, like her mother, had witnessed the apocalypse that had swamped their homeworld of Ethera more than two years ago, had seen countless millions of human beings consumed by the horror of the invasion. She knew well what was behind them, and that their only future lay somewhere ahead.

Valiant had dropped out of super-luminal velocity into the Chiron system, the farthest point they had been able to reach before the ship's internal reserves of hydrogen had been exhausted. The system was virtually uncharted, located as it was on the very outermost boundary of the explored cosmos. Unexplored moons, exotic nebula and high volumes of stellar-radiation and cosmic rays made a beautiful vista a deadly trap for the unwary. Or the desperate.

The sound of running boots echoed down the corridor behind the cockpit and an elderly man burst through the swirling clouds of vapour, his chest heaving and his left arm glistening with moisture and mechanical fluids, the metallic glint of his bionic prosthetic visible beneath the cuffs of his jacket. Stefan Morle, Ishira's father and the ship's engineer, leaned one hand against the frame of the cockpit door and wiped sweat from his brow.

'What's the story?' Ishira demanded of him.

'The engine bays are fine,' Stefan replied, 'but we've lost power conduits and cooling from a third of the ship after that last hit. Another couple of blows and that'll be it.'

Ishira looked down once more at the dark shape in the rear-view monitor pursuing them across the void, and then at a schematic of the attacking vessel. A Veng'en cruiser, a big one too, heavily armed and likely manned by countless warriors hell-bent on spilling the blood of humans. She glanced at her instruments, gauging velocities and trajectories, and then looked over her shoulder at her father.

'Divert all remaining power to the engines. Give her everything we've got. All that's keeping us alive now is our speed.'

Stefan nodded as he looked at Erin. 'How are you holding up?'

Erin smiled, a brave face thinly veiling her fear. 'I'm fine.'

'We can't run forever,' Stefan cautioned his daughter. 'You know that, right?'

Ishira nodded and gave a barely-perceptible nod of her head toward the fearsome star laying directly in their course.

'We won't have to run forever.'

Stefan glanced at the star, and Ishira saw his expression crease a little as he concealed his own fear and pain deep inside.

'Can we reach it before..?'

'We can reach it,' Ishira insisted. 'Maximum orbital velocity and the star's gravity will do the rest. We won't even know what's happened until...'

'No other options?' Stefan persisted.

'Surrender, and...'

Ishira broke off and Stefan nodded. 'I'll switch the power across.'

Stefan turned and hurried away from the cockpit. Erin looked at her mother.

'What are we going to do?'

Ishira smiled at her daughter and gently cupped her jaw in her hand. 'We're going somewhere even the Veng'en will not be able to find us.'

Erin smiled again but somehow Ishira knew that her daughter was not entirely fooled, that even a nine-year old girl could see that their situation was hopeless.

Valiant was a merchant ship that had been in the family for two decades, running the mineral line between distant asteroid clouds, Caneeron, and Ethera, bringing home valuable minerals to industries in the core systems for trade and construction. Barely two hundred fifty cubits long, Valiant and her compliment of twelve miners and crew had been on the outer limits of the Tyberium Fields when the apocalypse had struck and the Legion had overwhelmed mankind.

The distress signals had arrived first, all of them several hours old by the time they had travelled across the Ethera system and reached Valiant. Hundreds of them, thousands, the clamouring of millions of voices crying out in pain and fear and filling the communication channels until, one after the other, they had fallen silent until nothing had remained but the hiss of static.

Ishira had immediately set a course for the inner system despite the protestations of her crew. Ishira's mother was on Ethera, as was her brother. It soon became clear that they could not have survived the calamity.

Nobody aboard was under any doubt that something horrendous had occurred on Ethera, but Ishira knew that Valiant was only equipped and supplied for a three-month mining cruise: if the devastation back home was as bad as the distress signals indicated, they would need supplies before they could flee the system permanently. Thus, she pushed on in both the vain hope that she could re-stock their holds and the even slimmer chance that the rest of their family had somehow made it out alive.

Valiant reached as far as Caneeron before it became clear that they could go no further, the communication channels filled with the digital hymn of the Word's complete control over humanity's technology base. On the way in they had passed a handful of refugee vessels packed with terrified passengers, the last survivors of mankind fleeing their only home.

Ishira had guided Valiant into the docks at Caneeron and together the crew had loaded everything and anything they could aboard her before blasting out of the system with a handful of Colonial cruisers in hot pursuit, their crews entirely consumed or controlled by the Legion. It had taken all of Ishira's skill as a helmsman and all of her wily father's experience as a commander to outwit the Legion and escape into deep space. But with only a small mass-drive to propel *Valiant* toward other star systems, and with only enough supplies aboard to last perhaps a year, it had become a long and lonely journey through a hostile cosmos.

'They're closing on us!'

Erin's panicked voice snapped Ishira out of her reverie and she scanned her instruments once more as she keyed the ship's intercom system.

'Transfer the power now!' she called.

A series of gauges on the cockpit panel before her shifted colour as her father drained power from the shields and other systems, then redirected the supply toward the engines. One thing that Valiant had as an advantage over the lumbering Veng'en cruiser was speed: designed to run the trade routes for maximum profit against minimum time, Valiant's sub-luminal acceleration far outstripped that of the big cruisers.

Her father's voice replied over the intercom.

'That's it, you've got everything, now get us out of here!'

Ishira saw the engine displays register an excess of power and she threw the sub-luminal throttles fully forward. Valiant surged as she accelerated and Ishira felt herself pushed back into her seat as the freighter soared away from the big cruiser.

She scanned her instruments and constantly updated her position in her mind, a natural ability to calculate angles and velocities inherited it seemed from her brother, Carnoy, a recruit in the Colonial Fleet's flight training program who was likely now dead along with several billion other human beings.

'They're falling back,' Erin shouted with delight as she pointed at the rear-view display.

Not for long, Ishira knew. Although slower to accelerate due to their massive size, once fully underway the cruiser would soon begin to overhaul Valiant. And that was exactly what Ishira was counting on as a new plan formed in her mind.

Ishira keyed the intercom again, this time broadcasting to the entire ship.

'All personnel, strap in immediately. Prepare for tactical manoeuvring.'

Stefan reappeared in the cockpit doorway and stared at his daughter. 'What are you going to do?'

'How many planets does this system have, pa?' she asked as she scrolled through the ship's data logs.

'Chiron? I don't know, it's unpopulated because of the dying star. Maybe three or four, several moons I think but it's not a good idea to...'

'Four,' Ishira said as she found the correct entry, 'two of them with breathable atmospheres. One is too close to the parent star, but the other...'

Stefan moved to stand alongside her seat and he frowed heavily.

'You don't know what's out there, Ishira,' he said. 'It won't likely be any safer on one of those planets than it would be to turn back and welcome the Veng'en aboard.'

'You got any better ideas?!' Ishira shot back. 'It's either try to survive or fly this ship straight into the heart of that damned star and...'

Ishira cut herself off as she saw Erin staring at her wide eyed.

'Rock, hard place,' Stefan said. 'How are you going to lose the Veng'en cruiser?'

'I'm not,' Ishira replied. 'I'm going to force them into an overshoot, and then duck back toward the nearest habitable moon and hunker down. The Veng'en cruiser's mass is sufficient enough that it will take them too long to reverse their course and keep track of us.'

Stefan bit his lip as he strapped himself into a seat. 'They'll flip her and fire their engines at maximum thrust to do that,' he said. 'It's a military vessel. They'll be back onto us too quickly.'

'Not if we're close enough to that star,' Ishira said.

Stefan and Erin fell silent.

Ishira knew that the gravitational pull of the star, combined with the Veng'en cruiser's mass, would produce enough force to prevent it from slowing easily, whereas Valiant's nimble hull and powerful engines would quickly propel her on a new course and buy them the time they needed to hide.

'Here we go,' Ishira whispered as the first glowing tendrils and veils of ejected stellar material flashed past Valiant. 'Brace for turbulen...'

The first wave of stellar radiation and billowing solar wind pummelled into Valiant like the blow of a giant hammer and shuddered through her. Giant hull braces groaned and the keel strained as she was flexed by the violent forces acting upon her.

'Point oh-two-four luminal velocity,' Ishira said, trying to keep her voice calm and avoid upsetting Erin.

'Too fast,' Stefan said, 'we won't be able to pull out!'

Ishira did not reply as she gripped the controls more tightly.

Valiant shuddered again as she was pummelled by wave after wave of stellar gases, many of them heated to thousands of degrees as the star cast off its atmosphere in a vast nebula, the solar core growing before them. The star's surface was a blinding mass of boiling solar storms, massive plumes of hydrogen gas soaring billions of cubits above the solar plane and spiralling out into deep space.

Valiant's systems began malfunctioning as the barrage of high-energy particles began breaching her hull plating.

'We're getting too close!' Stefan insisted.

'Stand by,' Ishira said as she prepared to reverse course under maximum thrust.

It was Erin's voice that broke through her concentration.

'Mummy, they're gone!'

Ishira glanced down at the rear view monitor and was shocked to see the Veng'en cruiser falling far behind, a silvery speck now that was already slowing hard as Ishira checked the tactical display.

'They're turning around,' Stefan said in amazement.

Ishira slammed Valiant's manoeuvering thrusters into full power and hauled back on her control column. The freighter gradually flipped over and her engines, still at maximum thrust, directed their energy in the opposite direction as Ishira reversed course. The deceleration once again thrust her back into her seat as she stared at the tactical display.

'They're not just turning around,' she said, 'they're running away.'

The display flickered and distorted and then blinked out as the tremendous energies around the ship interfered with her instruments. Valiant slowed gradually to a stop amid the boiling veils of solar ejecta and then began accelerating back the way she had come. Stefan unstrapped himself from his seat and peered out into the swirling gas clouds. His experienced old eye tracked the diaphanous veils and detected something that Ishira had not.

'There's something out there,' he whispered.

Ishira squinted through the viewing panel. 'I don't see anything.'

A silence descended in the cockpit as the freighter began to accelerate away from the flaring star, the thick veils of gas billowing past outside and shimmering with irridescent colour as though alive. Ishira changed course to avoid the Veng'en cruiser's flightpath.

'Temperature's decreasing,' Ishira reported as she scanned the instruments. 'The hull's holding up and the Veng'en are still fleeing. I'll set a course to stay inside the stellar veil, maybe we can sneak out without being noticed.'

Stefan peered out into the turbulent vista. 'I don't like this. Why did they pull back so suddenly?'

'Maybe they've just given up, got bigger fish to fry.'

Stefan shook his head.

'The Veng'en don't run away from anything and...'

Erin's scream pierced the air as something vast loomed from the gas clouds, a blackness as deep as all eternity. Ishira did not have the chance to even react with the controls when the darkness enveloped the ship and the brilliant nebula surrounding them vanished from sight.

Ishira barely had time to think about the cold dread filling her belly when she felt herself losing consciousness as the cockpit lights around her began blinking out one after the other. Beside her, Erin slumped in her seat. Ishira reached out for her daughter but it was already too late.

As absolute darkness consumed her Ishira felt her hand fall across Erin's shoulders as a fearsome chill enveloped the ship to a noise that reminded Ishira of thin ice cracking, and then she passed out.

***

Dean Crawford

II

The sunlight burned brightly on Ethera, the sea a sparkling blue and the sound of children's laughter filling the air to compete with the cries of grandiose four-winged seabirds wheeling gracefully against a hard blue sky. Grandsons, grand-daughters, nephews, nieces, brothers and sisters. A vivid memory in motion, so close and yet so far, never to be seen again.

Captain Idris Sansin leaned back in the tired leather chair that he had brought with him from Ethera to his final command and stared at the image on the wall of his quarters. One of several dozen arrayed around him, they only moved when he looked at them, sensors embedded within the images detecting the direction of his gaze. The memories of times long past drew his eye away from the cabin's dull grey walls and bulky fittings, the hallmark of a military command, and transported him back to happier times. A bitter-sweet melancholy enveloped him in its sombre embrace, reminding him that even when times were good he had rarely been there to enjoy them, too busy on deployments with the Colonial Fleet. He himself appeared in none of the moving images, separated from his family then as now.

The Atlantia's hull hummed softly around him, the huge frigate's mass-drive in full flow and propelling the vessel at super-luminal velocity across the cosmos. A small data screen embedded in the wall over his desk displayed velocity, bearing and crucial status updates such as fuel-remaining, fighter-wing readiness and ordnance available. Position, also a key issue, was only ever calculated based on the frigate's last-known location: travelling at velocities beyond that of light stripped away all visual information from around the ship, meaning that no crew actually knew *for sure* if the course they had laid out prior to leaping would result in them reaching their destination until the mass-drive was disengaged. That said, no vessel had been more than a couple of planetary diameters off course in decades…

Idris stood from his chair and crossed the cabin, examining the images more closely, listening to the sounds of the past and trying to let them carry him away, however briefly, from the cold comfort of his command.

Since fleeing Ethera some two and a half years ago, free time had become a scarce commodity aboard the Atlantia. Over a thousand personnel were crammed aboard the former prison ship, many of them civilians housed in the sanctuary, a natural-gravity chamber in the heart of the ship filled with forested hills and idyllic valleys that provided a respite from the ship's cramped corridors. Two fighter-wings, several hundred marines and numerous drones, Corsair bombers and all of their combined crews and maintenance teams completed the nightmare of logistics involved in just keeping Atlantia functional.

Only during super-luminal cruise was the ship's compliment stood-down, a brief respite and a preparation for whatever lay ahead when the Atlantia emerged into conventional travel. Yet even in the absence of normal combat operations there was little rest for a captain, especially the last one alive.

Idris glanced down at his desk. A single sheet of slim, clear plastic glowed with administrative tasks that flashed for his attention, a new one added to the list every few minutes. Requests for repairs, promotions, demotions, shortages of materials alerts regarding fuel, food and water, training clearances for the Marines to practice boarding and defending the ship, concerned officers watching over the increasingly restless and fearful civilians in the sanctuary who were being kept in the dark about their destination and disliked everything that they were being forced to endure. Sick-bay was short of medicines, maintenance short of manpower and the Marines short of NCO's and officers to help shoulder the burden of General Bra'hiv's command.

Idris looked up at a steel mirror bolted to one wall. His reflection stared back at him, grey hair and tired eyes, his back still straight and his shoudlers broad but his posture gradually folding beneath the weight of his duties and the fatigue of his years.

A spent force.

Idris would have laid down on his bunk for respite but embedded into the ceiling above it was another data screen identical to the one on his desk, there to update the captain of a military vessel during every single waking hour, minute and second. In time of combat patrols it had been known for some captains to develop the ability to literally sleep with one eye open, certain threatening patterns in the data displays such as flashing red alerts waking them up at a moment's notice, ready for immediate action.

He perched instead on the corner of his desk and pinched the corners of his eyes between finger and thumb. He was deep in thought when a soft, insistent beep infiltrated the privacy of his misery.

'Go ahead,' he said in reply to the beep. The intercom opened a channel and a voice carried through the cabin.

'Cap'n to the bridge.'

'On my way.'

Idris inhaled a deep breath and then walked out of his cabin, the door opening automatically.

The corridor outside bustled with ensigns and officers, all of whom immediately froze and saluted.

'As you were,' Idris snapped as he saluted sharply and strode a few cubits down the corridor to where it opened out onto the bridge entrance and the elevator banks.

He strode toward the bridge doors, the two marine sentries posted there snapping to attention as he passed by and the doors opened.

The Atlantia's bridge was circular in design, mirroring an observation platform above it that allowed a panoramic view of the surrounding cosmos, and was accessed by two flights of stairs flanking the bridge. Arrayed around the edges were various command stations covering all aspects of normal operations, and in the centre was the captain's chair flanked by that of his Executive Officer, Mikhain, and that of the Commander of the Air Group, Andaim Ry'ere. Both men stood to attention; Mikhain the older, shorter and stockier of the two, a veteran of many Colonial fleet actions, and Andaim the image of youth but already an old head on young shoulders, a fighter pilot by training and now commander of the Atlantia's compliment of twenty eight Raython fighter-interceptors and three Corsair bombers.

'At ease,' Idris said to them. 'Status?'

'Super-luminal cruise stable,' Mikhain replied briskly, 'all systems fully operational but we're increasingly low on fuel and supplies. We'll need to drop out of super-luminal within a few hours now, captain.'

'CAG?' Idris asked.

'All fighters fully operational, all crews rested and ready for duty sir,' Andaim replied. 'Two Raythons ready for immediate defensive launch when we drop out of super-luminal. We're planning to reduce training sorties to conserve what fuel we do have.'

Idris nodded, and as he looked at his chair he saw another data-sheet identical to the ones in his cabin, half a dozen more tasks now blinking for his attention. He managed to conceal his irritation as he picked the sheet up and dutifully studied it for a moment.

'Civilian unrest?' he uttered as he read one of the notifications.

'Some of the natives are a bit unhappy down in the garden,' Mikhain replied with scarcely concealed distaste and using a slang name for the sanctuary that suggested nothing but rest for the civilians within. 'We're getting complaints about the working hours down there, managing the solar farms.'

'They'd rather we all starve to death?'

'There are a few vocal members clamouring for a say in what's happening with the Atlantia. Since Counsellor Dhalere died, they haven't got anybody to speak for them.'

Idris sighed and nodded. Dhalere had been infected by the Word and had died as a result, her bloodstream infested with countless tiny machines controlling her every movement, her every action. The Legion. By the time her affliction was realised it was too late and the resulting fight for control of *Atlantia* had almost ended their battle for survival once and for all.

'There are rumours,' Andaim added. 'They've heard we're pursuing a Veng'en ship and they're not happy about that. Having a Veng'en living down there in the sanctuary doesn't help much.'

'It'll do their zenophobia good,' Idris replied. 'And military matters are not their concern.'

'We can't keep them in the dark forever,' Mikhain pressed. 'I don't like it, but right now I reckon keeping them informed of the situation might keep them contained. The last thing we need on our hands right now is an insurrection aboard ship.'

The Veng'en, a war-like race, had fought many long wars with humanity over the centuries, but the devastating effects of the Word's destruction of mankind had overflowed into their own territories and now they sought out humans and murdered them wherever they could be found. In a near-fatal encounter, the crew of the Atlantia had managed to form a tenuous bond with the crew of a Veng'en cruiser and now, in the hopes of forming a stronger alliance with the Veng'en at large, Idris had ordered the Atlantia to follow the Veng'en home at a safe distance. It was an unpopular decision and Idris knew it, but he had a slight advantage in having a Veng'en ally aboard, Kordaz, who had seen through prejudice and realised that, no matter what had gone before, Idris Sansin and his crew sought to right the wrongs of the past and destroy the Word, whatever it took.

'The people cannot rise against us,' Idris replied, 'because even if they did they would have nowhere new to run, nothing new that they could bring to the table.'

'A lot of people don't always think before they act,' Mikhain replied with a tight smile. 'That's *our* job.'

Idris nodded.

'Okay, increase the sentries around the sanctuary but do it quietly,' he replied. 'I don't want the people thinking we're deploying martial law. Send a few of General Bra'hiv's Marines to act as eyes and ears down there and let us know what's going on?'

'Captain?' Idris turned to see the ship's communications officer, Lael, gesture to the main display panel. 'The Veng'en cruiser has dropped out of super-luminal and her course has changed.'

'Already?' Mikhain asked. 'We're nowhere near their homeworld, Wraiythe.'

Idris turned to look at the main viewing panel. Entirely black during super-luminal cruise, overlaid on that featureless canvass was a limited stream of information drawn from the gravitational trail of the Veng'en cruiser they were tailing. The mass-drives that powered large vessels such as Atlantia at super-luminal velocity left a wake in space-time, much like a sailing ship through water. The subtle frequencies of the wake revealed information about the craft that had left it: velocity, heading and hull mass. The captain's experienced eyes scanned the data, seeking information about when the cruiser had ceased super-luminal flight, usually revealed by a "back-wash" in the frequency of the wake as the craft's deceleration produced a new signal that radiated back down its path of flight at an equal velocity.

'It pulled out a few hours ago,' he said. 'Where is she now?'

Lael glanced down at her instruments as she replied.

'The estimated coordinates suggest she's in the Chiron system.'

Idris looked at Andaim, who spoke for the first time.

'Chiron's an outlying world,' he said, 'right out beyond the frontier of human exploration. Not much there because the system's parent star is dying and consuming the inner, habitable planets.'

'He's right,' Mikhain said as he examined a display console. 'Several planets, three of them gas giants, two smaller terrestrial worlds. One of the smaller planets has likely already succumbed to the parent star, the other won't be far behind.' The XO frowned as he scrolled down his screen. 'Unexplored mostly, but the system's on colonial records as being a brigand lair.'

Idris raised an eyebrow. 'Criminals?'

'The system's so far from Ethera and the local group of planets that it was apparently used by anybody fleeing justice as a haven,' Andaim said. 'Chiron's planets are rich in minerals, but the distance was too great for merchant vessels to make much profit from trade routes and the dying star flares violently enough to dissuade pilots from heading there.'

'Except those who don't wish to be found,' Idris murmured. 'But why would the Veng'en stop there?'

'Maybe they're low on supplies too,' Mikhain hazarded.

'Or maybe they've realised we're following them,' Andaim countered. 'We can't be sure they'll offer any quarter. They still don't trust us.'

Idris stared at the data on the screen as he weighed the pros and cons of the Atlantia's predicament, and then he made his decision.

'We too are running low on supplies. Prepare the fighter screen for launch and bring us out of super-luminal on the edge of the system. If any unlicensed armed craft approach us without making contact first, blow them to hell.'

***

III

'They're not going to like this.'

Lieutenant C'rairn strode down a corridor toward the sanctuary, flanked by two non-commisioned officers and trailed by a dozen armed Marines of Bravo Company. Civilian contractors and petty officers leaped out of their way and pressed their backs to the walls to let the heavily armed troops through, their boots rumbling against the deck plating.

'Ain't for them to choose what they like.'

To C'rairn's right walked Qayin, a six-foot-five giant of a man with alternating gold and blue locks that hung to his shoulders in tight braids and flickering bioluminescent tattoos that glowed like rivers of magma against his bitumous skin. Recently promoted to the rank of sergeant in the wake of the battle against the Veng'en cruiser, he bore his shoulder insignia with the same brash disinterest as the facial tattoos signifying gang-kills on the mean streets of Ethera. *The Mark of Qayin*. Like all of Bravo Company's Marines, Qayin was a former convict who had once been a prisoner aboard Atlantia Five, the high-security wing towed behind Atlantia years' before. Now, those former murderers, gang-bangers and drug-dealers made up one half of Atlantia's infantry defence. The other half consisted of Alpha Company, made up of career Colonial Marines and led by General Bra'hiv.

As the Marines reached the sanctuary deck, more civilians watched them with suspicious expressions as they passed.

'They're afraid,' the lieutenant observed under his breath, 'of us.'

'They're supposed to be,' Qayin replied. 'You don't get control without discipline.'

'You don't get help without respect.'

'Respect has many forms,' Qayin grinned tightly, his massive hands cradling a plasma-rifle as he looked down at C'rairn. 'Don't much matter if it's love or fear.'

C'rairn did not reply as they halted at the entrance.

The sanctuary was a cylindrical sub-hull buried deep inside Atlantia that rotated to provide a natural gravity, rather than the quasi-gravity created by the powerful magnetic plating beneath Atlantia's decks that pulled down on the iron inserts fitted to the crew's uniforms.

'Two at a time,' Lieutenant C'rairn ordered them. 'Captain's orders are clear: observe, don't provoke anybody, see what you can learn. Talk to the people, okay?'

The Marines nodded as one, most of them probably keen just to get into the sanctuary and away from Atlantia's drab, cramped corridors.

'Remember to re-weight your fatigues to zero before you enter the sanctuary,' C'rairn reminded them. 'I don't what any of you landing in a crumpled heap, unable to stand up.'

C'rairn turned to the sanctuary entrance and hit a button. A shaft door opened, some three feet square and leading into a steeply declined chute made of a flexible, metallic material.

Because the sanctuary rotated within the Atlantia's hull to create normal gravity, it was not possible to simply "walk" in. Instead, the flexible chute allowed access, dropping the entrant into the sanctuary via the gravity it created through centrifugal motion, the chute attached to it via disc-seals and bearings that allowed it to move freely as the sanctuary rotated. A similar system allowed crew members to exit the sanctuary at the opposite end.

Two Marines stepped forward and jumped into the chute one after the other with a six second interval - enough for the first to land and get out of the way before the next Marine landed on top of him. Each soldier removed his magnetic armour and dumped it in a steel bin beside the entrance before pulling themselves into the chute and vanishing as they accelerated away.

Qayin hauled himself inside the chute, his broad shoulders barely fitting as he dove in, and the tug of the sanctuary accelerated him gradually until he was flying down the chute. A waft of cool, clean air breathed across him, as fresh as heaven after weeks of heat and the stale odours of Atlantia, and then he flew out into mid-air and landed on a soft, deep pile of freshly cut grass. Bright, warm sunlight shone down on him and he squinted as he rolled to one side and landed smoothly on his feet, then stood up and sucked in a lungful of the clean air.

The sanctuary was a vast valley, its immense scope partly an illusion created by powerful screens that cast a vivid, bright blue sky overhead and a distant ocean stretching to infinity in the distance. Behind Qayin, a waterfall crashed into a cool lagoon from cliffs that marked one end of the sanctuary's cylindrical shape, the other somewhere out across the distant ocean. Steep hills to one side and vast blue sky above completed the illusion of a Utopian paradise far removed from the cold, lonely vacuum of space outside the Atlantia.

Created as a reminder of home for crews serving aboard the prison-ship, the sanctuary now represented the only remaining part of home that was still populated by human beings. Most survivors of the apocalypse knew that in reality their homeworld was long gone, now the lair of the Word and its Legion.

Qayin watched as the last of the Marines landed in the sanctuary and gathered around Lieutenant C'rairn.

'You all know what we're looking for,' he told them. 'Rumours, evidence of conspiracy, any hint of discord among the civilians. No sudden moves though, okay? Let's get the people to talk to us instead of barging into their homes and making them hate us.'

As they turned to leave a second platoon of Marines approached them, led by General Abrahim Bra'hiv, a squat and powerfully built man with shaved steel-grey hair and cold blue eyes. Alpha Company had been sent in to patrol first, easing the civilians into the idea of having soldiers in the sanctuary before letting Bravo's former convicts wander about. The Marines of Bravo Company snapped to attention as Lieutenant C'rairn saluted.

'At ease,' Bra'hiv growled, his voice as rough as sandpaper.

'Anything we should know about?' C'rairn asked.

'They're as tight as a clam's ass,' Bra'hiv replied in typical fashion. 'Nobody's talking to us and they're already suspicious of the patrols. Seems like they now consider the sanctuary their personal home and us as intruders.'

'We don't have time for this, baby-sitting civilians when there's proper training to be done,' C'rairn agreed.

'Captain's orders,' Bra'hiv replied. 'May not like 'em but we've got to carry them out.'

Qayin was paired-off with a younger, junior-ranked soldier named Soltin, a wiry street-youth whose neck was laced with cheap tattoos mostly hidden by the collar of his fatigues. Qayin led the way, striking out across a grassy knoll that led down toward dense forest within which countless tiny homes were scattered.

The path ahead wound through a deep gulley lined with trees that climbed steep hills to either side of them. Qayin knew from much-cherished time spent down here for Rest & Recuperation that the gulley opened out onto an area of farmland that in turn met the "shore" of the ocean, no doubt where many of the oft-complaining civilians spent much of their idle time seeking new things to moan about.

Qayin's eye drifted upward and he watched the trees above. Steep hills gave access to the tops of trees further down, and as he scanned the higher branches he saw birds nesting deep inside the leafy canopy. A few species native to Ethera had been carried aboard, adding to the illusion of being home instead of on duty aboard the old prison ship.

The path opened out onto a gathering of compact homesteads and instantly Qayin's instincts were tugged as he saw sharp gazes directed at him. A few of the menfolk exchanges glances and it was as if an unseen switch had been flipped. One man turned and walked into the nearest homestead as the others shifted position, continuing with their chores but placing themselves between Qayin and the homestead that the lone man had vanished into. At the same time three women began walking toward Qayin, awkward smiles on their faces.

'Welcome,' one of them greeted him with a grin so forced it seemed she was trying to bend an iron bar with her lips. 'How are you?'

Qayin smiled back as he towered over her.

'I'm very well indeed, thank you,' he replied in a delightfully pleasant accent. 'Now, what are you all hiding?'

The woman's smile slipped as shadows passed behind her eyes.

'We're not hiding anything,' she insisted. 'We're just trying to make a living. Please, won't you come inside for a drink?'

The woman gestured to one of the other homesteads and Qayin grinned again.

'I'd love a drink,' he said. 'Let's go into that home there.'

He pointed to the homestead and the women shook their heads. 'Oh no, that one's being renovated and fumigated. Infestation of skin-ticks, very nasty and...'

Qayin walked past the women and made for the homestead, Soltin jerking into motion alongside him.

'Whatchya doin'?' he asked.

'Stay sharp,' Qayin snapped.

The three men ahead of them looked up and immediately began moving to intercept the Marines. One of them, a bulky looking man with a thick beard, pointed one thick arm at Qayin.

'You ain't welcome here!'

Qayin did not slow down until he was within six cubits of the three men, all of whom were armed with crude weapons such as pitch forks and other gardening implements. As per strict rules, nobody but Colonial Officers and Marines could bear arms aboard the Atlantia.

'Just 'cause I ain't welcome doesn't mean I can't be here,' Qayin replied. 'What's in the homestead?'

'Nothing of your business,' the bearded man replied.

'Everythin' aboard ship is our business,' Qayin replied. 'I don't want to force my way in, but if I have to I will.'

'Likewise,' the bearded man replied, 'I don't want to have to stop you.'

He gripped his fork tighter in his hands, and Qayin flicked the power switch on his plasma rifle. The magazine hummed into life.

'Your fork against my rifle,' Qayin grinned. 'Fancy your odds?'

'You ain't got no right!' the bearded man growled. 'You're all just murderers, not soldiers. You can't tell us what to do.'

'I can,' Qayin replied, 'but I'm not. I'm askin'. What's in the homestead? Your women said it was an infestation of bindweed.'

The bearded man nodded. 'That's right.'

'Actually, they said it was skin-ticks,' Qayin replied, his smile vanished now. 'What's in there?'

'You can't go in.'

'I can, and I am,' Qayin said as he marched forward.

'Stay where you are!'

The man who had vanished inside the homestead burst out, a plasma rifle cradled in his grasp that he powered up and aimed at Qayin.

'Weapon!' Qayin roared.

Soltin dove for cover as Qayin leaped in the opposite direction, the two Marines instantly creating two targets instead of one and forcing their attacker to choose. Qayin hit the ground and rolled as he aimed back at the farmer. 'Drop the rifle!'

The farmer fired, two shots ripping across the open space between Qayin and his assailant and blasting the ground where he had just stood. The fearsome rounds of super-heated blue-white plasma incinerated the earth and started small fires in the grass.

'Don't shoot!' Qayin yelled at Soltin.

His command was too late, drowned out as Soltin fired and hit the farmer straight in the chest, his plasma round blazing straight through the man's rib-cage in a flare of blue smoke. The man toppled backwards onto the ground, the rifle falling from his grasp as the women behind Qayin screamed in horror.

'Stand down!' Qayin yelled as he scrambled to his feet and dashed toward the fallen man's body.

Even before he reached the farmer's side Qayin knew that the man was dead, a smouldering black cavity of cauterised flesh the size of two bunched fists hollowed out where his heart should have been. He cursed and then looked up ahead at the darkened maw of the homestead.

Qayin aimed his rifle into the darkness and advanced. To his credit, he heard Soltin silently move into position behind him without orders, covering Qayin as he entered the homestead. Despite Soltin's returning fire, the fact was the farmer had fired first. Repercussions, if there were any, would come later.

The interior was dark and Qayin hesitated in the doorway as his eyes adjusted to the gloom. He could hear the women outside huddled around the farmer's dead body, their sobs haunting the homestead as Qayin moved forward, but the building itself was silent.

A simple living room extended into three bedrooms, the home a single-story with a bath stall attached to the rear. Even here, in the sanctuary, there was little room for luxury and most of the accommodations were sparse and functional in their dÃ©cor. On first sight everything appeared normal, but it was not the sight of the interior that bothered Qayin. It was the smell.

Death had an odour and Qayin knew it well, the rank, stale aroma of flesh in a state of decay. Qayin, one finger resting on the trigger of his plasma rifle, advanced toward a corridor at the back of the living room that led to the bedrooms.

A soft gurgling sound attracted his attention and he turned into the second room and froze in the doorway.

A single mattress contained a man's body, limbs trembling and twitching as though live current were surging through his veins. Sickly, pale foam trickled from his lips and stained the mattress beside his head, and his eyes were wide and feverish as they stared at the ceiling above him.

Worse, the man's naked body was laced with a miasma of thick purple lines that criss-crossed his skin as though his veins had burrowed out of his flesh to envelop him like writhing snakes.

'What's going on?' Soltin called from behind him.

'Big trouble,' Qayin replied. 'That's what.'

***

IV

'Almost a thousand tonnes. Not a bad catch.'

Captain Taron Forge fell rather than sat into his chair in the cockpit, casting a practised eye over the instruments as he pulled off leather gloves and let them hang in mid-air. The nebula outside the cockpit shimmered and glowed as the spacecraft accelerated through it and turned away from the star's powerful, flaring surface.

The *Phoenix* was not a large spacecraft, powered by twin engines mounted on strakes either side of a bulky, long-nosed hull, but what she lacked in size she more than made up for in manoeuvrability and durability. Capable of both atmospheric and space flight, super-luminal velocity and heavily armed, the merchant ship had long ago ceased to be the benign haulage craft she had been laid down as.

Taron did not like the term "pirate". He preferred to be known as a freestyle businessman.

The broad, wedge-shaped cockpit looked out over the dense starfields as Taron's co-pilot, Yo'Ki Yan, guided the Phoenix toward the habitable planetary orbits. A diminutive woman with long black hair pinned back in a pony tail and exotic, dark and slanted eyes against olive skin, Yo'Ki's small stature belied her lethal nature. Taron's partner in crime for many years now after he had liberated her from a slave-market way out beyond the Icari Line, she was a skilled pilot and a talented killer, when the need arose. She conveyed her displeasure with a sideways glance at him.

'What? So she's a civilian vessel. We've done worse, right?'

One of Yo'Ki's perfect eyebrows lifted a little higher.

'Okay, so maybe we haven't,' Taron muttered and waved away the air between them. 'Times are harsh and pickings are slim. You think we should let them go or something?'

Yo'Ki simply stared ahead out of the viewing panel.

'I didn't think so,' Taron replied. 'We gotta eat, right?'

A soft sigh and a shake of Yo'Ki's head that rippled her glossy black pony-tail.

'Oh, so now we're starving ourselves to death?' Taron asked her. 'Why not save ourselves all this trouble and just fly to Ethera and hand ourselves over to the Legion? What about fuel? What about repairs to the Phoenix?'

Yo'Ki's sculptured lips formed a slight smile as she rolled her eyes.

'Yeah, yeah,' Taron uttered. 'Space is littered with parts and debris now. Just that little matter of finding what we need among all the junk before we end up floating across the cosmos for all eternity. You got any better ideas on how to make a living out here, I'm all ears.'

Yo'Ki's slim hand reached out for the cable jettison switches on a panel above her head.

'Don't you dare touch that!'

Taron's hand moved faster as he blocked her access to the switches. He glared at her and noticed her little shoulders shaking and her black hair shimmering as she chuckled to herself in silence.

'Very funny,' Taron grumbled as he re-took his seat. 'I wonder how much I'd get for a talented comedienne on Chiron these days?'

Yo'Ki's plasma pistol was in her hand in a flash and aimed right at Taron's face, rock steady and with two dark eyes blazing behind it.

'What? Lost that sense of humour already?' Taron mocked with a wry smile.

Yo'Ki glared at him for a moment longer, and then the pistol was spun through her fingers and vanished back into the holster on her belt as she turned back to guiding the Phoenix through the vastness of space.

Taron continued to smile to himself as he glanced down at a monitor that displayed an image of the mining craft being towed behind the Phoenix. The data Taron had collected suggested her holds were empty and she was low on fuel and supplies, but the ship still had value, as did her crew.

'I'm going to check on the cargo,' Taron said as he stood up. 'You stay here and keep the joy alive.'

Taron strode out of the cockpit down a narrow corridor into an austere circular living space. Beyond were other passages leading to cabins, engine room and gun turrets, of which there were four mounted fore and aft, above and below to deter attacks from unknown vessels.

Taron passed a steel mirror on his way to the observation room and caught a glimpse of his reflection as he did so. He was tall, with rangy limbs and tousled brown hair, his father's features ever present in his own like a ghost that refused to let him be. The rugged, loose-fitting spacer's clothes that he wore broke the illusion, far removed from the stiff Colonial uniform of his father.

Taron reached the observation platform, little more than a ladder really that accessed a small bubble projecting from the upper surface of the Phoenix's hull. Taron turned as he saw his ship's surface, and then looked behind. There, tethered securely, was the slender freighter and behind it the brilliantly flaring star receding into the distance.

Scanners had detected a dozen or so human beings aboard and she looked like one of many merchant ships plying the trade routes around the Tiberium Fields. Or at least there had been, until the Word and its Legion scattered humanity from the core systems out toward the Icari Line and beyond.

Around the cockpit of the captured freighter was a shimmering field of energy, as though the ship had been caught inside some kind of net and trapped there. Taron knew nothing of where the energy field originated, other than him winning it from a drunk Caneerian rogue two years previously during a Voltan match. The Caneerian had protested the next day with considerable violence, claiming that as he had been drunk he could not have played well enough and demanding a rematch. When Taron refused, the Caneerian had drawn his weapon.

Taron had drawn faster.

The energy field possessed a remarkable property: placed within reasonable range of biological life, it sent that life into a sort of comatose state. It worked on all life forms that Taron had tried it on, and that was many in the past couple of years as he had captured vessels and plundered their wares. Something to with the frequency of brain waves, or so he and Yo'Ki assumed, it also shut down low-voltage electrical systems. A carefully kept secret, it had made him one of the most successful brigands yet to curse the trade routes and one of the most wanted. That was until nobody cared about anything other than their own survival after the Etherean apocalypse that had claimed so many lives. So much for human ingenuity, he figured.

The energy field was constructed by an unknown race, and recovered from an unknown location. Its original owner, before his unfortunate demise, had claimed he had no idea where the thing came from, a claim that Taron believed. The Icari Line, which held back all military and law-abiding civilian craft, presented no such barrier for the brigands, corsairs and escaped felons and convicts fleeing the core systems. Racing out into the unknown void, they had encountered things that could not even adequately be described using words alone. Many had barely survived long enough to describe their astonishing experiences. Nobody knew what else lay out there, beyond the charted systems.

A speaker down below beeped softly.

Taron turned and saw a small planet in the distance, a bright speck moving against the infinite stars. He descended back into the ship and made his way back to the cockpit as Yo'Ki worked the Phoenix's controls, slowing her toward orbital velocity as the planet grew larger before them.

'Sending identification signal,' Taron said as he flipped a switch.

A pulsed light beam emitted a flickering signal toward the planet's surface, which was in turn detected by receivers planet-side. A few moments passed and then a signal was picked up by the Phoenix's sensors in reply. Taron scanned it and then took the controls from Yo'Ki.

'Okay, let's see how much they'll take for her.'

Taron manoeuvered the Phoenix into position, the planet Chiron looming to fill the viewing panel as against its churning oceans a bright metallic speck appeared, rocketing up toward them.

It took several minutes for the advancing shuttle craft to reach orbital altitude and perform the delicate process of docking with the Phoenix, but Taron was waiting at the hull ports as the seals activated and the docking lights changed from red to green. Yo'Ki waited alongside him, both of them armed.

'Stay sharp,' Taron said as he hit the docking port access panel and the shield doors hissed open, a brief cloud of vapour tumbling from them as the two vessel's internal atmospheres equalised.

Five figures emerged from the vapour through the narrow docking port, four of them lithe and well-armed, one in the centre portly and squat. Slick black hair, squinting eyes and oily skin reflected the ship's internal lights as the man surveyed Taron and Yo'Ki.

'Taron, my boy,' the man greeted him. 'Once again you exceed my expectations.'

'Salim Phaeon,' Taron replied coolly. 'How much for the freighter?'

Salim chuckled, the laughs shaking his belly and rippling the jewels on his garishly coloured long coat.

'Down to business already, Taron?' Salim asked. 'And how are you, my beauty?' he asked Yo'Ki. 'Have you thought any more about my proposal? We have wonderful living standards on Chiron and you will be well cared for, especially by me.'

Yo'Ki did not move as though her entire body were cast in stone. The silence drew out and Salim's gracious smile withered.

'How much?' Taron repeated.

Salim sighed, as though finally accepting that they would not be sitting down to discuss old times over a drink and cakes.

'Taron, you push too hard. You need to relax a little. Negotiations like this should not be rushed, they require delicacy and tact and…'

'Fifty thousand,' Taron said.

Salim's eyes widened. 'I'd have sold my own mother for less.'

'That says more about your mother than the mining ship. Take it or leave it.'

'For that piece of old junk?' Salim growled. 'How many bodies on board?'

'Twelve, all alive,' Taron replied. 'They're an additional thousand apiece.'

Salim's eyes narrowed, a cruel gleam twinkling deep inside them.

'Perhaps I should ask you to pay *me* sixty-two thousand in return for not blowing your ship to hell.'

The four men flanking Salim activated their plasma rifles, the magazines humming into life.

Taron grinned. 'All talk, Salim, no action. Look behind you on the wall.'

Salim turned. Either side of the hatch were two plasma charges, each with a flashing red light. The oily man turned back to see Yo'Ki with a detonator in her hand, her expression still completely unreadable.

'You think your boys will shoot us both and grab that detonator before they get sucked out of here with you, Salim?' Taron asked.

Salim glared at Taron for a moment longer and then he burst out laughing, his great belly rippling as he shook his head.

'I wouldn't have expected anything less from you, Taron,' he chuckled. 'Forty thousand for the ship and its crew. No more.'

'Fifty.'

'Forty five and we're done.'

Taron weighed up the price in his mind. 'All in advance, all in minerals.'

Salim inclined his head. 'Then we're done. My men will present you with the minerals, then collect the vessel and transport her to the surface. Can I extend my hospitality to you and your beautiful consort?'

'She's not a consort,' Taron replied. 'Annoy her too much and she might blow that detonator just for the hell of it.'

Salim gave Yo'Ki a nervous glance and then forced a smile through it. 'Of course, although I'm surprised at you Taron. I thought you liked my girls and their… offerings. Come down, stay a while. You might find you like it.'

'People to see, places to go, Salim,' Taron replied. 'I'll see you next time we pick up anything of interest, agreed?'

Salim attempted to hide the scowl that shadowed his features as he cast a longing glance at Yo'Ki, barely managing to keep the awkward grin on his face.

'As you wish, captain,' he purred and then clicked his fingers. 'The merchandise, now!'

His men deactivated their weapons and scurried back through the docking port to carry out his orders.

'You can put the detonator away now, my dear,' Salim said to Yo'Ki. 'Our business is done and we can be civil with each other.'

Yo'Ki did not move.

'She doesn't like slavers,' Taron informed Salim. 'You know that.'

'I am not a slaver,' Salim replied as his lips formed a smile, 'more a humble foreman.'

Salim's men returned, each with a bulky metallic chest that had no magnetic alignment, enabling them to push them through the air before them. They positioned the chests well inside the Phoenix and then backed away, their hands back on their weapons.

Taron pulled a scanner from his pocket and passed it over the two chests. A long silence drew out until he was satisfied that both chests were filled with minerals and neither contained explosive devices.

'Normal procedure,' Taron said. 'Seal the port, and then we'll un-dock and release the freighter to you.'

Salim bowed graciously as he backed away but his eyes never left theirs.

'Of course, and I extend my thanks to you for this new acquisition and its unexpected bonus aboard.'

Taron frowned. 'What bonus?'

'The crew,' Salim smiled. 'You did not know that there is a woman and a young girl aboard?'

Taron felt a pulse of shame as beside him Yo'Ki raised the detonator in her hand. Salim's men's weapons snapped up to point at her.

But Salim simply grinned.

'Destroy us and you'll doom the woman and child too,' he replied. 'You'll have sixty seconds to leave before I have my men blow the Phoenix into ashes.'

Salim slipped through the docking hatch, and moments later the hatch hissed shut. Yo'Ki lowered the detonator in her hand as Taron deactivated the charges. He turned as he heard a dull thud and saw Yo'Ki thump the wall of the corridor.

'There's nothing we can do,' Taron said. 'Our scanners aren't powerful enough to determine everything about the people aboard that ship.'

Yo'Ki glared sideways at Taron.

'What the hell do you want me to do about it?' Taron asked. 'Cut them loose? Salim will have his gunners tracking our every move, we wouldn't even get a shot off. I'm sure they'll be just fine, okay?'

Yo'Ki stared at him for a moment longer and then she whirled and stormed away in disgust.

'Women,' Taron uttered under his breath as he followed her. 'Can't live with 'em, can't shoot 'em. What can you do?'

***

Dean Crawford

V

'How the hell did this happen?'

Idris Sansin stood on the command platform of Atlantia's bridge as General Bra'hiv completed his report, the Marine standing erect and with his chin held high as he spoke.

'There was nothing that Sergeant Qayin could have done, sir,' the general explained. 'The civilian opened fire and the sergeant's subordinate returned that fire in the heat of the moment in self-defence. I would be extremely reluctant to reprimand him considering the circumstances.'

Idris nodded, his brow deeply furrowed.

'The civilian should never have been armed in the first place,' he replied. 'Do we have any idea where he got his rifle from?'

'It was an older design, obsolete by military standards. It's likely he smuggled it aboard when we abandoned our prison orbit two years ago. There could be others, captain. I'd recommend a thorough search of the entire sanctuary to root out any contraband weapons.'

'I'd concur with that,' Mikhain, the Executive Officer, added. 'The civilians are restless, especially now that one of their own has been gunned down by our Marines, and men of Bravo Company for that matter.'

'Bravo Company are well trained soldiers,' Bra'hiv snapped back at the XO, 'as much Marines as Alpha Company.'

'That's not how the civilians see it,' Mikhain retorted. 'They see murderers and thugs dressed up as soldiers and let loose to wander the ship.'

'The civilians can see what they damned well like! As long as they're opening fire on my men they'll get what they deserve and...'

'The civilians are ruffled enough without door-to-door searches,' Idris cut across the two officers. 'They already feel abandoned and alienated. I'm not about to turn their homes over because one farmer decided his right to privacy overruled our right to patrol this ship.'

Mikhain inclined his head but his tone was not conciliatory.

'So you would advocate us letting them self-rule, or carry concealed weapons, ready to use the moment they decide our security personnel have crossed a line?'

'I would advocate earning their trust back,' Idris replied. 'Force has already been shown, lethal force. Right now, asking questions will get us further than tearing down doors.'

'Such as what the hell were they hiding in that homestead?' Mikhain suggested. 'Why haven't we been informed of what the general's Marines found in there? Why keep us in the dark?'

The XO's accusing glare was directed at General Bra'hiv, but it was the captain who replied.

'I'll inform everybody, once I have all the facts.' A soft beep alerted the captain and he strode across to his chair where a flashing light called for his attention. He pressed the light. 'Sansin.'

Idris, it's Meyanna. Can you come down to sick-bay for a moment? There's something here I want you to see.'

Idris deactivated the console and turned to Mikhain. 'XO, you have the bridge. Alert me as soon as we're ready to drop out of super-luminal into the Chiron system. General Bra'hiv, keep your men on watch outside the sanctuary only for now. It'll give the civilians time to adjust to what's happened.'

'And formulate further discord?' the general pressed. 'We should be watching them at all times, remind them of who's in control here before they take up arms against us!'

'Yeah,' Mikhain snorted, 'a bunch of farmers with pitch forks against your Marines. That'd suit you just right, eh general?'

Bra'hiv scowled at the XO, his fists clenched like balls of rock by his sides.

'That's enough,' the captain snapped. 'General, if you will?'

With a last glare at the XO, Bra'hiv spun on his heel and stormed off the bridge. The captain turned and peered at Mikhain as he passed by.

'Tow the line,' he growled.

Mikhain nodded as Idris walked past him and off the bridge.

The journey down to the sick bay took only a couple of minutes, the bay located conveniently close to the bridge where most of the senior officers' quarters and stations could be found. Idris walked into the sick-bay where two dozen beds lined dull grey walls to see Meyanna Sansin, his wife, treating numerous patients for sickness and injuries sustained during the ordinary working life of the ship. Although they had not seen combat for many weeks, Atlantia's compliment of well over a thousand passengers, service personnel and maintenance crew ensured that somebody, somewhere aboard always needed attention.

Meyanna turned to him as he walked in, and although her long brown hair and bright smile looked perfect to a bystander he could immediately sense in her expression that something was wrong.

'Thanks for coming down,' she said as she stood from treating a burn on the arm of a crew chief from down in the landing bays.

'For you, anything but I don't have long,' Idris said, playing along with her attempt at concealing the import of whatever it was she was hiding. 'What's up?'

'This way,' she beckoned for him to follow.

The sick-bay was arranged into four wards separated by thin, portable panels, and beyond the wards was Meyanna's laboratory, a sealed section of the bay behind fixed transparent walls where she could work as ship's physician without fear of contaminating the nearby wards.

Idris followed her inside the laboratory which she sealed behind them. Meyanna touched a control on a wall-panel and the transparent walls turned opaque.

The laboratory had taken on a new role in the aftermath of humanity's fall, chiefly that of studying their most implacable foe, the Legion. In the wake of a battle aboard the merchant vessel *Sylph* one of Atlantia's most trusted officers, Evelyn, had recovered a single Hunter, one of several types of tiny robotic machines employed in their billions by the Word in order to kill or convert humans to its cause.

He glanced across the laboratory to where a magnetic chamber contained a black metallic device the size of a human eyeball. Like a writhing insect suspended helpless in the web of some unseen spider, the Hunter was entrapped within magnetic fields generated by the chamber, forced to hover in mid-air where it could not attack anything. Equipped with razor-sharp mandibles and programmed to destroy anything human, Hunters were lethal if allowed to propagate.

'Have you learned anything about the victim found in the sanctuary?'

'Yes,' Meyanna said, 'he's presenting entirely new symptoms.'

'The Legion?' Idris asked.

'No,' Meyanna said. 'There has been no new outbreak. This is something else.'

'Disease then?'

'Worse, I'm afraid,' Meyanna said as she stepped across to a privacy rail and pulled back the curtain.

Idris turned and saw a man strapped to a bed and wearing only his underclothes. His wrists and his ankles were restrained by leather straps, his torso likewise pinned in place to minimize his movements as he writhed. His skin was sheened with sweat, his hair matted and his eyes wide with a volatile mixture of pain, anger and desperation. Worse, his veins were discoloured across his entire body as though his skin were laced with dark vines.

Idris stepped closer to the man and saw white foam frothing from his mouth, a plastic wedge gripped between his teeth.

'What happened to him?' he asked.

'It's not what happened to him that's the problem,' Meyanna replied. 'It's what he did to himself. I tested his blood, and he's full of Devlamine.'

Idris felt as though his heart missed a beat. Devlamine, the *Devil's Drink*.

The drug Devlamine was a crystal, a volatile mixture of chemicals that had been the staple of violent street gangs since long before the apocalypse. The spawn of an exotic carnivorous flower found in the deep tropical forests of Ethera's equatorial belt, the crystals formed over many years and then were deposited by the flower to draw in prey, usually insectoids and small mammals, by essentially making addicts of them over time, the animal trails they created moving to and from the flower drawing in yet more creatures that then also became addicts. Eventually, one after the other, their addiction became so acute that they climbed up into the flower and were thus consumed.

Cultivated by organised criminal gangs and exported across Ethera and the core systems, Devlamine had become the scourge of society and ultimately the drug that the Legion had first used as a carrier to infect mankind. In its normal form it provoked a sense of euphoria that was so powerful it literally caused users to lose hours or even days of their lives while comatose in a blissful Utopian dreamworld, far from the horrors of reality around them. Grieving relatives saw lost ones again, terminally ill patients ended their lives in serene delight, and reckless youths seeking the next illegal high sent themselves into an oblivion of ecstacy, often never to return.

It was said, by some, that it was the Legion's ability to manipulate the drug in which it had hidden that caused the destruction of mankind to be so complete: the Infectors that infiltrated the minds of addicts did not initially directly control their host: the supply of the drug did, hijacked by the tiny Infectors infesting their brain stems to deliver the Devlamine precisely when and where it was needed to ensure compliance, and withdrawn when that obedience was challenged.

'How far gone is he?' Idris asked.

'Hard to say,' Meyanna replied. 'But I'd say he's at least a couple of months in, maybe a little more. Maybe he lost his supply or it was stolen, but he crashed real quick. My response team got him out quickly and quietly, but word of the shooting spread fast.'

'Too fast,' the captain agreed. 'The people with whom this man shared his home kept his affliction quiet while they tried to treat him, so nobody in the sanctuary actually knows why that farmer was shot. An outbreak of

Devlamine withdrawal will be seen as a weakness on our part for allowing the drug aboard ship and a threat to the civilians themselves. The last thing I want is them marching on the bridge again.'

'They need to see direction,' Meyanna replied, 'but they also need to know that they're part of the group. They feel isolated down there and regularly complain that they don't know what's going on. Maybe informing them of everything would help the situation?'

'And give the people distributing this disgusting cocktail the chance to hide their supply?' Idris challenged. 'Not a chance. They need to be controlled. We need to stamp down on this fast.'

'Controlled, stamp,' Meyanna echoed his words, 'you see how you're bludgeoning them to conform to what you think you need? The majority of the civilians will still be clean. You need to trust that they have enough eyes and ears to find out who's doing this for you, not lock them in their homes.'

Idris exhaled noisily.

'I don't have the luxury of letting them find out in their own good time who's behind this,' he replied. 'If they'd been able to achieve that they'd have done it already. What if the drug makes its way into the military population? Keep this to yourself for as long as you can,' he insisted. 'I'll re-task the Marines to start rooting out who's behind this as best they can.'

'Where the hell did it come from?' Meyanna asked. 'We had no drugs aboard ship before the apocalypse other than those used for medical purposes. I couldn't have concoted Devlamine in here if I'd wanted to.'

'I don't know,' Idris replied as he cast the dying man one last glance. 'Will he make it?'

'If he doesn't get a hit of Devlamine in the next few hours?' Meyanna asked. 'No, he'll be dead.'

Sansin thought hard for a moment, but his train of thought was interrupted as a tannoy announcement echoed through the ship.

'All personnel, sub-luminal velocity deceleration in ten minutes.'

'We're coming up on a habitable system,' Idris said. 'There may be supplies but the Veng'en cruiser we're following may also be waiting for us, I have to go.'

'Get to the bottom of this man's addiction,' Meyanna insisted as the captain turned to leave. 'If we have an outbreak of drug abuse aboard ship, what cohesion remains among the ship's company will be lost forever.'

***

Dean Crawford

VI

Ishira awoke to the touch of cold air upon her skin and a feint sliver of light suspended before her in the darkness. She shifted position and immediately realised that her wrists were bound behind her back and that her shoulder hurt where it was pressed against a thin foam sheet on the cold floor.

'Erin?'

Ishira scrambled to her feet in the darkness, her first thought for her daughter's safety. The empty tone of her voice told her that she was in a bare cell and exposed to the open air that she could smell drifting in through the narrow gap ahead. Ishira staggered forward in the darkness, her legs weak and her head groggy as she peered through the gap in a pair of heavy doors and out into the world beyond.

The smell of sea salt and the whisper of waves crashing somewhere far away below her drifted across her senses, and she realised that she was suspended hundreds of feet in the air above the turbulent surface of an ocean. She looked down and her balance wavered as she saw that her tiny prison was swaying back and forth, giving her vertiginous glances of the precarious drop. Waves thundered against a rocky cliff-face far below, churned white and grey as a brisk gale whipped the ocean into a frenzy.

'Erin!?'

Her voice sounded small and she realised that nobody would be able to hear her above the roar of the seas below. She cried out again anyway, calling for her daughter, and almost fell over as the tiny prison jerked upward and swayed dangerously as it began to climb. Ishira dropped onto one knee, nausea from the movement and darkness swimming in her belly as the cell rose up, the sound of some kind of mechanical winch hauling it and then swinging it away from the cliff's edge.

Ishira groaned as the nausea intensified, but then the cell thumped down with a metallic clang onto solid ground and her senses returned to normal as a dull crunch was followed by the doors to her cell being swung open as brilliant sunlight blazed inside.

As she struggled to her feet a giant hand grabbed her upper arm and yanked her out of the cell. Ishira stumbled out into the bright sunlight, squinting as she tried to focus on her surroundings.

She was standing upon a rocky cliff-top that stretched as far as she could see in either direction across the shore of a vast ocean that sparkled like liquid gold in the sunlight. The sun in the sky was bloated, radiating immense veils of glowing gas that were visible even against the pale blue heavens above, and those skies rippled and shone with glowing aurora that flowed like gigantic rivers of light through the heavens.

She turned and saw large, rusting cranes mounted upon the cliff's edge, and below them ranks of metal cells like the one she had been incarcerated inside, dangling from hooks that were attached to precariously thin metal wires stretched taut between bracing towers erected at key points along the cliff.

'My daughter, Erin,' she gasped as she turned to the man who had liberated her.

A huge, muscular creature leered down at her with wide dim-witted eyes, a drooling mouth spilling copious volumes of saliva down a threadbare vest. An Ogrin, a feeble-minded race often enslaved by unscrupulous traders and brigands.

The back of the Ogrin's enormous hand smashed into her chest and propelled her backwards into the ground. Ishira cried out as she slammed onto the rocky earth, and immediately other hands lifted her up again. Ishira realised that she was one of dozens of captives being picked out of their hanging cells along the cliff by dozens of Ogrin who shoved and cajoled them into lines.

'Don't aggravate them,' an electronically-translated voice cautioned her. 'They're ordered to throw into the sea anybody who disobeys them more than once.'

Ishira looked into the eyes of a Caneerian miner, human but his skin touched with the faint blue tint that all Caneerians had evolved, the legacy of generations of evolution causing blood to flow more thinly near the skin on Caneeron's icy veld. Far away from his cold, distant homeworld, like many who had never left before he spoke only his native tongue rather than Etherean. Bulky and muscular but also appearing tired and lethargic, his gravelly voice whispered to her.

'Face the front, stay in line. You'll survive longer that way.'

'My daughter, Erin,' Ishira whispered. 'Have you seen her?'

The Caneerian shook his head and said nothing as the Ogrin lined them up and linked their manacles together with strong wire cord before their leader, a creature even bigger than the rest, yanked the front of the cord and the prisoners were hauled into motion behind him.

Ishira tried to quell the fear for Erin poisoning her guts as she made an effort to start thinking. She took in the ocean again and noticed for the first time the immense thunderheads far out across the horizon, flickering with distant storms of unimaginable ferocity. A brief glance at the dying star dominating the sky and she realised that the planet itself was also in its death throes.

'The oceans are starting to evaporate,' the Caneerian said, noticing her gaze. 'The heat and vapour cause giant storms, and the aurora up there are visible day and night.'

Ishira glanced up at the glowing auroral veils, the result of energetic particles from the dying star hammering into Chiron's magnetic field.

'How long?' she asked.

'A few weeks at best,' the miner replied. 'The magnetic field won't last much longer, and once it's gone those cosmic rays will hit the surface and all life will be extinguished. Including us.'

Caneerians were not known for their inate optimism, probably a result of living on a cold and lonely planet of ice that endured storms that could last for weeks. Caneerian miners were even less jovial, due to spending most of their working lives beneath the surface of Caneeron and thus not even enjoying the modest sunshine the world had to offer.

'I don't intend to be here to find out,' she replied.

The miner gave a snort.

'You won't be with that attitude,' he informed her. 'You won't survive the night.'

'Who owns this place? Who's in charge?'

'You'll see soon enough,' the Caneerian replied.

'What's your name?'

'Who cares? We're all doomed anyway and...'

'Then I'd like to know who I'm doomed with, okay?'

The Caneerian peered over his shoulder at her and then shrugged his big shoulders. 'Dantin.'

'Ishira, pleased to meet you.'

'Sorry it's not under better circumstances.'

'Me too.'

The Ogrin led them between two peaks on the headland, following a meandering path between barren expanses of hardy grass and gnarled, twisted trees long dead. As they crested a rise that descended on the other side of the headland between the two peaks, a vast valley revealed itself. Watercourses flowed down from distant highlands toward a river system that swept in from the mainland and wound its way toward the ocean somewhere far to Ishira's right. Huge sprawling plains of vividly coloured foliage swept into the distance, nature's elegant touch colouring the wilderness even as mankind's rough caress destroyed it.

But it was the gigantic object set in the heart of the valley that took Ishira's breath away.

A vast space cruiser lay in dock alongside the river, supported by immense beams and cradles and tended by hundreds of men and machines. To Ishira's practiced eye the ship looked Colonial, of an older model, her slab-sided fuselage and stubby engine nacelles reminiscent of the *golden age* of space travel when just being functional was enough, architectural aesthetics left to artists and dreamers. The vessel towered high above the swarm of slaves labouring around her, her upper hull partially obscured by low cloud drifting through the turbulent sky and the tiny specks of Chiron's birdlife wheeling and turning as though flocking to the side of giant cliffs, their hawkish cries distant and muted by height.

Around the cruiser was arrayed a flotilla of docked spacecraft. Ishira counted at least fifty of them, of varying types and origins and ages. She felt her heart leap as she recognised *Valiant* docked alongside a boarding platform.

'That's my ship!'

The Ogrin glared at her as they lumbered alongside the prisoners, and Dantin shook his head.

'It *was* your ship,' he replied. 'Now, it's theirs.'

The Caneerian nodded toward a towering scaffold set against one of the peaks, banners flying from its heights as though it were some kind of palatial residence. The odd contrast of make-shift metal and colourful exuberance bothered Ishira immensely as they were led by the Ogrin beneath the massive bow of the grounded Colonial frigate, showers of sparks raining down around them from high above as slaves worked on repairing huge hull panels and giant power conduits.

Ishira saw sitting among the colourful scaffolds ranks of men, all of them watching the arriving prisoners with satisfied grins on their faces and large tankards in their hands. Clouds of smoke drifted from pipes and root tobaccos, the men variously lounging on casually arranged beds or leaning against pillars and surveying the miserable horde as it approached.

The lead Ogrin stopped at the foot of the scaffolds, the seemingly tiny wire cord held in one giant fist, and looked up at the watching men.

'Your subjects, my lords,' he intoned in a voice so deep it sounded as though the earth had moved beneath them.

One of the men, a tall and wiry man with deeply tanned features and long black hair tied behind his head, stepped forward. A colourful trench coat billowed in the wind as he tossed something down that wriggled and screeched as it tumbled toward the giant Ogrin below him, and the creature caught it in mid-air and hungrily gobbled whatever it was to the sound of a wet crunch.

'Chironian spice rat,' Dantin explained. 'They've got the Ogrin well and truly addicted to them.'

'That thing was a drug?' Ishira asked.

'Kind of, it's full of sweet juice from the trees that it lives on here. It eats the fruits like a parasite, more than enough to go around. They're lethal to humans, but these Ogrin can't get enough of them.'

Ishira narrowed her eyes as she stared at the men gathered above them. 'How come the Ogrin don't just get it themselves?'

'Because access to it is tightly controlled,' Dantin smiled tightly, 'and the Ogrin were never very good at handling plasma rifles. They're totally at the mercy of these men.'

Ishira looked up at the men and as she did so they parted and another joined them from within the scaffolds. He was squat, his long, thick black hair pulled back from oily olive-coloured skin and pinned in braids down his back. Oddly effeminate make-up adorned his eyes, contrasting sharply with his thick and hairy forearms as he strode out to survey the new arrivals. A cold gleam in his eye told Ishira everything that she needed to know even before his voice broke out over the captives.

'Welcome to Chiron!' he boomed jovially. 'You may thank us later for liberating you from the grasp of the Legion and bringing you here to our lair. Your lives are now saved, and they belong to us.'

Ishira couldn't help herself. She strode out of line and glared up at the squat man.

'Who are you, where is my family what the hell are you doing with my ship?'

A few captives working nearby drew a sharp intake of breath and for a moment it seemed as though the wind stopped blowing as the squat man stared down at Ishira. Then, a ripple of chuckles fluttered among the men behind him and a grim smile curled from his lips like a snake basking in the sun.

'My my,' he intoned, 'where are your manners, my dear?'

'Give me a plasma pistol and I'll show you where I'll shove my manners.'

The men behind the squat man burst out laughing. Their leader continued to smile but his voice crackled with restraint.

'My name is Salim Phaeon,' he replied. 'Your daughter is safe, as is your father. As for your ship, well, we promise to take good care of it now that it's ours.'

Ishira strained against her manacles as she tried to walk closer to Salim.

'Like hell it is,' she spat.

An Ogrin's massive hand clamped onto her shoulder and drove her to her knees with such force that she thought she would be buried up to her neck, pinning her down. She kept glaring at Salim as he stepped down from his platform and strode to stand before her.

'Then welcome to hell,' he smiled without warmth.

In the distance Ishira could see Valiant, her hull gleaming in the brilliant sunshine as cloud shadows drifted across the landscape around them.

'A fine craft,' Salim observed. 'Perfect for what we have in mind.'

'She's *mine*,' Ishira hissed.

Salim stepped to her and tutted as he rolled his eyes in a parody of concern. 'You really must understand, my young friend, that you do not own anything. You, all of you, are now mine and any resistance will result in consequences, you understand?'

Ishira strained against the Ogrin's grasp.

'Drop dead,' she spat.

Salim lifted one podgy hand and clicked his fingers.

Up on the scaffolds the lounging men parted as two women in garish, revealing clothes that showed more flesh than they covered walked out, swaying their hips in a seductive manner with a smaller, similarly dressed woman pinned between them. Ishira gasped as she saw Erin, her hair brushed out and her soft skin covered in make-up as though she were some kind of living doll, her expression confused and apprehensive.

'For our entertainment,' Salim said by way of an explanation.

Ishira yanked her head to one side and sank her teeth into the Orgi's hand on her shoulder as though she hadn't eaten for a month. The giant gaoler screamed and tore his hand away and Ishira leaped up like a coiled spring at Salim. Her body rocketed toward his as she jerked her head back and smashed her forehead against the pirate's nose.

Salim's nasal cartilage collapsed with a dull crunch as the wire restraint brought Ishira up short in time to see Salim stumble backwards and collapse onto the ground, his face a bloodied mess. A rush of gasps and whispers fluttered across the prisoners as the pirates up on the scaffolds whipped pistols and rifles up to point at Ishira, plasma magazines humming into life.

The Ogrin's giant, bloodied hand smashed across Ishira's chest and hurled her to the ground as Salim, his eyes blackened with rage, hauled himself to his feet and drew a long, curved blade from his belt as he glared down at her.

'You will learn your place,' he sneered, 'or others will suffer!'

Salim turned and the curved blade flickered in the sunlight as he threw it. The blade flashed through the air and thumped into the chest of a skinny looking man with thin, grey hair and a pallid expression. The blade buried itself to the hilt in the man's scrawny chest and he stared down at it with an expression of bewilderment.

'No!'

Ishira's cry rang out as she watched the man's legs crumple beneath him as he collapsed, his eyes rolling up in their sockets as his heart bled out inside his chest.

'This is what will happen,' Salim roared, wiping blood from his face, 'upon every act of insubordination. This is how we punish those who oppose us! Those closest to you will take the punishment, and that punishment shall be death! Get them to work!'

Salim's last was directed at the Ogrin, who jerked the prisoners into line and forced them to march toward the towering bulk of the cruiser nearby.

Dantin hauled Ishira up to her feet, his features stormy with anger as nearby the dead man was cut from the line.

'Now do you understand?!' he hissed. 'Stay quiet, before you get anybody else killed!'

Ishira turned as she saw an Ogrin drag the dead man's body away by the ankle and hurl him over the edge of the cliffs. High on the scaffold she saw Erin led out of sight by the pirate's consorts, her features twisted with despair.

***

Dean Crawford

VII

The scramble claxon burst through the field of Evelyn's awareness like a hammer through glass, shattering the blissful oblivion of sleep as a bright, unwelcome light flickered into life above her head.

A data panel mounted scant inches from her face revealed a scramble order, flashing red as a priority command from Atlantia's bridge. Evelyn groaned and dragged one hand across her eyes in an attempt to wipe the sleep from them. She rolled over, and in the dim light she reached down and pulled from beneath her pillow a small cache of what looked like miniature stones wrapped in a clear gel. Carefully, she reached into the gel and broke the seal. A rich, thick fluid seeped out as Evelyn sucked it from the gel and let it settle under her tongue.

For a moment nothing happened as the fluid was absorbed into her body, and then suddenly the lethargy and the weariness faded away like a dream interrupted. Evelyn flopped onto her back for a moment, staring up at the flashing red icon on the screen as she felt the drug hit her bloodstream and begin powering through her nervous system, and then she reached out without looking and hit a switch on the wall of her bed.

The side of her bed slid automatically open to reveal a tiny living space. A pair of long, slender legs, the skin tinted a pale blue, landed alongside Evelyn's bed as her room-mate Teera dropped from the bunk above and turned to look down at her, all bright eyes and excitement as she pointed at the small cabin's data screen.

'Scramble Alpha Flight, that's us!'

Evelyn ran a hand through her hair as she rolled out of the bunk and stood up, one hand reaching out without thought for the flight suit hanging ready on the wall.

'I'm on it,' she yawned.

Evelyn hauled on her flight suit and caught the flask of energy-fluid that Teera tossed her as she quickly dressed, the two women moving about each other in the tiny cabin with well-practiced precision.

'Didn't you get any sleep?' Teera asked.

'Do I look that bad?' Evelyn replied as she glanced in the steel mirror on the wall and saw her bleary-eyed countenance peering back at her. The effects of the Devlamine were starting to blow away the cobwebs of sleep, a distant supernova light glowing ever stronger somewhere deep in her tired eyes.

'We always look good Eve,' Teera soothed, 'you're just less good today than normal.'

Evelyn zipped up her flight suit and yanked on her boots as she drained half of the energy-drink and tossed it back to Teera.

'Let's get out of here.'

Teera led the way as they exited their cabin and jogged down the corridor outside, the usually bustling passageways more quiet than normal as the crew got their heads down during the long-range cruise. The captain's brief had been that Atlantia had sufficient reserves for a four-day super-luminal leap, and with two days still remaining that meant something had come up.

Even as they jogged, a tannoy broadcast an emergency alert claxon and the voice of the ship's Executive Officer snapped and echoed through the ship.

'All stations, alert-four, alert-four.'

A minor alert level then, Evelyn recalled. Something in the path of the ship or an un-planned emergence into sub-luminal cruise.

'Maybe the Veng'en cruiser's stopped off somewhere?' Teera called over her shoulder as she ran. 'It'd be great to get some real fresh air!'

'Don't get your hopes up,' Evelyn replied. 'Pretty much every planet I've landed on so far has been more dangerous than staying aboard ship.'

Teera laughed Evelyn's warning off. Teera was younger than Evelyn by several years, with short-cropped blonde hair and bright blue eyes that matched her skin: the pale blue tint that mimicked the bloodless skin of Caneerians was a legacy of being the fifth generation of humans brought up on Oraz, a moon that orbited the blue star Rigelle in an outlying system. Despite Teera's youth she had earned her wings and joined *Reaper* Squadron a short time before Evelyn, and had built up a small but impressive tally of combat victories.

They jogged together out onto Atlantia's flight deck, where two sleek Raython fighters were mounted side-by-side on powerful magnetic catapults that ran from the for'ard bay toward huge launch doors that were currently closed. Technicians swarmed over the two fighters, cables snaking from internal circuitry and the fighters' ion engines glowing blue as their internals were kept spun-up for a swift emergency launch known as Quick Reaction Alert, or QRA.

'Evelyn.'

Evelyn turned and saw the CAG walking toward her through the throng. Teera nudged Evelyn in the ribs and whispered to her.

'Your beau's here!'

'He's not my beau!' Evelyn snapped back, but Teera was already making her way toward her fighter.

'You're up,' Andaim said as he reached her side. 'Two alert Raythons will be ready on the cats once you're launched.'

Evelyn knew the drill. In fact all pilots did, so there was no need for Andaim to brief her.

'Shouldn't you be on the bridge overseeing tactical?' she enquired demurely.

'You know I like to be down here among the Raythons,' Andaim replied 'The bridge always feels detatched from the action.'

An awkward silence filled the space between them despite the noise of the engineers and the whining ion engines. Andaim opened his mouth to say something, and then he hesitated as though he'd already forgotten what it was.

'I've got to go,' Evelyn said. 'They call it a scramble for a reason, y'know?'

Andaim blinked and nodded.

'Of course, get going. I'll be in touch from tactical, okay?'

Evelyn briefly felt as though she were being mothered, but a tingle of warmth filled the pit of her belly. She turned and jogged away from the CAG so that she could better conceal the smile on her face, and then climbed the steps to the cockpit of her Raython. Her name was emblazoned in stencilled letters beneath it and a gold diamond painted just after: her designation as a section leader, awarded for meritous combat performance and leadership. She levered herself into the cockpit as the aircraft's crew-chief helped her with her harnesses, other maintenance crew hurriedly unplugging power lines as they swarmed around the fighter.

'Reaper One, radio check.'

'*Five by five,*' Teera replied as she closed her canopy.

Just before her cockpit closed Evelyn heard the tannoys announcing the drop out of super-luminal cruise, and wondered what was awaiting them outside in the cold vacuum of space beyond the huge bay doors barely two hundred cubits ahead. With no time for a briefing, she and Teera would be updated seconds after launch.

Her cockpit came alive as she activated the avionics and started the engines as the ground crews rushed away and huddled down in sealed bunkers close by. The Raython hummed with restrained energy as her ion engines came fully on-line and Evelyn completed her pre-take off checks. She made sure her plasma cannons were charged but not activated and ran her throttles up to launch power, then settled back and glanced at a series of warning lights high up on the launch bay walls as the voice of Atlantia's communications officer buzzed in her earphone.

'Sub-luminal cruise in three, two, one… disengaging!'

The huge bay seemed to shudder and the light became briefly polarised as the Atlantia surged out of faster-than-light travel and decelerated in the blink of an eye as the mass-drive disengaged. In a flash the lights on the bay wall turned from green to red and ahead a sudden billowing mist of escaping air was sucked into oblivion as the launch bay doors lifted.

Evelyn's Raython surged forward as the magnetic catapults threw the fighter down the launch bay, her body slammed back into her seat under the tremendous acceleration as she threw the throttles wide open. Running lights flashed past her in a blur and the huge launch bay doors whipped past scant cubits above her head as her Raython hurtled beneath them and was flung out into the blackness of space.

Evelyn flicked a switch on her instrument console to activate her weapons as her eyes took in a spectacular panorama. The vast starfields vanished ahead into a brilliant, rainbow nebula of billowing gases cast off in a tremendous halo by a yellow star in the distance. Photo-receptive shielding in her canopy protected her eyesight from the blinding glare of the star, revealing the beautiful colours spanning the inky black heavens.

'Reaper Two, weapons hot.'

'Copy, Reaper One,' Evelyn replied. 'Battle flight, go.'

Evelyn broke hard left and the two Raythons separated as they raced away from Atlantia, Commander Ry'ere's voice reaching Evelyn from Atlantia's bridge as she manoeuvered.

'Reaper Flight, stay sharp, system may be populated, unknown numbers, unknown allegiances. Form CAP at twenty thousand cubits.'

'Copy, Reaper Flight, Combat Air Patrol at twenty, Reaper One.'

Evelyn levelled out into position a thousand cubits away from Reaper Two and on a parallel course. She glanced down at her displays.

'Chiron system,' she said over the intercom to Teera. 'That's a frontier post isn't it?'

'Bunch of moons and smuggler hideouts, way out from the core systems,' Teera confirmed. *'Nothing much here as far as I know.'*

Evelyn scanned the vista ahead and figured it out.

'Resources,' she replied as she looked at the immense billowing clouds of ejecta. 'That stellar nebula will contain billions of tonnes of hydrogen, oxygen, helium and metals.'

'I've got a planetary body, dead ahead.'

Evelyn squinted ahead but could see nothing against the terminal halo ejected by the dying star. She glanced down at a tactical display and she spotted a planet, its orbit marked around the parent star and a brief data list scrolling alongside it.

'Chiron IV, habitable surface and atmosphere, undocumented life-forms,' she murmured as she read the list. 'Second of two habitable worlds in the system.'

The first is already burned out,' Teera confirmed. *'Too close to the parent star when it started to swell.'*

Chiron's parent star had exhausted its fuel of hydrogen and begun burning helium in its core, in doing so producing more heat than the star's mass could contain and thus casting off its atmosphere into space in gigantic outbursts. The once–stable star had thus swelled to many times its original size, consuming those worlds in close orbit around it.

'Looks like Chiron IV's days are numbered,' Evelyn said. 'Instruments are recording violent climatological change. The oceans are evaporating and the atmosphere's already breaking down under the cosmic rays from the parent star.'

'Lot of storms too,' Teera reported.

Evelyn spotted the planet ahead, a tiny speck of black against the brilliant sunset hues of the dying star. She glanced at her instruments and called out to Teera.

'We're at twenty thou', start CAP orbit.'

'Roger that.'

CAP, or Combat Air Patrol, was their assigned role. Both aircraft set up a mutually supporting racetrack orbit between the Atlantia far behind and Chiron IV, ready to intercept any foreign craft while the rest of the air wing was prepped for patrol.

'I'm not seeing any sign of the Veng'en cruiser,' Teera reported.

'Me either,' Evelyn replied.

It wasn't her job to question policy, but privately Evelyn and a lot of the other pilots were concerned about the captain's decision to attempt to recruit the Veng'en to their cause. A violent and untrustworthy race who had despised humanity even before the emergence of the Word and its Legion, the Veng'en had actively pursued and destroyed human vessels fleeing Ethera in the wake of the apocalypse in the hope of containing the Word's spread. Nobody knew how many men, woman and children had died at the hands of Veng'en commanders keen to slake their bloodlust.

There were many other races, further flung and likely still free of the Word, to whom the Atlantia could implore for help. Captain Sansin's ploy of turning enemies into friends risked even greater losses than had already occurred should the Veng'en's War Council reject any form of alliance with humanity.

I've got something,' Teera reported.

Evelyn glanced at her holographic tactical display and spotted a small target moving away from Chiron IV. The track was accelerating with almost fighter-like rapidity away from the planet Chiron, but was still close enough that it would be fighting against the planet's gravity and unable to make the jump to super-luminal velocity.

'Looks like a freighter climbing out of orbit,' Evelyn replied. 'No transponder code.'

'Unlicensed, two hundred fifty tonnes,' Teera confirmed.

'And she's fast,' Evelyn noted as she checked the vessel's course and velocity. 'Looks like she's spotted us and doesn't want to play.'

'Let's give her a run for her money, shall we?' Teera suggested.

'Roger that,' Evelyn replied. 'Reaper flight, *buster buster!'*

The Raythons rocketed at full power toward the target, the merchant vessel turning away from them and making a desperate attempt to escape the two fighters.

***

VIII

'Damn she's quick,' Evelyn replied as she glanced at her instruments and noted that the fighters were already nearing their maximum velocity.

She spotted the freighter visually against the brilliant sky as a tiny black speck and a small aiming reticule appeared on Evelyn's canopy, projected over the target with range, velocity and trajectory information.

'*She's building up to super-luminal,*' Teera guessed. '*I'm detecting a mass-drive spinning up.*'

Evelyn gauged the distance between them and the freighter, and made her decision. 'Transfer all power to engines, give them all we've got. Let's catch her up before she leaps.'

'*That's risky!*' Teera called. '*We're at thirty thousand cubits already!*'

'Atlantia can still see us,' Evelyn replied, 'and I don't want this one getting away.'

Evelyn deactivated her weapons, shields and all non-essential devices, including her radar, and re-routed the power to her engines. The Raython accelerated further, now travelling at over a thousand cubits per second as it raced in pursuit of the merchant vessel. Although accelerating ever faster in the vacuum of space, all craft had a natural maximum velocity and range based upon how much fuel they had remaining in order to be used to slow down again. Faster than the Atlantia, if a Raython exhausted its fuel at maximum velocity, at a distant enough range, there were no other craft that could ever catch up with it again. The pilot would be forced to eject on a trajectory that would slow them down enough to be rescued, thus losing the valuable fighter to the void of space.

'Almost there,' she said, looking briefly over her shoulder to see Teera's Raython keeping pace, a tiny silvery speck against the star fields.

'*Reaper Flight, Atlantia, pu.. b... ne.. cont...*'

The communication from Atlantia crackled with bursts of static interference caused by Chiron's massive stellar storms.

'*We're losing Atlantia,*' Teera warned. '*Tactical orders are to always remain within comms range!*'

'Stay on target, I've almost got her,' Evelyn replied, the Devlamine coursing through her veins shielding her from hubris or doubt and super-charging her determination.

The freighter's hull glinted in the light, and Evelyn saw her powerful engines glowing white hot as they propelled her toward a velocity high enough for her mass-drive to engage. Long, slender and sleek, the freighter was perfect for high-speed trade.

'Why is she running?' Teera asked.

'Probbaly thinks we're infected with the Word,' Evelyn replied. 'Don't activate weapons, we'll just pull in alongside and signal that we're not infected.'

'I'll go wide,' she reported. *'Get out in front of them.'*

It was a simple fact that most of the human race had been infected by the Word, which was now hunting down any survivors with extreme prejudice. Any survivors were thus extremely wary of anybody they encountered, and would likely flee a heavily armed frigate upon first sight and...

'It's turning toward us!'

Evelyn looked up in surprise to see the digitised track on her viewing screen veer suddenly onto an intercept course.

'It's doing *what?*'

'They're engaging us!'

Evelyn barely had time to think when the onrushing ship zoomed toward them and a burst of plasma fire rocketed toward her Raython. Evelyn hauled her fighter over and yanked hard on the control column as she rolled around the salvo, the plasma shots zipping past outside as she glimpsed the ship flash by at terrific speed.

'Defensive break!' Evelyn yelled.

She hauled the Raython around a tight turn as she saw Teera's Raython flash by in the opposite direction, each covering the other's tail as they reversed course to engage the unknown ship.

'She's out of range!' Teera called as they levelled out on a pursuit course.

The craft was now drawing away from them, already out of effective weapons range.

'Damn,' Evelyn cursed.

The pilot, whoever they were, was good and didn't lack courage. Charging two Raythons head-on was the last thing they would have expected the unknown craft to do.

'Maintain a pursuit course,' Evelyn ordered as she glanced at her instruments and noted that the fighters were already again nearing their maximum velocity.

'Where's Atlantia?'

Evelyn glanced at her displays and grinned to herself. The frigate was nowhere to be seen, and she realised that the captain must have reacted to what was happening.

'She's deploying countermeasures, hiding herself,' she replied. 'They're going to sneak up on this guy and intercept him. Stay on his tail.'

The two Raythons streaked through space, the fleeing spacecraft ahead leaving a faint ion trail behind it as it raced clear of Chiron's gravitational field. Evelyn kept one eye on her display as she waited for the Atlantia to reappear. Against the vast blackness of space, even a large vessel like a frigate was essentially invisible unless illuminated, and even with the veils of stellar material glowing all around them the Atlantia would be just a speck until the last moment.

'*Got her!*' Teera yelled.

The Atlantia reappeared on their displays, far ahead but almost right in front of the fleeing craft's path.

'Prepare to intercept!' Evelyn snapped.

There was only one thing that their quarry could do and that was alter course to avoid the frigate, which would keep her inside Chiron's gravitational influence for a little longer and give the Raythons a further chance to intercept and get in close.

'*There she goes, breaking left!*'

Evelyn laid in a fresh intercept course as she turned left, Teera just ahead of her, and the Atlantia also altered course to close in from the far side of the engagement. Evelyn spotted new contacts appearing as more fighters were launched by the Atlantia to aid the chase.

'You're not going anywhere now,' Evelyn grinned.

Her grin vanished as she saw their quarry reverse course in a tight, aggressive turn and race back toward her.

'*They're engaging again!*' Teera called.

A flash of plasma burst past Evelyn's cockpit and she saw the spacecraft bank heavily and turn as it raced past her canopy.

Evelyn hauled the Raython over into a hard turn in response, disbelief in her voice. 'They're closing for a fight!'

To her amazement the craft turned rapidly with her Raython as she looked up out of her canopy and saw it matching her position, vying to turn more tightly and get in on her tail. A bolt of plasma fired straight up at her from turrets mounted on the craft's upper fuselage caught her unawares and she yelped with fright as she rolled the Raython and jerked it out of the line of fire.

'Weapons hot!' Evelyn yelled. 'Engage!'

She saw Teera's Raython rushing down upon the craft as Evelyn kept it busy.

'I've got her,' Teera replied as she settled neatly down in the turn behind the ship, which flashed by above Evelyn.

Evelyn reversed her turn, rolling to keep the two spacecraft in sight above her as she moved to support her wingman.

'Firing now,' Teera called.

Evelyn waited for the shots from Teera's Raython, but nothing happened. The spacecraft broke hard right but Teera's Raython continued silently on out into space.

'Teera, what's wrong?' No answer came from the Raython. 'Teera, respond!'

Silence filled Evelyn's cockpit and then a burst of plasma fire smashed into her Raython as the freighter's turrets opened fire. Sparks flashed through the cockpit to the sound of warning alarms and the acrid stench of burning circuitry as Evelyn pulled hard right to throw off the freighter's aim.

'I'm hit!' she yelled.

One of her engines flamed out even as she scrambled to shut off fuel lines and isolate fires while throwing the fighter about in evasive manoeuvres. She craned her neck back and saw the freighter following her, plasma blasts flashing by as it tried to hit her again.

'Atlantia, Reaper One, respond, ETA?'

'Reaper One, Renegade Flight, ETA three minutes.'

Damn, not quick enough.

Evelyn broke hard left as she shut off the damaged engine, and then on an impulse she threw the throttles wide open and kicked in a boot full of rudder. The Raython yawed violently and span on its axis to point back at the pursuing freighter.

Evelyn saw the ship track through her sights and she fired twice, her senses heightened by adrenaline mixing with the Devlamine coursing through her veins. Two plasma rounds leaped from her weapons, one flashing past the ship but the other striking it square on the bow with a bright flare of dissipated energy as the ship's shields absorbed the blow.

The freighter rushed overhead, forced to overshoot as Evelyn's remaining engine slowed her down dramatically in her new orientation, and she felt the vibrations from the craft's engines as it roared by. She flipped the Raython over once more and tried to pursue, but with one engine out it was useless.

She was about to call it in when a new voice emerged over the radio.

'Renegade three and four in position.'

Andaim Ry'ere's calm tone startled Evelyn and she glanced down at her display to see two more Raythons streaking by far ahead, cutting the freighter off once more. She looked right and saw several Raythons rushing toward her, the fighters marked by blue boxes projected onto her canopy.

Evelyn looked at the freighter and she knew that it could no longer escape as a warning salvo was fired across its bow to explode in bright flares of blue-white light.

'What took you so long?' she demanded of the CAG with a smile.

'It's fashionable to be late,' Andaim replied. *'Cover Reaper Two, immediately.'*

Evelyn switched her attention to Teera's stricken Raython still flying out into the void in a straight line as though nobody were at the controls. She pursued the Raython, calling for Teera to respond, until she drew alongside and got a good look at the fighter.

Teera was still inside, her head slumped forward in her cockpit, which was covered in what looked like some kind of energy field.

'The freighter must have dumped something on her,' she reported back. 'Teera's not responding. Deploy a rescue vehicle. I'll hack her fighter's control computer, slow her down and shut down her engines.'

'Copy that,' Andaim replied. *'We've got things here.'*

Evelyn glanced over her shoulder and saw the distant speck of the unknown freighter being circled by several Raythons as, further away, the Atlantia closed in. Over the radio, she heard Captain Idris Sansin's voice broadcasting on all channels.

'Unidentified craft, stand down and prepare to land or we will blow you into a thousand pieces!'

***

IX

Evelyn's damaged Raython wobbled as she guided the craft in for a landing, the fighter drifting into the landing bay and hovering above the deck on its magnetically-opposed landing pads as she nursed it over its landing spot and set it down.

As she began shutting the fighter's systems down other fighters landed around her, with Teera's Raython being eased in under remote control via Atlantia's technical crew as a medical team and several dozen armed Marines stood-by in the sealed bunkers lining the bay to receive the craft.

The landing bay emergency lights remained on and the bay doors stayed open, forcing the rest of the pilots to remain in their cockpits as, escorted by two more Raythons, the freighter they had pursued eased into the Atlantia's landing bay.

She was larger than Evelyn had assumed during the fight, her fuselage scorched with plasma damage both old and new. A few dents and nicks marred her hull plating, the long nose at her bow and broad viewing screen growing into a larger mid-section. The two horizontal strakes either side of the main hull held her four ion engines and she could see the plasma turrets that had fired at her and Teera, their barrels scorched black by the heat.

The freighter extended three heavy-duty landing pads in a tricycle pattern, blasts of vapour flaring from her exhaust nozzles as her pilot balanced her, and then the landing struts sank down as they took some of the weight of the ship against the magnetically-charged decks and she landed.

From the bunkers, Marines in atmospherically-sealed battle suits rushed across the deck and surrounded the freighter, plasma rifles aimed up at the ship as behind it the last two Raythons landed and the huge bay doors rumbled shut.

Evelyn saw the atmosphere being reintroduced into the landing bay, and then the lights turned green and she instantly hit the switch to open her canopy as she tore off her harnesses and leaped out of the cockpit. The temperature was bitterly cold in the wake of the vacuum of space, but tolerable now that massive deck vents were billowing hot air in trembling clouds to re-heat the internal atmosphere.

The ground crews swarming to the Raythons with boarding ladders and refuelling hoses never even got close to Evelyn as she vaulted down onto the deck and hurried across to Teera's Raython.

The Marines guarding it remained at a safe distance as technical crews scanned the strange energy field bathing the fighter's nose and canopy.

'What is it?' Evelyn demanded.

One of the technicians glanced at her, saw that her shoulder insignia outranked his by a good margin, and replied instantly.

'We don't know. Scanners don't recognise the material at all, although it is negatively charged and attracts to the surface of the Raython.'

'What about Teera?'

'Lieutenant Teera Milan is alive and appears to be asleep.'

'Get that thing off her,' Evelyn ordered.

'We don't know what it will do to her if we remove it, or us,' the technician replied. 'We can't just rush over there and yank it off and...'

Evelyn stormed past the technicians and broke through the Marines to grab one of the fire crew's hoses. The fireman shouted in protest at her but Evelyn ignored him as she strode closer and aimed the nozzle at the energy field on Teera's fighter and opened it up.

A blast of thick fire-retardant foam blasted the nose of the Raython and the glowing material flickered as it was lifted by the force of the flow and slid sideways, tumbling like a fabric that was somehow alive as it folded over upon itself and then tumbled from the Raython's nose and slithered down toward the deck. The bay's zero-gravity allowed it to hang in mid-air, suspended amid a galaxy of foam droplets.

Evelyn shut off the hose and dropped it as she dashed to Teera's cockpit and hit the emergency release handles embedded into the fuselage wall. The canopy hissed open just as Teera lifted her head and stared bleary-eyed at Evelyn.

'What happened?' she mumbled.

Evelyn looked back at the medical teams. 'Get over here, now!'

She jumped down as the medics rushed up to the fighter, and immediately stormed past them toward the freighter looming nearby, encircled by armed Marines.

'Get that thing open, now!'

General Bra'hiv pulled his helmet off and waved her down.

'Easy there lieutenant, the ship could be infected by the Legion and we don't know who or what is aboard and...'

'I don't care!' Evelyn snapped. 'You get them out here and let me crack their head for...'

Evelyn was interrupted by a loud hiss of escaping air as from beneath the freighter a boarding ramp descended on hydraulic rams. She drew her plasma pistol and activated it even as Bra'hiv took up position, ready to confront whoever or whatever walked down the ramp. Evelyn positioned herself behind the general's right shoulder and took aim to cover him.

The ramp hit the deck with a loud metallic clang, and the clouds of released vapour swirled for a moment and then dissipated as the sound of boots marched down the ramp and a voice called out from inside.

'How many of you are infected?!'

General Bra'hiv opened his mouth to speak, but Evelyn's voice rang out.

'None. Get out here, *now*!'

A long silence hung in the air in the wake of Evelyn's shout and then a pair of boots appeared through the vapour, followed by a long pair of legs casually striding down the metallic ramp. As Evelyn watched, a tall, swarthy man with tanned skin and a casual set to his shoulders descended the ramp, a plasma blaster in one hand and caution writ large on his features as he hesitated.

The man looked about him at the armed Marines, the landing bay packed with Raython fighters and the hustle and bustle of a busy Colonial frigate.

General Bra'hiv aimed his rifle directly at the man. 'Drop your weapon and get down on your knees!'

The man stayed where he was. A pair of icy grey eyes fixed upon the General's. 'I'm not going anywhere or doing anythin' until I know what's going on here.'

'You're under arrest, that's what's going on,' Bra'hiv snapped. 'Get on your knees now or I'll order my men to fire.'

The grey eyes flicked across the gathered Marines but again the man did not move. His reply rang out clear across the landing bay.

'Yo'Ki!'

In an instant the freighter's plasma turrets activated with a hum of energy as two more popped out from concealed panels beneath the spacecraft's hull and swung around to point at Evelyn, General Bra'hiv and the gathered Marines.

The man's features twisted into a sly grin as he looked at the general. 'One shot and I'll have my ship blast this entire landing bay into molten slag, understood?'

Bra'hiv growled under his breath alongside Evelyn and then called back. 'You're not in a position to make threats!'

'Yes I am,' the man replied. 'But I have no desire to hurt anybody. You pursued me, remember, and I assumed that this was a vessel infected by the Word. There are enough of them about, former Colonial rigs filled with those little machines tearing up the cosmos. You're going to arrest me for trying to save my own life?'

Evelyn stared at the man for a long moment, and then she lowered her pistol and holstered it. The man noticed her move and gestured to her.

'Now, that wasn't so tough was it?' he asked. 'The lady here knows where I stand.'

Evelyn gauged the angle of the freighter's plasma cannons and determined that they could not shoot directly at her without hitting Taron. She stepped out from behind the general with her hands in the air.

Evelyn strode forward and up the ramp toward the man, and stood before him for a moment. He could have been twenty years old or forty, it was hard to tell. Lean and with a casual stance that belied a good degree of physical fitness, the pilot looked the image of restrained violence. His disregard for the danger he was in, and for what he had done to Teera, angered Evelyn even more.

'Here's where I stand,' she said.

Evelyn dropped her hands and swung a bunched fist straight across the man's jaw, the impact a dull crack that echoed across the landing bay. The pilot fell backwards and slammed onto his back on the ramp as Evelyn pointed down at him.

'Try using the damned emergency comms frequencies next time! You nearly got my wingman and I killed!'

The man stared up at her as he massaged his jaw, and an annoying smirk curled from his lips as he slowly got back to his feet.

'Shut down your weapons,' Bra'hiv ordered the pilot.

'Call off your men,' he replied past Evelyn.

A voice came from behind them. 'You don't give orders on this ship, captain.'

Evelyn turned as Andaim appeared at the foot of the ramp and surveyed the scene, his flight helmet tucked under his arm. He took one look at the new arrival and seemed to make a decision.

'General, order your men to stand down for now,' he suggested.

The general scowled but Evelyn could see that the CAG no longer considered the pilot much of a threat. Bra'hiv waved his men down and they lowered their weapons. The pilot's grin broadened.

'I knew you'd all see sense,' he murmured, and then he called back into the interior of his ship. 'Shut her down, Yo'Ki!'

Moments later, the humming plasma turrets whined down and the pirate captain holstered his pistol and pointed at his own chest.

'Captain Taron Forge, at your service.'

Evelyn blinked. 'Forge?'

Taron rolled his eyes. 'An unfortunate legacy.'

Andaim stepped up and looked Taron up and down. 'I'll be damned, the son of Tyraeus Forge, one of our finest fleet admirals.'

'Ex-admirals,' Taron reminded the CAG. 'The damned fool vanished during the apocalypse.'

'Not exactly,' Evelyn said as she recalled her encounter with a man who was no longer a man but a hideous cannibalisation of man and machine.

'You're not going to make my day even worse and tell me that my old man's still alive are you?' Taron asked.

Before Evelyn could reply, Andaim took a pace closer to Taron. 'We'll be asking the questions, and you'll be coming with me.'

Andaim reached out for Taron's arm. In an instant, Taron gripped Andaim's forearm and turned violently, hauling Andaim aside. The CAG crashed down onto the ramp and Taron's plasma pistol flashed into his hand with near-magical speed and aimed down into the CAG's face.

Evelyn stepped forward, but this time Taron's grin was cold.

'You only get one opportunity like that, sister,' he snapped, and then looked back down at Andaim. 'I don't take orders, expecially from a damned Colonial Officer. I'm here because you wanted me to be, because you pursued me. Any of you try telling me what to do one more time I'll blow this ship's landing bay apart just for the hell of it, understood? Now, you answer me a question: what the hell do *you* want?'

It was not Andaim that answered, but Captain Idris Sansin, flanked by a squad of Marines.

'We want to know what's going on out there, and you're going to help us,' he boomed.

***

X

'Are you kidding me?'

The Executive Officer, Mikhain, dragged one hand across his forehead as he marched up and down in his tiny cabin. He glanced at Ensign Scott, a young man he had taken under his wing. Idealistic and devoted to the Colonial cause, he like many younger crew members understood Mikhain's concern over Captain Sansin's methods and sympathised with the direction he wished to take.

'I'm not, sir. Taron Forge has been given temporary quarters aboard ship, captain's orders. In return the captain wants information from him'.

Mikhain struggled to comprehend what Captain Sansin was hoping to achieve.

'First a Veng'en hitch-hiker and now he's entertaining a damned pirate?'

The Ensign shrugged. 'It would appear so, sir.'

'We're doomed,' Mikhain murmured to himself. 'This can't go on.'

'Sir?'

'That's all for now, Ensign. Thank you.'

The Ensign saluted crisply and whirled on the spot before marching out of the cabin. The door hissed shut and Mikhain leaned on his desk as he tried to figure out a suitable course of action.

While the captain was dallying with a known brigand, the Atlantia's problems were mounting and becoming more serious with every passing day. The unrest among the civilians had become endemic and increasingly volatile, especially in the wake of the shooting of a farmer who was now being lauded by his peers as a model citizen who was merely defending himself against Colonial aggressors in the form of Bra'hiv's convict-Marines. Mikhain was being asked to control the situation while the General and his better-trained Marines were messing about in the landing bay guarding a single unregistered vessel and its strange weapon, an energy veil of some kind.

Supplies were woefully low, including water, and yet no shuttles had been sent down to the surface of Chiron IV to replenish them despite repeated requests from the civilians. The sanctuary's blue sky and clouds were limited in their ability to generate a true micro-climate, the space there not large enough to generate sustained rainfall and thus recycling was key to their continued survival. Sooner or later, stocks needed to be replenished.

Then there was the issue of the man found sick in his bed in the sanctuary. Mikhain knew that he was currently in the sick-bay under twenty-four hour guard, with no reports on either his condition or its cause. Many of the crew and civilians were fearful of a repeat infection of the Legion aboard ship, especially as it was being rumoured that a live Hunter was still being held somewhere in Meyanna Sansin's sick bay. Combined with the captain's insistence that the ship should follow a Veng'en cruiser home into its own home planetary system and attempt to enlist the Veng'en into helping humanity fight back, despite the fact that the species hated humanity with all its black heart, support for the captain's leadership was at an all-time low.

Mikhain turned and marched out of his cabin. Located just a few cubits from the bridge, on the opposite side from the captain's quarters, Mikhain did not turn toward the bridge but instead marched in the opposite direction. He entered the elevator banks and travelled down through the ship toward the enlisted quarters, the billets where the majority of the crew bedded down.

Mikhain had made it his business to get a feel for the mood of the crew. Aboard a big ship like the Atlantia it was possible to be on cruise for months and still see new faces, which made it too easy for a senior officer to view the crew as a nameless mass of automatons. But Mikhain felt that monitoring them, having a good sense of their needs and wishes, made them the most powerful ally aboard the entire vessel.

Ensign Scott was invaluable in learning the chow-room gossip, but for a personal touch Mikhain liked to show up unannounced and let the men speak to him. Given the chance to air their grievances, and then being shown that action was taken to alleviate their discomfort or unhappiness, Mikhain had patiently and skillfully begun to win their allegiance a man at a time.

'XO on the deck!'

The duty sergeant's call as Mikhain entered the chow-room sent some eighty men bolting to their feet over their meals. Mikhain waved them down casually.

'At ease gentlemen, don't let your food go cold. It tastes bad enough hot.'

The men chuckled as they settled back down behind their meals, but the hum of conversation had fallen silent now that the Executive Officer was in the room and they listened expectantly as they ate.

'A quick update,' Mikhain said as he stood with his hands behind his back and surveyed them. 'I understand that many of you feel that you're working blind, unaware of what's happening on the bridge and annoyed that you're being kept in the dark when this ship is your home as much as it is mine and the captain's.'

A ripple of agreement drifted through the hall.

'I understand,' Mikhain said. 'All of our lives are on the line here, and it's your right as much as it is mine to know everything that's going on aboard the Atlantia. While I cannot divulge every little piece of information as it comes in, I can share the following: we are now within the Chiron system, which has a habitable planet still in orbit around a parent star, which itself is nearing the end of its life. In time, we hope to replenish our stocks before moving on.'

'Moving on where?' asked a petty officer.

'That will be for the captain to decide. At this time, our objective is still to continue on toward the Veng'en system and...'

A loud barrage of curses and shaking heads assaulted the XO, and he sighed. Truth was, he knew that would be the response and that's why he'd said it.

'I know and I understand,' he continued. 'It makes no tactical sense but at this time we have no realistic military option against the Legion and insufficient strength to mount an assault on Ethera alone. We need allies, plain and simple.'

'So find allies, not existing enemies!' somebody shouted.

'Or lead the Legion to Wraithe and let the damned Veng'en deal with it!'

A ripple of laughter rolled around the hall.

'We've already got one of the leathery bastards living down in the sanctuary,' another man called. 'What's next? Inviting the whole damned race aboard?'

More laughs, bitter this time.

'Kordaz saved the lives of several of our people,' Mikhain replied as their voices calmed. 'He, perhaps alone among the Veng'en, has some understanding of humanity and is now a true ally. It may be hard to swallow and we may not like it, but Kordaz earned his place among us and I'd rather fight alongside him than against him. Kordaz is not the problem here.'

'What about those damned machines being kept in secret labs?' called a Marine.

'Or that man who got shot in the sanctuary?' shouted another. 'Are we killing our own people now while inviting pirates aboard?'

'The man shot in the sanctuary was attempting to protect his son, who is sick,' Mikhain reported. The chow-hall fell immediately silent and Mikhain knew what was on their minds. 'It is *not* the Legion,' Mikhain cautioned, 'that much I know for sure. Doctor Sansin is performing tests now to try to understand what has happened to the victim. As for the machines, there are no longer any Infectors aboard the Atlantia. Only a single Hunter is being kept in stasis aboard ship for tests, and it is not the type of Legion machine that can self-replicate itself – it's too large.'

'Are you sure?' asked the Marine. 'It's a hell of a risk to have that damned thing aboard, isn't it?'

'We can't learn how to defeat our enemies without first studying them,' Mikhain pointed out. 'The risk is worth the reward if it results in a means to prevent the Legion from advancing further. I'll be back in a few days, and hopefully I'll have some more answers for you.'

'XO!' shouted the duty sergeant.

The men shot to attention and Mikhain was about to leave when one of the soldiers stood up. The towering Marine with blond, short-cropped hair and angular features atop a massively muscled frame made his way toward Mikhain. The XO turned and walked out of the chow-hall with the huge Marine following, and as the buzz of conversation returned to mask their conversation he turned to the soldier, whose shoulders bore the insignia of a corporal.

'What can I do for you, corporal?'

'I was demoted recently,' the corporal said, 'unjustly.'

'That would be the concern of General Bra'hiv,' Mikhain replied. 'You should take your concerns to him and…'

'My rank was taken by Qayin,' the corporal growled. 'One of the former convicts that Bra'hiv holds so damned dear.'

Mikhain hesitated thoughtfully. 'What's your name?'

'Djimon.'

'When did this happen?'

'Six months ago,' Djimon growled, his fists clenching at his sides.

'I recall that the report says that you left Sergeant Qayin to die aboard the Sylph instead of covering his retreat.'

'The Sergeant confirmed that I was mistaken in believing that he could not have escaped regardless of my covering him or not.' Djimon replied. 'I was still demoted.'

'Qayin,' Mikhain murmured. 'A former killer-convict and gang leader. I presume you would like to take Sergeant Qayin to task over this?'

'I'd like to skewer his guts on my bayonet,' Djimon snarled, 'sir.'

Mikhain nodded. 'That won't be necessary, but I can report that there are many officers and crew who are deeply dissatisfied with the captain's leadership.'

Djimon's expression changed instantly. 'What do you mean?'

Mikhian was aware that the Marine knew precisely what he was suggesting. The XO could tell by the soldier's Alpha Company shoulder insignia and his general demeanour that Djimon was a career Marine, a devoted soldier of the Colonial Forces. Mutiny or indeed any form of insurbordination would be anathema to him unless provided with the correct motivation.

'We need a second voice on the bridge,' Mikhain explained carefully. 'The captain is taking too much upon his own shoulders and it's starting to cloud his judgement. There is no Admiralty to act as a check to his actions and even I as Executive Officer am often ignored. I want to make him aware that his is not the only professional opinion aboard ship and that he needs to listen to his officers more keenly if we're to survive this.'

Djimon's eyes narrowed and he glanced over his shoulder at the chow-hall. 'That's why you've been coming down here giving these little pep' talks of yours,' he said.

'I'm keeping the crew informed as much as I can,' Mikhain replied. 'The captain keeps trying to maintain the old model of *need to know*, but we're not part of a fleet anymore and everybody's live are at stake. I want people to understand the situations we're involved in so they then understand our responses to those situations. People don't like being kept in the dark when their lives are on the line.'

Djimon nodded slowly, watching the XO with wary eyes. 'What would you have me do?'

'Nothing much,' Mikhain replied. 'Just keep an eye on things under General Bra'hiv, let me know if anything starts happening that you think is out of order, any events that the command structure tries to sweep under the carpet, understand?'

'What's in it for the crew?'

Mikhain smiled. Djimon was indeed a model soldier, more concerned about the people and the ship around him than his own personal gain.

'Information, clearer leadership, and hopefully a more cordial atmosphere and sense of mutual trust than we have right now.'

'You want to share information?' Djimon challenged. 'You find out what Qayin's up to. He's often missing when off duty and nobody knows where he goes. He ensures the rosters are such that I'm always on duty when he is not, so I cannot follow him.'

Mikhain's eyes narrowed. 'What do you think he's doing?'

'I don't know, or I wouldn't be asking would I?'

Mikhain nodded. 'I will assign you briefly for some extra duties, and you can use that time to find out what, if anything, Qayin is doing.'

'And that pirate ship we captured?' the Marine asked. 'More allies for the captain that none of us want?'

'The pirate is an unknown quantity,' Mikhain admitted. 'He thought that we were an infected vessel so he ran. Now he knows we're clean, he's as interested in us as we are in him. He's cooperating willingly with our inquiries.'

***

XI

'I'm not telling you anything.'

Captain Taron Forge slouched in a chair with his boots propped up on the edge of a table and one arm draped across the chair's back rest.

'We agreed we'd share information.'

'We agreed we wouldn't shoot at each other,' Taron corrected. 'The rest is open to negotiation.'

The captain's dining cabin was larger than his personal quarters and had been designed specifically for entertaining dignitaries who did not wish to chat among the austere grey walls of the rest of the frigate. Panelled in beautiful, deep Etherean pine and with lush carpets underfoot, it seemed a world away from a ship-of-the-line in deep space.

Captain Idris Sansin leaned against one wall with his arms folded as he watched the smuggler before him.

'You were leaving the system,' he said. 'What were you doing here?'

'Sight seeing,' Taron replied. 'Have you seen the aurora down there on Chiron? Absolutely beautiful.'

'I have the impression aurora aren't really your thing, Taron.'

'And what would you know about it?'

'Quite a bit, actually.'

A screen on the wall of the room illuminated and data scrolled down it, dominated by two images of Taron Forge. The smuggler smirked.

'Fame at last,' he murmured, and he glanced across at Yo'Ki who was draped across another chair. 'See, I was cute when I was younger.'

His co-pilot glanced at the images and shrugged without interest. Idris looked at the first image of Taron on the screen, resplendent in a Colonial uniform.

'Taron Forge,' Idris said, 'son of the late Tyraeus Forge. You were commissioned as a fighter pilot in the Colonial Service and served five years before being dishonourably discharged for various crimes.'

'Something I'm very proud of,' Taron announced.

'Drunk on duty,' Idris read with interest from the screen.

'It had been a tough day.'

'Striking a senior officer.'

'He deserved it. How we laughed, afterward.'

'Dereliction of duty, causing the deaths of several fellow pilots...'

'We were all being *sent* to our deaths,' Taron said, all humour vanishing from his voice. 'They all followed orders like little sheep. I didn't and it saved my life.'

'The admiralty seems to think that you were guilty of cowardice,' Idris pointed out.

'You *think*?'

The smuggler raised an eyebrow. Idris looked at him and knew that, whatever this layabout rogue might be guilty of, cowardice was not likely part of it. He had willingly engaged half a squadron of Raythons in combat only a couple of hours previously, and thus displayed a reckless but inspired skill for flying.

'What happened then?' Idris asked, 'in your own words.'

'Go to hell,' Taron snapped back. 'I already told the admiralty what happened years ago, and they decided to bury my statement during the Court Martial. I don't answer to authority any more.'

'You don't want to clear your name?'

'My name is clear to everybody that matters to me,' Taron replied, and gestured with one casual waft of his hand toward Yo'Ki.

'Yo'Ki Yan,' Idris said as he looked at Taron's exotically attractive co-pilot. 'Wanted by Colonial Police for the murder of at least three men and maybe as many as seven in the charted systems, a former inmate of the colony's most dangerous prisons and in and out of jailhouses all your life.' Idris grinned without warmth at them both. 'What a beautiful couple you make.'

Taron's jaw creased with that annoying wry smile.

'Double standards, captain,' he said. 'I noticed that half the Marines in your landing bay were plastered up to their necks in gang-colours.'

'They've learned the error of their ways,' Idris replied. 'I wonder, can you?'

'Already did,' Taron said, 'the moment I got the hell away from the Colonial Forces.'

'Indeed,' Idris noted as he looked at the second image of Taron on the screen. 'You disappeared after your discharge...'

'Dishonourable,' Taron reminded the captain.

'...dishonourable discharge and only re-emerged two years later after a shooting match with a Colonial Patrol out near the Tyberium Fields.'

'I was minding my own business collecting minerals when I was attacked.'

'Yes, but you were collecting those minerals from a legally certified mining vessel that you'd fought and disabled.'

Taron shrugged. 'Picky, picky. They were damaged and I was helping them off-load their cargo.'

'Cut the crap, Taron. You're a pirate and smuggler, nothing more, and you spend most of your time tearing up people's lives for profit.'

'I only hit the big corporate ships,' Taron said defensively. Yo'Ki shot a severe glance at her captain, and he shrugged. 'Okay, times have been hard, but I *mostly* only hit the soulless corporations. They don't notice the financial loss like the small operators.'

'You're all heart,' Idris uttered. 'What's down there on that planet, Taron?'

'Nothing much,' Taron replied. 'We were restocking water and other essentials. If there were any mining operations here, they cleared out a long time ago. You know that star's about to go bang, right?'

'The star doesn't have enough mass to go supernova,' Idris pointed out.

'Nope,' Taron agreed, 'but sooner or later it's going to blow out the Mother of all Solar Flares and when it does, everybody inside its orbit will be toast. That's one light show I don't want to see, hence our rapid departure from the system.'

Idris's eyes narrowed.

'You're a very clever man, Taron,' he observed. 'Your Colonial records state that your inventiveness and improvisation skills were unmatched.'

'At least they got something right,' Taron beamed.

'They also said that those skills made you a natural liar and deeply untrustworthy.'

'Like I said, they didn't get everything right. What do you want with me, captain, and what the hell are you doing here anyway? How come the Atlantia didn't get swallowed up by that whole mess on Ethera?'

'Same reason you didn't,' Idris explained. 'We were outside the main systems. Atlantia had been retired from front-line duty and was acting as a prison ship. We had a chance to flee.'

'You should have stayed away,' Taron replied.

'That would be cowardice.'

'That would be smart,' Taron retorted. 'Ethera's gone, captain.'

'And we're taking it back.'

Taron stared at the captain for a moment and then glanced at Yo'Ki. The silent killer watched Idris for a moment and then shook her head slowly and looked away.

'And we want allies,' Idris added.

A long silence descended upon the cabin.

'Us,' Taron said flatly.

'You,' Idris nodded. 'You have skills, a fast ship, knowledge and…'

'I'd sooner sign up to the Legion,' Taron snapped. 'It was the Colonial government who created the Word, the Legion and this whole damned mess. It was people like my father, like you, who allowed it to get out of hand and kill millions, billions of people.' Taron stood up and pointed a finger at Idris's chest. 'You stand there and tell me and Yo'Ki here about how we've killed people? Well newsflash for you, numbskull; we only ever fired in self-defence, we shot straight and the people we killed were all kinds of evil. You, on the other hand, wear the uniform of an organisation that has killed entire worlds because your little toys got out of control and now you want *our* help to sort it out?'

Idris stood resolute before the pirate's tirade.

'Yes,' he replied, 'because you're human beings and we're becoming an endangered species real fast.'

'No thanks to the Colonial government,' Taron shot back. 'I'm speechless, really. You'll be telling us next that you're off to the Veng'en homeworld to ask *their* help in cleaning your mess up.'

Idris ground his jaw a little. 'We were on our way there when we stopped for supplies here.'

Taron stared openly at the captain and for once it seemed as though the cocky pirate was at a loss for words. He shook his head and turned away as Idris went on.

'We have only two choices: keep running for all eternity and let the Word grow more powerful as time goes by, dooming our children and their children and who knows how many more generations to fight the war that we didn't have the guts to fight for ourselves – or take the fight home to Ethera with what we have and destroy the Word for once and for all.'

'Destroy the Word,' Taron echoed as he slumped back into his seat and waved the captain's words aside as though they were of no more substance than air. 'Seems to me the Word has done the rest of us all a favour by destroying the Colonial Fleet.'

'You don't mean that.'

'Don't I?'

'You're the son of a Colonial hero. There must be at least some patriotic blood running in your veins.'

'Clean out.'

A panel by the captain's door beeped softly. 'Yes?'

Technical has completed their analysis of the pirate shroud, as they're calling it,' came Lael's response from the bridge. *'It turns out that the shroud emits a low-frequency energy field that conflicts with both biological brain-wave patterns and some forms of electrical circuitry, causing interference in alpha and delta-wave signals and…'*

'The short version, Lael.'

'It knocks people out, captain.'

'Thank you.'

Idris turned away from the panel and then opened the door to the cabin. From outside walked Andaim, General Bra'hiv and Evelyn. Taron Forge raised an eyebrow as the door slid shut behind them.

'Another greeting?' he enquired as he looked at Evelyn. 'You've quite a temper and not a bad right-hook. I could use somebody like you to…'

'We're not here to discuss Evelyn,' Idris snapped.

'First name terms?' Taron noted immediately. 'Not bad for a girl who hasn't spent much time in space. How'd you get into the cockpit of a Raython?'

Evelyn strolled toward Taron and leaned toward him, a soft smile on her lips. 'Nobody dared get me back out again. How's the jaw?'

Taron's grin broadened as beside him Yo'Ki glowered silently at Evelyn.

'You sure you're in the right place?' Taron mocked her further. 'Seems like you're far too free a spirit to be chained to a Colonial frigate.'

'Better than a common thief dwarfed by his father's shadow,' Evelyn shot back.

'Enough small talk,' Andaim interjected, watching the interplay between Evelyn and Taron with what looked like concern. 'Right now, we want to know everything about every pirate you've come into contact with in the past few months.'

'Sure you do,' Taron replied. 'Your captain's already asked, though, and I politely declined.'

'We're politely insisting,' Andaim snapped. 'Unless you want your ship dumped out the back and left to plummet in a fiery descent toward Chiron.'

Taron did not move but his expression turned cold.

'Go ahead,' he replied. 'And I will spend my dying breath killing as many of your crew as I possibly can, as will Yo'Ki.'

In response the co-pilot produced as if by magic a silvery, curved blade that flashed in the light as she idly spun it over in her hand.

'This will get us nowhere,' Evelyn said as she stood back from Taron. 'If you're both all done with the bravado? We need information about any pirates, smugglers or other like-minded captains you may know of operating in this system – their numbers, armaments and intentions.'

'There are no pirates in this sector,' Taron replied. 'They're as scattered and disorganised as everybody else. What did you think would happen to us? That we'd all gather together after the apocalypse and play happy campers on Chiron?'

'Like attracts like,' Andaim said, 'and scum always gathers together at the bottom of the bowl.'

Taron chuckled in delight. 'I'm not about to divulge what little I do know about pirates to some jumped-up little boy who only got his CAG badge because there was nobody else left aboard to take it on. If you want credits for hunting pirates son, you'll have to find them someways else.'

'We're not interested in hunting pirates,' Idris replied for the CAG. 'We're looking to recruit them.'

***

XII

'We're looking to what?'

Both Andaim and Evelyn stared at the captain in surprise. General Bra'hiv grabbed Idris's arm.

'You want to employ pirates?! They're nothing but common criminals. I wouldn't trust them as far as I could throw them.'

'You've seen how it's worked out for your Marines,' the captain pointed out. 'Bravo Company has fought with considerable valour on numerous occasions. I don't doubt that pirates would likely be as ferocious on our behalf, with the right motivation.'

'The right motivation,' Taron drawled. 'I reckon that what motivates pirates and what you *think* motivates them are two different things.'

'Is that so?'

'Let's assume you're successful in recruiting them to your cause,' Taron suggested airily. 'And let's assume that you defeat the Word and take back Ethera with a fleet of scum by your side. What then? You think that they'll all settle down and have little pirate children and grow old together?'

Idris folded his arms.

'The end game for our allies is a bridge we can cross when we get there,' he said. 'Right now all I'm interested in is building a fleet and equipping it to fight.'

'Fight whom?' Taron asked. 'You're not going to get a pirate fleet to attack the Word. They know damned well that the entire infected Colonial Fleet is ranged against them and won't go within a dozen light years of Ethera, Caneeron or any of the core systems.'

'You could ask them,' Evelyn suggested.

Taron looked at her. 'Sure, they'll jump into line the moment I click my fingers.'

'They might,' Idris said. 'It doesn't matter whose colours we're flying under, the fact is that the Word hates humanity and will hunt it down and destroy it wherever it is to be found. You and your kind are no safer than us or any other species in the cosmos right now.'

'You're all so damned *noble* aren't you?' Taron uttered as he got to his feet once more. 'All for the cause of humanity despite being the proximal cause of its near-extinction. That's where you differ from what you call "my kind", captain. We walked away from humanity long ago because it sucked, and if we're all about to become extinct then our natural response is to get drunk and have a good time until the end of days, you understand what I'm saying? You ever seen how much wonderful junk is floating around out there waiting to be found and sold for what meagre enjoyment the survivors of your apocalypse can get before they expire?' Taron shook his head. 'You go fight your war, but we're done here.'

Yo'Ki got to her feet and followed Taron to the door.

'Have a nice life, captain,' Taron waved airily over his shoulder without looking as the door to the quarters opened.

Two massive, hulking Marines stood in the way, their weapons aimed at Taron.

'I'm afraid leaving is not an option, captain,' Idris said.

'Keeping us here won't make a difference,' Taron replied. 'You're wasting your time.'

'The energy shroud you were using to incapacitate crews and capture plunder,' Idris asked. 'Where did you get it from?'

'I won it.'

'Where does it comer from?'

'Nobody knows,' Taron replied as he rolled his eyes.

'*Nobody* knows?' Evelyn asked.

'Well somebody does, obviously, because they must have found it in the first place,' Taron admitted. 'But the thing could be a thousand years old or built last year, I have absolutely no idea.'

Idris turned to Andaim and the general.

'Just how far could brigands like Forge here have gone beyond the Icari Line?'

'Mass-drives have been available for commercial use for over a century,' Andaim said. 'Including return journeys, it's plausible that some human craft might have travelled hundreds of light years out into the cosmos.'

The Icari Line, proposed and enforced by the Icari, a race whose existence was supported by the atmospheres of giant stars and who themselves existed as little more than rays of light, was an invisible and yet rigidly enforced barrier to human expansion that had been observed for decades. The rules had been simple: there were things out in the cosmos that humanity was not yet prepared to face. Stay within the boundaries of the Icari Line and wait for permission to expand further. Nobody questioned the wisdom of the Icari, beings who had existed for countless millennia and who had chaperoned equally countless civilisations through the minefield of *first contact* with other spacefaring species and beyond.

'You're so naiive,' Taron smirked at Andaim. 'You don't even consider who has come wandering into and out of Etherean systems when our ancestors were still throwing wooden spears at each other. Humanity is a young species, compared to many.'

'He's right,' Bra'hiv agreed. 'There could be countless things like that shroud littering the galaxy that we don't even know about yet.'

'That's what I'm counting on,' Idris Sansin replied.

'What are you thinking?' Andaim asked.

'I'm thinking,' Idris said, 'that perhaps a change of plan might be in order.'

Idris had spent a lifetime serving the Colonial Forces, and during those long decades he and his fellow officers had seen countless things that they could not explain. Spacecraft whose performance defied human experience that vanished as soon as they appeared. Terrifying but beautiful species whose existence seemed to be on a plane different to that of the human experience, much like the Icari. Fearsome black holes, blazing supernovae, super-dense neutron stars spinning six hundred times per second and bizzare life forms that lived upon the precarious edges of all three natural phenomena, places where humans would be vaporised in an instant were it not for the protection afforded by their spacecraft.

Occasionally, artifacts or even entire craft were found drifting in the deep void, light years from the nearest systems and pitted with the impacts of tens of thousands of years' of micrometeorites – the relics of advanced species long extinct. Carefully concealed by the Colonial government for fear of alarming the general public, the study of these relics had often advanced human knowledge and technology by decades in a single bound.

But brigands like Taron Forge were under no obligation to hand over such items.

'The Word's knowledge is all built upon *human* knowledge,' Idris mused. 'Its experiences are bounded by our own, right up to the holocaust. It is now learning on its own but until its field of exploration exceeds our own…'

'… it knows only what we know,' Andaim finished the captain's sentence.

Evelyn caught on a moment later.

'If we could find a weapon against which the Word has no defence, we could strike back, hard.'

Idris nodded as he peered at Taron.

'Have you seen anything else like that shroud before?' he asked.

For once, the pirate captain seemed interested in the conversation.

'You hear things from time to time,' he admitted. 'Rumours, pilots being confronted by things they can't explain or escaping with their lives from some bizarre threat. Some of it is just bar-room bragging, but not all. That said, if you believed some pilots you'd think they all had a stash of planet-destroying weapons tucked away somewhere.'

Captain Idris Sansin nodded as he regarded the pirate. 'You got a stash down there on Chiron?'

'There's no stash,' Taron replied. 'We don't carry enough stores to need one.'

Idris smiled.

'You're a smart guy, Taron,' he observed, 'smart enough not to carry all your weapons in one holster. Your ship's holds are not that large, so you'd likely be trading in valuable minerals rather than parts and materials. I wonder what'll happen if I send a troop of Marines aboard her and let them see what they can find?'

Taron's casual air vanished in an instant. 'Over my dead body.'

'I can arrange that.'

Taron's hand flashed to his plasma pistol and the watching Marine's plasma magazines hummed into life again as they took aim at Taron and Yo'Ki.

'How do you want to play this?' Idris asked. 'A shooting match here, followed by your deaths and our searching of your ship anyway? Or some cooperation from you, and we let you go on your merry way?'

'Why the hell should I trust you?' Taron snapped.

'You can't,' Idris admitted, 'but then again, I don't have any real reason to detain you here either. Yet.'

Idris let the word hang in the air for a long moment. Taron glared at the captain and his hand remained on his pistol, but his shoulders sagged.

'Chiron IV,' he replied, 'northern hemisphere. You'll probably pick up a faint energy signal. I have weapons there.'

'Weapons?'

'I don't know how they work,' Taron replied. 'But it's my guess they'll go off with a hell of a bang. You'll need a shuttle and a tech-crew to move them. You find the weapons, then you let us off this damned ship.'

'Agreed,' Idris nodded and glanced at Evelyn. 'Lead a shuttle down there as escort. If you find anything, report back immediately.'

'Yes sir,' Evelyn replied and spun on her heel to march out of the room.

'Andaim,' Idris said, 'back her up with the alert flight, just in case.'

The CAG nodded and hurried off in pursuit of Evelyn.

'Guard,' the captain snapped. 'Escort Captain Forge and his co-pilot back to their ship, but do not allow them to take off without my permission.'

Taron joined his co-pilot and cast Idris a last glance. 'You're playing a very dangerous game, captain,' he observed.

The pirate walked out of the room, and General Bra'hiv confronted Idris.

'We can't trust him,' Bra'hiv said. 'He'll do anything he can to get control of the situation.'

'In time of war,' Idris replied, 'you can't be too choosy about your allies.'

'You can be a bit more bloody selective than this,' Bra'hiv hissed. 'Veng'en warriors first and now him? You any idea how this looks to the crew and the civilians, captain?'

Idris glared at the general.

'If you have any better ideas of how to move forward, general, I'd love to hear them.'

'I'm not saying that we don't need to take chances but…'

'Yes you are,' Idris snapped back. 'Right now we need to get every human being we come across on our side, one way or the other. We don't have many friends out there, general. I'm not about to throw away any opportunity to make new ones.'

'Pirates don't give a damn about us,' Bra'hiv insisted. 'You heard what Forge said.'

'Then we won't give a damn about them. But I'm not going to miss the chance to try and make allies, is that clear?'

Bra'hiv ground his teeth in his jaw. 'Aye, cap'ain.'

'Prepare a Marine landing party to join the techs in the shuttle crew,' Idris ordered. 'I want weapons and boots on the ground in case anything goes wrong.'

Bra'hiv saluted crisply and whirled away, leaving the captain to wrestle over the dilemma of whether his course of action really was the best one.

***

Dean Crawford

XIII

'Easy now.'

Dr Meyanna Sansin lifted a saline line and injected a painkiller into the feed. Slowly, the writhing, incoherent man strapped to the bed began to relax, his breathing becoming more regular. His skin was mottled with dark purple lines and slick with sweat despite his skin being cold to the touch.

Meyanna sealed the line once more and tapped the time and date onto a display screen beside the bed. She could see that the patient's seizures were becoming more regular and more acute, and the required dosage of medicine higher to combat them. Much more, and she feared she would end up killing the patient herself.

'How's he doing?'

Meyanna turned to see her husband entering the laboratory chamber, a series of transparent double-doors that sealed the laboratory's atmosphere from that of the ward beyond.

'Stable, but his seizures are getting worse.'

Idris Sansin moved to stand beside the bed and looked down at the civilian caught in the throes of extreme withdrawal from Devlamine.

'I'm going to need him to tell us where he got the drug from.'

'I can't do that,' Meyanna said. 'If he regains consciousness too early he'll suffer untold agony. Even if he did mention a name, we wouldn't be able to tell if he was telling a lie in order to be sedated again to avoid the pain. It would be a form of torture, and we both know that the results gained under duress are unreliable.'

'There could be other addicts aboard.'

'It's not the addicts you need to worry about,' Meyanna insisted. 'They can be treated once we know who they are.'

'They're not going to just march forward.'

'They will when the supply dries up and they enter withdrawal,' Meyanna replied. 'That's where you need to focus your efforts – find the supplier and shut them down.'

Idris nodded, and smiled. Meyanna was the rock in his life in so many ways, and despite working countless hours to keep the sick-bay running she still had enough wits about her to see problems clearly.

'I haven't figured out a good way of doing that yet,' he admitted. 'The toughest thing is figuring out who is definitely clean and getting them on the case.'

'Andaim? General Bra'hiv? Both of them are as straight as an arrow.'

'Yes,' Idris agreed, 'but it's for that reason that nobody else aboard ship would open up to them and reveal who is supplying and growing the drug. It's no good me sending the Marines in and rooting out the supplies of the drug if we don't also isolate its source. They'll just grow more of the damned stuff.'

'You need somebody to get on the inside,' Meyanna understood. 'Somebody that the suppliers might believe would become an addict.'

'Maybe one of the former convicts, one of the Marines?'

Meyanna winced. 'Chances are they'd do such a good job of infiltration that they'd *become* addicts, doubling the problem. Too risky.'

'Which leaves Qayin.'

'Qayin?!' Meyanna gasped in surprise. 'You'd let that rogue in on this? He was a gang-leader and a drug dealer, wasn't he? You let him in there and he'll end the supply all right, by taking over the operation!'

'That's my point though,' Idris said. 'He was a dealer, not a user. Qayin's too smart to let a drop of Devlamine anywhere near his body. He'd know how the drug grows, how people might hide it because he's likely done it himself.'

'You realise that makes him sound like a possible suspect for being behind this?'

'I do,' Idris acknowledged, 'but if he's the source then he'll have a hard time maintaining his operation while trying to be seen to stamp it out at the same time. It might also give him an out if he's behind it all – he can heroically discover the supply and the mysterious owner can escape unpunished.'

'Qayin's not going to let a stash go if he's got one. He'll keep something back.'

'But the current supply will end and we'll know Qayin's behind it. We win, both ways.'

Meyanna sighed. 'I guess Qayin's the best shot we've got.'

'I like the way you say "*we*",' Idris smiled, 'makes this ship feel like a family business.'

'Which reminds me,' Meyanna said, 'there are all kinds of rumours floating around right now among the crew and civilians. My nurses report them to me, because no patient ever says much to me directly as I'm your wife.'

Idris nodded. The sick-bay was a valuable source of ship-board gossip, a gauge by which the captain could measure the mood of his crew via his wife's regular updates. Her staff, it turned out, were inveterate gossips themselves and loved nothing more than to share what they heard on the wards with Meyanna.

'What's the latest?' he asked.

'They think that the command structure is becoming a dictatorship,' she replied.

'Seriously?'

'There's a lot of discord among the ordinary people who don't feel as though they're getting a say in things. Most believe that you're not interested in them and that they're regarded by the military as having an easy life and that they should just stop complaining.'

'There's some merit in that sentiment.'

'They're people,' Meyanna insisted. 'As long as they think that their needs are being considered, they'll be happy. Right now, their requests for supplies are being ignored and their sanctuary guarded by armed Marines who have recently shot dead one of their own. You do understand how that might make them feel?'

'Of course I do,' Idris replied, 'but right now I can't deal with them and run the ship. They'll just have to get through this.'

'They *have* been getting through this, just as we have for three years now,' Meyanna pointed out. 'They need a break. We all do.'

'Are you saying what I think you're saying?'

'Make planetfall,' Meyanna replied. 'Stand the ship down for a few days, give people a chance to get some real fresh air and a change of scenery. There's a planet down there with a habitable atmosphere. If the parent star flares we can pull out long before anybody gets hurt. Believe me, it'll do them good.'

'We're at *war*,' Idris insisted. 'We can't just go take a break for a few weeks!'

'We'll be at war for a long time yet,' Meyanna pointed out. 'How long do you think the people will go before they take matters into their own hands? It happened once before under Counsellor Hevel, and before you say it – it doesn't matter that he was infected. The people still followed him of their own free will and they almost took the ship from us.'

Idris sighed and rubbed his temples. 'I'll think on it.'

'Do that, before it's too late.'

*

'Stay low.'

Soltin responded without a word as he crouched down in the foliage. The leaves of the trees above them whispered in the breeze, the air cooler beneath the canopy as the sunlight dappled the forest floor nearby as they watched.

The order had come discreetly directly from the captain via General Bra'hiv: two men were to infiltrate the sanctuary and maintain a watch. Qayin, as a former drug smuggler, was to lead the small team and use his expertise to obtain information on the drug operation within the sanctuary and attempt to disrupt or bring to an end the supply chain.

Qayin, virtually invisible amid the dense vegetation, observed a lone man walked along the isolated path through the forest. Stocky, with thick arms and a bald head, the man moved almost silently and was casting his eyes up into the canopy above their heads.

Qayin remained absolutely still, as he and Soltin had done for the past two hours. It took at least a quarter of an hour for the local wildlife to settle down after they had set up their observation post, mimicking the work that Colonial Special Forces had once done before they were wiped out during the apocalypse. Concealed in a low gulley in the woods, Qayin had chosen a spot that he would have used as a dealer hoping to conceal merchandise, and begun a watch cycle designed to pick out the man at the source of the Devlamine supply.

'That was quick,' Soltin breathed in a soft whisper.

'Local knowledge,' Qayin explained but said nothing more as the man approached closer.

The trees he had seen on earlier patrols, densely packed on the hillsides, provided the ideal hiding place for small, portable stashes of Devlamine. Their height amid the branches would prevent easy detection either by sight or by sensors, yet also provide easy access for the dealer.

The man wore a sack over his shoulder, which he dropped to the ground beneath the trees and opened the drawstring. From within he hauled a length of rope attached to a metal grapple. The man stood beneath a large tree and looked up, swinging the grapple in ever expanding loops beside him before letting it fly up into the canopy. The grapple looped itself over a thick tree limb some twenty feet above the ground and caught firmly.

The man tugged hard on the rope to test its strength, and then he climbed up with surprising agility and vanished into the canopy above.

'So that's where they're hiding it,' Soltin said.

Qayin nodded. Given the sanctuary's nature there were actually few places that such things could be hidden without observation. The sanctuary was large, but not so large that it could not be thoroughly searched, the soil barely a cubit deep and the waters of the shoreline shallow enough to wade in.

Qayin crept forward, Soltin following as they moved silently out across the pathway between the dense trees and slowed alongside the dangling rope.

'What do we do now?' Soltin breathed.

Qayin grinned. 'That's easy.'

Qayin activated his pulse rifle and aimed up into the trees.

'You're going to kill him?!' Soltin gasped.

'He's a drug dealer,' Qayin replied. 'No use in keeping him alive.'

'But he might lead us to the suppliers!' Soltin urged.

Qayin did not reply as he took aim. He breathed softly as he picked out the shape of a man huddled on a thick limb high in the canopy, and then held his breath as he squeezed the trigger.

The plasma rifle jolted down in his grip as the forest was shattered by the crack and whine of a plasma blast as Qayin's shot rocketed up into the canopy and seared its way through the leaves. Qayin shot Soltin a dirty look as the younger Marine's glove forced the rifle down at the last instant.

They heard a cry of shock and Soltin jumped back as the thick rope dropped from out of the trees and landed in a dense coil at Qayin's feet.

'What the hell did you do that for?' Qayin hissed.

'It's not our place to kill civilians,' Soltin shot back. 'No matter what they're doing.'

Qayin swallowed his anger and kept his rifle aimed up into the trees as he called out.

'You're under arrest, by the authority of Atlantia's command crew,' he bellowed. 'Give up your weapons now or you'll be blasted from that tree by my platoon!'

A long silence enveloped the tree, the wind rustling through the leaves, and then a plasma pistol dropped out of the canopy and hit the path nearby with a deep thud.

Qayin lowered his rifle as Soltin retrieved the pistol, and keyed a microphone.

'Sergeant Qayin,' he reported, 'sector four. We got one.'

***

Dean Crawford

XIV

'I can't wait!'

Teera's excitement was palpable as her Raython joined into close formation on Evelyn's wing, the two fighters circling the Atlantia as it hove into position in high orbit above Chiron IV.

'Stay sharp,' Evelyn cautioned. 'We don't know what's down there.'

The blue planet's oceans glowed as the sunrise appeared, a dazzling burst of brilliant light that swept the clouds and coasts far below in a haze of pinks, reds and orange.

'Roger that,' Teera replied. *'But really, I just want to breathe fresh air again.'*

'I know what you mean.'

Evelyn had, along with a handful of convicts and crew, been the last person to walk on a terrestrial planet with a breatheable atmosphere well over a year previously. Although the scrubbers aboard Atlantia did a remarkable job of cleaning the air supply, and the sanctuary provided a welcome relief from the rigours of ship-borne duty, neither could quite perfectly replicate the smell of a planetary atmosphere.

Evelyn looked down at the planet's vast sphere beneath them, too huge to fit in a single glance, and saw writhing coils of aurora sweeping through the planet's skies like beautiful kaleidoscopic ribbons of light that seemed to beckon her toward them. She knew that they were a gorgeous but deadly phenomena, a sign of the cosmic rays bombarding the planet's weakening magnetic field, and suddenly she saw them reach out toward her. Like giant golden glowing hands with hooked fingers that seemed to wrap around her Raython, she saw them loom before her and pass through her field of vision. Evelyn blinked, and the illusion vanished. With a start she realised that she was coming off the Devlamine high, and would need another dose soon because in the same instant she realised that she was sweating lightly and felt strangely cold.

'Ranger One, aloft and joining.'

'Copy that, Ranger One, you have the lead,' Evelyn replied as she snapped herself out of her reverie and spotted the shuttle on her holographic display, closing in on them.

'Reaper Two, guard formation, weapons cold.'

'Roger.'

Teera's Raython broke out of close formation and the two fighters formed up on the shuttle as it turned toward the planet's surface.

'Lock onto any source of power you can find,' Evelyn said. 'It should be Taron Forge's stash. We'll pick that up first and then scout for supplies.'

I've got a good source of energy from the northern hemisphere, near the coast,' came the Ranger pilot's reply. *'Elevation four-seven-oh, my mark. Atmospheric descent in ten seconds.'*

'Copy, your mark,' Evelyn replied as she keyed in the location. 'Let's go.'

The three craft nosed down toward Chiron's surface, all three of them also turning into a de-orbit position and firing their retro-thrusters forward as they spread out to avoid collisions. At Chiron's orbital speed of twelve thousand kilometres per hour, it took almost sixty seconds of burn before they really began descending at speed.

Evelyn tilted her Raython's nose up a little as she saw the temperature rise on her instruments and noted the flare of orange light around the fighter's nose as it hit the upper atmosphere at close to five thousand kilometres per hour. The fearsome flames of re-entry fluttered and glowed around the three craft for several minutes as they descended, slowing rapidly. Evelyn's cockpit shuddered around her and the little fighter's wings rocked but she held the craft steady until the turbulence passed.

The immense horizon gradually flattened out around her and the inky blackness of space was slowly replaced by a powder blue sky in front and a sweeping sunrise behind as they raced the aurora across the sky, veils of light flashing past like luminous clouds.

I've got lethal levels of radiation up here,' Teera reported as she scanned her instruments. *'This planet doesn't have much time left.'*

The shuttle descended into a broken cloud layer, Evelyn formating on its left wing as Teera took up position on the far side. The clouds raced past and the Raython shook with turbulence, enough so that Evelyn found herself smiling. In space there was minimal sensation of flight, but down here in an atmosphere she could feel every bump in the air, every thermal and every cloud as they raced down through them.

I've got a lock on the energy source,' Ranger One called.

Evelyn glanced at her displays and frowned. A large, powerful source of energy appeared before her as well as signs of large constructions.

'What the hell has he got down here?' Teera asked across the radio as she too saw the energy source ahead of them.

Evelyn felt a pulse of alarm as she got a handle on just how much energy she was looking at.

'He's not alone,' she called. 'Reaper Two, weapons hot, now! Ranger One, abort!'

The shuttle pulled back up, climbing toward the cloud layer, but Evelyn realised that it was already too late. The blue sky twinkled as multiple metallic objects caught the dawn sunlight, the objects travelling fast on a direct intercept course. A series of alarms burst into life in Evelyn's cockpit and made her jump as warning sensors flashed bright red at her.

'What the hell?' she uttered, and then she realised.

'Multiple contacts, stern quarter, all armed!' Teera yelled. *'It's a trap!'*

'Damn him,' Evelyn cursed as she thought of Taron Forge. 'He set us up!'

*

'How many?'

Captain Idris Sansin paced the Atlantia's bridge like a caged lion as he watched the trap unfold in the skies above Chiron IV and listened to the XO's reply.

'Fourteen, maybe more, but the signal's weak. It seems like they're running some kind of electronic interference. Our sensors did not detect them.'

The captain turned and looked straight into the eyes of Taron Forge, who was leaning against a support post on the bridge alongside Yo'Ki with his arms casually folded across his chest.

'You planned this,' he snarled at the pirate.

'You forced me into it.'

'How many are there?'

'Too many,' Taron replied, 'far too many.'

Idris whirled away and pointed at the XO.

'Launch the support fighters immediately and prepare an extraction force.'

'Too little, too late,' Taron murmured from behind the captain.

'Broadcast a warning on all frequencies, battle fleet in the vicinity code,' Idris ordered Lael.

The communcations officer sent the signal immediately as Idris turned back to Taron Forge.

'If even one of my people are hurt or killed, I'll have your corpse impaled on a post outside Atlantia's bridge as a warning to the others.'

Taron smiled back at the captain.

'Do as you will, but it won't change a thing. Your pilots down there are totally out-numbered and out-gunned. They won't last a moment if they try to fight.'

Idris clenched his fists and turned to watch the tactical display as the Raythons rushed headlong into the teeth of the attack, Teera's alert call coming through broken and distorted by interference.

'Multiple contacts… bearing ten-zero-elevation… minus oh-four!'

'Identity?' Idris demanded.

Mikhain scanned his tactical display as he replied.

'No identification squawks on any frequency, no registration codes or known colours broadcast.'

Sansin took his seat on the bridge and his practiced old eye scanned the charts, tactical displays and the radar tracks of the incoming vessels.

'Launch the CAG with the alert-five aircraft,' he ordered. 'I want support for Reaper Flight out there right now.'

'Aye, sir,' Mikhain responded.

The captain surveyed the displays. 'How many contacts now, exactly?'

The Atlantia's communications specialist, Lael, replied moments later.

'Twenty seven individual craft,' she said. 'Various exhaust readings from all of them suggesting varied types.'

Idris looked at Mikhain, whose expression had darkened to a scowl. 'Brigands.'

The captain nodded.

'No distinguishable formation,' he observed of the onrushing craft, 'no apparent colours or planetary flag, multiple craft types liberally deployed. They must have been here for quite a while.'

Brigands, buccaneers, corsairs, privateers and pirates were as much a part of Etherean legend as many other planets, first on terrestrial oceans and then upon the far greater canvass of the cosmos. By their very nature they were marginalised, their crews often comprised of escaped convicts and wanted felons, those who did not wish to conform but instead to disrupt, to profit from the suffering of others. Despised and despising, pirates had naturally migrated to the furthest known, least hospitable and generally uninhabited systems. Only the most pioneering of exploratory vessels had regularly encountered pirates in the farthest reaches of explored space, such as the mineral-rich Tyberium Fields, and they had generally been required to carry heavy weaponry to deter attacks from such marauders.

Three decades previously Idris Sansin had been the commander of a smaller vessel, the *Ventura*, a well-armed Colonial vessel manned by three hundred personnel and equipped with two full squadrons of Phantom fighters and the rather aptly-named Corsair bombers. The Ventura had been tasked by the admiralty with sweeping the shipping lanes of the Tyberium Fields, actively seeking out pirates after they had conducted several daring raids on massive but lumbering corporate merchant vessels.

During the course of the six-month cruise the Ventura had captured or destroyed seventeen pirate craft, many of them stolen years before from law-abiding crews who had then been set adrift in escape capsules in deep space. Not all had been found before their survival systems had exhausted their fuel.

There had been no quarter given to those pirates found guilty of causing the deaths of employees of the mining companies or of killing owner-operators. Vetoing the normal Etheran laws, the high court had deemed that as the killings had occurred outside of Etherean space, so the normal rights afforded convicted criminals did not apply. Thus were some forty eight pirates put to death for their crimes. Interestingly, given Etherea's liberal society, there was minimal outcry at the sentences – one of the most feared ways to die in modern society was to be cast adrift in space, to tumble endlessly into the void and slowly freeze to death. By contrast, as it was noted in the media, a swift death by controlled plasma charge administered to the guilty pirates was virtually painless.

'What the hell are they doing here?' Mikhain asked out loud. 'That star could destroy Chiron any moment if the planet's magnetic field is overwhelmed.'

'That,' Idris said, 'is a very good question. Lael, what's the history of pirate activity in this system?'

Lael scanned the records.   .

'The instability of the star and its distance from the core systems put it out of the range of almost all but military vessels, making it something of a haven for criminal enterprise. There are some charts based on a visit by a mining company that operated out here some decades ago, but they cleared out when the star became too volatile and their operating profits too low to justify trading this far out.'

Idris stood up from his chair and began pacing back and forth as he spoke.

'They have a lot of vessels, a lot of firepower.'

Mikhain stared at the captain for a brief instant. 'You're not thinking of talking to them?'

Idris glared at Taron. 'Who's down there?'

The smuggler shrugged. 'You want your people back, you'll need me to liase with the brigand force down there. You don't let me go, who knows what will happen?'

Idris ignored the smuggler.

'Maintain an open channel,' he suggested to Lael. 'Let's see who we're actually dealing with here.'

*

'Defensive break, go!'

Evelyn hauled her Raython into a hard right turn toward Teera's fighter and was immediately caught by surprise by the immense G-forces that drove her into her seat. Even with the Raython's on-board computers preventing her from over-stressing the airframe, she herself was unfamiliar with the strains of atmospheric flying and her vision turned almost immediately grey.

Evelyn broke off the turn as she saw Teera's fighter sweep overhead, vapour trails spiralling from the wing tips and puffing in clouds above the fuselage.

'Watch the G-forces!' Evelyn yelled.

Teera's Raython rolled onto its back and plummeted from the sky for a moment before rolling upright again and pulling out of its dive.

'*I blacked out!*' she called back.

Evelyn didn't have time to reply as a flash of plasma fire rocketed past her Raython and the onrushing interceptors flashed by her. She glimpsed various types of craft including at least three dirty-looking Raythons amid a mixture of old bombers, modified survey craft and civilian transports.

'Keep your speed down,' Evelyn advised as she turned once more, keeping the G-forces low. 'Try to out-turn them!'

The Raythons swept around their turns but Evelyn could tell instantly that they were at a disadvantage. The motley formation of craft turned wildly across the skies, less agile than Evelyn's fighter but their pilots more experienced at atmospheric combat and able to push their craft closer to the limits of their performance.

The equation was simple: experience and numbers had put the odds in their attacker's favour.

'Cover the shuttle, stay between it and them!' Evelyn ordered.

The sky seemed suddenly filled with enemy craft, their wings flashing with metallic brilliance against the cold blue sky as Evelyn rolled and pulled through a series of defensive manoeuvres, breathing hard and tensing her legs to keep the blood in her upper-body as the forces of gravity worked against her heart to drag it all down from her head.

Another salvo of shots raced past her canopy and she broke hard left and dragged her throttle back as she rolled inverted and looked behind her. Her head span as she did so but she spotted a small craft race by, overshooting her as she slowed. Evelyn rolled upright as she slammed the throttle open and the Raython accelerated in pursuit of the craft, which turned hard right in an attempt to shake her off.

'Got you,' Evelyn snarled.

Her plasma cannons locked onto the fleeing craft and Evelyn fired once.

Two blue plasma shots zipped away from her Raython and one crashed into the craft's upper hull with a bright orange fireball and a trail of black smoke. The craft emerged from the blast and rolled slowly onto its back as it began diving toward the planet's surface.

'Splash one!' Evelyn called.

She rolled away as a series of plasma blasts detonated off her port wing, rocking the Raython violently.

'We're out-numbered!' Teera cried, and Evelyn looked up to see her wingman's fighter twisting through a cloud of enemy craft all swarming to get a shot off at her.

'Break left, full power!' Evelyn called.

Teera veered toward Evelyn's Raython and flashed by overhead as Evelyn aimed at the pursing group of craft and opened fire randomly at them all. Plasma blasts smashed into two of the craft as the rest of them scattered.

'Where the hell did they get Raythons from?' Teera asked.

Evelyn keyed her microphone.

'Atlantia, Reaper Flight, do you copy?'

A hiss of static rippled in Evelyn's ears.

'We're being jammed,' Teera reported as her Raython opened fire on another of the attacking craft. *'They can't hear us!'*

'Where's the shuttle?' Evelyn called, a sheen of sweat now beading on her forehead, her hands clammy on the controls as a dull nausea spread through her stomach. 'The alert fighters will be here soon enough if Atlantia can't make contact! We just need to hold them off for long enough to…'

A new voice broke into the transmission frequency.

'… to escape? That, I'm afraid, is no longer possible.'

Evelyn gripped her controls more tightly. 'Who is this?'

'The person targeting your shuttle craft,' came the reply. *'Surrender immediately or you will be blasted from the skies.'*

'We have a frigate supporting us and several squadrons of fighters all ready to…'

'So do we,' came the reply. *'Surrender now! If your supporting fighters don't turn back, we'll blast them from existence too.'*

Evelyn rolled her Raython level and searched the skies around her. She saw at least twelve craft all manoeuvring to shoot her, six more of them trailing Teera's Raython as a salvo of plasma blasts showered past her craft.

Almost immediately one of them struck Teera's Raython and a plume of flame and smoke erupted from her tail.

'I'm hit!' Teera yelled. 'Shutting my starboard engine down!'

The voice returned to the radio.

'You're running out of time.'

Evelyn spotted the shuttle high above them and surrounded by four craft, one of which had manoeuvred into position directly above it to prevent it from climbing away any further. A large, X-winged vessel with a cruel, hooked nose like a beak, it dwarfed the shuttle it was shadowing. Two smaller vessels were sitting in a perfect firing position, directly behind the shuttle.

Evelyn made her choice.

'Reaper Flight, weapons cold, stand down.'

'Are you kidding me?' Teera snapped. 'I can handle these...'

'Weapons cold, now!' Evelyn bellowed at her wingman, and instantly Teera's Raython stopped manoeuvring, the cloud of craft around it settling into firing positions behind her as the voice called across the radio once more.

'That, my young friend, is the first good decision you have made this morning.'

'Who the hell are you?'

'You will be guided to land,' the voice ordered. 'Deviate from your assigned flightplan by so much as a wingspan and your flight will end in a real hurry, understand?'

***

XV

'What the hell's happened?!'

Captain Idris Sansin stormed across the bridge toward the XO, Mikhain.

'We've lost contact,' Mikhain reported. The ambush was successful, captain. It looks like Reaper Flight has stood down.'

Idris whirled and approached Taron Forge.

'You knew they were down there,' he growled. 'What else have they got?'

'A lot more than you think,' Taron replied.

'I knew he was dirty,' Mikhain snapped as he rushed out from behind his console at Taron.

The XO swung a punch at Taron, but the pirate batted it aside with one hand as he turned and rammed one flat hand under Mikhain's jaw. The XO's momentum sent him flying past Taron and he sprawled onto the deck in time for Yo'Ki's pistol to aim down at his head.

'Manners, Mikhain,' Taron smirked at him.

The captain grabbed Taron's arm. 'I want my people back.'

'I want a place in the sun and more money than I know what to do with,' Taron replied, 'but that's not going to happen right now, is it?'

Mikhain got to his feet, his features twisted with fury.

'I told you that this was a bad idea!' he snapped at the captain as he pointed at Taron and Yo'Ki. 'These scum cannot be trusted! We should have blasted them the moment we laid eyes on them, not invited them up here!'

'Noted,' the captain growled back.

'Is it?!' Mikhain demanded. 'Is it *really*?!'

The bridge fell silent as the crew watched the XO glare at the captain.

'Secure that,' Idris replied. 'This isn't the time or the place.'

'And what is the time and place?' Mikhain snapped. 'We've lost two Raythons, their pilots, a shuttle and a platoon of Marines, all because you didn't listen to what I or anybody else advised!'

The captain peered at Mikhain. 'I listened to all of the advice.'

'And rejected it!'

'That's my job, if needs be!'

'It's the work of a dictator!'

The two senior officers stared at each other for a long moment across the bridge, and then Lael stepped in.

'We none of us have time for this right now,' she insisted. 'We have people to liberate from that planet and likely not much time to do it, if that star is anything to go by.'

The captain appeared to shake himself from his study of the XO and glanced at Taron Forge.

'Who's down there, exactly?'

'Cut me loose and I'll go down and talk to them,' Taron suggested. 'Maybe negotiate the release of your people.'

'Over my dead body,' Idris snapped. 'Where are the alert fighters?' he asked Mikhain.

The XO mastered his anger and marched back to his tactical station.

'Descending, but they're not going to get there in time to make a difference. Evelyn would not have surrendered lightly, even against those odds.'

Idris stared at the tactical screen for a moment. He could see the shuttle surrounded by enemy craft.

'Call the alert fighters back,' he ordered. 'Lael, transmit a dialogue request on all open channels to the planet's surface.'

The XO and communications officer relayed the commands, and almost immediately Andaim's voice spoke from the cockpit of his Raython.

We should maintain a presence captain,' he advised. *'If they're taking hostages we should do what we can to keep pressure on them. Regular patrols to prevent anybody from leaving the surface. It'll keep their craft on the ground too.'*

Idris nodded.

'I agree, make it happen. Then get back aboard the Atlantia immediately, I need you here.'

'They've taken Evelyn, captain, and if we get a chance to...'

'They're not going to make any mistakes, Andaim,' the captain insisted. 'Evelyn made her call and stood down, and besides there are thirty other hostages down there too. We need them all back alive and I won't risk their lives with a reckless rescue attempt. Land immediately, is that understood?'

'Aye, captain.'

The communication channel to the bridge shut off just as General Bra'hiv marched onto the bridge and saluted the captain.

'We have a prisoner, sir.'

'A what?'

'My Marines found one of the civilians hoarding Devlamine down in the sanctuary. He'd placed his stash up in the treetops, which was why we didn't find anything during the initial searches.'

Idris rubbed his forehead thoughtfully. 'He talking?'

'I haven't got started on him. I thought you might want to have an ear in on the conversation.' The general looked at the tactical displays and frowned. 'Where's my platoon?'

'On the surface,' Mikhain reported, 'as hostages.'

'Hostages?'

'They were ambushed,' the captain explained. 'It looks like our new friend here found himself a get-out clause.'

Bra'hiv glanced at Taron and Yo'Ki without interest. 'I'd prefer them both to be locked up in the brig,' he said.

'That might be the safest place for everyone,' Taron murmured as he looked at the captain and the XO with interest. 'You guys are likely to destroy each other long before the Word shows up.'

Idris stared at the pirate for a moment.

'Win, lose or draw Taron, you're a human being and that makes you just as much of a target for the Word as we are. If there are people down there then they could have been tracked, so why isn't the Word here?'

Taron smiled, shrugged his shoulders. 'Who knows?'

Bra'hiv's side-arm snapped out of its holster so fast it seemed as though it were alive, the pistol pressed against Taron's jaw before Yo'Ki could pull her own weapon.

'*You* know,' Bra'hiv snarled. 'It's up there in that head of yours. Either share it now or I'll share the contents of your head in a totally less pleasant way.' Bra'hiv activated the plasma magazine and the pistol hummed into life. 'In your own time, captain.'

Taron glared down at the shorter, stockier man, but he made no attempt to draw his own pistol. His idle tones carried across the bridge to the captain.

'You want me to help you, captain?' Taron asked Idris. 'Get this little squirt out of my face first.'

The captain forced himself to keep a lid on his anger at the pirate's flippant insults, and nodded to the general.

'Stand down general, and let him speak.'

'You can't trust a word he says unless there's a weapon pressed to his head,' Bra'hiv warned. 'His kind knows nothing but lies and theft.'

'He knows what's down there,' the captain said, 'and for now that will have to be enough.'

Bra'hiv held his position for a moment longer, and then he deactivated his pistol and stood back from Taron.

The pirate smirked at the general.

'What's down there is Salim Phaeon,' he said simply.

A silence enveloped the Atlantia's bridge at the mention of the name.

'Salim,' the captain echoed as though spitting out something unpleasant. 'He is alive?'

'Very much,' Taron replied. 'In fact, as far as I can tell he's never been happier.'

'Who is Salim Phaeon?' Bra'hiv asked.

Idris placed his hands behind his back as he replied.

'Salim Phaeon was one of the most feared brigands ever to come to the attention of the Colonial Forces, back when I was in command of an active ship of the line, Ventura. He was leading a flotilla of pirate vessels and causing mayhem in the Tyberium Fields before we were called in to flush them out and engage them directly, to protect the shipping lanes out near the Icari Line.'

'You've met this man?' Mikhain asked.

'Not in person,' Idris replied. 'But I have engaged him in combat and in doing so killed several members of his family. Salim is not going to want to do any kind of deal with me. If we negotiate, it'll have to be with somebody else acting as commander of this vessel.'

Mikhain stood a little more upright behind his console.

'I would be happy to play that role, captain.'

Idris peered at the XO. 'It's *captain* now, is it? And there was I thinking that you no longer held my command in the highest respect.'

'It's not your command that I disrespect, sir,' Mikhain replied. 'But what I think does not matter right now. Getting our people back aboard before this Salim murders them is what matters.'

Idris nodded thoughtfully.

'I want to know what Salim is doing down there,' he said to Taron. 'Why is he holed up on this planet, in a dying system?'

'Why do you think?' Taron asked rhetorically. 'Because it's a dying system very few vessels ever ventured out this way. There has been a smuggling settlement on Chiron IV for decades, not that any of you thought to search for one.'

'The system was off-limits due to the stars' instability, Admiralty's orders,' Mikhain uttered.

'Since when do pirates obey the Admiralty?' Taron murmured in response. 'The system's instability provides the perfect cover for Salim's operations.'

'And now?' Bra'hiv asked. 'The Admiralty is long gone, nobody is hunting Salim so why is he still here?'

'The star,' Taron said and tilted his head toward the bridge's main viewing panel, where an image of Chiron IV and its parent star dominated. 'It emits vast amounts of energy, magnetic fields, cosmic rays and such like. As it turns out, the Legion doesn't like to play when the sun's shining too brightly.'

'They're driven away?' Idris asked.

'Can't say for sure,' Taron admitted, 'but whenever an infected ship has entered the system it's always pulled away again before reaching too deep. Many of the ship's Salim's men have plundered were found because they fled here and managed to escape pursuit by the Word.' Taron grinned. 'Out of the frying pan…'

Idris turned away thoughtfully but it was Mikhain who responded.

'This could be the kind of place we were looking for after all,' he suggested. 'A safe haven, as long as we keep an eye on solar activity. That star could take decades to become truly dangerous.'

'Or it could flare up tomorrow and blast Chiron IV's atmosphere into oblivion,' Bra'hiv countered. 'This isn't a safe place.'

'Nowhere is truly safe,' Mikhain replied. 'But a planet in a zone where the Word will not travel isn't something we can lightly pass by.'

Idris stared at the deck for a long moment. 'We need supplies,' he said, almost to himself. 'That really is something that we cannot pass by. Chiron IV there is more than big enough for us and Salim's fleet.'

'And this time we'll be ready for them,' Mikhain added.

'You're forgetting,' Taron murmured, 'that he's holding several of your crew hostage. He may not allow you to descend toward the surface again.'

Idris's features creased into a grim smile.

'Then we'll have to test his resolve,' he growled. 'I'm not about to let my crew be pushed about by a common criminal.' He turned to Lael. 'Activate all electronic counter-measures and broadcast at full power. Salim's going to hear what we say whether he likes it or not.'

'Her won't listen to you,' Taron reminded the captain smugly. 'You'll need us to liase with Salim.'

Idris, his fists clenched by his sides, bellowed out a new command.

'Guards, get them both out of here and into a holding cell!'

Two Marines thundered onto the bridge and grabbed Taron and Yo'Ki, disarming them and turning them toward the exits. Taron's voice called back to Idris as they were escorted from the bridge.

'Only way out of this for your people is to listen to me, captain,' he called. 'We're useless to your captured crews in a prison cell.'

Idris waited until the smuggler was off the bridge before he turned to Mikhian.

'We need a solution to all of this and fast.'

'What about the prisoner from the sanctuary?' Bra'hiv asked again. 'We need to find out where he's getting his Devlamine supply from.'

'We will have to deal with him later,' Idris replied. 'Right now we may have a hostage situation and that takes precedence. Have your men ready to move at a moment's notice, general.'

As the general saluted and marched from the bridge, Mikhain stepped up.

'Who is going to play the role of captain, in your stead?'

Nobody answered for a moment as the captain turned to look at Mikhain. He looked as though he was about to reply when the bridge doors opened and Andaim strode onto the bridge.

'Reporting for duty, captain,' Andaim said.

Idris turned to face the CAG, and he grinned.

'Welcome aboard, *captain.*'

Andaim frowned in confusion, and Idris did not see the scowl darken Mikhain's features behind them.

***

XVI

'Get out of your ship with your hands where we can see them!'

Evelyn punched her harness lock as she watched a group of flamboyantly dressed men encircle her Raython fighter. Their faces were tanned and several were scarred or laced with tattoos, both human and other species alike, some of which she had never seen before. All were heavily armed, their weapons trained on her as she flipped a switch and her canopy opened.

A blessed gust of fresh, wind-swept ocean air swept across her face as she stood up in her seat and clambered out of the cockpit. A vast ocean glittered in the sunlight, nearby cliffs bathed in glowing yellow light from the sunrise, their wind-swept tops a hundred feet over her head. For a few moments her cold sweat and nausea was blown away by the crisp, clean air.

Evelyn jumped down and landed on soft earth for the first time in months as the men advanced around her.

'Hands behind your head!' one of them bellowed.

Evelyn slowly raised her hands and placed them behind her head as she watched Teera being likewise detained nearby. The shuttle had landed but not yet opened its rear ramp. Heavily armed and not likely willing to surrender without a fight, the Marines inside might charge out with guns blazing. Evelyn kept one eye on the shuttle as a brigand approached her.

His face was heavily pock-marked like the surface of a battered moon, and wiry stubble sprouted here and there around a mouth filled with yellowing teeth that stank of old tobacco. A thick, stubby cigar was clenched between them as he peered closely at her with a jaundiced gaze and lifted his rifle up to rest on his shoulder.

'Well, aren't you a pretty little thing? I'd like me a piece of you.'

Evelyn smiled at him and then drove her knee deep into his groin with a grunt of effort.

The man's cigar blasted from between his teeth and spun over Evelyn's shoulder as he dropped like a stone to his knees, the rifle swinging back down to point at her. Evelyn grabbed the weapon and ducked down beside the man's body for cover as she grabbed his scrawny beard and yanked him sideways.

The pirate spun about awkwardly as Evelyn twisted the rifle around and jammed it up under his armpit. She activated the magazine and faced the men surrounding her.

'Come any closer and I'll fry his brain!' she snapped.

The men looked at each other and then to her dismay they began laughing.

'Do it, honey,' one of them called. 'Old Feyzin stinks to high heaven anyway!'

More laughter and the men closed in further.

'You can't shoot us all, missy,' another of them sneered.

Evelyn glanced at the shuttle craft. A small group of men were approaching the rear ramp with their weapons aimed at it, but it still had not opened. She looked back at the pirate who had spoken to her.

'I don't have to shoot you all,' she replied. 'Just a few will do.'

She pushed the rifle harder against Feyzin's ribcage and heard the old man wince in pain.

The pirates hesitated, unsure of how to respond.

Evelyn saw the shuttle's ramp emit a wisp of vapour as it cracked open.

'Come now missy,' said the advancing pirate. 'There's nothing to fear here.'

Evelyn grinned at him without warmth. 'Yes, there is.'

The shuttle's rear ramp suddenly dropped and hit the earth with a deep thud and instantly a salvo of plasma blasts cracked from its depths and cut down several pirates in a hail of fire as the Marines rushed out from the shuttle's interior and fanned out, firing as they went.

The pirates confronting Evelyn whirled in surprise at the sudden noise and Evelyn opened fire. Her first shot blasted Feyzin's head clean off of his shoulders and her second dropped the nearest man before he had even realised that she was firing at him. The plasma blast blazed through his chest in a cloud of smoke and burning flesh as he screamed and toppled backwards.

As the pirates scattered Evelyn ducked into cover behind the nose of her Raython and saw Teera jerk her head backwards into the face of the man holding her and break free of his grip. She dashed for her fighter and rolled beneath it as a haze of plasma fire ripped the air around her.

The Marines spread out, firing controlled bursts at the pirates and cutting them down one by one. Evelyn fired at another man, his colourful billowing coat slowing him down as he ran. Her shot hit his cheek and blasted the top of his head off, his body collapsing in a rolling heap.

The pirates retreated toward their own craft, taking shelter behind them as the shuttle closed its rear ramp and its engines whined into life. Evelyn yelled across to Teera.

'Get airborne and cover them! We're getting out of here!'

The shuttle's pilot spun the craft in mid-air and aimed its small plasma cannons at the various pirate craft landed around them. The cannons fired a crackling blaze of plasma rounds that smashed into parked craft and sliced through their metallic hulls in bright flashes. A series of explosions shattered the air, thick clouds of black smoke boiling up into the perfect blue sky.

Teera dashed for her Raython's cockpit and clambered into it as Evelyn laid down covering fire against the pirates closest to her wingman's fighter. The shuttle's cannons hammered the ground around the pirate's craft and two more of the parked vessels crumpled amid explosions as they were hit.

The Marines, still laying down heavy but controlled fire, moved position as they headed toward a series of low bluffs for better cover. Evelyn whirled for her Raython's cockpit and made to climb aboard when a huge blast shattered the air above her.

Evelyn threw herself instinctively to the ground and glanced up as she saw the shuttle spin sideways through the air as it trailed a dense coil of black smoke. Even as she watched a second blast smashed into the shuttle and it exploded in a massive fireball that showered burning fragments down onto the beach and littered it with debris.

Evelyn, her ears ringing from the blast, struggled to her feet and turned to see a large vessel bristling with weapons hovering over the cliffs. The X-winged vessel's long, cruel, hooked nose extended back toward a large hull, a billowing cushion of heat haze rippling beneath the craft as it moved out over the ocean and descended, turning to face back toward the beach with its heavy weapons aimed at the Marines.

As the craft was expertly hovered just a few cubits above the beach, a ramp lowered and dozens more pirates and giant, lumbering figures hefting heavy weapons descended onto the beach and advanced toward the Marines' position.

Evelyn felt her shoulders sag as the pirates, backed by their ship, marched without fear and their leader, a swaggering man with a loud hailer, called out above the roar of the ship's engines.

'Surrender, now, or this is all over!'

Evelyn looked across at the Marines, and after a few moments the soldiers lowered their weapons and emerged from cover. Evelyn reluctantly stood up and held her weapon in the air as the pirates marched up to her and grabbed the pistol from her grasp, spun her around and slammed her down onto her knees on the beach.

Her arms were yanked behind her back and bound firmly by heavy metal manacles, and then she was dragged to her feet and shoved toward the surrendering Marines, a pistol barrel jammed hard under her ribs.

The large vessel changed position, its engines blasting clouds of sand across the beach as it hovered toward more stable ground and settled down onto a series of landing pads that extended from beneath the hull. As Evelyn was shoved toward the Marines and forced onto her knees to join them on the beach, a portly man descended the pirate gunship's ramp as its engines whined down into silence, his robes colourful and his skin oily. The man approached the Marines and pilots and paused to look about him at the smouldering debris and dead bodies on the beach.

He shook his head and tutted.

'Now there was really no need for any of this, was there?'

Evelyn looked up at the man but remained silent. She realised that the Marines surrounding her were all watching her expectantly, and then she got it: with the shuttle pilot dead, she was now the ranking officer.

'My name is Salim,' said the portly man with a cold smile, 'and you are all now mine.'

'Our ship is in orbit, the frigate Atlantia,' Evelyn shot back. 'They will begin a bombardment any moment.'

Salim looked down at her for a moment and then up as he surveyed the flawless sky above. He looked back down at her, the smile still affixed to his face.

'Strange, then, that I have taken your ships, killed several of your people and apprehended so many more, yet nothing has happened?'

'They're biding their time.'

'And you're wasting yours,' Salim smirked, and then he looked up at the huge creatures looming over them, thickly muscled and with simple, flat faces.

'Take them to the camp!' he ordered.

'You're making a mistake,' Evelyn insisted. 'We were here only for supplies. Now you've started a war.'

'I think, my dear, that this war has been fought for many years,' Salim corrected her. 'Chiron IV is our home and you're trespassing. If your frigate's commander makes any attempt to attack us, it will be you who is killed first.'

Even as they were about to be led away, a pirate hurried up to Salim and whispered into his ear. The portly man grinned broadly and glanced at Evelyn.

'It would seem that your commander cares for you after all,' he purred. 'Captain Ry'ere has requested that we begin a dialogue for your release.'

Evelyn almost frowned in confusion at the pirate's use of Andaim's name as the Atlantia's captain, but she managed to check herself. Whatever was going on up there, Captain Sansin would not be talking to the pirates.

'Rest assured,' Salim promised them. 'I will talk to your captain as a matter of common courtesy, but none of you will ever leave this place alive.'

***

Dean Crawford

XVII

The vessel in which Evelyn was manacled touched down, the interior vibrating as it landed and her fellow captives shaken in their seats.

'Where the hell are they taking us?'

Teera's whispered question was not heard by their giant captors, whom Evelyn had learned were called Ogrin and who squatted around the ship on giant, flat feet, their grim faces hung low and their eyes devoid of anything other than the most basic of intelligence.

'I don't know,' Evelyn replied, and tried not to think too hard about it.

Fact was, she knew damned well the practices that pirates enjoyed, chiefly those of slavery and debauchery when not hunting down prey in the shipping lanes. Many of the most gruesome stories of pirate activity were myth, enhanced in the retelling, but others were not. Entire slum-cities of captives had been discovered during the great Colonial crack-down on piracy a few decades previously, thousands of slaves liberated from endless years of back-breaking labour under the cruel gaze of their piratical foremen. Whether building new spaceships, mining or running sweatshops printing fake cash or forging fake minerals, the pirates wasted very little time on worrying about their workers' rights.

The rear ramp of the ship was lowered, daylight and fresh air wafting inside as the engines wound down and Evelyn was led outside with a push and a shove. She stumbled out into the bright sunlight and almost immediately her breath was taken away as she looked up at the huge frigate looming over them.

'I'll be damned,' Teera gasped. 'That's Arcadia!'

Evelyn stared up at *Arcadia*, one of several sister-ships to Atlantia and a former Colonial frigate retired from combat duties almost a decade before and employed in the prison service. The huge vessel seemed even larger when viewed on foot, her keel resting on huge docking cradles and her hull towering over the landscape around them.

'How the hell did they get Arcadia?' Teera wondered out loud. 'The prisoners must have escaped somehow, like they did on Atlantia.'

'Except they were successful in taking the ship,' Evelyn replied, realising what might have happened and where so many pirates and criminals had managed to turn up in the same place at once. 'They're reparing the damage.'

Evelyn scanned the Arcadia's hull and spotted signs of battle damage, workers high up on her surface welding giant hull panels back into place or repairing damaged power conduits.

'The prisoners could not have arranged all of this on their own,' Teera said as they were led beneath Arcadia's hull, the wind brisk as it was channelled beneath the bow of the ship high above them. 'It's too big a task.'

'It must have been planned,' Eveyln agreed, 'maybe after the apocalypse.'

Despite the extreme level of security that had surrounded the orbital prisons, the inmates always somehow found a way to communicate with the outside world. Corrupt guards, blackmail and the near-permanent threat of physical violence had often resulted in major criminals running their operations from inside high-security prisons. In a weakened and panicked state after the apocalypse it was not unthinkable that the crew of Arcadia, perhaps divided and in disarray, could have been overwhelmed by a concerted pirate attack alongside an internal insurrection.

The prisoners were led in a long line down to the base of a low cliff, dominated by what Evelyn assumed was the equivalent of a pirate's headquarters, elaborate banners fluttering in the wind. But there were no brigands visible, only a single hulking Ogrin whose dull, deep tones carried over each of the Marines and crew as he recited what had clearly been dictated by his piratical owners.

'You will be assigned tasks,' the Ogrin growled. 'Undertake them or you will be punished. If punishment does not stiffen your resolve, you will be killed.'

'Not exactly a worker's union then,' Teera muttered under her breath.

Then, the Ogrin spoke again. 'The women will be separated and tasked with serving the gentlefolk.'

Evelyn's eyes widened as she was yanked from the line along with Teera.

'Serving the *gentlefolk*?' Teera almost laughed. 'Boy, they're gonna get a shock when they meet us.'

Evelyn said nothing, watching instead as the Marines were sectioned off into groups of six, each under the watchful eye of an Ogrin, and led toward the Arcadia's towering hull. From her viewpoint Evelyn could see literally hundreds of workers labouring across the hull, and who knew how many more were inside, working to repair the ship's systems?

'This way!'

Evelyn was grabbed by an Ogrin's giant hand and shoved toward the pirate's palace, which in reality was little more than a tower of scaffolding affixed to the cliffs and panelled with old hull plating. A couple of mounted plasma guns sat in unmanned turrets, ready to quell any uprising or attack on the makeshift fortress.

The Ogrin prodded them up a flight of steps and into the pirate's lair. The rush of the ocean and the rumbling wind became a muted backdrop as Evelyn walked into what looked like some kind of lounge. The air, so fresh outside, was pungent with the sickly odour of countless types of tobacco and alcohol, the light dim and lethargic.

A pair of brigands slumped against sagging couches, their eyes watching Evelyn and Teera with interest but not a single muscle in their bodies moving. Likely doped to the eyeballs, Evelyn figured as she was led past toward another, larger room.

The second room opened out and was ringed with ornate banners hanging from the walls, some of them the captured planetary colours of plundered vessels, others the garish flags of pirate captains themselves, personalised designs depicting fiery beasts of the air or hellish skulls as though the owners believed themselves some kind of cult leaders.

Salim sat in a large bejewelled throne glittering in the low light that looked as though it had been yanked from the capital ship of a mining tycoon with far more money than sense or taste. He sat slumped there, his shining black eyes fixed on Evelyn and Teera as they were led to stand before him.

Salim was surrounded by a harem of women of all ages, some probably reaching their fifties, some not yet into their teens. Some were not even quite human but examples of rare *Hybrids*, the result of illegal breeding programs run by pirate clans over the years in an attempt to create the perfect "companion" species. Selectively mated for their personalities, sexuality and obedience, *hybrids* were typically exotic looking in nature and although Evelyn had never laid eyes on one before she knew what they were the moment she saw them.

There were four in all, all of them with dark, slanted eyes and deeply sun-burnished skin. Long, luscious hair was either glossy jet-black or sparkling blonde, and their limbs were rippling with bioluminescent tattoos reminiscent of Qayin's gang-colours. Evelyn knew however that their greatest assets remained internal, not external: genetic enhancements that allowed for improved sexual performance and diminished self-awareness.

Hybrids were banned for good reason: they were slaves bred deliberately to be too dim to understand what they were. The Ogrin, Evelyn had no doubt, had suffered the same fate.

'Welcome,' Salim said, 'to our house of peace and mutual respect. You will be well cared for here, my lovelies.'

Evelyn looked down and into the eyes of a young girl who was watching her with an alert, curious gaze. A new arrival Evelyn guessed, and not yet even a teenager.

'I doubt that you've got any idea what mutual respect is, Salim,' Evelyn replied. 'I like to treat as I find.'

'Is that so?' Salim asked.

'Sure it is,' Evelyn said. 'Which is why I'm going to make sure that you spend the rest of your life in a prison serving other people instead of being here using human beings as slaves.'

'My people are content,' Salim replied. 'You will be too.'

'Like hell,' Teera spat. 'First chance I get, I'll shove my pistol up your ass and pull the trigger.'

The blows came from behind, like giant hammers that drove Evelyn to her knees as she heard Teera cry out in pain and thump to the ground alongside her. Behind them, the Ogrin stood with clenched fists held in mid-air where they had struck across Evelyn's shoulders.

'I like to see spirit in my girls,' Salim said as he stood and descended toward them. 'It gives me more pleasure as I break them.'

'Only thing broken here is your head,' Evelyn managed to cough in response. 'Let us go and the Atlantia might not pummel this place into the ground.'

'Your ship will not fire upon us,' Salim replied without concern. 'There are too many innocent victims for their bleeding liberal hearts to fear over. They will be forced to negotiate with us and they will be unsuccessful. We will hold on to you and the other prisoners as a guarantee that the ship will not return here, ever. Then, they will leave.'

'I think you underestimate them.'

'I think you over-rate them,' Salim countered. 'There is no colony any more, no Colonial forces, no government, no nothing. There is no cohesion and without that there is no law and no reason for them to try to get any of you back. Cutting your losses, it's known as.'

'We'll never serve you,' Teera spat.

'That's what they all say,' Salim shrugged. 'But then they see what happens to those who oppose me.'

As if on cue an Ogrin appeared, dragging something behind him on the ground. Evelyn felt a pulse of alarm as she recognised the body of a woman, the limbs bouncing loose on the ground and the eyes rolled up in their sockets. The Ogrin dragged the body by its long brown hair in front of Salim and let it drop with a thud to the ground.

Evelyn stared in shock at the woman's body, laced with deep lacerations from a plasma whip.

'Mom!'

The young girl near Salim's throne leaped down and tears sprung from her eyes as she dashed to the fallen body and threw herself upon it. Salim watched the girl for a moment and then looked at Evelyn.

'You can either live like the lovely girls behind me, in comfort,' he said, 'or you can end up like Ishira here.'

Evelyn was about to answer when an Ogrin burst into the throne room. Salim's features twisted with rage at the intrusion and he opened his mouth to protest, and then he fell silent.

Evelyn turned to see a Marine pushed onto his knees in front of Salim, and she felt her heart skip a beat as she looked at him. He was shivering, his face sheened with a cold sweat and his hands quivering like leaves in a gale. His eyes darted left and right as though he was some kind of cornered animal seeking an escape, but it was as though he could not see anything, a blind man surveying the darkness.

But what chilled Evelyn to the core were the jagged purple lines lacing his skin, faint but visible.

Salim walked toward the man, who was held in place by the Ogrin's giant hand.

'Well, well, well,' Salim purred, 'what have we here?'

He looked down at the Marine and turned his face left and right with one podgy hand, examining his prize. He glanced at one of the nearby watching pirates, who grinned slowly as he looked the Marine over.

'That's cutting out,' the pirate drawled. 'He's in withdrawal, probably Feykon Ice, maybe even Devlamine.'

Salim looked at the stricken soldier for a moment longer and then peered curiously at Evelyn.

'You have Devlamine on board your ship?'

'What's Devlamine?' Teera asked.

'Some kind of drug I think,' Evelyn replied, playing her part smoothly even as her blood ran cold in her veins and she tried to ignore the cold shivers rippling beneath her skin. 'No, I don't think so.'

Another pirate entered the throne room, strolled casually up to Salim and murmured something in his ear. Salim's grin spread to cover his face as he nodded and turned back to Evelyn.

'The negotiations are to begin,' he said. 'Your people are not coming down here for you in force I'm afraid, just as I said.'

Evelyn bit her lip as she tried not to reveal her consternation to Salim. The oily pirate gestured down to Ishira's comatose body.

'If you disrupt the negotiations, or otherwise displease me in any way, I shall have her killed and her body hanged by the cliffs as a warning to everybody else, understood?'

Evelyn said nothing and beside her Teera remained silent also. Salim nodded, taking their silence as a tacit agreement, and then gestured to a viewing panel mounted up on one wall of the throne room.

The panel glowed into life and then a face appeared.

'Greetings,' Salim said, spreading his arms as he stood before the panel. 'My name is Salim Phaeon, and you are?'

A young, handsome face with a square jaw and hard eyes stared back at Salim.

'My name is Captain Andaim Ry'ere of the Colonial frigate, Atlantia.'

***

XVIII

'Captain Ry'ere,' Salim's voice poured into the Atlantia's bridge like honey laced with poison. 'Such a pleasure to hear a new human voice, even if it does belong to a Colonial Officer.'

Andaim stood on the command platform in front of the captain's chair, and for a moment he realised that this was how it felt to command a frigate. Everything was on his shoulders and there was nobody to take the fall for him if he got things wrong. He could feel the eyes of the command crew upon him as he spoke.

'I'm afraid it takes more than a global apocalypse to stop the Colonial Fleet,' he replied.

'A shame,' Salim murmured. 'And now you have come here to destroy everything that I have created. Why, captain? Why could you not have simply passed us by and continued on your way?'

'Chiron IV is not registered as belonging to any nation or planetary system,' Andaim informed the pirate king, 'so we can come and go as we please. We need supplies, nothing more. You should have let *us* be.'

'We believed you to be agents of the Word,' Salim explained with a slow shrug. 'We feared that you would attack us here and murder our people.'

'Your people?' Andaim asked with feigned interest. 'Are they all your family?'

'You could call them that,' Salim supposed. 'We all work toward the same cause.'

'And what would that be?'

'Freedom from oppression,' Salim smiled.

'We're detecting upwards of a thousand people down there, Salim,' Andaim reported, 'and considerable construction work, although you appear to be jamming our sensors.'

'Professional caution,' Salim explained demurely.

'And now you have several of our people with you as well,' Andaim went on. 'I take it that they too are now working towards freedom from oppression?'

'They are my guests,' Salim said, 'and my guarantee that your frigate will not attack my compound. They will remain here now until our work is done and we leave, upon which time you may collect them and go on your way and...'

'Don't have time for that, Salim,' Andaim cut him off. 'We're on a mission and we're in need of all hands to complete it. Either you hand over our Marines and pilots, or we'll come down there and get them ourselves.'

Salim's smile turned cold.

'That would be most unfortunate,' he purred, 'for your crew I mean. They'll be executed before your first shot lands.'

'More of your professional caution?'

'My resolve,' Salim snapped back. 'The lives of your people are under my control and you will do precisely as I say. I will allow you to collect supplies from the planet's surface at a location geographically distant from my compound, and then you will leave. There will be no further negotiations.'

Salim looked as though he was about to draw his hand across his throat at somebody off screen to cut the transmission. Andaim took a step forward.

'There is another way.'

Salim peered at Andaim. 'Another way to what?'

'To both resolve this crisis and find a way forward.'

Salim's sneering smile returned. 'A way forward?' he echoed. 'I'm intrigued, captain.'

Andaim took a short breath.

'Our mission is to return to the core systems and retake Ethera from the Word,' he explained. 'We have already defeated the Legion in combat, twice, and have found weaknesses in its defences. The Word is neither infallible nor omnipotent. Together, we can defeat it.'

Salim stared out of the screen at Andaim, his round face devoid of emotion as though he were unable to digest what he had just heard. Then he almost coughed out a loud belly laugh that echoed loudly around the Atlantia's bridge. Behind Salim, on the screen, Andaim could see and hear other pirates laughing along with their king.

'Together,' Salim echoed again as he recovered from his mirth. 'My, captain, you are a bold and brave one. You are offering an alliance with us, against the Legion?'

'We are an endangered species,' Andaim replied. 'There cannot be many free humans left in the cosmos. Finding them and urging them to join our cause is the only way we can confront and defeat the Legion.'

Salim slowly shook his head, the smile still winding its way across his face like a snake.

'I don't want to defeat the Legion,' he replied. 'The Legion destroyed the Colonial Fleet, for the most part, and the damned government on Ethera. The Legion did us a favour for which I am truly grateful, and I have absolutely no intention of marching back into the core systems to reinstall a bloated, self-congratualting government to hunt us down again.'

'We're not interested in retribution against anything or anyone but the Word,' Andaim insisted.

'I'll believe that when I see it.'

'You can see it now,' Andaim said. 'It's right in front of you. Half of the Marines you captured are former convicts, liberated and given the chance to fight alongside Colonial personnel in the war against the Word. All have been pardoned. Ask them.'

'Ask them?' Salim echoed. 'You know what I'd like to ask them?'

Salim clicked his fingers and a huge humanoid figure lumbered into view with something in his massive hand. Andaim saw the shivering, sweating form of a Marine, his teeth chattering and his face lined with ugly purple lines.

'What I'd like to ask them,' Salim went on, 'is where they got their Devlamine, because they're going to give it all to us.'

Andaim bit his lip as he formulated a reply. There was little point in lying – pirates of all people would know what withdrawal symptoms from powerful drugs would look like. But an admission of no knowledge of the drug's use aboard ship would weaken his own position and give Salim confidence that he could control the Atlantia via his hostages.

'The Devlamine was brought aboard ship after she deployed, probably by convicts smuggling the drug through to the prison. The man you're holding is suffering from withdrawal because there is no Devlamine left. What little we found we destroyed. We have another man in our sick bay suffering in the same way, and we don't know if he'll make it through the night.'

'A tragedy,' Salim purred. 'We were looking forward to growing Devlamine down here. Tremendous sunlight right now, perfect conditions. But, you know what bothers me captain? Devlamine withdrawal occurs under two conditions: prolonged abstinence, or in the wake of an overdose. In the case of abstinence, the user develops seizures as the body reacts to the lack of the drug. But in an overdose, the user's veins swell and their heart rate doubles as the body is overcome by the amount of Devlamine in their bodies.' Salim gestured down at the shaking Marine. 'This is not abstinence, captain. This is the result of an overdose, and an overdose means that there is an excess of supply aboard your ship.'

Andaim cursed himself silently but he maintained an impassive expression.

'That would be for our chief physician to decide,' he replied. 'Overdose, abstinence, it doesn't make much difference, we destroyed what we found. Any Devlamine aboard the Atlantia is in small quantities and not worth the effort of tracking down. Frankly, I think that anybody dumb enough to use drugs doesn't deserve our effort in supporting them.'

Salim grinned.

'So do I,' he replied and drew a thick, stubby pistol from his belt. 'Much better to make a profit from them instead!'

Salim leaned down and shoved the pistol against the Marine's head as he spoke to him.

'You tell me where you got your supply and I'll not just let you live, I'll keep your supply moving and you can join us.'

'You're making him promises with a gun to his head,' Andaim cut in, hoping that the soldier would hear him. 'Good luck with that.'

The Marine peered up at Salim through the veil of his suffering. Andaim knew that Devlamine, once entrenched in a victim, required truly hellish agony to remove. Few had lived to describe their ordeal, and those that had painted a canvass of agony so awful that most were unable to coherently describe it without breaking down, even years after beating their addiction.

The Marine shuddered again as he spoke.

'Give me a fix,' he gasped, 'and I'll tell you all you need to know.'

Salim glowered down at the Marine. 'Tell me now, or your suffering will end real fast!'

The Marine smiled back through gritted teeth. 'Go ahead. Either way, I'll feel better.'

Salim cursed and drove a boot into the Marine's stomach as he turned and aimed his pistol at the screen.

'If you're not gone within twenty four hours, I'll start executing hostages!' he screamed. 'Devlamine is the only currency that will save their lives!'

Salim fired and the plasma shot blasted the viewing screen and cut the transmission off. Andaim's shoulders sank as the tension lifted from them, and he glanced over his shoulder to where Captain Sansin was standing with Mikhain well out of sight in the shadows of the bridge.

'The drug's use is more widespread than we feared,' Andaim said. 'Even the Marines are using it.'

Sansin strode to the command platform, his hands behind his back. Mikhain emerged also, his face swollen with anger.

'You should have let me handle this,' the XO uttered to Sansin. 'Now they're after a Devlamine supply too.'

'It's something to bargain with,' Idris replied. 'We didn't have that before.'

'You're actually thinking of going along with it?' Mikhain gasped.

'We need our people back.'

'You'll be condemning countless hundreds of other hostages to drug addiction,' Mikhain snapped back. 'You know damned well that there are slaves down there, lorded over by that pig Salim! It'll give him that bit more control over those people, keep them enslaved to their drug supply and...'

'I know what he'll do with it!' Idris shouted. 'Be quiet!'

The XO stared at the captain as he paced up and down on the bridge for several long moments, the crew watching him.

'Salim allowed us the chance to gather supplies,' he said to Andaim.

'An olive branch of sorts,' the CAG replied. 'He wants to give us what we need and see us leave as soon as possible.'

'Do we have any idea what he's building down there?' Idris asked Mikhain, all the anger suddenly gone from his voice.

Andaim was always impressed by how Idris conducted himself. His rage at Mikhain's playing constant Devil's advocate was only ever in the moment, and he always returned to his normal calm self as he sought a solution to the many problems that he faced.

'It's big,' Mikhain replied, somewhat deflated. 'Probably as large as Atlantia, but he's doing a good job of blocking our sensors so we can't get a good look at it. Even the optical scopes are seeing nothing but distortions, so Salim's directing his shielding directly at us.'

It was a common tactic to use lasers with randomly changing frequencies and wavelengths to distort the light from ground-based installations when viewed from orbit, twisting the images into meaningless ripples of light that took powerful computers many days to unravel.

Idris nodded. 'We need somebody to go down there and take a look.'

'Only way to be sure,' Andaim said. 'I could maybe take a Raython and try to get below the aurora without being detected.'

'Too risky,' Idris said. 'Salim will cheerfully cut the throats of a hostage or two if you're spotted.'

'It needs boots on the ground,' Mikhain said. 'Bra'hiv might be able to figure out a way to get somebody down there.'

'Do it,' Idris agreed. 'Send a signal to Salim that we'll be sending a shuttle down to the opposite side of the planet to gather supplies. Make sure it has a flight path that gets reasonably close to Salim's compound.'

Mikhain whirled away as Andaim approached the captain.

'We're going to have to launch an assault, eventually,' the CAG insisted. 'Salim's not going to give up without a fight.'

'I know,' Idris replied. 'But right now we need to keep him thinking that he's got us over a barrel. Military options are what we use when every other possible course of action has been rejected or has failed.'

Andaim nodded. 'We still have the Devlamine angle. If we can find the source we might be able to barter a deal out of them.'

'And we have Taron Forge,' Idris added.

'I wouldn't trust him as far as I could throw him,' Andaim muttered.

'That's what I'm counting on.'

The captain drew Andaim close and spoke to him so that nobody else aboard the bridge could hear.

***

XIX

The cell was small, no more than ten feet by eight, with bare walls of steel grey metal devoid of seams or edges. A small seat occupied one corner of the cell, the door barred and the access panel closed, a lone man, stocky and bald, trapped within.

'How long has he been in there?' Idris asked as he watched a monitor in the observation room that showed the interior of the nearby cell.

'A few hours,' General Bra'hiv replied, 'and I can tell that he's sweating about something.'

'Has he had any visitors?'

'Two,' Bra'hiv confirmed, 'one from his wife and another from his lawyer, or a civilian who's playing the role at least.'

The Atlantia's brig was small, capable of holding no more than twenty prisoners aboard ship under high security conditions and armed guard. Most all military vessels had them, but it had always been exceedingly rare for the cells to be occupied by anyone from the ship's compliment – most captives were enemy combatants or captured criminals. Idris had watched many a Veng'en trapped like a caged animal in such cells via the concealed cameras that monitored the unfortunate occupants, but now he was looking at an ordinary man very much out of his depth.

'Bring him out,' Idris ordered. 'And make him feel like he's the most wanted man on the planet. I want him to fold and fast.'

General Bra'hiv left the observation room, and moments later Idris watched on the viewing screen as two Marines burst into the cell. The captive startled as the soldiers rushed in screaming *down down down* and roughly manacled the man. They hauled him out of the cell, his legs dragging on the ground behind him as they hefted his body down the corridor outside.

Idris remained silent and still as the man was dragged past the observation room and into an interrogation room just down the corridor. He waited for a few moments until the soldiers would have strapped the captive into a seat, and then he opened the observation room door and walked down the corridor outside. General Bra'hiv emerged from the interrogation room and waited for the captain.

'He's ready,' Bra'hiv announced, speaking loudly enough to ensure that he was being heard by the man in the room behind him. 'How rough do you want this to be?'

'As rough as it needs,' Idris replied. 'If he doesn't talk, he doesn't survive. I take it that your men will dispose of him without fuss?'

'Nobody will even know he was here,' Bra'hiv replied. 'We'll make sure it looks like a suicide.'

A voice cried for help from within the room and was instantly muffled. Idris strode with Bra'hiv into the interrogation room to see the captive strapped into a steel seat, a Marine on one side of him holding a rifle and a Marine on the other with one gloved hand shoved over the captive's face.

'Outside,' Bra'hiv ordered the two Marines. 'You weren't here, understood?'

'Yes sir!' the two soldiers snapped in response and marched out of the room.

The door slammed shut behind them and the captive stared in horror at Bra'hiv and the captain.

'You can't do this!' he whined, his eyes wide with shock and fear. 'You can't do this!'

'We are doing this,' Bra'hiv replied without emotion.

Idris watched as the general reached into his pocket and produced a metallic device that looked like two steel pincers with a black handle. Bra'hiv activated the device and it hummed into life as a bright blue spark crackled between the tips of the two pincers, a bright plasma glow that flickered in the low light inside the room.

'You know what this is?' he asked the man.

The man nodded frantically. 'It's a plasma torch.'

His voice had risen an octave while dropping in volume as though his throat was constricted.

'The walls of this cell are sound proofed,' Bra'hiv went on. 'Mainly, it was done to allow confessions from convicts and gang members to be made without fear or reprisals from former allies, but now it serves another purpose. People outside can't hear you screaming as your limbs are severed.'

The man's face turned pale white and his voice trembled as though vibrations were rumbling through his lungs.

'I don't know anything,' he blubbed.

'We know that you were caught with Devlamine in your possession,' Bra'hiv snarled. 'We know that people are dying of Devlamine overdoses in the sanctuary, and we know that somebody is supplying the drug. Right now we have a major situation unfolding that requires us to recover all of the Devlamine aboard ship. Do you understand what I mean?'

The man, his eyes fixed on the crackling plasma torch, nodded frantically. 'But I don't know where it is.'

Bra'hiv's features formed a cold smile.

'Allow me to refresh your memory,' he snarled as he lowered the torch toward the man's hand.

'You wouldn't dare,' the captive shouted in defiant rage. 'This isn't legal! You can't do this!'

'Supplying drugs is illegal,' Bra'hiv countered. 'Dealing them is illegal. Being armed in the sanctuary is illegal. We don't have time for courts and due process here, and lives are at stake because of that filth you're peddling down there to men with families and children. I don't give a damn about your rights, your reasons or even your life because right now all I see before me is a cowardly dealer of death. I have no reason to care whether you survive this encounter or not, so to hell with you.'

Bra'hiv lowered the torch until the tremendous heat caused the hairs on the man's hand to curl up and singe as a whiff of smoke puffed from his skin.

'No, please, *no!*' the man screamed as the pain bit deep. 'I'll tell you what I know! I'll tell you!'

Bra'hiv held the snarling, crackling plasma torch inches above the man's fingers as he leaned close and his gaze burned into the captive's.

'Who supplied you, Olag?' the general growled.

Olag held the general's gaze for a long moment, and then suddenly his face folded in upon itself and his shoulders trembled as he wept openly. Tears rolled down his cheeks and he looked away from Bra'hiv as he blubbed his response.

'They told me if I spoke, they'd kill my wife.'

Bra'hiv leaned even closer. 'You don't tell me, I'll *kill* you.'

Olag sucked in a sharp intake of air and managed to control himself.

'Then do it, because I won't risk her life for mine,' he snapped.

Bra'hiv held the torch in place for a moment longer but it was Idris who spoke.

'Tell me what you *do* know.'

Olag looked at Idris for a long moment, his cheeks still glistening with tears.

'I don't know who supplies the drug itself,' he said. 'All I know for sure is that there are three guys who control the growth of the crystals in the sanctuary. They have a farm that's tucked away somewhere near one end of the forest and they keep it under cover. A couple of the guys reckon they have their kids play nearby to act as a watch.'

'That's the farm sorted,' Bra'hiv growled at Olag. 'What about the processed nectar, the source of the Devlamine crystals themselves? It must also be stored somewhere.'

'I don't know,' Olag insisted. 'They don't tell me that, I swear!'

Idris thought for a moment.

'These *guys* that you mention, how much access do they have to the rest of Atlantia outside the sanctuary?'

Olag sniffed mightily as Bra'hiv slowly drew the plasma torch away from him, his eyes still fixed upon the brutally bright weapon.

'Two of them are engineers,' he explained, 'so they can move about pretty much wherever they like. My guess is that the supply isn't coming from inside the sanctuary but from outside, somewhere in the ship.'

Bra'hiv backed away another pace and this time he shut off the torch as Idris paced closer to Olag.

'Give me their names,' he ordered.

'I can't,' Olag moaned miserably. 'They've already made it clear that they'll take it out on my wife if any of them are caught. You don't mess with these people, they'll kill without hesitation.'

Idris, his hands behind his back, stared down without compromise at Olag as he spoke.

'Due to you, I now have a number of my finest officers facing possible death because of what you've done, not to mention at least one dying man in the sick bay and others that will appear as soon as we stop this drug supply. Believe me, we will stop it, sooner or later. How little do you think I care about your survival, or that of your wife, when compared to officers who have risked their lives to protect us all?'

Olag stared back up at Idris, his resolve stiffening once more.

'I will not sacrifice my wife to save my own life,' he snapped.

'I'm not asking you to,' Idris replied. 'I'm asking you to provide me with names. I will then ensure that your wife is placed in protective custody before any searches or arrests are made. Nobody will touch her until this is all over, understood?'

The prisoner looked back and forth between the captain and General Bra'hiv.

'How can I trust you?' he spat. 'This bastard just threatened to cut off my limbs, kill me and make it look like a suicide!'

Idris shook his head.

'None of it would have happened,' he said. 'I just wanted to let you know that we mean business. No matter how hard it becomes I *will* destroy this drug trade, and I *will* remove anybody from this ship who tries to slow me down, do you understand? My men will not torture you or anybody else, but I absolutely will authorise Maroon Protocol for anybody involved in the trade who does not redeem themselves by helping me shut it down.'

The captive swallowed thickly. Maroon Protocol, the procedure for marooning undesirables on foreign planets, was an age-old custom much feared by civilians who had often never set foot on another planet. The sort of things parents threatened misbehaving children with, or travellers told tales about over camp fires in the wilderness.

'Tell me the names of your accomplices and where they keep their supply,' Idris repeated, 'or I'll ensure you and your wife's safety from the dealers by placing you on Chiron IV and damned well leaving you here.'

Olag closed his eyes, and then revealed the location of three homesteads in the sanctuary.

'Get on it,' Idris ordered the General.

***

XX

'Okay, this is how it's going to go down.'

Qayin stood before a platoon of Marines from Bravo Company, formed of former convicts who had once been incarcerated on Atlantia Five, the prison hull Atlantia had once guarded. Beside him, Lieutenant C'rairn watched but did not intervene, giving Qayin space to command the men.

'We work in groups of four,' Qayin went on, 'two to search each premises, two to stand watch in case anything goes wrong or anybody attempts to run.'

'Why can't we search in greater numbers?' asked Soltin. 'More chance of somebody getting away if we're only four per house.'

'We need to hit all three homesteads as once,' Qayin explained. 'The people talk and they talk fast – word will get around and stashes will be hidden before we can get to them if we take too long or advertise our presence.'

The exterior of the sanctuary was quiet, the interior mimicking night time. Qayin knew that the human body was at its weakest in the small hours before dawn, and the ship-time routine was based around the twenty-six hour cycle of the sanctuary, which itself mimicked Ethera's day and night cycle. Used in order to allow crew the chance to maintain some sense of time when on cruises in deep space that might last months, now that same cycle gave Qayin and his team the chance to hit hard and fast against minimal resistance from the civilian population.

'Alpha Company will be moving in from the for'ard hatch,' Qayin went on, strolling up and down in front of the men as he spoke, the bioluminescent tattoos on his face glowing in the dim light. 'We'll come in from the aft entrance, further limiting escape routes for any dealers inside the sanctuary. Guards will be posted outside the exits also, just in case anybody manages to slip by us. Any questions?'

'Just one.'

The lone voice at the back was that of Corporal Djimon, the towering mass of muscle standing almost a full head above the other Marines.

'Yes, corporal?' Qayin asked.

'Nobody has explained how the Devlamine came to be aboard in the first place. Few members of the crew have been off-ship since we left Ethera over two years ago, and as a military vessel the drugs would not likely have been aboard beforehand. Thus, somebody among the crew who has left Atlantia during our voyage is responsible for bringing drugs aboard ship.'

'When we apprehend the dealers we'll find out who brought the drugs aboard,' Qayin said. 'Kind of what we're here for don't you think, genius?'

Djimon did not react to Qayin's flippancy, letting his words carry the accusations he harboured.

'I'd have thought that only a user or dealer would recognise Devlamine in its crystal form if they'd seen it. Somebody with a history of dealing, for instance.'

Qayin grinned, his teeth bright against his dark skin.

'And somebody like that would also be pretty good at rooting out the same problem,' he replied. 'We'll deal with who's done what when we find them. Right now our job is to search every homestead inside the sanctuary on our list, clear them of any drugs and arrest the possessors. No hesitations, but weapons cold for those searching the premises. Call out the occupants before entering and keep them under guard. I don't want anybody else panicking and opening fire on us, okay?'

The Marines snapped to attention and Qayin turned to the lieutenant.

'Let's go.'

C'rairn turned and opened the sanctuary's entrance chute, and with military precision the Marines jumped inside one after the other, accelerating away as the sanctuary's motion and gravity pulled them in.

*

The light was not the same as it was on Wraithe. Even the stars were not in the same places.

Kordaz lay across the broad beam of an Etheran pine and stared up at the night sky. Though he knew that it was an elaborate illusion and that the entire sanctuary was a construct of human ingenuity, if their skills could be called that, Kordaz could still reflect that the human condition was no different to his own species, the Veng'en. Deep in space and far from home, both species tried to replicate something of their homeworlds to ease the loneliness of the void, to break the monotony of grey corridors, darkened bridges and harsh electrical lighting. The Veng'en deliberately cultivated dense vegetation to clog the interiors of their battle cruisers, the corridors filled with mist and vapour just like the jungles of home.

The wind whispered through the trees, cold compared to the hot, humid breath of Wraithe's vast tropical forests. Kordaz had taken to wearing a thermal layer over his scaled skin since Captain Sansin had allowed to him make his home in the sanctuary, but apart from that he remained much as he had on Wraithe, the trees his domain. Food, disgusting as it was, was provided by the crew and the civilians with whom he shared the sanctuary, though he saw them little. That he was feared and hated by the human inhabitants of the sanctuary was beyond doubt – the Veng'en and the humans had been at war for decades before the apocalypse that virtually eradicated humanity, each inflicting terrible atrocities upon the other in a seemingly endless series of territorial disputes and major fleet actions.

Kordaz knew well that his people were war-like, born to survive in the dangerous jungles in which they had evolved, but even so humans were shockingly adept at violence and combat, ingenious in their ability to surprise at the last moment when their defeat seemed imminent. Yet also they proved ridiculously empathetic toward their fellow man, often discarding certain victory in battle rather than abandon their own on the field. Many gains had been made by the Veng'en over the years simply through the act of abduction of senior human officers and negotiations for their release.

Kordaz glanced down through the forest canopy, through black veils of leaves toward distant homesteads set near the edge of a plain filled with crop fields. The peace of this place seemed at odds with his mental image of humanity and that shared by his fellow Veng'en. Veng'en schooling had taught them that humans routinely raped and pillaged each other's towns, often delighting in eating the young of their enemies. Kordaz now suspected that some of those stories may have been somewhat enhanced by the retelling, especially as he knew of several human younglings living in the nearby farmsteads that were clearly doted upon even by humans with no family ties to them and…

A scent drifted across Kordaz's olfactory and he instinctively tensed, ready for combat. He lay still, his face still staring up at the stars, but his eyes swivelled to the east and his ears twitched.

Kordaz's eyes were big, baleful and currently almost filled with an "X" shaped iris that was fully expanded to draw as much light as possible toward the centre of his eye. The adaption allowed for better night vision in misty conditions within the jungle, directing and focusing light in the centre of the eye to better detect movement. Now, in the clear conditions of the sanctuary, Kordaz could see almost as clearly as in daylight on Wraithe.

He spotted them almost immediately, moving quickly but quietly through the forest toward the clearing to Kordaz's right. Four men, Marines, all armed. The metal, rubber and plastic of their weapons and armour was what he had smelled even before he'd heard them, the air circulating around the sanctuary drawing their scent toward Kordaz.

Kordaz rolled off the tree limb, one arm catching his fall and letting him swing into motion as he plummetted down and across to another large limb. Powerful legs landed and compressed and then launched Kordaz with impressive force through the air two-dozen cubits above the ground. He flashed silently across the sky and landed with all four claws against the side of a thick trunk and listened intently.

The Marines walked fast beneath him, weapons not activated but held at the ready. He could faintly make out the glowing tattoos of the big man, Qayin. A dangerous individual, Kordaz new, untrustworthy by nature and yet now a leader of men. As Kordaz watched, the Marines hurried out into the clearing and encircled the first of the homesteads.

*

'Where d'ya think they got the crystals from?' Soltin asked in a soft whisper as they crept forward.

'Does it matter?' Qayin hissed. 'General said that guy we found is now in the sick-bay after over-dosing himself, and the one we caught gave the names of his accomplices.'

'There wasn't any in the prison before it got blown away,' Soltin pointed out, refusing to abandon his train of thought. 'Corporal Djimon had a point. Only contact we've had with other possible sources since is the Veng'en cruiser we've been following and that wreck, the Sylph.'

The Sylph had been a merchant vessel found adrift some months before, her crew having fallen victim to the Legion. The battle with the Veng'en for possession of the ship's supplies had almost been the end of the Atlantia.

'Probably the Veng'en cruiser that turned up later,' Qayin said. 'They grow stuff inside their ships to make it more like the jungles they evolved in. Maybe somebody picked some of it up in there.'

'But there were no civilians aboard her, except for the captured members of the Sylph's crew.'

Qayin nodded thoughtfully. The captain and a small number of senior officers of the Sylph had been liberated from the Veng'en in the aftermath of the battle, and as such they may have been carrying small quantities of the drug upon their person. A small matter to pass a few crystals into the hands of a willing civilian aboard the Atlantia and cultivate more of the drug. Once the crystals were crushed and processed, it would generate a healthy income to the person controlling access to the drug.

There was no money aboard the Atlantia, much as there had been no cash in the high-security prison Atlantia Five. Yet that had not stopped Qayin from becoming very wealthy as he served his time. Privileges, materials, a private cell and other luxuries were afforded by protection rackets, accumulation of ill-gotten gains and outright theft of weaker prisoners forced to submit to Qayin's crew. Even drugs administered to sick prisoners could be stolen, accumulated, mixed and sold back to others with sufficient wealth to afford them. Qayin knew the workings of drug management well, and he knew how to root out the problem.

'If they're growing the stuff here then they'll need it to be out of sight and out of mind, that's why we're not hitting the farm first,' he said. 'Most people aren't into drugs, too afraid to give it a try. It's the weakest minds that use them, the easiest led. Anybody else would report the runners or the growers and the whole operation would be blown, 'specially here in the sanctuary.'

'How come that guy ended up in the sick bay then?'

'Greed,' Qayin murmured. 'Whoever's growing the flowers has allowed too much to go on sale, hasn't controlled his market. Drug money ain't no good to nobody if there's enough to go 'round. You gotta make it scarce, keep 'em hopin' for their next cut, you wanna make 'em pay enough to take the risk of growin' the stuff in the first place.'

Soltin nodded thoughtfully as they moved.

'Most of 'em are just ordinary people,' Soltin said. 'They ain't doing the crystal trade.'

Qayin nodded in agreement.

'Which makes somewhere outside of the sanctuary the perfect place for dealers to hide their gear,' he replied. 'They don't crap on their own doorstep.'

Qayin had always ensured that no drugs or weapons contaminated his own cell when he was incarcerated aboard Atlantia Five. Such risky items had always been carried by his lieutenants or lower ranking gang members, removing the likelihood of Qayin himself being associated with any crime. Sure, the correctional officers, or "sticks" as they had been known after their liberally deployed electrified pacification batons, frisked Qayin often enough and knew damned well that he had been behind a stabbing or some other heinous crime, but they'd never pinned any of it on him.

The platoon slowed as it approached the assigned cabin, and Qayin raised a clenched fist and pulled it downward twice. The Marines melted into the shadows as they crouched down. Qayin waited for a few minutes, listening for movement within the cabin but nothing stirred, the occupants either absent or asleep.

'Now!'

Qayin's voice hissed in the silence of the night and instantly two Marines rushed to the front door of the homestead and attached a small device that automatically unlocked the door. The door opened and the two men hurried in, Qayin listening as the two soldiers rushed into the cabin's bedrooms with weapons held at the ready and cornered the occupants before they had even realised their homes were being invaded.

Silent, swift and without drama.

'Close them down!' Qayin whispered into his microphone with satisfaction.

A brief, muted commotion of shouts were cut short and silence reigned once more. Qayin watched and waited as a man was led from the homestead, his wife behind him holding a baby and a small child being led behind them, rubbing the sleep from his eyes.

'Okay, search everything,' Qayin ordered.

The man, a tall and robust looking civilian with a thick beard, pointed at Qayin and his voice boomed out into the night. 'Who the hell do you think you are?!'

'We're just following orders,' Qayin replied.

'You're convicts ransacking my home!'

Qayin spotted a light go on in a homestead some distance away.

'Please sir,' Soltin said calmly, 'we're not accusing you or your family of anything, but there is a need for us to search every premises and…'

'There is a need for you and your damned captain to keep us in isolation and treat us like second-class citizens!' the man roared. 'You've already killed one man and now you're here tearing up my home, and for what?!'

'We're searching for illegal contraband,' Qayin insisted.

'Illegal under whose laws?!' the man shouted. 'Ours or yours? And what contraband?'

'I'm not at liberty to say, sir,' Qayin replied.

'The hell you aren't,' the man snapped and reached out to push Soltin aside.

'Take it easy, sir,' Soltin said as he pushed back.

The man's clenched fist swung in the darkness for Soltin's face, and Qayin jumped in and blocked the blow as he twisted the man sideways and slammed him onto the ground.

'This is harassment!' the man seethed.

Qayin placed manacles on the man as Soltin tried to keep the wife and child calm.

'Get the search done as quickly as possible,' Qayin ordered, 'and keep things quiet before everybody knows we're here.'

Soltin ushered the wife and children away as Qayin hauled the man up onto his feet and propelled him away from the farmstead. He guided the irate citizen toward the cover of the trees and into the deep shadows. Qayin grabbed the man's shoulder and spun him about as he gripped him around the throat and slammed him against the unyielding trunk of a tree.

'Give me one good reason I shouldn't gut you like a fish right here and now,' Qayin hissed.

The man's eyes bulged but he managed an awkward grin. 'Because you need me as much as I need you.'

'Not now I don't,' Qayin growled and squeezed harder. 'I told you, supply and demand rules all. You sold too much Dev' and some idiot overdosed and is now in the sick-bay. If he survives, he's going to start squealing about who supplied him.'

The man choked, his body shaking as his skin flushed a deep, unhealthy shade of red.

'It wasn't me who sold out,' he gasped, his hands trying and failing to dislodge Qayin's. 'Everything was fine but then one of my guys got greedy.'

'I don't give a damn who it was, it was your responsibility.'

The man gargled his reply.

'Yeah, well it's yours now, 'cause if they come for me then I'll send them straight to you.'

Qayin grinned in the darkness and with his free hand he raised his rifle up to the man's neck. The plasma magazine hummed into life.

'What makes you think you'll be in a fit state to do anything?'

Qayin squeezed with all of his might and the man's throat collapsed beneath his grip. The man's eyes widened and he grasped desperately for Qayin's face. Qayin released the man's throat and stepped back as the man collapsed to the ground, his mouth gaping as he tried to call for help. But his throat was too tightly constricted and nothing came out but a whistling, wheezing breath.

'Give it to me, now,' Qayin demanded.

The man reached beneath his jacket and produced a small, dense block of a crystalline structure that was encased in a sort of gel and wrapped in clear plastic. Qayin grabbed the Devlamine and stuffed it beneath his body armour.

'Where's the rest of your stash?'

'I don't have any more,' the man gasped.

Qayin aimed his rifle at the man's head and he covered his skull uselessly with his hands.

'Okay,' he cried out. 'It's in barrels, astern down in the keel access tunnels. We stored it in coolant containers to disguise it!'

Qayin raised his rifle, and as the man looked up Qayin brought the weapon's butt crashing down across the man's temple. The man's head snapped sideways and he slumped onto the soft earth, his breath rattling in his throat as he whimpered in pain.

Qayin lowered the rifle and looked over his shoulder at the homestead. The Marines were guarding it as their companions exited the building. Qayin could see by their body language that they had found nothing of use inside, which was what he had expected.

Qayin's hand rested instinctively on a bayonet attached to his webbing belt, but then he turned and saw the man's wife and children being questioned by Soltin. Qayin thought for a moment and then he shouldered his rifle and stood back.

'Get up,' he ordered the man slumped at his feet. 'Get inside your house and clean yourself up. You ever breathe a word of this to anybody, I'll arrange a real nasty accident for you and your family, you feel me?'

The man nodded, scrambled to his feet. Qayin grabbed him by the collar and pulled his face close as he snarled at him.

'There's a dealer in custody already, one of yours most likely,' he growled. 'He sold you out, so he takes the rap for dealing and supplying? Tell him that I know where his family lives. If he squeals names, they die. That way, we both get free of this, understood?'

The man nodded frantically. Qayin released him and shoved him away. Qayin saw his wife spot him and rush across to his side, heard her gasp of despair at her husband's facial injury as she threw her arms about his neck and led him toward their home. Qayin walked back toward the Marines and Soltin glanced at him.

'What he hell happened to him?' he asked.

'He tried to escape into the woods,' Qayin replied. 'I had to bring him down hard.'

'You find his stash?' Soltin asked. 'We didn't find anything inside the home.'

'No,' Qayin said. 'I'm pretty sure he's dealing, but maybe the threat of arrest will be enough to turn him around.'

'If he's a dealer we should be arresting him right now,' Soltin pointed out. 'Captain's orders, remember?'

Qayin gestured to the homestead.

'He's got a family,' he replied. 'We arrest him then they've got nobody here to help them. It's not the dealers who are the priority, it's the source.'

Soltin raised an eyebrow. 'Man, you've actually got a heart? I thought there was nothin' but hot air in that chest.'

'Who knew?' Qayin uttered. 'Let's move out.'

The Marines departed the homestead and began marching toward the next in the line, Qayin at their head.

The big sergeant never saw Kordaz watching them from up in the trees. The Veng'en watched as the Marines led their captives away, and then a soft beeping alerted him to a communicator attached to his belt. Kordaz opened the device and immediately wondered why he was being summoned to the launch bays.

**

Dean Crawford

XXI

'This is your chance to shine and win friends.'

Kordaz stared down at Lieutenant C'rairn and said nothing.

'You'll be the toast of the ship,' C'rairn added.

'I'll likely just be toast,' Kordaz growled, his guttural dialect translated by a throat-mounted vocal resonator.

Kordaz had made his way under the captain's orders to the launch bay as soon as he'd seen Qayin's Marines leave the sanctuary. The launch bay was dominated by a single shuttle and a platoon of Marines boarding it, along with canisters being loaded aboard that would return filled with whatever resources could be scavenged from Chiron's surface. In addition, the shuttle's lower hull had been fitted with a large, flush-fitting tank with which the pilots could scoop water from suitable fresh-water lakes while in flight.

Attached to the top of the shuttle was a single escape pod.

'The pods are reliable,' General Bra'hiv assured the Veng'en. 'They can take a hell of a beating.'

'Have you ever seen one survive a re-entry?' Kordaz asked.

'Just because I haven't seen it, doesn't mean it cannot happen,' Bra'hiv replied.

'The capsule will jettison as soon as you're through the atmosphere,' C'rairn explained. 'Being on the top of the shuttle will protect you from the worst of the entry-burn. The pilots will detach you and you'll free-fall for two minutes before a parachute will deploy and slow your descent until touch down.'

'Why not just throw the capsule out of the back of the shuttle once we're safely through the atmosphere?' Kordaz asked.

'The descent phase masks craft from radar and sensors while in the upper atmosphere,' Bra'hiv explained. 'The heat and light will prevent Salim and his people from detecting your presence. Once clear of the shuttle, the pod on its own is too small to track. If the shuttle slowed in normal flight and opened its rear ramp, they might detect it.'

Kordaz's long snout and scaled facial features made it hard for him to express emotions, but he gave it his best shot.

'A frigate filled with soldiers and your damned captain chooses me for this mission?'

'You're getting a free ride home aboard Atlantia,' Bra'hiv replied. 'You gotta take a fall sometime.'

'Very droll,' Kordaz murmured. 'Weapons?'

'Close quarters blades only for you,' C'rairn cautioned. 'Chiron IV is uninhabited so it's plausible that Salim's men could detect an active plasma magazine out in the wilderness and you'd be bombed out of existence. You'll be supplied with some chemical explosives to be used on targets of opportunity, if required, to assist us. Plenty of wildlife down there though, so as long as you stay out of sight they should never even know you're there.'

'Wildlife?' Kordaz echoed. 'Any idea what form it takes?'

C'rairn and Bra'hiv glanced at each other. The general shrugged. 'Another good reason to stay out of sight.'

'Rescue, if I become injured or am spotted?' Kordaz inquired with what might have been a hint of weariness.

'The captain cannot reveal this deception for fear of hostages being killed,' Lieutenant C'rairn replied, 'so if everything goes to hell your best bet is to run like the wind and hunker down somewhere. We'll get to you eventually.'

Kordaz rested his hand on an elaborate, mirror-polished blade attached to a simple belt around his waist. A wickedly-hooked weapon with several different cutting edges and a spike pointing out of the back of the hilt, it was a ceremonial *D'jeck*, used in mortal combat between warring Veng'en back on Wraithe when judicial means were unable to resolve a dispute.

'You just lost two fighters, a shuttle, a platoon of Marines and two pilots down there, but you'll *get to me eventually*?' Kordaz uttered. 'I won't hold my breath. I need to speak to the captain before I leave.'

'There's no time,' C'rairn replied, 'and the captain's got his hands full right now. Get this mission out of the way and I'm sure he'll find a slot for you.'

'It's important,' Kordaz insisted, certain only that he could trust nobody other than the captain with what he knew.

'So is this mission,' Bra'hiv replied cheerfully. 'Unless you'd rather I report to the captain that you're unwilling to undertake it, or perhaps afraid?'

Kordaz scowled at the general as he turned and in a single bound leaped onto the top of the shuttle. The open capsule was laying on its back and attached via clamps to the hull, the lid opened. Kordaz took one last look at the crew on the deck below and at the ship around him, and tried to force an unfamiliar emotion of regret from his mind as he clambered down into the capsule and closed the lid.

The capsule sealed itself and almost immediately he felt rather than heard the shuttle's ion engines whine into life, the vibrations humming through the capsule. The launch bay was evacuated of personnel and then after a short delay and the sound of warning claxons the atmosphere rushed out of the bay in a whorl of white vapour as the shuttle lifted off and accelerated away.

Kordaz looked out of the capsule's viewing window and saw the landing bay lights flash by and then the vast bow of the Atlantia drifting past far above him, her hull scarred by years of travelling the cosmos and stained a dull rusty colour from being constantly bombarded by cosmic rays and dust.

The frigate vanished as the shuttle turned beneath him and aimed at the planet, out of Kordaz's sight. Moments later the ship tilted slightly as it angled itself for primary descent, and Kordaz glimpsed the Atlantia once more, already far away and glinting like a jewel suspended against the dense starfields. He turned his head and saw the flaring star entombed in its glowing death throes disappearing over the shoulder of Chiron IV, and he realised that not only was he about to be plunged alone and virtually unarmed onto a planet he had never before visited, but that he was also going to be deployed at night.

Kordaz cursed and then yelped as a sudden, severe vibration slammed into the shuttle and a fearsome red glow illuminated the edges of the capsule. Kordaz gritted his teeth and clenched his clawed fists as the shuttle plunged into the atmosphere, shuddering and rattling as the immense forces at work around it attempted to tear the vehicle apart and consume it in a fiery halo.

Warning sensors began blaring for attention in the capsule and Kordaz saw a temperature gauge shoot up as the shuttle plummeted toward the planet's surface. The viewing panel cracked as he stared at ferocious jets of flame flickering around the edges of the shuttle's hull, reaching out for him. The stars in the inky blackness outside glittered and shimmered in the heat and an alarm screeched in Kordaz's sensitive ears as the capsule's own hull reached critical temperature.

Kordaz let out a cry of alarm as the whole capsule shook as though it were being torn from its mounts. He grasped for the handholds inside as suddenly a heavy jolt slammed his head back against the rest and the capsule tumbled as it was ejected from the shuttle's hull, the terrific noise vanishing as though a switch had been flipped.

Kordaz's ears hummed with the memory of the din of re-entry and he grimaced as he felt himself flipped upside-down, the capsule spinning wildly. He glimpsed clouds far below glowing a strange green and orange beneath immense veils of light rippling across the skies. The capsule rolled over and over, spinning as it plummeted toward the surface at a velocity Kordaz did not want to think about. The clouds below seemed to grow larger with frightening rapidity, looming toward him, and then the sky and the aurora vanished and turbulence buffeted the tiny capsule as it rocketed ever downward through dense clouds and was plunged into utter blackness.

Kordaz glanced at an altimeter inside the capsule, the feint green glow like an anchor to reality. The figures upon it were in human script and as such meant little to him, but the terrifying speed with which they were counting down told him all that he needed to know.

Kordaz didn't pray. No Veng'en did. But every now and again, in times of extreme stress, even a Veng'en could not resist the temptation to address a higher power.

'I'll kill you!' Kordaz bellowed in his darkened prison.

A reply came as a deafening crash right above Kordaz's upside-down head sent a tremor of terminal fear racing through his body. The capsule jerked right-side up and immense G-forces slammed into Kordaz's body as it did so, and then all was silence.

Kordaz, his breath sawing rapidly in his throat and both of his hearts racing in his chest, pressed his head against the viewing panel and peered up to see a parachute canopy billowing above him, just visible against the darkened sky. He looked down and then jerked his head back just before the capsule slammed into the ground.

Kordaz was pitched onto his back again and he felt the capsule being dragged along the ground by the chute. He hit the buttons to jettison the lid, and as it popped open he pulled the parachute cutting-cord hard and then scrambled out of the capsule. The parachute billowed in the wind and then collapsed onto scrub foliage on a low hillside nearby. Kordaz crouched in the darkness, one hand on his *D'jeck* as he peered into the gloom and tried to calm his wildly beating hearts.

The smell of oceans and salty air caressed his senses, and his eyes swiftly adjusted to the planetary conditions. The clouds above glowed from the ethereal auroral light above them, and as Kordaz turned on the spot he realised that the shuttle pilots had done an immensely competent job. Beyond low hills no more than ten thousand cubits away a bright glow lit the night sky and reflected off the clouds as only man-made light could do.

Kordaz hurried across the plain and gathered up the parachute, rolling it into a tight ball and depositing it inside the capsule. He worked fast, dragging the capsule into bushes of scrub foliage and then camouflaging it as best he could. Within minutes the capsule looked much like a rock covered in ferns and mosses, the lid open and the bundled parachute breaking up its sleek lines to help disguise its presence.

Kordaz turned and took a pace toward the distant light.

A growl stopped him.

He froze. He could see nothing and no scent marred the air. With the wind in his face he knew that the threat must lay behind him and most likely had purposefully approached him from downwind. A predator's natural instinct.

Kordaz turned, his wide eyes seeking movement in the darkness. The faint glow in the clouds above gave him just enough light to pick out shapes in the gloom, and that was when he saw it and several thoughts flashed through his mind in a beat of his hearts.

Twice as large as a Veng'en, likely double the body-mass too. Fangs. Huge, hunched shoulders and muscular forelimbs with crouched, shorter hind legs. A leaping, ambush beast, not a long-distance runner, with a backbone and spinal column just like so many species on other worlds. Dense, dark fur and large, padded, clawed feet.

Yellow, soulless eyes.

Kordaz slowly drew his *D'jeck* with one hand and the weapon glinted in the faint light. He saw the creature's gaze flick briefly to the weapon but sensed no understanding in the gaze, only recognition of the movement. The creature shifted postion, crouching down lower as its fearsome eyes narrowed. Kordaz braced himself as the beast prepared to launch itself at him.

A hellish scream erupted from the animal and reverberated through Kordaz's chest like war drums as the beast leaped into the air and bounded toward him.

Kordaz jumped to one side as with his free hand he hauled the parachute out of the capsule and into the air, the huge canopy billowing open. The beast plunged into the parachute and landed with the fabric rippling around it as it clawed to free itself and let out another enraged roar.

Kordaz leaped through the air and landed upon the animal's back as the chute slid free, its shoulders as hard as rocks and the fur thick and smelling of soil and the oil of its skin. The animal, its head still wrapped in the chute, reared up as Kordaz lifted the *D'jeck* and plunged it down with all of his might into the back of the animal's neck.

The polished blade smashed down through flesh, gristle and bone to a terrific scream of pain as Kordaz shifted to a two-handed grip on the weapon and, careful not to impale himself on the spike poking from the handle, he twisted the weapon sideways and then hauled it out of the animal. The serrated blade tore upward and took ragged chunks of flesh with it.

The beast groaned in agony and hurled itself sideways in an attempt to crush Kordaz. The Veng'en leaped clear and rolled across the ground, then came up into a crouch with the *D'jeck* held ready.

The beast got up onto all fours as the parachute ripped open and fell away from its face, and shook its great head. Kordaz saw it stagger slightly as blood poured from its wound, the terrible damage wrought by the *D'jeck* on its spinal column taking its toll.

The animal looked at Kordaz and he heard its tortured breathing wheeze from gigantic lungs, and then its legs gave way and it slumped forward onto its belly, the air from its snout blowing dust as it struggled to stay alive.

Kordaz watched it for a moment, and then he slid the *D'jeck* back into its sheath and marched away toward the light.

**

XXII

'You've got to be kidding me.'

Teera stood in the barred cell alongside Evelyn and looked down at the pile of robes that an Ogrin had just tossed into the cell. Similar in style to those worn by the hybrids, they were designed to expose the maximum amount of flesh and be as easy to remove as possible.

The Ogrin stared at them expectantly. Neither Teera nor Evelyn moved.

The Ogrin humphed, turned, and stomped away from the cells.

'We need a way out of here,' Evelyn said.

'And off this planet,' Teera whispered beneath her breath. 'The Atlantia was cleared to gather resources, right? The captain would have made every effort to put somebody on the ground near us.'

'Probably,' Evelyn replied as she surveyed the meagre clothing offered them. Right now, she felt a lot more secure in her flight suit. 'But it's not going to have been easy. I'm guessing that the Arcadia's shields and radar are all fully active, so that'll be what's giving Salim's compound its cover and defences.'

The Ogrin returned, and this time he was dragging a body behind him. Evelyn and Teera stood back from the cell doors as two pirates, flanking their giant charge, opened the doors. One stood guard with a plasma rifle aimed at Evelyn and Teera as the other yanked the door back and the Ogrin hurled the comatose woman's body into the cell. The door slammed shut behind her as Teera dropped to her knees alongside the woman.

'An idea of what's going to happen if you don't comply,' one of the pirates murmured with a confident grin. 'We'll give you one hour to convince her to capitulate. If she does not, you'll all be hanged outside the compound as a warning to others. Think on it, why don't you?'

The pirates strolled away, followed by the Ogrin. As soon as they were gone Evelyn joined Teera, who was lifting the woman up into a sitting position and holding her there. The woman blinked, her eyes hooded and her hair in disarray.

'Erin,' she gasped.

The woman's voice was rough, her throat dry. Evelyn spotted a small cantina of water on a shelf in the cell, a vague gesture of humanity from their captors. She fetched the cantina and let the woman drink from it.

'Who's Erin?' Evelyn asked her.

141

The woman stopped drinking and gasped for breath as she slumped against Teera.

'My daughter,' she replied. 'They're holding her and my father, Stefan.'

'I think we saw Erin in the throne room,' Evelyn replied. 'She's unharmed.'

'For now,' the woman replied wearily.

'What's your name?' Teera asked.

'Ishira,' came the exhausted reply, 'captain of the merchant vessel *Valiant*.'

'How did you end up here?'

'We were fleeing,' Ishira replied. 'We were searching for supplies when we got jumped by a Veng'en cruiser. We fled across the system and managed to evade them, but then we got captured by some damned pirate and...'

'Whoa, back up a moment,' Evelyn cut her off. 'You saw a Veng'en cruiser?'

Ishira nodded as she drank a little more from the canteen. 'Came out of nowhere. We'd only just arrived in the system, and I guess the flare star's output was screwing up our warning receivers and radar. They opened fire but we out-ran them.'

Evelyn sat back on her haunches thoughtfully.

'We were following a Veng'en cruiser,' she said. 'Sensors said it dropped out of super-luminal close to the Chiron system.'

'Could be the same one,' Teera acknowledged. 'But why start messing about hitting merchant ships? They were on their way home, right?'

'You don't know where the cruiser went?' Evelyn asked Ishira.

'No,' Ishira replied. 'We were getting closer to the parent star when they just vanished, turned back for some reason.'

Teera and Evelyn exchanged a glance.

'Maybe they saw the pirates coming?' Teera ventured.

'Veng'en wouldn't run just like that,' Evelyn said. 'If they were chasing one human vessel and others turned up they'd have considered it a bonus. Something else must have happened to them.'

Ishira looked up at them both as she began to recover her senses.

'What the hell were you doing following a Veng'en cruiser? Who are you?' Then she saw Evelyn's shoulder insignia and the patches on her flight suit. 'Atlantia?! You're Colonial?'

'Atlantia's in orbit right now,' Evelyn confirmed.

Ishira apparently found a fresh surge of energy as she scrambled to her feet.

'Then get them the hell down here!'

'A bit tricky,' Teera replied. 'We're hostages here and Salim Phaeon has a large force at his disposal. Carpet-bombing the compound with so many innocent lives at stake isn't an option.'

'Nor is leaving us here!'

'Nobody's leaving anybody,' Evelyn assured her. 'But our captain isn't going to make a move against Salim until he's sure that he can do so without endangering too many lives.'

'Human shield,' Ishira uttered in disgust. 'Salim is a pig and a coward.'

'Our sentiments exactly,' Teera grinned. 'Which is why we'll do everything we can to disrupt things from our end.'

'Great,' Ishira said as she put her hands on her hips. 'Where do we start?'

'By putting these robes on,' Evelyn replied.

Ishira's jubilant expression folded in upon itself. 'You want us to do *what*?'

'Put the robes on,' Evelyn replied as she picked up one of the flowing gowns. 'We can't do much good sitting down here in a cell.'

Ishira stared at the gowns, mortified. 'I just went through hell to avoid wearing those damned things.'

'Then you're an idiot,' Evelyn snapped back. 'Best chance we have to get out of here is to not be locked in these cells. Your daughter is up there right now. You think you're doing her any favours by getting yourself killed down here?'

Ishira fumed in silence as Evelyn tried to work out which way round the gowns went on.

'This isn't exactly my sort of thing,' Teera said as she unzipped her flight suit. 'And we can't conceal weapons in them.'

'We'll cross that bridge when we come to it,' Evelyn said as she glanced at Ishira. 'You said your father was here too?'

'Working on the Arcadia, I think,' Ishira replied. 'We got separated when we arrived.'

Evelyn thought for a moment and then she looked at Teera.

'If the Arcadia was captured recently, it's unlikely that Salim's people could have completely hacked her systems and computers.'

'Doesn't matter much, does it?' Teera asked. 'There's no way we can get a team down here to check, and a Marine assault is out of the question.'

'We might not have to,' Evelyn said as she slipped out of her flight suit and draped the slender robe over her shoulders. 'We might be able to use the Boarding Protocol.'

'The what?' Teera asked.

'All Colonial capital ships share the same computer codes and contain hidden overrides that are designed to allow remote control from a sister vessel.'

'You mean Atlantia could take control of Arcadia?' Ishira asked.

Teera stared at Evelyn and grasped her own head with one hand.

'Of course,' she replied. 'I remember something of that from the training. The codes were designed so that if a ship was successfully boarded by attackers, the rest of the fleet could both contain and control them, turning the attack into a capture.'

Evelyn's and Teera's military training had been compressed into six months instead of three years, and much of the detail had been missed in order to bring them to combat-ready status, but pilot chatter and building experience meant that many of those missed details were steadily being filled in. Both Mikhain and Captain Sansin had occasionally spoken of the Boarding Protocol, which had only been used once during a battle between a Colonial scout vessel, *Patriot,* and a Veng'en cruiser, code-named *Rage,* during a confrontation a decade previously.

Ambushed during a routine patrol on the Icari Line, the Patriot had been hopelessly out-matched by the much larger and more powerful Rage. Choosing to flee, Patriot's captain had elected to head not for Etheran space but instead for the nearest Colonial outpost. The faster Patriot could have made it to the outpost ahead of Rage, but her captain was unwilling to risk the lives of the outpost's personnel should the Veng'en push their attack further. Instead, he undertook an ingenious deception.

Nearing the outpost, he sent an alert signal ahead and then deliberately weakened his own aft shields, allowing the Veng'en cruiser to achieve a hit on the smaller vessel. Feigning crippling damage, the Patriot slowed and the Veng'en cruiser both caught and boarded her. The Veng'en boarders reached the bridge, only to find it abandoned. Calling their own crew aboard their ship for assistance, they were surprised to receive no reply.

The Patriot's captain and crew had counter-boarded the Veng'en cruiser, now short of armed personnel, and successfully took the bridge. Moments later, the Colonial outpost took control of the Patriot and sealed her, trapping the boarders inside. In the space of an admittedly tense hour, the Patriot's captain took his crew from certain defeat to complete victory with barely a shot fired, an event that had gone down in Colonial history and earned the captain his promotion to admiral.

'The problem is,' Teera pointed out, 'we don't know if anybody is aware on Atlantia that there's a Colonial frigate down here.'

'They will,' Evelyn replied. 'That's our job. As long as Salim or his people are talking to Atlantia, we need to be there to try and send a signal to let them know what's down here. As soon as they figure it out they might be able to take control of Arcadia and shut her defence systems down, then launch an assault to liberate us.' Evelyn looked at Ishira. 'All of us.'

Ishira looked at Evelyn for a long moment and then she stooped and picked up one of the robes.

'This had better be worth it,' she uttered.

Evelyn looked down at herself and tried to ignore the sickly flushes washing through her body, provoked by more than just the cold. It could not be long before the withdrawal fevers that she had heard about began, horrific pangs of agony that wracked the sufferer's body for days or even weeks on end.

The robes were of a creamy-white satin fabric, two lengths over her shoulders that reached down to a clasp at her waist, and two more lengths that extended almost to the ground. Her mid-riff was bare, far more skin showing than was covered, and the tiny shoes that came with the robes were thin-soled and not good for running or fighting of any kind.

'We're not going to be able to thump our way out of here,' she warned Teera and Ishira. 'We'll need our wits for this, understood?'

Her two companions nodded, and they waited together for the Ogrin to return.

***

XXIII

Qayin strode through the ship toward the holding cells, a hundred thoughts skimming around through his mind like flashes of awareness in an immense darkness.

The farmer in the sick-bay was still unconscious and unable to communicate with Doctor Sansin, a state of affairs that Qayin would very much like to become permanent. But security was high around the patient's bed, with little chance of Qayin making his way inside without being observed. Likewise, there were now three Devlamine dealers in custody, and only the threat of violence against their families forcing them to maintain their silence. Qayin knew that his threat could only hold for so long before the men folded. He needed a way out and off Atlantia, the sooner the better.

On Chiron IV an entire armada of pirate vessels were commanded by a man whose exploits out beyond the Icari Line were almost legendary. Qayin did not like what he had heard about the man, but then he did not like what he had heard about most pirates, or even drug dealers for that matter. There were no such things as friends in Qayin's business, only accquaintances who gained or lost favour through their ability to supply or pay for goods. Nothing much else mattered, really, and that was the kind of lifestyle that Qayin yearned for once again.

The complexities of proper relationships frustrated him at the best of times. The constant sacrifices, both large and small, to maintain the trust of people who thought of themselves as friends was a drain on Qayin's patience that he could ill afford. Stuck aboard Atlantia Five as a high-security convict for two years and another two aboard Atlantia herself as a Marine had driven him almost insane. Now, liberation was at hand, a chance to break free from the stifling coils of Colonial life that no longer existed anywhere else in the cosmos anyway. Every order, ever command and every duty strained the limits of his endurance, but not for much longer.

Qayin entered the cells, the two Marines guarding them stepping aside as they recognised him. Both were former convicts and servants of Bravo Company but, to themselves, servants of Qayin. Loyal men, who knew how to fight and who had expressed a desire to leave the Atlantia a the first reasonable opportunity. Qayin nodded discreetly at them as he strode into the cells and down to where a lone man was sitting on a bench staring at the deck.

Qayin knew a little about Taron Forge, not least of all that he was the estranged son of the celebrated Admiral Tyraeus Forge, a man as famous as Salim Phaeon for entirely opposing reasons. A valiant commander with many courageous battle actions to his name, lost now to the Legion.

Taron looked up at Qayin without interest at first, but then he spotted Qayin's bioluminescent tattoos and a sparkle of curiosity twinkled in his expression.

'The Mark of Qayin,' he murmured.

'Pleased to meet you,' Qayin replied.

Taron stood and looked the Marine up and down. 'Last person I'd have thought would stoop to becoming a Colonial foot soldier. What happened?'

'Cicrumstances,' Qayin replied. 'Better to be free up there than locked away down here.'

'That depends on what you call "free",' Taron pointed out. 'You here to escort me to more comfortable surroundings?'

'No,' Qayin said. 'I'm here to make you an offer.' Taron's eyebrow lifted and he glanced over Qayin's shoulder. The big Marine turned and saw a petite but somehow dangerous looking woman with exotic features watching him in silence from the opposite cell. 'Both of you,' Qayin added.

'What kind of offer would that be?' Taron asked. 'Working for the Man?'

Qayin shook his head, his gold and blue locks shimmering and his glowing tattoos sparkling as though with mischief.

'Working for yourself,' he replied, 'through me.'

Taron eyed the Marine thoughtfully. 'Just the kind of thing Sansin would pull as some sort of loyalty test, I presume. See if I can be trusted?'

Qayin stepped closer to the bars.

'See the guards by the block entrance?' Taron glanced to his left, and when Qayin was sure he was looking at the Marines he spoke again. 'They're my men, not Sansin's or anybody else's. Half of Bravo Company is waiting for my word to pull the hell off this damned ship and get back to business.'

Taron watched the two Marines for a long beat and then looked back at Qayin.

'What's your trade?'

'Devlamine, but I'll shift whatever turns a profit.'

'User?'

'Seller,' Qayin grinned, 'supply and demand is all I'm interested in.'

'Where's your market?'

'Chiron IV. Salim already knows the drugs are aboard Atlantia, and the captain is searching for them as we speak. He won't find them yet because they're well enough hidden, but the wider the search goes the sooner they'll be found. Captain plans to exchange the entire stash for Salim's hostages. I disagree. Best place for them is with the customer, don't you think?'

'Where is your supply?' Taron demanded.

'Safe, below decks,' Qayin assured him.

Taron glanced at Yo'Ki before he spoke. 'What's your price?'

'Salim's reckoned to have a lot of ships down there, a lot of merchandise he's picked up since the apocalypse. We trade for transport and supplies, and make sure we hold back the crystals that are the Devlamine source. Keep Salim dependent on us for supply.'

'The small matter of getting the Devlamine down there?'

'Leave that to me,' Qayin replied. 'I can get you both out of here with the Devlamine, and back to Chiron.'

'And I take it that your Marines will be coming along?'

'If not now, then imminently. Captain will be forced at some point to launch an assault, and we'll be there. A small matter to switch sides once we're on the ground.'

Taron frowned.

'And if any assault by Atlantia is successful? You'll be trapped down there with Salim and blasted to hell.'

'No gain without risk,' Qayin countered. 'Sansin won't bombard the compound if there's even the hint that he'll hit his own people. Better than that, there are ships down there for the taking. If we can't get off with Salim's crowd, we'll just take what we need ourselves.'

'My ship's not for the taking,' Taron growled.

'Yours is free,' Qayin grinned. 'We're on the same side, remember?'

'We're all on our own side.'

Qayin smiled broadly. Taron was nobody's fool, and he was clearly thinking much along the same lines of Qayin: look after Number One, and then worry about everybody else if you felt so inclined.

'You know Salim personally,' Qayin said. 'I don't. You're the link we need to make this work, somebody Salim trusts and will listen to. I don't doubt that he'll be interested in a direct line to the drugs and having a few dozen trained Marines to add to his arsenal.'

'You want to join his little clan?' Taron asked.

'Only for as long as it takes to cut Atlantia loose,' Qayin replied. 'The rest we'll figure out from there on in.'

'We'll be leaving as soon as the dust settles,' Taron said as he glanced again at Yo'Ki.

'Then we're clear,' Qayin said finally. 'We focus on getting free of this damned ship, and then after that we all decide where we want to go. I'm guessing anywhere but here is just about fine for the both of you?'

Taron watched his co-pilot and Qayin saw her nod fractionally.

'Done,' Taron replied. 'You get us out of here, we'll get you and your men to the surface and help the trade with Salim. Then we're even.'

'I'll be in touch,' Qayin said.

The Marine turned and marched off the block, a satisfied grin on his face.

*

Corporal Djimon leaned over the computer console in the control room outside the cells and watched as Sergeant Qayin strode away, an expression of delight etched into his features and his glowing tattoos fluorescing brightly enough to be visible on the monitor.

The guard seated behind the monitor looked up at the corporal.

'You want me to call it in?' he asked. 'Sergeant Qayin has every right to be here if his men are guarding the prisoner and I saw no evidence of suspect behaviour.'

Djimon shook his head. Both Qayin and Taron had spoken softly enough to not be heard by the camera's microphones.

Alpha and Bravo company shared shifts on guard duties, each taking responsibility for the onerous task on an alternating basis. Both of the guards present were Bravo Company and likely loyal to Qayin, as were so many it seemed, and if questioned by would say nothing untoward had occurred. Likewise, General Bra'hiv would not see any cause for concern. He did not share Djimon's dislike of Qayin, although he did still harbour a healthy mistrust of the former convict.

Djimon stood up and took a deep breath as he considered his options.

'No, leave this with me.'

***

XXIV

Meyanna Sansin stood before the magnetic confinement chamber in her laboratory and peered at the Hunter hovering within, entrapped by intense magnetic fields. She shivered as she moved from side to side and saw the small machine's photoreceptors follow her. It both recognised her presence and appeared self-aware, reacting to her.

Alive.

And yet its circuitry was confined to too small a space for it to be truly intelligent, its reactions to her the programmed responses of an otherwise soulless machine.

Meyanna had spent many hours observing the Hunter. Captured by Evelyn from the merchant vessel *Sylph* many months before, it had been just one of countless millions aboard the ship. In her analysis, Meyanna had surmised that this Hunter had been constructed from the same metals and materials *Sylph* had been built from. Once aboard a foreign vessel, the tiny Infectors' secondary role after infecting humans was to replicate both themselves and then larger machines like Hunters, drawing on whatever materials and resources surrounded them.

What interested Meyanna the most was not what the machines were built of, however. She was fascinated by what they all shared, the internal circuitry and architecture that they must all possess in order to work as one, as a cohesive force. The fact that it was she doing the research and not somebody from the engineering department was because although the Legion was chiefly constructed from metals and plastics and computer circuits, their internal organs were far more the work of biology and chemistry.

Kordaz, the Veng'en who had joined the crew after the encounter with the Sylph, had revealed that Veng'en research had discovered that the Legion used chemicals with which to communicate and operate as large formations in perfect harmony. The method, clearly inspired by swarms of insects, allowed the Legion to move in their millions almost like a single, gigantic organism and overwhelm any foe in their path.

Meyanna's task was to unravel the complexities of their bio-mechanical circuitry and the language of their chemical communications, and then come up with a suitable defence or weapon to be used against them. If somehow they could learn to disrupt the Legion's ability to coordinate itself, or perhaps even completely prevent them from cooperating with each other, then the Word's most powerful weapon would be neutralised and the chances of their success in retaking Ethera massively improved.

'Sounds easy if you say it fast enough,' she murmured to herself as she looked at the Hunter before her.

Some other means of technical wizardy had clearly also been employed by the Word to enhance the performance of these murderous little machines. It could be anything from neuronal networking to some super-advanced programming to quantum computing: all that Meyanna could be sure of was that it would have its origins in human endeavour, for the Word's knowledge was all based on humanity's own immense store of information. Although the Word could learn independently, Meyanna was not required to undergo the same laborious task: here, she could reverse-engineer the Hunter and...

The machine's gaze switched position as Meyanna was examining it and turned to look over her shoulder. Meyanna whirled and saw a man's arms smashing down toward her.

She screamed and hurled herself to one side as a metal specimen jar smashed against the magnetic confinement chamber and shattered it. The twisted face of the drug-addict glared at her, his eyes jaundiced and poisoned with delirium and rage as he staggered toward her, incoherent words and drool spilling from his lips as he screamed and ranted.

Meyanna whirled and hit an alarm switch on the wall that sent a blaring claxon screeching through the sick bay. Instantly, half a dozen nurses and orderlies dashed toward the laboratory, but the sick man was standing between Meyanna and her escape, one trembling arm pointing at her, ripped IV lines dangling from veins and trailing blood in slick red smears across the floor.

'You're killing me!' the man gasped in agony.

Meyanna worked her jaw and tried to find her voice.

'I'm trying to save you,' she managed to reply. 'You're sick from the drugs! You overdosed! Who gave you the drugs?!'

'I'll kill him,' the man growled. 'I'll kill him!'

'Who gave you the drugs?!' Meyanna demanded.

The man scowled and swung a fist at her.

Meyanna ducked and as the clumsy punch raced past she lunged forward and drove her shoulder into the man's belly. His breath blasted out of his lungs beside her as she barged past him and dashed for the laboratory door, one hand slamming into the locking buttons and deactivating the pressure seal.

The doors hissed open and the nurses plunged into the laboratory, one of them carrying an anaesthetic gun that he immediately fired straight into the patient's chest. The main wailed as the projectile buried itself in his flesh, one hand grasping blindly for it, and then within seconds his legs quivered beneath him and he plunged to the deck just in time for the other nurses to restrain him in a well-ordered, oft-practiced drill. Within moments he was back on his bed, his wrists and ankles restrained and IV lines re-inserted.

'What happened?' Captain Idris Sansin burst into the sick-bay, drawn from the bridge by the sudden alarms. 'Are you okay?'

'I'm fine,' Meyanna replied, hugging herself as her husband's hands gripped her shoulders. 'He must have worked free of his restraints.'

Idris glanced at the now comatose patient. 'This is getting out of control. Anybody on that drug who starts withdrawing is going to become dangerous.'

'Have there been any more?' Meyanna asked.

'Not yet,' Idris replied. 'But it can only be a matter of time. Damn it, we need to know who's behind this and recover their stash. It's the only thing Salim Phaeon seems interested in.'

Idris held his wife close in an embrace, but then he felt her stiffen.

'Don't move,' she whispered in his ear.

Slowly she took his shoulders and turned him around. Idris saw the entrance to the laboratory, and to his left the magnetic containment chamber that housed the...

'It's gone,' he uttered in horror.

The chamber's glass walls had been smashed by the patient's attack on Meyanna, and the magnetic field had been disrupted by the impact. The Hunter, for so long lodged in the chamber, had escaped.

'Don't move,' Meyanna repeated.

She eased past her husband, slowly, carefully. The laboratory doors were still open, the nurses having rushed in without realising that the chamber was breached. Right now, Meyanna did not care about the doors. Her eyes were fixed upon the blood stains smearing the laboratory deck.

There, on the tiles, was the Hunter.

'What's it doing?' Idris asked as he spotted the machine.

The nurses behind them were silent and still now, aware of the escaped Hunter and likely pertified of what the tiny machine might do. Meyanna herself, however, had no real fear of the machine. Too large to self-replicate at the molecular level like the Infectors, and not small enough to infect humans itself, it was unable to cause much disruption aboard Atlantia on its own. What transfixed her attention now was the machine's activities on the deck.

The Hunter was crouched over the blood the patient had trailed and it had extended a small proboscis from its nose that was visibly sucking up the blood before it. Meyanna approached silently, moving behind the Hunter as she reached behind her and picked up a plastic container from a desk, ready to trap the Hunter inside it.

The machine appeared unaware of her advance, and as she watched she saw it increase its consumption of the spilled blood. To her amazement, within a few moments the blood was dripping from its tail as though it had passed through the machine's internals and been excreted.

Meyanna crouched down behind the Hunter and dropped the plastic box over it. The Hunter ignored her completely.

Slowly, the captain and the other nurses edged forward until they were all staring at the trapped machine as it sucked blood from the laboratory floor.

'I thought that it would have run away,' Idris said, 'tried to hide and start messing with the ship's electrical systems.'

'Me too,' Meyanna replied. 'I don't know what this means. I need that chamber fixed, and fast. The Hunter can chew straight through that box if it decides that it wants to.'

'Get on it,' the captain snapped at the nearby nurses. 'Contact engineering and tell them I said to give you whatever you need.'

The nurses stumbled over themselves to carry out the captain's orders as fast as they could, and Idris watched as his wife examined the Hunter.

'It looks as though it's extracting something from the blood,' she said.

Idris looked at the Hunter, and then at his wife.

'The Devlamine?' he ventured.

Meyanna stared at the Hunter for a long moment as she recalled how the Legion had taken control of the human race back on Ethera years before.

It had been the Infectors that had replicated in silence through some eighty per cent of humanity before being commanded by the Word to attack, decimating humankind in a single, cruel blow. But the very start of the infection, the common vector that had gotten those first Infectors into society, had been Devlamine.

'They recognise the drug,' she murmured.

Devlamine, a street drug of unrivalled potency, had been the perfect vector because its crystalline nature had allowed Infectors to bury themselves and survive outside of their human hosts until the drug was consumed. They then, having gained access to the spinal cord and the brain of their host, were able to both control the flow of Devlamine in the body and also enhance its effects, turning the host into a virtual robot that they alone could control.

'It's stocking up,' Idris confirmed, clearly thinking the same as her. 'The Hunters must have carried Devlamine at one point too.'

Meyanna got to her feet as two engineers hurried in with a sheet of glass and a pair of magnetic plates, giving the Hunter at her feet a wide berth as they moved to repair the damaged containment unit.

'Hunters sometimes carried Infectors aboard and would deliver them hypodermically to victims,' Meyanna recalled. 'The Infectors would carry Devlamine into the victim with them and use it to control them regardless of whether they were already addicts or not. Our little friend here does not possess any Infectors, but it would still probably pick up the Devlamine as a matter of course if it detects any.'

Meyanna turned and looked at the patient now laying silently on the nearby bed.

'We need that Devlamine,' she said to her husband. 'Not to give to the pirates down there, but to use as a draw for the Legion.'

'What do you have in mind?' Idris asked.

Meyanna almost smiled as a plan formed in her mind.

'What if we could load an accelerant with enough Devlamine to draw in Hunters and Infectors?' she asked rhetorically. 'Then we could fire on them and incinerate them a million at a time.'

Idris thought about it for a moment, and as always he then thought bigger.

'Or a billion,' he said. 'There's no reason we couldn't deliver Devlamine in ordnance, maybe torpedoes, and then fire on them.'

'They'd be destroyed quickly enough that they would not be able to pass signals on to warn other units of the Legion about what had happened to them,' Meyanna went on. 'And the resulting fires would burn up any chemical trails they had laid.'

'It's brilliant,' Idris said. 'Now all we need is to find what Devlamine is aboard ship and take control of it. I can't believe I'm about to say this, but we need to cultivate as much of that drug as we can.'

'What about Salim?'

Idris thought for a moment, and then made a decision.

'I've got an idea.'

***

Dean Crawford

XXV

'Say what now?'

Taron Forge watched the Marine Lieutenant as he unlocked the doors of Taron's cell.

'You're free to go, captain.'

Taron remained where he was, suddenly unwilling to leave the relative safety of his cell and uncertain of what the Marine had in store for him. He looked at the adjoining cell where Yo'Ki was likewise being released. She glanced across, suspicion writ large across her exotic features.

'Just like that?' Taron asked.

'Just like that,' Lieutenant C'rairn confirmed. 'Captain says you're no damned use to us and doesn't want to waste our limited resources having to feed you both, not to mention your ship taking up space in the bays. So, get out of here.'

Taron stepped out of the cell and was even more surprised when C'rairn produced Taron's pistol and handed it to him, the magazine fully charged. Yo'Ki's weapon was also returned to her in likewise pristine condition.

'What's to stop your captain blowing us out of existence the moment we lift off?' Taron asked.

'We don't care,' C'rairn replied with the briefest of smiles. 'But like I said, the captain doesn't want to waste resources so he won't bother shooting you down. Best for you to just get the hell off of our ship before somebody wastes a few calories and cuts your throat, know what I mean?'

C'rairn rested one hand on the sheathed knife on his webbing belt. Taron managed a grin, but he began walking.

'Thank your captain for a wonderful stay won't you?' he suggested as he joined his co-pilot.

'Escort them to the launch bay,' C'rairn ordered the two Marines who had accompanied him. 'Make sure they get aboard their ship immediately.'

Taron kept walking and ignored the two Marines who fell into step behind them and followed as they walked toward the launch bay, several minutes away across the ship.

'I don't like this,' Taron uttered beneath his breath.

Yo'Ki shrugged.

'I'm not complaining either,' Taron said. 'But, this ain't right. Salim's got hostages down there and we're the captain's only real bargaining chip so far as we know, and he's just going to let us go?'

Yo'Ki glanced sideways at Taron and lifted one perfectly shaped eyebrow.

'Sure, maybe we aren't that important,' Taron shrugged. 'Kind of degrading, you know what I mean?'

Yo'Ki jabbed him in the ribs with one elbow but said nothing as they kept walking.

Taron led the way to the launch bays and walked out to see rows of Raython fighters parked beside each other along each wall, and at the far end of the bay the Phoenix waiting for them, her main ramp still raised as they had left it.

'You see anything amiss?' Taron asked Yo'Ki.

She shook her head, her long black pony-tail swinging and catching the light. All around them maintenance crews were swarming over the Raython fighters and three older bomber craft that Taron recalled were named Corsairs – an appropriate name considering the circumstances.

Yo'Ki tapped Taron in the side as they walked and nodded toward the Corsairs. Taron spotted instantly the heavy plasma weapons being loaded into their bomb bays. Each capable of delivering a two-megaton blast, sufficient to level several city blocks, the bombs would decimate Salim's compound on Chiron IV.

'They're going for it,' he uttered to his co-pilot. 'They're going to level the compound.'

Taron looked over his shoulder and saw plasma torpedoes being loaded aboard Raython fighters, increasing their air-to-ground capability instead of self-defence against Salim's fighter screen. As Taron slowed and looked behind him, down the far end of the bay, he saw almost a hundred Marines hauling on their battle kit near a pair of shuttles.

Taron stopped where he was as he stared at a sight he had not seen for almost ten years: a fully armed, fully equipped and manned frigate and fighter squadrons preparing for open battle. Taron thoguht about the Devlamine that Qayin had promised was waiting somewhere below Atlantia's decks, and of the huge demand for the drug elsewhere in the cosmos. If they walked now, the deal would be lost. And then he thought of the kind of people Qayin and Salim represented, the form humanity would take if they alone prevailed in the wake of the apocalypse.

Taron looked at the Phoenix, her sleek hull and powerful engines seeming to beckon him toward her, offering escape, a place where he wouldn't have to care.

Yo'Ki watched him in silence, waiting.

'Damn it,' Taron uttered, and turned back toward the launch bay exit.

*

Captain Idris Sansin scanned the tactical display on Atlantia's bridge as his crew hurried to perform their duties in preparation for battle.

'Are the Raython's fully fuelled?'

'As much as they can be, captain,' Mikhain replied. 'The Corsairs are armed with plasma-bombs, full escort will be in attendance, and the Renegades are armed with extra air-to-ground ordnance to back them up.'

'Good,' Sansin replied. 'Prepare the launch sequence, full tactical. I want every single one of those fighters and bombers off the deck and into planetary descent in double-quick time, no delays, is that clear?'

'Aye, captain!'

Sansin looked up as a commotion near the bridge entrance caught his attention and he spotted Taron Forge and Yo'Ki confronting the two hulking Marines standing guard outside. Taron was jabbing his finger into one of the soldier's chests and looked as though he was about to draw his sidearm when Sansin called out.

'Let them in.'

The two Marines stepped aside abruptly enough that Taron almost fell between them. The smuggler walked onto the bridge with his co-pilot following silently behind as he strolled directly up onto the command platform.

'What the hell's going on here?'

'None of your business, Taron,' the captain replied as he studied a meterological chart of the weather on Chiron IV below them. 'You have your clearance to leave. Get off my ship before I have you forcibly ejected.'

'You're going to launch an assault on Salim's compound.'

'And people say you're slow.'

'There are at least a thousand people down there,' Taron snapped. 'You hit them with plasma bombs when you can't differentiate between friend and foe, the collateral will be unthinkable.'

'You put us in this position,' Idris reminded him. 'This is what happens when you don't cooperate. You've left me with no choice.'

'You'll kill your own people!'

'Not your problem,' Idris muttered without looking at Taron. 'You're still on my bridge. Guard?!'

The two Marines hurried onto the bridge as the captain gestured dismissively toward Taron without even dignifying the smuggler with a glance.

'Remove this man from my bridge immediately.'

Idris moved to turn away, but was yanked back around by Taron's hand on his shoulder.

'They have a Colonial frigate down there,' the smuggler said. 'Atlantia class. It's moored near the shoreline.'

All movement on the bridge stopped. Idris Sansin stared at Taron for what felt like an age before he finally managed to speak.

'A Colonial frigate?' he echoed, as though unable to believe what he was hearing.

Taron nodded. 'Captured a couple of months ago. Don't ask me how, because I have no idea. It's what they're using to shield the compound while they repair the damage to the frigate's hull. She's operational, captain, but if you bombard the site you might damage her beyond repair.'

Idris turned and looked at Mikhain, who also seemed to be unable to believe what he was hearing.

'We could double our strength in one fell swoop,' the XO said finally. 'Two frigates. We'd have more room, be able to employ better tactics, double our firepower in any single engagement.'

Idris nodded thoughtfully, but then he sighed.

'We'll have to hold off on the orbital bombardment and restrict the operation to airborne attack and a Marine landing.'

'Didn't you hear what I just said?' Taron said in amazement. 'You can't launch an assault with so many people trapped down there.'

'Like you said, collateral damage, but we'll gain a lot more when we've taken Salim and his smugglers out of the picture.'

Taron looked about him on the bridge as though seeking support, but nobody was looking at him. Every officer was fully engrossed in their duties.

'You're no better than Salim,' Taron uttered in disgust.

Idris whirled and stormed across to Taron, looming over the pirate with rage seeping from his pores.

'It's you who gave us no choice,' Idris snarled. 'You could have informed us about the frigate's presence beforehand and allowed us to overwhelm Salim's people with the element of surprise on our side. You could have given us information about numbers of opponents, weakness in their defensive structure, potential allies among their prisoners. But no, you sat here and whined about how you wouldn't do anything unless we gave you an incentive that was worth your while!'

The bridge fell silent as the captain raged into Taron's face.

'I just gave you that frigate,' Taron muttered in reply.

'Too little, too late Taron,' Idris went on, and drove a finger into the pirate's chest. 'We now have no other way of bringing our people back but to launch a full-scale assault on a man who happily uses children as human shields. The longer we leave it, the harder it will be and the greater the number of casualties on both sides, no thanks to you!' Idris turned his back to the pirate. 'You're no longer welcome here because you're no longer a human being. You're a pirate and a criminal Taron, nothing more, and you have no place among us!'

Taron hovered for a moment as though uncertain of whether to storm out of the bridge or beg for the lives of people he did not even know. The smuggler glanced at his co-pilot, Yo'Ki, who raised a silent eyebrow at him. Taron rolled his eyes and placed his hands on his hips.

'Perhaps there is something that we might be able to do to help?'

'What could I possibly want of you two, Taron?' Idris uttered without looking up.

'I'll fly down there and see if Salim can be convinced to free at least some of the hostages, but I'm not guaranteeing a damned thing, understood?'

The captain concealed a quiet smile as he intently studied a tactical display and kept his back turned toward Taron.

'How can I trust you to do anything to help us?' Idris growled.

'I'm damned well here, aren't I?' Taron snapped. 'Don't pull my chain, captain. I can just as easily take off and leave the system.'

Idris, his hands behind his back, turned to face the smuggler.

'Guards, stand by,' he ordered as the nearby Marines activated their plasma rifles. 'Captain Forge is displaying frightening indications of goodwill.'

***

Dean Crawford

XXVI

The glow of the lights was a white halo that cast the darkened crest of the hillside into sharp relief, low clouds drifting by in a sullen sky and the glowing aurora visible between them, rivers of ghostly green light amid the frigid darkness above.

Kordaz eased his way up the hillside, the chill in the air bitter and his bones aching with the cold. The thermal suit he wore did little to protect him, continuous motion his only ally against hypothermia as he clambered over rocks and around thickened tufts of hardy grass.

From the distance he heard the muted clash of metal upon metal, the sound of mechanical engines and human voices echoing around him as he climbed the last few cubits to the ridgeline and then paused. He calmed his breathing, cautious of the clouds of vapour he was billowing out onto the cold air and of how easily they would be illuminated by the distant lights. Darkness was his only defence against capture, and he had little doubt about how a motley gang of pirates and smugglers would deal with a Veng'en intruder.

Carefully, Kordaz peered over the ridgeline and immediately his breath was taken away by what he saw.

The vast frigate was mounted on immense cradles forged from a mixture of the natural bedrock and shaped steel braces, box-like constructions containing row upon row of metal ovals capable of bearing the frigate's tremendous weight. Illuminated by countless arc lamps blazing like a galaxy of white stars, scaffolding had been erected around the frigate's lower hull, upon which countless workers slaved with welding torches. High above Kordaz other workers could be seen atop the frigate, swarming like ants across a whale's back as they conducted extensive repairs.

Kordaz scanned the compound and identified power conduits and cables, all snaking away to a bank of powerful generators erected near what looked like some kind of makeshift castle mounted against a steep hillside opposite, replete with banners and flags. He scanned the ship again and saw only faint illumination coming from within.

The fusion cores must have been deactivated to allow some of the repair work to go ahead, and therefore the power for the lights, power tools and shielding devices being emitted by the frigate was coming solely from the generators. Ten in all, each the size of a large house, they would themselves be powered by smaller fusion cores.

He cast his gaze back up to the towering frigate. Among the workers strode hulking figures that Kordaz recognised as Ogrin, a dim-witted species enslaved centures before by the Veng'en and others. Obedient and unchallenging, the Ogrin were routinely abused by their captors and forced to work endless hours, their huge strength and easily manipulated nature much in demand, especially outside the core systems where such factors as right-to-dignity laws championed by the Etheran government were given short thrift.

Beyond the frigate Kordaz could just make out an open plain upon which were parked countless fighters, freighters and other assorted craft, likely all pilfered by the smugglers during their normal course of operations out in the Tiberium Fields and beyond. Kordaz could see at least three craft whose origin were unknown to him, created by a species yet to be documented by the governments of the core systems. The Icari Line, generally respected by all species including the Veng'en, represented no barrier to those who flew under no flag and obeyed no laws.

Kordaz reached down to his belt and retrieved a small camera with which he proceeded to take high-resolution film of the site. He knew that the Atlantia would not be able to receive his imagery from its orbital position on the far side of the planet, so the best way to inform Captain Sansin of what was waiting for him on the surface was to board the captured ship and send the information directly to the Atlantia by creating a priority fleet signal. Kordaz knew that only a signal sent from the same ship creating the interference would get through, otherwise Colonial frigates would not have been able to communicate in battle while running those jamming signals. If what he was looking at was indeed a sister ship to Atlantia, then the required codes for getting the signal through would be on board.

There was, however, a major problem.

Kordaz put the camera away and looked at the power generators arrayed near the strange pirate stronghold. The chances of him getting aboard the frigate and then infiltrating the bridge and manipulating the controls without being spotted there were slim. He recalled that like Atlantia the frigate would possess a War Room, a smaller bridge that was used by the command structure if the main bridge was damaged or otherwise compromised, perhaps by boarding enemy or some such, but even that would be impossible to breach without being spotted. That was the whole point of such a room: to prevent boaders from taking control of the ship.

Kordaz would have to settle for second-best. He eyed the distance from the power generators to the nearest of two parked Raython fighters visible beyond the frigate's massive hull. His best chance was to kill the power to the frigate, giving Atlantia the opportunity to attack with an aerial assault and overpower Salim Phaeon's men with brute force and surprise.

Kordaz lay flat and turned side-on to the ridgeline to reduce his profile before he slowly rolled over it and descended down into the shadows toward the compound.

*

'How many are there?'

Meyanna Sansin walked as quickly as she could to keep up with General Bra'hiv as he led her through a winding path in the sanctuary's forest.

'Half a dozen and more coming in since we arrested the dealers and cut off the supply of Devlamine,' the general replied. 'I don't have time to chaperone them and my men are stretched too thin as it is down here. They need treatment, and many of the locals are refusing to let their loved ones out of the sanctuary and into the ship proper.'

'Why would they do that?'

'Because,' Bra'hiv smiled tightly, 'they believe us to be the enemy.'

'Then we need to show them that we're not an enemy,' Meyanna insisted. 'Do you know where the Devlamine farm is?'

'Yes,' Bra'hiv acknowledged, 'I have two men watching it as we speak.'

'Let the civilians know its location,' Meyanna said. 'Let them take control of it for us.'

'That won't change much,' Bra'hiv said, 'we still don't know where the main supply is, the liquified form of the drug that's already been harvested.'

'Doesn't matter if it can't be supplied to addicts,' Meyanna pointed out. 'You worry about the hidden stash. If the people think we trust them with this, they'll turn to our side far quicker than if you keep them in the dark.'

Bra'hiv led Meyanna to a small cluster of homesteads arranged alongside fields packed with crops, the homes backing on to the forest from which she and Bra'hiv emerged. A small group of Marines were standing guard unobtrusively nearby, a larger crowd of civilians gathered in a loose knot amid the homes.

'It's your show from here,' Bra'hiv told her. 'I'm pulling my men out of the sanctuary until I receive orders otherwise from the captain. We're not helping here, we're just creating discord.'

Before Meyanna could reply Bra'hiv clicked his fingers loudly and jerked his head to one side. Every one of the Marines split from their posts and marched on his position as the general led them away from the homes and back into the forest.

Meyanna slowly approached the gathered civilians, who watched her warily until they recognised her and saw the medical logo on the briefcase she carried. As if by some unseen command the women in the group suddenly rushed toward her and in a torrent of words spilled their suffering.

'My son, he's got a temperature of over a hundred.'

'It started last night, after he got back from engineering.'

'It's not drugs, is it? My boy would *never* do that! Would he?'

Meyanna waved the women into silence and spoke quickly.

'Are they exhibiting high temperatures, inflamed veins and arteries, elevated heart rate and excessive sweating?'

All of the women nodded anxiously, their eyes filled with a curious elixir of hope, dread and frayed nerves.

'All of your loved ones are experiencing Devlamine overdose,' Meyanna said sharply. 'You can deny it for as long as you want, but if they are not treated and soon they will all likely perish.'

Another flurry of desperate cries broke against Meyanna's medical expertise and she forced the women to calm down. Behind them, the menfolk were watching with cautious expressions.

'These victims need treatment,' Meyanna said. 'You see the command structure of Atlantia as some kind of enemy, but in truth this has surprised the captain as much as anybody and all they're trying to do is stamp the drugs out, fast. I'll treat all of the victims down here, but I'll need help from my staff and all of those suffering from withdrawal in the sanctuary in one place where we can treat them efficiently, no exceptions.'

One of the men strode forward. 'How can we trust you when your own people are suffering from this sickness, this disease of addiction? We heard that some of your soldiers are afflicted.'

'It's precisely *because* our military personnel are suffering that you can trust us,' Meyanna countered. 'Devlamine affects everybody. You all remember how it was the scourge of the docks back on Ethera? Do any of you want the same epidemic to strike here aboard Atlantia, our last home, perhaps the last home we'll ever have?'

Nobody challenged Meyanna, and she pointed to one of the homesteads.

'That one there,' she said. 'Have it cleared and bring every sufferer there as and when they are found. With them all in one place we'll be one step closer to stamping it out entirely.'

The women looked at Meyanna for only a moment, and then they scattered to do her bidding.

*

Mikhain stormed through the Atlantia's corridors, junior officers stepping out of his way and saluting briskly. He noticed none of them, his mind boiling with outrage. That Andaim had been selected as the Atlantia's captain's "face" for the duration of the orbit had been enough of a blow to his credibility in the eyes of the command team, but now things had truly gone too damned far. The Atlantia was in orbit above a pirate's haven with sworn officers held hostage under threat of death and the captain was apparently placing his faith in Taron Forge, a man known mostly for his hatred and betrayal of Colonial forces. Worse, the captain had entrusted the infiltration of Salim's compound to a traitorous Veng'en who showed little promise of loyalty toward mankind. Kordaz would as likely inform Salim of the impending attack rather than risk his own life. The attack would become a failure before it even went ahead, and any chance of liberating the hostages would be lost.

The captain of the Atlantia was no longer an asset: he was the greatest threat to mankind's continued survival. Mikhain felt certain that the only logical course of action was to ensure that the captain's increasingly erratic behaviour was brought to a halt before any more of the ship's crew were lost.

The Marine's barracks were located close to the launch bays along with the pilot's cabins. Placed for rapid deployment in an emergency, the barracks were split evenly between Alpha and Bravo Company. Mikhain headed directly for the former and strode in.

Corporal Djimon awaited him in the otherwise empty barracks, the towering Marine as immovable as a granite mountain and with features to match. He watched impassively as Mikhain approached.

'You've heard?' he asked.

'An airborne assault on the surface,' Djimon replied. 'The general's keeping the details sketchy, but we're figuring it's some kind of pirate lair and that hostages are involved.'

'That's it,' Mikhain confirmed. 'The damned old fool thinks that he can use Taron Forge to get on the inside and cajole Salim Phaeon into releasing hostages.'

Djimon stared at Mikhain for a long moment. 'How?'

Mikhain scowled at the corporal. 'I don't know because I'm not in the damned loop. Captain Sansin is playing this close to his chest and nobody seems to know what's going on.'

'Nobody from Alpha Company has been deployed that I know of,' Djimon gasped in disbelief.

'Precisely,' Mikhain replied. 'The captain has placed all of his faith in a morally questionable pirate in order to infiltrate Salim Phaeon's compound and liberate Colonial officers. What's the chances of Taron and Yo'Ki changing their minds about their allegiance to us when they get down there?'

'What about Qayin?' Djimon growled.

'To hell with him,' Mikhain replied. 'This is about saving Colonial lives!'

'I saw him,' Djimon said. 'He visited Taron Forge in his cell. I don't know what they talked about, but they both looked so happy I'd say they cut a deal.'

'Salim Phaeon,' Mikhain realised as he thought about this new and unexpected information. 'He knows about the Devlamine supply aboard ship and wants all of it. Qayin's going to turn against us and ally himself to Taron,' Mikhain said with rock-solid conviction. 'Damn it, I knew that man was up to no good.'

'We should report this to the captain,' Djimon insisted.

'No!' Mikhain forestalled the big Marine with one hand. 'The captain isn't listening to anybody but himself. Even if we reveal what's happening he'll push on regardless, he has no choice.'

'Then what do we do?' Djimon asked.

Mikhain clenched his fists by his side as he stiffened his resolve.

'Something neither of us will enjoy,' he replied. 'We must ensure that the mission fails and that the crew's faith in Captain Sansin's ability to command and Sergeant Qayin's loyalty is undermined.'

The big Marine stared down at Mikhain for a long moment as he processed what the XO was suggesting.

'We could lose lives on the surface,' he replied.

'Yes,' Mikhain agreed. 'Qayin, a Veng'en traitor and a damned pirate who should have been hanged years ago. How would you like to see Sergeant Qayin pay for his crimes? Stuck in a cell here on Atlantia surrounded by loyal Marines, or shot for his treachery?'

Corporal Djimon thought only for a moment longer, and then his glacial features cracked with a thin smile.

***

XXVII

Evelyn strode down onto the throne room with Teera behind her, their feet making barely a sound on the stony ground. The air was cold against her skin, but as they reached the throne room warm air billowed from heaters and enveloped her as they followed two giant Ogrin into the room.

Several pirates were lounging on couches and chairs, smoke drifting upward in lazy blue spirals from chrome tobacco pipes as they turned and saw her. Salim Phaeon, slumped on his makeshift throne, looked up and his thin black eyes widened as a satisfied smile curled like a snake across his face.

'My, my,' he murmured as he observed Evelyn and Teera. 'That wasn't so hard now, was it? And how fabulous do they both look?' he asked his companions.

A ripple of soft murmurs floated among the pirates, as though even the effort of speaking was too much for them.

Then, Salim caught sight of Ishira walking down into the room.

'Wonders will never cease!' he exclaimed, and Evelyn saw young Erin stare wide-eyed at her mother as she glimpsed her. Erin jumped up and dashed to Ishira's side, Ishira placing a hand on her daughter's head as she walked.

Salim hauled himself lethargically to his feet as he surveyed the three women all draped in the silken gowns, watching them as though with some kind of fatherly pride that made Evelyn's stomach turn over.

'Welcome, my ladies,' he addressed them. 'You will be far more comfortable here than in those drafty cells, no?' He clicked his fingers at the nearest Ogrin. 'Bring them food, and drink!'

The Ogrin turned and lumbered away as Salim gestured to the thick rugs arranged around the throne, two hybrids already sprawled upon it as though basking with half-empty drinks before them.

'Come, sit down, rest yourselves.'

Ishira and Teera strolled obediently to the rugs but Evelyn did not move.

'We're not here to be enslaved,' Evelyn told him. 'No matter how hard you try there is no way that any of us will become your subjects like these poor pathetic creatures.'

Evelyn gestured to the hybrids, who purred with what may have been amusement and shrugged the insult off.

'These creatures, as you call them,' Salim replied, 'are my friends and are free to move as they wish. They are neither abused nor harmed in any way and…'

'They're slaves,' Evelyn replied. 'Doesn't matter how you dress them up, Salim. You're a slaver, nothing more.'

'And you're a Colonial Officer,' Salim murmured, 'as is your friend here, but she understands that there is no choice for any of you. There are no laws except those that I create here. There is no more Etheran government, no more humanity at all for that matter. Your best chance of survival is right here, and in return we ask little.'

Salim's oily smile only annoyed Evelyn all the more.

'I want to speak to my captain.'

Salim chuckled, his jowls wobbling. 'I'm sure you do, but my conversations with your captain are well and truly over. In fact, if their ship does not leave within the next few hours, our conversations will be over too as I'll have you executed.'

'Then you won't find out where the Devlamine is,' Evelyn replied.

'I doubt that your own crew knows where the damned Devlamine is,' Salim snapped back. 'Either way, it will belong to us just as you do.'

'I can get them to bring it down here,' Evelyn promised, 'in exchange for our release.'

'They'll bring it down here in exchange for your *lives*,' Salim growled. 'And you'll be staying, whether you like it or not. You're our insurance that your captain does not attempt to launch an assault on our little home.'

'He won't, for now at least,' Evelyn replied, 'but I can assure you that they will not abandon us here either. In the past two years Atlantia has defeated an infected Colonial cruiser, two Veng'en battleships and the Word in close combat. If it means sacrificing us to ensure your pirate lair is neutralised, then if pushed to it the captain will not hesitate to do so. Sooner or later, one way or the other, the Atlantia *will* liberate us and when it does it'll be you and your men awaiting execution.'

Salim glared at her and the pirates around him wore concerned expressions as they awaited their leader's response.

'If he were that mercenary he would have attacked already.'

'He's considering his options,' Evelyn said. 'If I know him, when he hits us it'll be when there is no other way, and you're not giving him many options. If we truly are to be killed, then he will simply remove us from the equation and kill you anyway.'

Evelyn kept her gaze on Salim even though she could see Teera's eyes widening as a *what-the-hell?* expression spread across her features. Salim ground his teeth in his skull.

'We have a frigate of our own, in case you hadn't noticed?'

'Without either a coherent crew or properly trained pilots,' Evelyn reminded him. 'Atlantia has both and the advantage of orbit. You try to take off, they'll destroy you before you break orbit. Take it from me, Salim: you think you're in control here but right now all you've got is borrowed time and not much of it. Let me talk to my captain and maybe we can arrange something other than the death of every single person in this compound'

Salim's pirates were now watching Evelyn with guarded expressions, some of their hands resting on the butts of personalised plasma pistols and highly polished blades. Salim continued to glare at Evelyn, and then he made his decision.

'You're right,' he said finally, and looked across at one of the pirates. 'Establish a communications link with Atlantia.'

The pirate, without looking, reached out for a control panel and flipped a switch that sent a signal to the orbiting frigate. Salim stood and from his belt he removed the broad, elegantly curved blade that he wore. He stepped down off the throne mount and walked to Evelyn's side, and with one hand he raised the blade to her throat and moved behind her.

'Speak, my lovely,' he whispered, 'and it'll be the last sound you ever make.'

*

Captain Idris Sansin strode toward the Atlantia's bridge with General Bra'hiv at his side.

'Are your men ready?'

The general nodded.

'All aboard and as ready as they can be,' he replied. 'Are you sure he can be trusted? That *either of them* can be trusted?'

'We will trust them with this,' Idris replied. 'What about the sanctuary?'

'I've pulled all of the troops out but kept the guards on the exits. The civilians are getting more and more agitated and they're openly complaining about the lack of information they're getting from the command crew.'

'Let them complain,' Idris replied. 'Right now we don't have the time to handle a crisis down in the sanctuary. If they push back too hard, pull Meyanna out and seal the sanctuary until we've resolved the situation on Chiron IV.'

'Captain,' Bra'hiv cautioned,' 'I can assure you that if we seal the civilians in we'll have a full-blown riot on our hands. They're virtually threatening to down-tools as it is. Meyanna advised that we let them know where the Devlamine farm is and allow them to control it.'

Idris nodded, his wife's idea both fair and shrewd. Far from being redundant passengers aboard Atlantia, the civilians managed the farmland and growing sectors of the sanctuary, where all of the ship's food came from as well as managing the water and air recycling plants which were attached to the sanctuary. Almost a third of the civilians represented professional and essential members of Atlantia's crew: engineers, weapons experts, surgeons and technicians whose families lived in the sanctuary and who would have a say in the matter if those families were sealed in without a choice in the matter.

'Do it, and give them a voice too,' Idris replied with a heavy sigh. 'We need a new Councillor to speak for them.'

'Fine. Who?'

'I don't know,' the captain said. 'Let them decide, call a vote or something but make sure it's somebody whom we can trust too. I don't want a repeat of Councillor Hevel's attempted mutiny.'

'Speaking of people we can trust,' Bra'hiv said, 'I've been meaning to talk to you.'

'About whom?' the captain asked. 'Is Qayin up to no good again?'

'Not Qayin, as far as I know anyway,' Bra'hiv said as they walked, 'I was actually hoping to have a word about…'

'Captain!'

Idris looked up as Mikhain dashed around the corner toward them.

'What is it?'

'Salim is back in touch,' Mikhain replied and cast a brief glance at Bra'hiv. 'He wants to speak to the captain.'

'Where's Andaim?'

'On his way,' Mikhain replied breathlessly. 'We should be there to see what Salim has to say.'

Idris followed Mikhain toward the bridge, Bra'hiv still by his side.

'Who was it you wanted to talk about?' Idris asked.

The general shook his head, one eye on the XO as they walked. 'It's not important right now. Let's deal with Salim first.'

Idris followed Mikhain onto the bridge, the entire command crew snapping to attention. Ahead, he could see Andaim already standing on the command platform as Idris and Bra'hiv moved out of sight to one side of the viewing panel.

Andaim looked at Idris, his features calm and composed. Idris tried to look encouraging as Andaim straightened his uniform and nodded at the communications officer, Lael.

'Open the link,' Andaim said.

The screen flickered and then Salim's face appeared, his oily features twisted into a slick smile as he looked out at them. Beside his face was that of Evelyn, her elegant, almost elfin features pinched with a mixture of concern and anger, her eyelids flickering and her jaw tense. Against her throat was a wicked, highly polished blade held in Salim's podgy hand. Idris saw that she was no longer wearing her uniform and that her bare shoulders were draped with a thin silken gown. She looked pale, almost ill.

'Salim,' Andaim said, breaking through his consternation at seeing Evelyn's plight and taking the opportunity to speak first in an attempt to control the conversation. 'You've fixed your screen.'

'Be quiet and listen,' Salim snapped. 'The Devlamine, where is it?'

'The deadline you gave us is not yet up so we're still...'

'I've changed the deadline,' Salim growled. 'You've got an hour or your beautiful friend here will find herself headless and floating in Chiron's oceans. I've heard that the water is getting quite warm these days.'

Andaim swallowed and Idris saw the CAG's jaw tense up and his fists clench by his side. The fighter pilot's affection for the fiery and unpredictable Evelyn was virtually common knowledge on the bridge, even though the CAG had never spoken of it and Evelyn had never acknowledged it either. Seeing her under imminent threat of death would be precisely the kind of thing that might send Andaim into the dangerous realms of recklessness.

'That would not help either of our causes,' Andaim replied, keeping his voice calm. 'There is no need for bloodshed – you'll get your Devlamine. We have no desire to keep it on board anyway.'

'Good,' Salim sneered. 'Once the Devlamine is here, we will discuss your terms of surrender.'

'Our what?'

'You heard,' Salim added. 'You don't think for a moment that anybody here believes you'll just abandon your own people to us do you? Your friend Evelyn here has made that quite clear. I give you the chance now to surrender your vessel to us and be boarded, or I'll execute every last hostage right here and now.'

Andaim's eyes narrowed.

'If you execute every last hostage there will be nothing to stop us from bombing you out of existence, Salim.'

'You wouldn't dare take the chance,' Salim uttered. 'I know you people, and you take a moralistic delight in sacrificing everything just to save a single life, poor bleeding-heart liberals every one of you.'

Andaim smiled, his features cold now.

'But for the chance to blast a pirate's lair into boiling atoms?' the CAG replied rhetorically. 'I'd have to think long and hard about it.'

Evelyn's eyelids fluttered again in surprise. Idris stared at Evelyn, her green eyes flashing on the viewing panel, and he felt his heart leap.

'Think all you like,' Salim snapped. 'But if you're not down here in the next hour, with Devlamine and ready to receive guests, I'll kill every one of them and show it all to you.' Salim peered sideways at Evelyn, and pressed the blade against her long, slim neck. 'You ever cut a person's throat, captain?' he asked Andaim rhetorically. 'It sounds like slicing fresh vegetables, crisp and sharp. I don't want you to entertain the idea that I wouldn't do it so let me show you right now, just so we're clear.'

Andaim's will broke and he stepped toward the viewing panel, one arm reaching out in desperation.

'No, *stop!*'

Salim smiled, his eyes gleaming with malice. 'One hour, captain.'

The viewing panel closed as the pirate cut the communications link, and Andaim let out a breath as his shoulders sagged and he turned to Idris.

'Damn it, I lost us time,' he said.

Idris stepped up onto the command platform and he rested a firm hand on the CAG's shoulder.

'But you gained us a miracle,' he replied, and turned to Mikhain. 'Did you see it?'

'Just,' the XO replied, 'but I didn't get the full message.'

'What are you talking about?' Andaim asked.

'Remember when Atlantia Five was taken over by Qayin's gang?' the captain asked him. 'Evelyn had her mask on then, but she managed to send us a signal letting us know how many hostages Qayin's gang were holding in the prison.'

'Sure,' Andaim said uncertainly, and then he got it. 'Her eyes!'

'Signals coding,' Idris grinned. 'She was messaging us. XO, we have a new mission.'

'What is it?' Mikhain asked.

'To recover the Colonial frigate Arcadia from Salim Phaeon,' he announced loudly enough for the entire bridge to hear. 'She's down there in dry dock and Evelyn's let us know that she's not under her own power.

Salim has generators. If Kordaz manages to blow those generators, we can take the compound and Arcadia for ourselves!'

Mikhain stared at the captain in disbelief. 'We cannot assault their compound, they have hostages, and we can't know what Kordaz will do!'

'What we cannot do is miss this opportunity,' the captain corrected the XO. 'If we don't take it, we may never get another chance.'

'If it fails, we'll double our losses!' Mikhain gasped.

'No gain without risk,' the captain agreed. 'But to double our strength is an opportunity too great to miss, Mikhain. Agreed?'

The XO stared at the captain for a long beat.

'Agreed, captain' he replied, and then turned and marched off the bridge.

***

XXVIII

Mikhain strode down through Atlantia's 'tween decks, Corporal Djimon at his side as they headed toward one of the most secure sections of the ship. The War Room, a second bridge concealed deep inside the hull, was used in time of emergency to continue operating the ship's defences when the outer hull had been breached or the bridge compromised.

Mikhain led the way, the number of personnel around them diminishing with every step, the ship still on night detail and a smaller watch. Mikhain reached the War Room and paused by the main access doors. He listened, the giant Marine behind him remaining silent. No sound emanated from beyond the corridor they occupied, this part of the ship close to deserted at this hour.

'Give me the holo-pass,' Mikhain ordered.

Djimon silently obeyed, then stood with his plasma rifle at port-arms as Mikhain reached up to a panel on the wall and entered his personal security details and pass codes. One of only four people aboard with the ability to access the War Room when the Atlantia was not on battle readiness, Mikhain knew that he would have to act fast and then make every effort to cover his tracks. The panel beeped, and Mikhain held up the holo-pass.

A complex, multi-layered security pass issued to all officers and non-commissioned officers aboard ship, as well as the ship's senior physicians, a holo-pass both enabled access to restricted areas and also recorded the name of the person who had done so. The holo-pass bore the name and image of Sergeant Qayin.

'Was it difficult to obtain?' Mikhain asked.

'No,' Djimon replied. 'He is on duty, but I don't know where or what he's doing. Hurry, I'll have to return it and fast. As soon as I find him I want to track him until he reveals what he's been doing.'

Mikhain swept the holo-pass across the door's scanners and the War Room's doors opened. Mikhain turned and handed the pass back to Djimon.

'Get this back where it belongs, as fast as you can, and then find Qayin.'

Djimon nodded, took the pass and began marching back toward the barracks.

Mikhain entered the War Room and hurried to the communications station, a more compact version of the one on the main bridge manned by Lael. Mikhain eased around to the front of the station and watched the screens, observing Lael's inputs and monitoring her duties.

He activated the War Room's veiling systems, designed to prevent boarders who had accessed the bridge from figuring out what was happening in the War Room. The dual-operation system allowed officers in the War Room to control the ship, whereas invaders on the bridge would have little or no idea of their presence.

Mikhain accessed a free comms channel and opened a link on a new frequency. For a moment nothing happened, and then a screen opposite him flickered into life and a podgy, oily face stared out at him with a bleary, sleepy expression. A gloomy private quarters was visible in the low light behind him, and what looked like a hybrid woman slumbered alongside Salim.

'Who the hell are you and what do you want?' Salim uttered.

Mikhain realised that he was gripping the controls tightly as he spoke.

'To resolve our differences in a manner that prevents any further loss of life.'

'Get lost,' Salim murmured and moved to shut off the link.

'You're being deceived.'

Salim froze in motion, his glistening black eyes staring at Mikhain. 'By whom?'

'By the captain of this ship,' Mikhain replied, 'who in my opinion is putting lives in danger.'

Salim's eyes narrowed and he straightened up. 'You're the Executive Officer,' he noted Mikhain's shoulder insignia. 'What's happened? Finally got upset that your captain is half your age?'

Mikhain let a slow smile spread across his features. 'The captain is almost as old as I am.'

Salim raised an eyebrow. 'If so, he's got far better genes and....' Salim broke off for a moment. 'Andaim is not the Atlantia's captain?'

'No,' Mikhain replied. 'You need to hear what I have to say.'

'Who is the captain?'

'All in good time,' Mikhain snapped. 'I want guarantees first.'

'Guarantees of what?'

*

The vast lower hull of the frigate cast a deep shadow over the valley, the scarred and dirty belly of the spaceship sitting above where the solid ground had been cut away to provide support for the immense braces that held her in place.

Kordaz was no engineer, but as he crouched in the blackness beneath the huge ship he was forced to marvel at how Salim Phaeon and his ragtag group of pirates and slaves had constructed such an incredible dock. Each of the braces probably weighed a thousand tonnes, shaped from steel with the huge load-bearing ovals cast between them that must have taken hundreds of men weeks to construct. Ten braces in all cradled the vast ship, and countless more lengths of double-coiled steel cable kept the ship tethered in place, attached to both the upper hull and massive braces far out across the landscape.

The captors of the great Colonial vessel had been smart enough to place the frigate facing into the wind that gusted almost permanently off the churning ocean. Although Kordaz knew that the frigate was not capable of natural atmospheric flight, its ion engines, anti-gravity gyroscopes and directional thrusters were more than powerful enough when combined to allow for a controlled descent and landing on a suitable planetary surface.

Kordaz wondered briefly how the pirates could have achieved such a feat, and could only assume that many of the ship's crew now made up the labourers striving to repair the damage to the hull and prepare the ship for space flight. He figured that if the crew were still alive, then Salim was not entirely unable to use the frigate effectively as a warship. If he were allowed to get her into orbit, he could represent a real threat to the Atlantia. Then again, if Captain Sansin were to double his strength with a second frigate, and then continued on his planned path to Wraiythe... Kordaz forced the thought from his mind and focused instead on the task ahead.

Kordaz looked up and saw men high on the scaffolds, showers of bright glowing sparks raining down as they laboured. The slaves were on a twenty-four hour work schedule, Kordaz having seen shifts moving back and forth from rest areas to the north of the frigate, simple tents guarded both by pirates and by the lumbering Ogrin. He had been unable to count accurately the ratio of prisoners to pirates, but at a maximum he figured about a hundred fifty pirates and maybe a hundred or so Ogrin, against at least a thousand slaves.

Four to one, if the slaves could be given the chance to fight back.

Kordaz slid down into the deepest recesses beneath the frigate's hull, infiltrating a fissure fifty feet below the surface of the plain. The keel of the ship was so close above his head that he could almost touch it, and the cold wind whipped past him as it was funnelled and accelerated into the cavity below the giant hull.

Kordaz crouched down and moved fast, passing beneath the hull and climbing up the slope the opposite side. More showers of sparks drifted down ahead, the shouts and calls of men working high above carrying on the wind. He slowed, peering out from beneath the frigate as he sought the position of the nearest power generators.

He spotted one of them, barely a hundred cubits away, linked to the frigate via massive power cables as thick as four men. Each generator hummed in the darkness, powered by the miniature fusion cores contained deep inside. They would not give the frigate enough power to lift-off, for that could only come from her more massive internal cores, but they would be more than enough to power her internal systems, environmental controls, shields and perhaps even her weapons. The perfect protection against interference while she was repaired.

Kordaz rolled onto his back and looked up at the frigate's vast, slab-sided hull and squinted as showers of sparks drifted down nearby like burning rain. The workers were engrossed in their labour and the Ogrin guarding them completely absorbed by their duty, having insufficient awareness for much more than one task at a time.

Kordaz checked his surroundings one last time and then he dashed out from beneath the frigate and raced across the open, illuminated ground until he was once again swallowed by the safety of the shadows.

The hum of the generators filled Kordaz's ears and seemed to reverberate through the ground at his feet. A billowing cloud of blessed warmth surrounded them from vents set into the rear of each generator, and he realised that he had long ago lost all sensation in his feet and hands. The warm ground heated his feet and the hot air swirled around him, and he stood for a few moments and allowed it to thaw his muscles and seep into his chilled bones until the numbness and aching subsided.

The sound of voices above the hum alerted him and he ducked down close to one of the massive generators as two swaggering pirates, both armed with plasma pistols, strolled casually by. Kordaz figured that they represented what passed for a security patrol down here, but their pistols dangled lazily from their hands and they trailed smoke from pipes in glowing clouds under the bright lights illuminating the frigate. As Kordaz waited, he noticed a faint glow on the horizon out over the churning oceans, the first hint of a fast approaching dawn.

Kordaz waited for a few moments until he was sure that they had passed, and then he studied the cables snaking from the generators, each standing higher than his own head. He crouched alongside one of them and touched the surface with his hand. Thick, insulating sealant that would be at least a foot deep protected the current-carrying cable within.

Kordaz reached down to his belt and produced one of the chemical explosives that Lieutenant C'rairn had provided him with. He moved back to where the cabling was attached to the generators via massive bolts and found the cooling fans, drawing heat from the massive generator's interior and blowing it out into the otherwise cold night air. The cables were too large for the explosives he had been able to bring with him to destroy, but if he blew the cooling fans themselves then the generators would overheat all on their own within moments, and that would shut down the power supply long enough for Atlantia to launch an attack.

Kordaz removed the fan's protective grill and then reached up and attached the first of his eight charges inside the fan duct. Hot air blasted past his hand as he secured the charge in place, and then moved on toward the next generator. One by one, he slipped the explosives into place inside each generator and activated their detonation receivers. He reached the final generator and set the charge in place before turning and heading back the way he had come, seeking the safety of the shadows beneath the frigate.

He was almost there when he heard running boots rushing toward his position from all sides and a rush of shouts. Kordaz ducked out of sight as dozens of pirates flooded between the generators, weapons drawn and activated.

The Veng'en cursed as he saw them hunting for him, and drew his D'jeck with one hand as with the other he set the detonator for the charges down beside him on the dusty ground and slid it out of sight beneath dense foliage.

Kordaz moved from shadow to shadow away from the detonator, and then a loud shout alerted him to a pirate who was turning and aiming his pistol right between Kordaz's eyes.

The Veng'en leaped into motion, the *D'jeck* flickering in the low light.

*

Corporal Djimon lowered himself down into the deep shaft of an access panel, his bulky frame barely fitting inside as he levered himself toward the inspection corridor that ran the length of Atlantia's enormous keel.

He dropped onto the deck, his boots barely making a sound as he crouched in the darkness and peered into the distance. A row of ceiling lights each spaced two cubits apart stretched away into what seemed like an infinite distance, shadows between each pool of light and a cold, damp atmosphere clinging to his skin as he moved forward.

Sergeant Qayin had come down here before him, having snuck away from his duties with Bravo Company. Djimon had known that it would only be a matter of time before the criminal that Qayin truly was would reveal himself, and the corporal's conviction that Qayin was behind the entire drug operation aboard Atlantia was now cemented. He had no business being down here – nobody but engineers and senior officers conducting routine inspections would ever bother to descend so deep into the ship's bowels.

Djimon moved in a low crouch and eased his way forward. With Mikhain's special duties clearance he could move freely through the ship, and that was just as well because the vast size of Atlantia would mean a long search. Djimon had known that the best way to start that search was to stick closely to Qayin, and now his plan had paid dividends.

He could not see the big sergeant as he advanced, but that was almost certainly because Qayin's Devlamine stash would be hidden in one of the countless side compartments, access panels and storage areas dotted throughout the deep decks, even here at the keel. Djimon was no expert on engineering, but he knew that much of the ship's used fluids, oils and lubricants were stored down here out of harm's way in barrels that were then used as target practice for gunners and fighter pilots, their shots vapourising the chemicals and thus disposing of them.

Djimon edged forward, passing panel after panel, seeking some sign of where Qayin was headed, of where he had concealed his Devlamine. It had been six months since the encounter with the Sylph, the moment widely regarded as having been when the drug entered Atlantia. Six months of even covert cultivation could have produced hundreds of gallons of liquified Devlamine, ready to be consumed by ravenous addicts. Djimon figured he was looking either for one large stash, or lots of smaller ones. Either way, only a single hit was required to reveal both Qayin's guilt and the success Djimon was hoping would see him reinstated as a sergeant and...

Djimon froze as he spotted an access panel ahead that caught his eye as slightly different from the rest. The lights hit the multiple doors with an even sheen that stretched away into the distance, but this one was scraped and mottled, the signs of recent and regular operation.

Djimon closed in on the panel, half as tall as he was and fixed only by simple braces. There were no locks on the panels down here and Djimon marvelled at Qayin's audacity. Keeping the drug almost in plain sight, in a place where the sheer monotony of searching every single panel virtually guaranteed that they would not be found.

But then, not every searcher was Djimon.

He strode to the panel and opened the braces, the door sliding up under its own momentum via counter-weights at the rear. The pale light shafted inside the compartment, and Djimon saw rows of heavy blue storage tanks marked with signs warning of expended fuel. The corporal leaned in and popped the cap on one of the tanks, then sniffed the contents.

Sweet, sickly, a thick odour nothing like fuel.

Devlamine.

'On the ground, now!'

Djimon jerked back from the tank and drew his plasma pistol as all around him from surrounding panels leaped armed Marines, their weapons pointed at him and their flashlights blinding him.

'*Down down down!!* Drop your weapon!'

Djimon raised his pistol into the air as he dropped to his knees and called out.

'Coporal Djimon, Alpha Company!' he shouted. 'It's the Devlamine, I found it!'

The Marines surrounded him, rifles shoved in his face.

'Drop the pistol, now!'

Djimon set the weapon down on the deck alongside him and put his hands behind his head as he replied.

'Inform the captain, right now,' Djimon ordered.

The Marines did not reply, and then a familiar voice called out to him.

'Oh, we will corporal, we will.'

Djimon felt his guts plunge as he saw Qayin's glowing tattoos flickering in the darkness beyond the soldiers and their flashlights. Djimon belatedly realised that all of the Marines were from Bravo Company.

'I followed you down here, Qayin,' Djimon shouted. 'You knew where this stash was!'

Qayin's white smile flashed in the darkness as he shook his head.

'That's odd,' he replied. 'I can't remember anything like that happening. Way I see it, we wandered down here after you and caught you checking your stash, corporal.'

Djimon cried out and leaped to his feet as he reached out for Qayin, but he was slammed to the deck by the weight of half a dozen Marines and his wrists manacled behind his back. As he writhed and fought in fury, he heard Qayin's casual tones.

'Take him to the cell block and hold him there, *quietly*,' the sergeant ordered. 'No sense in making a fuss now, eh boys?'

***

XXIX

'How much was there?'

Captain Idris Sansin sat in his personal quarters and looked at his desk monitor as General Bra'hiv replied.

'Sixteen barrels of the damned stuff. We've transported it already, as per your instructions.'

'Who found the stash?'

'Sergeant Qayin,' Bra'hiv replied. *'He and his men followed one of Alpha Company's corporals whom he suspected of being behind the drug's proliferation. The corporal is now in holding.'*

'Qayin,' Idris breathed in reply.

The former convict was in many ways like Evelyn, the captain reflected. Both of them were unpredictable and yet loyal in their own ways, both clever and capable of extreme violence when a situation demanded. But whereas Evelyn's loyalty was virtually unquestioned aboard Atlantia, Qayin remained an unknown quantity.

'Have the Devlamine mixed with accelerant and loaded as we discussed. I don't want it useable by Salim and his gangs. Then deploy with Bravo Company to the surface,' Idris ordered, and then added after a moment of thought: 'Allow Sergeant Qayin to select his own men personally to join you.'

'That could be dangerous,' Bra'hiv warned, *'the men of Bravo Company are at the highest risk of defecting, especially around pirates when considering their criminal histories.'*

'That's what I'm thinking,' Idris replied.

'Seriously, captain?'

'Do it,' Idris confirmed as a beep from his office door alerted him to a visitor. 'Good luck, general.'

Idris cut off the communication and then flipped a switch to open his door. Mikhain strode in and stood to attention before the captain's desk.

'The assault is ready, captain,' he reported. 'We're as prepared as we can be, and this will be our best chance to attack. I still recommend an orbital assault now while we have the advantage of a tactically superior position.'

'We don't have enough information about what's inside Salim's compound yet,' the captain replied. 'I'm not about to commit our forces to a blind assault on an enemy of unknown resources and number.'

The cabin was hot despite the presence of an extractor fan and de-ioniser built into the walls. Images of the captain's family moved silently on the walls as they detected a human's gaze, the sound switched off unless commanded otherwise. Mikhain shook his gaze from them and focused on the captain.

'Sir, we have Evelyn's information. There is an Atlantia Class frigate down there that could double our strength in an instant and she's vulnerable. The longer we leave it to deploy our forces, the more chance there is that Salim will use that same vessel to attack us. With his rumoured flotilla of captured vessels he may have sufficient firepower to cause us a great deal of damage.'

'Noted,' Idris replied without looking up from an electro-sheet. 'You're forgetting about Kordaz, however.'

Mikhain scowled and waved away the air between them.

'I'd be surprised if we ever see the damned Veng'en again, and I don't know that I'd trust any information he supplies us with.'

'You really think that he'd side with Salim Phaeon, after all that he's done for us?'

'No,' Mikhain admitted, 'but he'd be looking to see our downfall assured just as much as the pirate's. If he's down there right now and he's looking at a second Colonial frigate, you really think he's not going to consider how that might affect his own people in the future. Our hand will be doubly strong against any Veng'en vessel we encounter and that's got to play on his mind just as it would on ours were the situation reversed.'

Captain Sansin sighed and set his engineering report down on the desk before him. He rubbed his eyes for a moment, pinched them between forefinger and thumb.

'I think that you underestimate the value of placing trust in people.'

'I think that you place too much trust in questionable allies,' Mikhain retorted. 'What the hell do you think Taron Forge will do when he gets down there to Salim's compound?'

'He'll provide Salim with Devlamine,' Idris replied.

'What Devlamine?' We don't have any to...'

Mikhain broke off, his eyes wide as the captain spoke.

'The Devlamine stash was located by Bravo Company's Marines. It turned out an Alpha Company corporal had hidden the stash below decks.'

Mikhain forced himself not to try to clear his throat as he spoke. 'Do we have a name?'

'Corporal Djimon,' Idris replied. 'An otherwise exemplary soldier, although he has in the past been reprimanded for misconduct during operations. He's being held in the cells.'

'Has he revealed anything more, captain?' Mikhain asked, his throat tight.

'Not at this time, but he's locked down right now and somebody we can deal with later. Our priority right now is to recover our people from Chiron IV,' he said. 'It is also to recover the Arcadia from Salim Phaeon.'

'You're risking lives by not taking immediate action!'

'I'm saving lives by not listening to you!' Idris shot back and bolted upright out of his seat. He towered over Mikhain, his big hands balled into fists by his side. 'If you'd had your way, you'd have already bombarded the compound and killed many of the people we're trying to save. By taking our time we're increasing their chances of survival.'

'Or condemning them.'

Idris shook his head as he stepped out from behind his desk.

'This is why we had an admiralty and direct contact with Ethera during time of siege or stalemate,' he said. 'Such decisions cannot rest upon the shoulders of just two senior officers.'

'So put it to a ship-wide vote,' Mikhain suggested.

'And have unseasoned civilians casting their opinions on military matters for which they have no training and no experience?'

'You've told General Bra'hiv that you want them to have a voice.'

'I don't want to hand them the damned command!'

Mikhain tried to keep his voice level. 'We only ended up in this situation because you insisted on following a Veng'en cruiser to Wraiythe. We would never have set foot on Chiron IV if it were not for...'

'You can't possibly know that,' Idris shot back. 'We would have needed supplies whether we were following another ship or not. What's your point here, Mikhain?'

The XO stared at the captain for a long moment.

'I'm just trying to offer an alternative voice for your...'

'You're offering your opinions against mine,' Idris cut him off, 'at almost every opportunity. If I didn't know better I'd say that you're thinking that I'm not longer fit to command and that you should be the one up there giving the orders.'

'I didn't say that captain and...'

'You didn't have to!' Idris almost shouted. 'It's written all over your face, Mikhain! You want this command, you always have. Why do you think I chose Andaim over you to act as captain of this ship when communicating with Salim?'

Mikhain tried to work his jaw but it felt suddenly numb. 'I, I don't...'

'You think it's because I trust Andaim more than you?'

Mikhain kept his expression as neutral as he possibly could. 'I have no idea, sir.'

'No, you don't,' Idris replied. 'And that's the problem. You cannot act while observing your own performance, Mikhain. You command from a bubble of experience and authority, but you never look at the bigger picture from the perspective of those whom you command.'

Mikhain frowned. 'I don't think I'm following.'

'You, if you had felt it necessary, would have ordered a full assault on Salim's compound the moment you'd realised that Evelyn was telling you the Arcadia was down there.'

Mikhain raised his chin. 'Yes, I would have.'

'And yet you would therefore have left Atlantia with a greatly reduced Marine presence in the face of the great civilian unrest that you also can't seem to shut up about.'

Mikhain blinked as he realised what the captain was driving at.

'The civilians would be contained and...'

'It's not about whether they would be contained,' Idris snapped. 'It's about balancing what you want to do with what you reasonably *can* do. I need the entire ship on my side so that I can deploy Marines without having to worry about whether the Atlantia will be here when they get back. What you don't understand, Mikhain, is that while you feel strong in a position of command with squadrons of fighters and platoons of Marines at your back, the truth is that we're *weak*. We are *divided*. We are *insecure*. One false move, one error of judgement and this whole house of cards could fall apart, especially if Salim even catches a whiff of the fact that we're only half as strong as we look right now.'

Mikhain swallowed thickly.

'I had not considered that, sir.'

'No, you had not,' Idris agreed. 'Many of the people down there on that planet are our most loyal officers and Marines. Countless others are slaves who have no defence against their piratical overlords and would no doubt welcome our intervention. But if we bombard them from orbit and then launch Marines in an assault, endangering them ourselves and perhaps subjecting them to possible execution from their pirate overlords, casualties from friendly fire and injury from plasma blasts, how do you think they'll feel about us then Mikhain?'

The XO stood for several long seconds, and then it was as though his lungs emptied in one great blast as his shoulders sagged.

The captain watched his second-in-command for a moment before continuing.

'I chose Andaim to act as captain because I know that he has strong feelings for Evelyn,' he said. 'Those emotions would temper him, prevent him from going to far in his negotiations with Salim Phaeon. Andaim feels as though he has failed, that he has shown weakness before Salim and that he has weakened our position as a result. In fact, he has strengthened it.'

Mikhain frowned. 'How?'

'Because Salim now thinks that Atlantia's captain can be manipulated, an illusion that I'm happy to maintain. I actually have no intention of bombarding Salim's compound from orbit – I just want Taron Forge to head down there with that impression, and to pass it on to Salim in his negotiations, to make them think that I will sacrifice people if it's necessary. I have every intention of recovering Arcadia into our hands and liberating those slaves and hostages the pirates might be holding. You're always telling me how we should give the civilians aboard Atlantia a voice.' Idris looked into the XO's eyes. 'What would you think the best way of liberating the slaves down on Chiron IV would be?'

Mikhain took only a moment to process what he had heard.

'Turning them against the pirates, provoking some kind of revolt,' he murmured. 'They must outnumber the pirates three to one.'

'At least,' Idris agreed. 'We're not going to assault the compound. We're going to arm the slaves and let them revolt together, backed by our Marines.'

'But it's suicide!' Mikhain exclaimed. 'A single platoon down there can't hope to succed, and we'll never deploy in time to support them. It's like you want the damned mission to fail and...'

Mikhain stared into space as a sudden rush of revelations tumbled down upon him. Using Taron to get Bravo Company's Marines down onto the surface, the cargo of Devlamine as a draw. Sending Qayin instead of Bra'hiv or C'rairn.

'You're switching the crew out,' Mikhain realised. 'You're putting people you do not trust down on the surface and dumping the Devalmine with them.'

'People with no interest in supporting either Salim Phaeon or us,' Idris replied. 'Given the chance they'll flee at the first opportunity, thus weakening Salim Phaeon's position by provoking a retreat and strengthening our own in the confusion.'

'We'll deploy as soon as the chaos starts,' Mikhain imagined the confrontation. 'Salim will have his hands full trying to contain the revolt and control his own people.'

'And will be outnumbered and then out-manoeuvered by our Marines,' Idris completed the picture. 'Our Raythons will control the skies at the same time, without Atlantia having to launch a single missile against the surface.'

Mikhain's eyes sparkled at the intrigue even as a terrible guilt and dismay poisoned his innards.

***

XXX

The whine of massive ion engines awoke Evelyn with a start. She lifted her head from the bed of soft, clean pillows and cushions that were arranged in massive piles around Salim's throne room, saw Teera and Ishira likewise look up.

Salim appeared from his private quarters and strode across to one of the broad shuttered windows. He threw it open and the dawn sunlight streamed in and with it a panoramic view of the ocean. There, sweeping in toward the compound, was a freighter that Evelyn recognised instantly.

'The Phoenix,' Ishira growled as she spotted the craft. 'That bastard's the one who put us here.'

'Taron Forge,' Evelyn acknowledged.

The freighter swept past the compound and turned in mid-air as it hovered before settling down onto its landing gear. The whine from its engines faded away as Salim stood with his hands on his hips and turned to two Ogrin waiting patiently nearby.

'Escort him here,' he ordered.

The two Ogrin lumbered obediently away and Salim turned to two sleepy looking pirates, each with their arms draped around a hybrid.

'Go with them,' Salim snapped. 'Taron's too slippery to be left with those imbecilic oafs.'

Both pirates grimaced at the intrusion into their slumber, but they both hauled themselves to their feet and grabbed plasma weapons as they set off in pursuit of the Ogrin.

'What are you doing back here so soon, Taron?' Salim asked himself out loud.

Evelyn waited until Salim left the throne room, and then she turned to Teera.

'Why have they let him go?' Teera asked.

'I don't know,' Evelyn admitted. 'Maybe he's managed to escape somehow?'

'You captured Taron Forge?' Ishira asked, one hand draped over her daughter's still-sleeping body.

'We intercepted him as he was leaving the system,' Evelyn explained. 'I can't believe they've just let him go, or that he escaped Atlantia. There must be a reason for this. Stay sharp, the Phoenix may be our only chance to get back to the ship.'

'And then what?' Ishira asked as she grabbed Evelyn's arm. 'Your captain bombs the hell out of this compound and kills who-knows-how-many people? I'm not going to just sit here and let that happen!'

Evelyn was about to respond but then Salim reappeared, and walking alongside him with his customary loose-limbed stride was Taron Forge, followed by Yo'Ki. The pirate was listening to Salim and chuckling on cue, but his gaze was scanning very detail of the throne room.

Taron spotted Evelyn immediately and she felt suddenly a little odd as the pirate's gaze took in her flowing robes and excess of visible bare skin. The captain managed to cover his surprise well, averting his gaze back to Salim with what might have been gentlemanly discretion, had Evelyn not been aware of his true nature.

'... and so you see, captain,' Salim said, 'things have changed dramatically.'

Taron allowed himself to look again at the hybrids alongside Evelyn, Teera and Ishira. Erin recoiled away from Salim and Taron as they approached and scuttled for the protection of Ishira's embrace. Salim barely noticed, but this time Evelyn saw a clearly visible dismay in Taron's eyes at the sight of a small child fleeing from him. For a brief moment she wondered whether beneath the gruff, cocky exterior there might actually lurk a human being.

Salim turned as he walked past Evelyn and he slumped onto his throne, one hand reaching down to rest on Evelyn's bare shoulder.

'I even have a new harem to keep me company,' Salim boasted.

'You don't move your hand, you'll lose it,' Evelyn hissed as she turned her head and made to bite Salim.

Salim jerked his hand away and Taron laughed. The pirate king glared down at Evelyn.

'We had an agreement.'

'I agreed to wear a robe,' Evelyn corrected him, 'nothing more.'

'It looks good on you,' Taron said as he appraised her. 'You should wear girl's clothes more often.'

Ishira replied before Evelyn could open her mouth. 'Try this for size.'

Ishira leaped up and swung a punch across the pirate's cheek with a loud crack that made everybody in the throne room wince. Taron's hand flashed to his face in shock as he stared at Ishira and then at Evelyn.

'What the hell *is it* with you women?' Taron uttered to a smirking Yo'Ki as Salim chuckled heartily.

'It looks like we both have trouble with them.'

'That's for stealing my ship and placing myself, my daughter and my father into slavery for this fat pig!' Ishira shouted as she pointed at Salim.

Salim's mirth vanished and he leaned forward in his throne.

'Your daughter can suffer a lot more, if I choose so,' he growled.

Ishira glared at him but she said nothing more as she returned to Erin's side and placed one arm protectively over her daughter.

'Now then, captain,' Salim said, 'with the introductions out of the way, why are you here?'

'I've got trade for you,' Taron informed him. 'Something that I think you'll be very interested in.'

'And what might that be?' Salim enquired.

Slowly, Taron reached into his jacket and produced a small pouch of clear plastic gel that held tiny spheres of what looked like jewels. Evelyn's heart skipped a beat as she recognised what it was. Taron tossed the pouch to Salim, who caught it and held it up for closer examination.

'Devlamine,' Taron said. 'Some of the purest I've ever seen.'

'Where did you get it?' Salim demanded.

'For me to know,' Taron replied. 'Let's just say I have a contact.'

Evelyn stared at Taron as an image of Qayin popped clairvoyantly into her mind. For a moment she wondered whether something had happened aboard the Atlantia that had changed the state of play.

'You only left yesterday,' Salim murmured. 'I take it that you have also met our Colonial friends? I doubt that they would have let you through to land here.'

'That's where I met my contact,' Taron confirmed. 'The ship's command crew and compliment are fracturing. Looks like most of them want off the ship or at the very least away from its captain. One of them made me an offer, and I'm extending that offer to you.'

'Why?' Salim asked with a smile that conveyed no warmth whatsoever.

'Because it's good business,' Taron replied. 'Devlamine is in short supply, you could use it here and I can get it for you.'

Salim set the small pouch down beside him on the throne and then interlaced his hands beneath his chin as he regarded the pirate captain.

'Taron, I have hostages here,' he said, and gestured with one fat finger toward Evelyn and Teera. 'I have in my possession an entire platoon of Marines from the Atlantia. I can demand anything I want from that ship's captain and I know that I will get it. Have you met him, Andaim Ry'ere?'

Taron nodded.

'He's weak, Salim,' he reported. 'It won't take much to send him over the edge. His crew have no faith in his leadership and from what I heard the civilian compliment are already talking of mutiny. If we get enough of that Devlamine into circulation aboard Atlantia and here among the slaves, complete control will be possible.'

Salim nodded slowly, his eyes never leaving Taron's.

'And what would you want from this deal?' Salim asked.

'Sole supply rights,' Taron replied, 'a reasonable currency payment in minerals and any goods that will find a market out beyond the Icari Line. I know you have quite a stash here Salim. And..,' Taron's voice trailed off as he cast his eye over the watching hybrids and captives. '… any fringe benefits available.'

Salim's smile broadened.

'Captain, as ever you drive a hard but fair bargain,' he said. 'And I can only possibly reply with a single word. Guards!'

Taron's smile vanished as twenty or so pirates poured into the throne room, all heavily armed and with their weapons aimed squarely at Taron and Yo'Ki. Both reached for their plasma pistols but Salim shook his head and wagged a finger at them both.

'I wouldn't if I were you,' he cautioned. 'What a terrible mess you would make all over my throne room, and in front of children.'

Taron, his eyes fixed on the surrounding pirates, glared at Salim.

'What the hell is this?'

'This, my foolish young friend, is what happens when you lie to old Salim.'

'Nobody's lying,' Taron snapped.

'Are they not?' Salim asked rhetorically. 'Then, perhaps you might like to explain to me why you have not yet mentioned Captain Idris Sansin?'

Taron stared at Salim for just a little too long. 'Who?'

'Hand over your weapons, now!' Salim yelled as he drew his polished blade and pointed it at Erin's head. 'Or I'll take her head off!'

Taron glanced at the child, who was clutching Ishira's robe and hiding from the blade that hovered inches from her throat. Evelyn saw him look into her eyes too, and then the pirate lowered his pistol. Moments later, Salim's thugs moved in and snatched the pistols from both Taron and Yo'Ki.

Salim relaxed and shoved his blade back into its sheath as he looked at Taron.

'There, that wasn't so bad was it now?' His gaze drifted to Yo'Ki. 'I shall look forward to seeing you in your robes, my dear.'

Yo'Ki remained silent and still as Salim clicked his fingers and one of the hybrids reached out lazily with one arm and flicked a switch.

A communications link opened up with the Atlantia and moments later an image of the frigate's bridge appeared. Andaim's face filled the screen, his jaw tense and his bearing upright as he began speaking.

'Salim, I'm glad that you've contacted us. We have news for you regarding...'

'Silence, silence,' Salim waved Andaim away dismissively. 'I have no desire to speak or even listen to you. I want to speak to your captain.'

Andaim frowned. 'I am the Captain of the Atlantia, and I have the authority to...' Salim drew a plasma pistol from his waistband, activated the magazine and aimed it at the Marines kneeling nearby. He kept his eyes on Andaim as he pulled the trigger.

The blast was deafeningly loud in the confines of the throne room and Evelyn whirled in shock as the shot hit a soldier in his chest and blasted him backwards. The Marine landed on his back with blue smoke puffing from a blackened cavity where his ribcage had once been, his face twisted in a rictus of agony as his eyes stared silently at the ceiling.

A chorus of cries rang out in the wake of the blast, hybrids recoiling from the sight of a dead man's smouldering corpse. The throne room fell silent as Salim lowered the pistol, his nose screwing up slightly at the stench of burning human flesh now drifting through the throne room.

'Bring it out,' Salim snarled.

Two Ogri lumbered into view, the arms of a comatose Veng'en grasped in their massive fists. Kordaz was dragged between them, his chest lacerated by countless strokes of a plasma whip, his big yellow eyes dull and weak.

Salim stared hard into the camera, his eyes cold as he produced from behind him a thick, glowing plasma whip.

*

The homestead was half-filled with beds, each containing the writhing body of a Devlamine withdrawal sufferer. Anxious mothers and angry fathers hovered outside the homestead, held at bay by four Marine guards that Meyanna had insisted protect her staff from the large mob of civilians now crowded outside the buildings.

Meyanna carefully drew blood from one of the sufferers and marked the sample before placing it in a container with twelve others.

New victims were arriving by the hour, and Meyanna was stunned to see fearful but otherwise perfectly healthy people walk in to the homestead and admit to being users. Already there were thirty or more people in the homestead, most waiting for blood tests to determine how deeply entrenched their addiction had become.

'There are too many,' one of Meyanna's assistants said in a hushed whisper. 'We can't treat them all, we just don't have enough medicine for this. It could take them all weeks to fight off the addiction.'

Meyanna scanned the faces watching them, eyes dark, arms hugging themselves. Some tapped their feet or chewed their nails or played with hair, signs of deep anxiety. Others had fallen silent as their withdrawal took hold, their skin sheened with beads of sweat.

It was hopeless, she knew. All of them would have to go through the unspeakable agony of withdrawal, and if they survived to tell the tale they would likely never touch Devlamine again, a powerful antidote to the suppliers and dealers of the drug. But if they all died, the hostility of the civilians toward the captain and his command crew would only intensify.

'We have to be seen to be doing all that we can,' Meyanna replied. 'Nobody can ask more of us. Now, go and draw that man's blood, and then check on that patient's heart rate.'

The nurse hurried off as Meyanna stood. She was about to move to the next patient, a teenage girl with drawn eyes that had once been a bright blue but were now muddied by the misery of her affliction, but a woman approached her and touched her lightly on the arm.

Meyanna turned to see a tall, slim and dignified looking Etheran with earnest green eyes and light brown hair pinned back from a face devoid of make-up. She did not smile, but she spoke with a tone of hope.

'Could you spare me a moment, doctor?'

Meyanna turned and walked with her. The woman led her to the back of the homestead and turned to face her.

'My son,' she began, but her austere expression cracked almost immediately as she fought back tears. 'He is the man in your laboratory.'

Meyanna swallowed thickly. No matter how many times it happened, she could never quite get used to dealing with another person's loss and grief without feeling it burn in her own bones too.

'I'm so sorry for your suffering,' Meyanna whispered, 'and that of your son. We're doing everything we can for him.'

The woman nodded, managed a smile as brief as the passing of a ghost.

'His father was the man killed by the Marines,' she went on, still struggling to fight back tears. 'Before the shot was fired, my son was looking out of the window. He was sick already and had a fever, but I can assure you that he was fully lucid. He called out, was trying to warn his father of something.'

Meyanna's breathing slowed as she replied.

'What did he say, ma'am?'

'He called to his father that he should run. That we should all run. Because the man outside, the Marine, was the man who controlled the drugs and that he would kill us all.'

Meyanna swallowed thickly again. 'You have nothing to fear from him here.'

'Yes we do, because his soldiers, his gang, have been the ones guarding us until you showed up.'

'What is his name?' Meyanna asked.

'He's the big one with the glowing tattoos,' replied the woman. 'My son said that his name is Qayin.'

Meyanna only heard the last couple of words as she dashed from the homestead.

***

XXXI

Captain Idris Sansin sighed as he watched Andaim move away from the command platform and look across at him.

'How did he know?' Idris asked out loud.

'Taron Forge most likely,' Mikhain replied. 'He's the only person down there with something to gain by revealing what he knows to Salim. Everybody else would have remained silent in the hopes that the deception was part of a rescue plan. I told you that he could not be trusted.'

'And Kordaz?' Idris whispered in despair.

'I can only imagine,' Mikhain said. 'Somebody must have passed word if not Taron Forge. I'll look into it.'

'Make sure that you do,' Idris insisted.

There was no point in defying Salim any further so Idris stiffened his resolve, took a deep breath and strode up onto the command platform to take Andaim's place.

'Captain Idris Sansin,' Salim purred, his face glowing with the mindless satisfaction of malice. 'I truly thought that I would never lay eyes on you again, yet here you are.'

'Salim,' Idris acknowledged him, 'I've been thinking the very same thing.'

'I don't doubt it,' came the response. 'I suspect, given your current predicament, that you are far less keen to meet face to face than I am.'

'I have a job to do,' Idris replied, 'and that's to get my people back unharmed.'

'A job which you are failing spectacularly,' Salim observed. 'One of your soldiers is already dead, another half-way there with crippling Devlamine withdrawal, and from all I hear your ship's compliment is on the verge of mutiny. All in all, I'd say that my presence here is just what you need.'

'What the hell does that mean?'

Salim got up from his throne, the camera following him automatically. 'That you've reached your limits as a commander, Idris. You've overreached yourself and cannot realistically keep your force together. Coming here was the best thing that you could have done, because now you're in a position to ally yourself to us and have the structure and discipline that your people so badly need.'

Idris could not help the bitter little smile that curled from his lips.

'Seriously, Salim? You think that you could command a ship like Atlantia, or Arcadia for that matter, handle the needs of a thousand people and fight a war all at once?'

'But Idris, I already do,' Salim purred as he slipped the glowing plasma-whip from his belt and it hummed into life once more. 'When I speak, people act. If they do not act, then they are punished!'

Salim whirled and the whip hissed as it lashed out and struck a hybrid woman across her thighs. The woman screamed and dropped to her knees, her face twisted in pain as she huddled over her legs. Salim turned and placed one foot on her shoulder, pinning her in place as he looked at Idris.

'I have over a thousand people down here, Idris,' he boasted. 'Each of them obeys my every command.'

'They're not obeying a damned thing you say,' Idris insisted. 'They're cowering because they're afraid, because you're nothing but a brutal dictator and a coward, and if anybody's facing an imminent insurrection it's you.'

Salim's expression of delight soured as he glared at the captain.

'Then perhaps now is a perfect moment for us to iron-out our differences and bring an end to this pointless posturing. I propose a simple trade, captain. You, for these hostages.'

Idris shook his head.

'You and I both know that if I come down there, you won't release a single person.'

'You question my word, captain?'

'All the time, Salim,' Idris assured him.

'Then you will abandon your people to die, in order to save your own skin?' Salim suggested as he gestured to the kneeling Marines and pilots arrayed before him. 'And you call me a coward,' he uttered.

'A coward hides behind his hostages,' Idris said. 'A true fighter would not need to, but then we both know what you really are Salim, don't we?'

The pirate king chuckled.

'You can invent whatever stories you wish, captain, but nobody's believing them.'

Idris raised an eyebrow.

'But Salim, didn't anybody tell you? Atlantia was a prison ship, and we have detailed video recordings of all prisoners who moved through the system for decades past, especially the high profile ones. Would you like me to share them with your hostages?'

A flare of panic bolted across Salim's features and he whirled to somebody off screen and dragged his hand across his throat. The communications link abruptly vanished.

Atlantia's bridge fell silent for a moment.

'What videos?' Andaim asked.

'There aren't any,' Idris admitted. 'The prison system kept recordings of interviews with major criminals, including Salim, but they were on Ethera. It's my guess that Salim will now try to find those same recordings on Arcadia and destroy them. It'll buy us some time.'

'What was in the recordings?' Mikhain asked.

'Salim, blubbering like a little baby as he was interrogated,' Idris said. 'He sold out on dozens of pirate clans and families, was directly responsible for our subsequent cruises being so successful in stamping out piracy in the Tiberium Fields. It got him a placement into a lower-security holding facility, from which he was unfortunately sprung a few months later.'

'We could really use those videos,' Andaim pressed. 'Maybe in the archives?'

'No,' Idris replied, 'they were on Atlantia Five and were lost with her. But it doesn't matter, just the mention of it and Salim's reaction is enough to start fostering doubt within his inner circle and maybe give a little bit of hope to those captive in his court. I saw Evelyn is still there. I doubt that she will remain under Salim's yoke for long.'

'We don't know what he's got on her,' Andaim said. 'She would have made her move by now. There must be something stopping her and the others from fighting back. There's a whole platoon of Marines down there too,' he added. 'They would not be sitting around as hostages otherwise.'

'Where is General Bra'hiv?' Mikhain asked. 'He could maybe figure out something from here and use the time that we've got.'

'No,' Idris replied. 'We have to move while Salim's hands are tied, prevent him from getting the upper hand. Our best bet is to hit him with another surprise.'

'Which is what?' Andaim asked.

Idris took a breath. 'Organise an escort,' he said. 'I'm going down there.'

'You're going to do *what?*' Andaim gasped.

'It's the last thing he'll expect,' Idris replied. 'Believe me, I know that man and beneath the act he's nothing, a coward.'

'A coward with a few hundred pirates behind him,' Andaim pointed out. 'This is a bad idea. He's not going to free any of those prisoners no matter what you do or say down there!'

'I don't expect him to,' the captain replied. He took Andaim's arm and led him off the command platform as he spoke softly. 'It's no secret that the Atlantia's crew and passengers believe me unable to command this vessel and are questioning every move I make.'

'That's not true sir, and...'

Idris cut him off with a wave of his hand. 'It's a fact. Meyanna has told me as much and I can't ignore the fact that we're not just a military vessel any more. We're a floating city, with people aboard that have needs other than defence. I need you to command Atlantia while I'm away, understood?'

'Me?' Andaim whispered harshly. 'What about Mikhain?'

'I have other plans for the XO,' Idris replied. 'Right now you're the only person I completely trust to command this ship with the best interests of its crew at heart.'

'Why?'

'Because Evelyn's down there,' Idris said. 'She's counting on all of us to do our jobs well, and that's more than enough to assure your loyalty.'

Andaim blinked. 'My loyalty would be assured anyway, captain, with or without...' He broke off for a moment. 'It's my duty, sir.'

'I know,' Idris agreed, and rested one hand on Andaim's shoulder. 'Then you'll understand that if my plans on the surface do not work and all is lost, you will command the Atlantia to bombard the surface, understood? Do not risk losing Atlantia.'

Andaim made to resist but he could see the look in the captain's eye: stern, forceful, decades worth of experience brooking no argument.

'Aye, captain.'

'Good,' Idris said. 'But bombardment is the last resort. We must instead make every effort to bring those hostages back alive and Salim's slaves with them. As soon as you see the shields on Salim's compound go down, hack Arcadia's systems from here and give us control via either the bridge or the War Room, whichever we connect to you from, okay?'

Andaim simply nodded.

'This will work, Andaim,' Idris promised. 'Just as long as we can get aboard Arcadia.'

The captain turned and moved across the bridge to Mikhain's side. The XO lifted his chin expectantly to receive his orders.

'I'm placing Commander Ry'ere in command of the Atlantia until I return,' Idris announced.

Mikhain's studied, loyal expression slipped slightly but he nodded. 'Understood.'

Idris regarded his Executive Officer for a long moment before he spoke.

'I want Salim to be under the impression that I don't have an experienced second-in-command to support me. As long as he doesn't know you're here, he'll continue to believe that the Atlantia is now under the command of a man who can be compromised using the threat of Evelyn's death.'

'I understand sir,' Mikhain replied, his expression strangely neutral. 'Where is Genereal Bra'hiv? If this engagement moves to a ground offensive, we'll need him here on the bridge or be able to liase with him.'

'Bra'hiv is fully occupied with planning any ground offensive we might launch,' Idris informed the XO. 'Many of Alpha Company are engaged with guarding the civilian contingent, so we'll be deploying Bravo Company to the surface. Order a shuttle to prepare for launch, and two Marines as my escort.'

'Only two?' Mikhain uttered. 'You'll be hopelessly outgunned and outnumbered.'

'Just the way I want it,' Idris insisted.

'But you're playing directly into Salim's hands with no support in place. He'll hold all the cards.'

'Not all,' Idris assured him, and turned to Lael. 'All stations broadcast, please.'

'Aye, captain,' Lael replied.

A claxon sounded throughout the Atlantia, echoing through her endless corridors and even across the sanctuary deep inside the ship. Idris took a breath and spoke loudly and clearly upon the otherwise silent bridge.

'Attention all personnel, this is Captain Idris Sansin speaking. As you may have heard, we are having some issues with brigands down on Chiron IV's surface. We came here for supplies and got more than we bargained for, and coupled with our problems aboard Atlantia we have found ourselves in a position where hostages have been taken and there are no easy solutions.' Idris paused for a moment before continuing. 'I take full responsibility for these issues, for the command of this ship and for the outcomes of all decisions that rest upon my shoulders. At this time, I have no option to ensure the safety of those hostages but to surrender myself in their 'stead. Commander Ry'ere is now in command of Atlantia, and will be until my return. Ensure that you follow his orders to the letter, for all of our lives may now depend upon it. Should I fail to return from this mission, I nominate the commander to the role of captain, to select his command crew as he feels fit.' The captain looked at each of his command crew in turn, and nodded. 'It has been my pleasure to serve alongside all of you. Captain Sansin out.'

Lael cut the feed and silence reigned in the wake of his broadcast. Idris turned to Mikhain.

'XO, the shuttle if you please. Have the Marines meet me on the launch bay.'

'Aye, captain.'

Idris answered with a curt nod, and then marched off the bridge.

***

XXXII

'Find them!'

Salim's podgy face flushed an unhealthy shade of red as he pointed one flabby arm at the Arcadia, several of his closest piratical allies marching off toward the frigate.

'That could take days,' Taron Forge murmured as he looked at Salim with interest, 'by which time this could all be resolved if you start thinking straight.'

Salim Phaeon glared at Taron as he paced up and down in front of his throne.

'What you think doesn't interest me, Taron,' he growled. 'You've always been a Colonial stooge no matter what you make others think. Still trying to get out from under your daddy's shadow?'

Taron appeared unperturbed as Evelyn watched him smile casually.

'Daddy's dead,' he replied without concern. 'But it looks to me like you've got something you don't want others to see.' Taron glanced at the injured hybrid nearby, where she had crawled with one hand massaging the wound on her legs from Salim's plasma whip. 'Had a hard time in the cells, did you? Got daddy issues of your own? Maybe you wanted him to come rescue you?'

Salim took two giant strides off the throne platform and swung a bunched fist at Taron's head. Taron did not attempt to avoid the blow and it connected with a sharp crack that sent him sprawling to the ground.

Salim drew his blade from his belt and pointed it down at the smuggler. 'I think that your time has come to an end,' he sneered. 'You no longer have any value to me alive but you could become a useful talisman dead.'

Salim lifted the blade, just in time for Yo'Ki to take one pace forward and turn on her heel as her left boot shot out and ploughed into the fat man's belly with a deep thud. Salim's face turned purple and his eyes bulged as he was propelled backwards into his own throne with a loud crash, the blade flashing through the air and clattering to the ground as he slumped.

Salim pointed at her as he fought to draw a breath.

'Kill them!' he rasped. 'Kill them both!'

Two Ogrin stepped forward, each of them carrying a hefty baton as thick as Evelyn's thigh. The two Ogrin raised their weapons but the sound of approaching ion engines stopped them in their tracks.

The watching pirates leaped from where they were lounging with weapons drawn as they dashed to the windows and peered out at an approaching craft.

'It's a Colonial shuttle!' one of them shouted to Salim. 'What the hell are they doing?'

The pirate king struggled to his feet, off-balance and flushed with pain and rage as he got his voice back and bellowed across the room.

'Get out there! Surround it!'

The pirates stumbled over each other in their hurry to get outside and confront the approaching shuttle. Evelyn watched them go and then leaned over close to where Taron was still sprawled on the ground.

'You up to something here, Taron?'

The smuggler shook his head. 'Your captain freed me, like I said. Just trying to make a living, honey.'

Taron's cocky smile, even in the face of death, only irritated her even further as she turned away and looked at Teera and Ishira.

'Get ready, this could be our chance.'

Both of them nodded and Evelyn watched as the shuttle settled down near the compound as pirates dashed out across the open ground, their rifles cradled in their grip as they took up positions around the shuttle.

'Keep them under guard,' Salim snapped as he pointed at Evelyn, Taron and the others. 'If anything goes wrong, start killing them at random.'

The two Ogrin loomed over Evelyn and Teera, the huge batons in their hands as Evelyn watched the shuttle's main ramp open amid a cloud of vapour. Then, to her amazement, Captain Sansin strode down the ramp with two Marines flanking him.

She heard Salim's gasp of surprise and thought she noticed a ripple of panic on his features as the sound of work on the nearby frigate faded away.

'Place him under arrest, right now!' Salim roared out across the compound to his men.

Evelyn heard Sansin's voice call back, deeper and with resolutely more force despite the distance between the two men.

'You'll do no such thing, Salim! Get your fat backside out here now or I'll have this entire compound blown to damnation and to hell with myself or your hostages! Or are you afraid to do your own dirty work? Still not got the guts for a face-to-face, Salim?'

The captain's voice rolled and echoed across the compound and Evelyn realised that the distant hiss and clatter of work being done to Arcadia's hull had fallen entirely silent. Along with everybody else in the throne room she looked at Salim, who stared wide-eyed at the distant form of Idris Sansin.

The pirate seemed to realise everyone was watching him and he suddenly roused himself into motion and began walking down toward the compound.

'Captain's keeping him off balance,' Evelyn whispered. 'Something's going on but I can't be sure what.'

She could see that one of the Marines was well over six feet tall, about Qayin's height but she could not be sure if it was the former convict or not. Both Marines were equipped with full environmental suits, their features disguised.

Salim strode out onto the compound and slowed as he approached Captain Sansin. The captain stood in silence, his hands behind his back as he watched Salim. Idris ignored the pirate crowd around him and kept his gaze fixed upon Salim, despite being aware that the hundreds of slaves nearby were openly watching events unfold.

The pirate stopped a few feet from Idris, careful to remain out of arm's reach.

'A long time, captain,' Salim said quietly.

'Not long enough,' Idris replied. 'I'd assumed you were long dead.'

'As I had hoped. I found that less Colonial forces attacked me when they thought that I no longer existed.'

Idris looked up at the towering bulk of Arcadia. 'And what, exactly, do you intend to be doing with this frigate?'

'Leaving the area, with all due haste,' Salim replied. 'We won her in battle, captain, and she belongs to us now.'

'Her crew?' Idris asked.

Salim shrugged his round shoulders slowly. 'None survived,' he replied finally. 'But you know how these Colonial types can be – they don't understand when they're beaten.'

'Unlike you,' Idris replied. 'It's been very illuminating watching you grovel like a whipped dog on those prison videos. I'm surprised that you folded so easily, given how hard it was for me to capture you. I guess cowards run faster than heroes.'

'I spent four years being abused by Colonial prison officers because of you,' Salim hissed, keeping his voice down but unable to keep the anger from his tone. 'They beat and whipped and used me like a whore, and every single second of it was down to you.'

Idris shrugged.

'It's no more and no less than you have done to others. No more or less than what you're doing now.'

'Give yourself up, Sansin,' Salim snapped. 'Hand yourself over and I'll free your crew.'

'I don't believe that for a moment, Salim,' Idris replied. 'You're not a man of honour and never will be. You'd cut your own mother's throat if the price was right.'

'For most, no,' Salim agreed, 'but to have your damned hide hanging on the wall of my compound, I'd give up almost anything. Your crew, for your life, and you have my word whether you believe it or not.'

'Release my people and I won't order Atlantia to bomb this compound into the Stone Age,' Idris replied. 'You don't have any plays left, Salim.'

The pirate king frowned and chuckled as he looked around, at the hostages behind him in the throne room, at the ring of pirates surrounding them, at the countless Ogrin and the huge frigate Arcadia.

'I think that you've overestimated your position, captain,' he said. 'There is no way back to Atlantia for you now. In fact I could have you shot this very instant and there would be nothing that you could do about it.'

Idris shrugged.

'Enough talk then,' he said. 'Do it.'

Salim's eyes narrowed and he called over his shoulder to one of the pirates. 'Any explosives aboard their shuttle?'

The pirate, holding a small scanner in one hand and a pistol in the other, shook his head.

'Nobody but the pilot still aboard, no shields active and no weapons detected. It's clean.'

Salim watched Idris for a moment longer.

'Then to hell with you, Sansin,' he spat.

Salim reached down and drew the plasma whip from his belt, activating it in one fluid motion as he swung it over his head and down toward Idris's chest. Captain Sansin leaped to one side and rolled as he hit the ground, the glowing whip humming through the air and missing him by inches as he came up on one knee and brought his hands out from behind his back, a small device contained within them.

Salim's quick eyes spotted the device and panic struck him even as he reversed the direction of his whip in an attempt to strike out at Idris's hand.

'Shoot him, now!' he roared at his men.

The pirates moved to take aim but they didn't even come close to firing before Sansin depressed a button on the device and ducked his head down.

A deafening blast split the air all around them and Idris saw from the corner of his eye the large generator banks began to explode one by one in a violent expanding fireball of flame and black smoke, scrap metal shooting through the air.

The pirates surrounding them dove for cover as Sansin pressed a second button on the device in his hand.

Across the compound the Phoenix's boarding ramp hissed open and amid the blasts of flame and noise dozens of Marines pounded down the ramp and opened fire into the crowds of pirates surrounding them.

***

Dean Crawford

XXXIII

Evelyn leaped up even as the shockwave from the first blast hit the throne room, and the Ogrin instinctively threw themselves away from it as pirates and captives alike ducked aside for cover.

She ran hard, crossing the throne room in two bounds as she hurled herself into the nearest pirate and drove her shoulder deep into his abdomen. The pirate doubled over as he was hurled into a wall, the breath driven from his lungs as his head cracked against the unyielding metal. Evelyn grasped the pirate's pistol and yanked it from his hands before driving the butt into the side of his head. The pirate slumped as Evelyn turned and swung the pistol to bear upon the two Ogrin.

She opened fire, the first shot smashing into an Ogrin's chest in a spray of burning flesh and blue-white plasma. The creature roared in agony as it toppled into its companion, both of them crashing onto the ground in a heaving tangle of limbs.

Kordaz rolled aside from the collapsing Ogri and darted away toward the exits, one hand covering his injured chest as several pirates shouted commands and tried to open fire on the fleeing Veng'en.

Evelyn fired two random shots into the pirates nearest her, sending them diving for better cover, and then she whirled and took careful aim at the Marines. She briefly registered looks of absolute panic on the soldier's faces as she aimed and then she fired. Her shot smacked into the metal chains pinning them in place, and the chains melted in a pile of glowing slag as the soldiers hauled themselves free and scattered with war cries across the throne room.

Evelyn rushed across to where Ishira was shielding Erin from the carnage as the Marines ploughed en masse into the pirates and wrestled them to the ground, the screams of mortal combat deafening with the blasts coming from the generators outside.

'With me!' she shouted at them as Teera leaped to her feet.

Taron Forge and Yo'Ki were already moving as the Marines took control of the throne room, and Evelyn looked at the unpredictable smuggler with renewed enthusiasm as she saw the soldiers pouring from within the Phoenix and laying down heavy fire against Salim's pirates.

'I knew there was more to you!' she shouted above the din.

'We're even!' Taron snapped. 'And we're out of here!'

Before she could reply, Taron and Yo'Ki dashed out of the throne room and began making their way toward the Phoenix.

'Let 'em go!' Teera yelled. 'They're not worth the effort!'

Evelyn turned as several Marines, now heavily armed with an assortment of weapons liberated from pirates now sprawled comatose on the floor all around them, formed up on Evelyn and watched her expectantly.

She shook herself from watching Taron Forge vanish and called her orders to them.

'Form an advance guard!' she ordered. 'Get everybody out of here, hybrids and other slaves included, and get them to Arcadia!'

'We're not going back in shuttles?!' a Marine asked in confusion.

'I don't think that's what the captain has in mind,' Evelyn called back. 'We're here to take Arcadia with us! Who wants to fight the Word with two warships instead of one?!'

A cheer went up among the Marines as they ran from the throne room and opened fire on pirates who were retreating from the battle raging across the compound, hoping for cover within the throne room. Caught between a blaze of plasma fire, they began scattering for their ships instead.

'It's working! They're running!' Lieutenant C'rairn shouted from the compound below as he led his Marines toward the throne complex. 'Let them go and head for Arcadia!'

The Marines began breaking away from the fight and running toward the frigate, and as Evelyn sprinted for the nearest access point she heard Salim screaming to his men as he fled toward the frigate.

'Seal the ship!' he bellowed. 'Don't let them aboard!'

*

Atlantia's bridge was deathly silent, every member of the command crew standing by at their stations and waiting for a signal to appear on the frigate's sensor arrays and reveal Salim Phaeon's compound. Andaim stood on the command platform in front of the captain's chair, his hands behind his back as he slowly paced up and down, sub-consciously mimicking Idris Sansin's own habit.

'Sensor sweep,' he said, his voice calm and yet easily heard across the entire bridge.

'Negative,' Lael replied moments later. 'Still no discernible data from the site.'

'How long have they been gone?' he asked Mikhain.

'Less than an hour,' the XO replied.

Andaim tensed his hands behind his back. The shuttle would have taken little more than thirty minutes to descend to the surface, and perhaps another ten to circle in and land at the compound. That left over twenty minutes gone where anything could have happened, including Salim Phaeon deciding to take no chances and blasting the shuttle out of the sky before it could land.

Andaim glanced at the Atlantia's internal tactical display and checked once again that all fighters were ready for launch, Renegade Flight sitting on the catapults in the launch bay ready to go, two Corsair bombers standing-by and Reaper Flight right behind them. Two shuttles of Marines were also waiting, and all of Atlantia's plasma cannons were fully charged for an orbital bombardment if the captain's plan failed and...

Meyanna Sansin rushed onto the bridge, her features flushed with anxiety.

'It's Qayin!'

'What is?' Andaim asked.

'He's the dealer, he's the source,' Meyanna replied. 'Half of his Marines are acting with him. You need to arrest him right now. Where is he?'

Mikhain looked at the commander, and Andaim's expression darkened.

'He's already well beyond our reach,' he replied as he turned to Mikhain. 'Damn it, we need to let the captain know and...'

'Contact, surface elevation two hundred and eight cubits above mean sea level!' Lael called out as her panel lit up and the tactical display on the bridge changed.

Andaim whirled as he saw a small, circular patch of the planet's surface suddenly shimmer and data start streaming onto the screens as Lael zoomed the Atlantia's sensors in on what had previously been nothing more than a blurred and pixelated patch of coastline.

'It's Arcadia!' Lael confirmed. 'Military registration codes and Identification Friend or Foe transponding on normal frequencies!'

'I've got gunfire,' Mikhain added. 'Multiple discharges!'

'Activate the sensor hack!' Andaim called. 'Launch Renegade Flight and back them up with both Corsairs and one shuttle of Marines!'

'Aye, captain!' Mikhain called and relayed the command.

Andaim turned and saw on a live feed screen Atlantia's launch bay door drop and two Raythons accelerate in a blur as they shot out into space, two more already lining up on the catapults behind them.

He whirled and saw the optical sensors trained on the Arcadia and the pirate compound far below. He could see the indistinct black shapes of Marines firing on fleeing figures, the signs of complete chaos and confusion, and he smiled.

'It's working,' he said. 'Salim's pirates are breaking up under the assault!'

'Sensor hack engaged!' Lael called. 'Synchronising now!'

Andaim waited, and then he saw Lael's face fall.

'What is it?'

'Synchronisation failed!' Lael called, a faint tremor in her voice. 'We're being jammed!'

'I thought that Salim's systems were down?'

Lael scanned her displays desperately, but it was Mikhain who called out next.

'It's not them jamming us! New contact, bearing oh-five-seven, elevation four two!'

Andaim felt something icy run through his veins as he turned and saw a new, large contact on the tactical displays. Data streams from the oncoming contact filled the side of the screen.

'It's Veng'en!' Mikhain shouted, now truly alarmed. 'Sheilds are up, weapons are charging! It's an ambush!'

Andaim felt his mind swamp with indecision, and for several long seconds he stared at the screen and did not move.

'Commander?'

Andaim turned, wide-eyed as Mikhain stared at him expectantly. A single line drifted through Andaim's mind: *If you're in danger of freezing, do something, anything, rather than just stand there looking dumb. Say something!*

Words spilled from Andaim's mouth as though of their own accord.

'Re-task the Raythons to Atlantia's defence!'

Mikhain nodded and relayed the order, and suddenly Andaim's brain re-engaged itself.

'Hold back the second Marine troop in case we need them!' he shouted. 'Stream all power to the plasma cannons facing the Veng'en cruiser and hail them on all frequencies!'

Lael nodded as she frowned at her screen.

'It's Commander Ty'ek's former vessel, captain,' she informed him. 'The one we were following. I thought that they were on our side now?!'

Andaim could not answer her and he saw the look in Mikhain's eye.

'I told the captain that following them was a bad idea,' the XO snapped. 'You can't trust a Veng'en as far as you can throw them.'

'Scythe fighters deploying from the Veng'en cruiser!' yelled a tactical officer from across the bridge. 'She's moving to engage!'

'Launch all Raythons in response!' Andaim fired his order back. 'But do not fire until fired upon!'

'Too late!' Mikhain shouted. 'All batteries on the cruiser firing now!'

'Brace for impact!' Andaim yelled. 'Return fire and get them on screen!'

Andaim hurled himself into the captain's chair as the main viewing panel changed from an image of Salim's compound to one of the huge Veng'en cruiser looming toward them, her starboard hull rippling with bright red flashes as her plasma cannons opened fire as they came to bear.

The Atlantia shuddered as the blows hammered into her shielded hull, each blast louder than the last as they battered their way up Atlantia's flank toward her bridge. Alarms and claxons rang out as the immense energy of each strike overwhelmed the shield generators and caused short-outs and electrical fires to spring up across the ship.

'Fires on decks three through five!' Lael called out. 'Sheilds holding but power is down by twelve per-cent!'

'Return fire, all batteries!' Andaim yelled.

A deeper ripple of thumps reverberated through Atlantia's hull as her massive cannons responded and blasted a salvo of huge blue-white plasma charges across the bitter vacuum of space between the two vessels. Andaim saw the blasts smash into the Veng'en cruiser's hull in flashes of light that flickered and flared like lightning.

'Direct hits!' Mikhain called out. 'The jamming is preventing us from assessing the damage to their hull!'

'Renegade Flight fully engaged!' Lael added. 'They're outnumbered two to one!'

'Get the Reapers out there!' Andaim shouted as he realised that a thin veil of blue smoke was drifting through the bridge as circuitry was being overloaded. 'All power to starboard shields, bring us about!'

The helmsman obeyed instantly, Atlantia turning slowly but far faster than the much larger Veng'en cruiser could manage. Andaim saw that the viewing screen was now showing a shower of plasma shots zipping between the tiny Raythons and Scythes fighting for their lives between the two massive warships.

'Reaper Flight launching!' Mikhain informed Andaim. 'Four Raythons on orders to hold back and defend Atlantia.'

'Good,' Andaim replied. 'Helm, full power, bring us right in front of her. I want all our weapons to bear upon her bridge and as few of hers able to respond.'

'That could expose our people on the surface to bombardment,' Mikhain warned. 'If we can see Arcadia, then so can they!'

'Then we had best be quick about it!' Andaim snapped back. 'If we don't win this battle real fast then there won't be anybody left to stop a Veng'en bombardment!'

Andaim turned to Lael. 'Have they responded to our hail?'

'Negative, captain!' Lael replied. 'No transmissions at all since they arrived!'

Andaim looked at the cruiser and saw it trying to turn to bring its weapons to bear on the faster-moving frigate.

'Why the hell are they attacking us?' he asked out loud. 'We made our peace with Ty'ek's crew before they left us.'

Before anybody could reply, Mikhain's voice rang out

'They're launching more craft! I've got four Veng'en *Raider* assault vehicles, all aiming for the surface!'

Andaim spotted the new contacts splitting away from the cruiser and turning for the planet below them.

'What the hell are they doing? Interceptors, engage and destroy!'

'We can't spare the Raythons, they're fully engaged!' Mikhain replied. 'If they turn away from battle they'll be pursued and shot down, you know this!'

'Send the Atlantia guard fighters instead!'

'We'll have no close-support!' Mikhain argued.

'I know damn well we won't!' Andaim yelled back. 'Send them in, now!'

The XO relayed the order and the four Raythons immediately broke away from Atlantia and raced to intercept the four Veng'en assault craft.

'How long until our weapons come to bear?' Andaim asked.

Mikhain scanned his display panel. 'Thirty seconds, maximum.'

'Can we break through their jamming and take control of the Arcadia?' Andaim asked Lael.

'The signals from Arcadia are too weak and the Veng'en jamming too strong,' Lael replied. 'They're on their own down there.'

Andaim looked at a secondary display on the bridge, several of Atlantia's optical sensors still trained on Arcadia and bearing witness to the battle raging below on the surface.

'*Reaper Three, splash one!*'

The call came out over the communications link, and Andaim saw one of the Veng'en Raiders explode as two Raythons hammered it with plasma shots.

'There are too many,' Mikhain said. 'They're getting through!'

Andaim saw two of the Raiders flare bright orange and red as they plunged into Chiron IV's atmosphere, little finesse required for their tactical descent and the less heavily-shielded Raythons unable to follow them at such velocity.

Andaim turned and looked at the Veng'en cruiser, his eye judging the rate at which the two massive ships were closing on each other.

'Hit them with everything we've got!' Andaim shouted. 'Ignore the Scythe fighters and disable the cruiser's bridge and sensor array! We've got to stop that jamming!'

'Aye captain!' Mikhain replied.

'XO, you have the bridge!' Andaim snapped.

Several heads looked up at the CAG in surprise.

'The captain's orders were that you held the command,' Lael reminded him.

'That was before the Veng'en ambush!' Andaim snapped back. 'We need every single Raython out there, right now, or this is all over!'

Andaim turned to Mikhain, the Executive Officer standing resolute but with shadows of uncertainty, or perhaps conflicting courses of action, passing behind his eyes.

'Captain's orders were explicit. No bombardment unless no other option remained, understood?'

Mikhain stared at Andaim for a long moment before he replied. 'Aye, understood.'

'You have command!' Andaim called as he turned and dashed off the Atlantia's bridge.

Mikhain watched him go and then realised that the entire command crew were watching him intently.

'You heard the captain! Target the cruiser's sensor arrays!'

***

Dean Crawford

XXXIV

'Covering fire!'

General Ibrahim Bra'hiv hunkered down behind an abandoned chunk of welded steel and fired twice upon a pair of pirates advancing upon his position. The first blast smashed the rifle from the hands of one of the pirates in a cloud of sprayed plasma and burning clothes and flesh. The pirate collapsed screaming to his knees as the second man narrowly avoided Bra'hiv's second shot and fled out of sight.

The Arcadia's bow was high overhead, a fine drizzle gusting down from low scudding clouds above as Bra'hiv's Marines tumbled into cover around him, firing as they went. High on the scaffolding Ogrin were marching up and down, cajoling the slaves back to work even as a battle raged beneath them and turbulent storm clouds rumbled overhead. Beams of bright sunshine burst through the turbulent firmament above, illuminating the falling drizzle in bright rainbow bands of light.

'There are too many!' Lieutenant C'rairn shouted across the compound as he crouched behind scattered debris amid the rippling grasses. 'We need to get weapons into the hands of the slaves!'

The pirates had fled as one, taking cover around or near their ships, but as they realised that they outnumbered the assaulting Marines two-to-one so their flight had ceased and they had begun to reform and fight back. A barrage of plasma fire rained down upon the general's position as he tried to locate Qayin's Marines.

'Where the hell is Qayin?' C'rairn yelled above the din.

Bra'hiv thought about falling back once more on Taron Forge's freighter, Phoenix, parked nearby, but then he spotted the smuggler and his co-pilot beating a hasty retreat toward it. Both were armed and both were being largely ignored by the other pirates firing on Bra'hiv's Marines, and that meant their only escape from the planet's surface was being swiftly cut off.

The general pressed one hand over his ear to shield it from the deafening blasts of plasma fire as he called out on an open channel.

'Sergeant Qayin, report in!'

A burst of static replied and Bra'hiv looked up and around again, seeking a glimpse of blue and gold.

'Sergeant Qayin, respond!'

'We're pinned down!' Lieutenant C'rairn shouted.

Bra'hiv looked up and saw the pirates advancing on the Marine's position beneath the Arcadia's bow, the weight of their fire too heavy for the Marines to move position. Bra'hiv braced himself. When facing superior firepower from a numerically superior enemy, there was no longer any tactical way to win the fight. All that remained was the psychological battle to snatch victory from the jaws of defeat.

'All hands!' Bra'hiv yelled. 'Prepare to advance!'

The Marines took up ready positions as they fired, some of them affixing bayonets in preparation for the suicidal charge.

The pirates would be aware that they were outgunning the Marines, and their blood would be up after the unexpected assault. Friends would have been killed, perhaps they would be themselves injured and in pain, keen for revenge. Advancing now on the Marine's position, there was only one thing to stop them, and that was for the soldiers to do the last thing that the pirates would be expecting from a defeated enemy: an advance and attack.

'Ready?!' Bra'hiv shouted. *'Now!'*

The Marines leaped up as one and charged, just as a blaze of plasma fire raced over their heads and ploughed into the advancing pirates. Bra'hiv blinked as he saw them cut down one after another, their advance faltering and stalling as their ranks collapsed into disarray.

Bra'hiv turned and saw Qayin high on the scaffolding behind them, surrounded by not just Marines but dozens of slaves, now armed with plasma rifles that showered down covering fire from their elevated positions.

'I'll be damned,' Bra'hiv smiled as he called out to his men. 'Take cover! Let's finish this!'

The Marines broke off their mass charge and repositioned themselves in cover as ahead the pirates fell back en masse. Bra'hiv huddled down and produced two plasma-grenades from his webbing, set the impact fuses and then lobbed them in amongst the fleeing pirates.

A double-blast thumped the air and Bra'hiv saw several pirates tumble and fall, their bodies aflame with super-heated plasma as they screamed and thrashed. Behind them, Bra'hiv saw Marines tumbling from the throne complex and firing as they went, catching the now-beleaguered pirates in a lethal crossfire.

The Marines began advancing toward the pirate's craft, but Bra'hiv called them back as he recalled their primary mission.

'Stand to! We need Arcadia!'

The Marines turned, falling back toward their general's position with Evelyn and others in tow as Bra'hiv looked about him.

'Where's the captain?'

As the bulk of Salim's pirates fled from view and the gunfire suddenly ceased, Idris Sansin emerged from cover and strode toward the general.

'About time,' he called.

General Bra'hiv saluted and for once his wide jaw split with a smile. 'Been waiting for you, captain. Arcadia is ours.'

Idris's smile faded as he looked at the frigate.

'Not yet it isn't,' he replied.

Salim Phaeon stood upon Arcadia's boarding ramp with his mirrored blade in one hand and a plasma pistol in the other, several of his pirates arrayed around him beneath the huge frigate as they held the line before him.

The Marines advanced down toward the frigate, General Bra'hiv at their head and Idris Sansin close behind. All around them the slaves were descending down from the scaffolding, armed with pistols, rifles and even welding torches distributed by Qayin and his men, angry glares directed at Salim and his fellow pirates.

Bra'hiv saw Evelyn, her pistol aimed at the pirates and a thin gown barely covering her body, joined by numerous captives as they moved among the Marines. Idris, unarmed, moved to the front of the crowd and pointed at Salim. His voice was loud enough to be heard above the sound of fleeing pirates boarding their craft and taking off in the distance.

'It's over,' he called, his voice echoing off the frigate's gigantic hull. 'Stand your men down and hand the Arcadia over or she'll be blown apart as soon as she reaches orbit.'

'I'd sooner die here than surrender to you, Sansin!' Salim shouted.

Bra'hiv spotted several Ogrin among the liberated slaves, no longer controlling them but being led by manacles draped over their necks like leashes. Dim they might have been, but Bra'hiv realised that they knew when then game was up. Deprived of firm leadership, they lost their obedience and became docile and quiet, especially in the face of hundreds of armed slaves.

'I can arrange that,' Idris replied. 'But if you stand down at least you and your men will get out of here alive. Take off, and you're going up against a fully armed frigate with two entire squadrons of trained pilots and hundreds of Marines. You and I both know how that's going to end.'

Salim's podgy features twisted with anger but he forced a smug grin across his face. 'Better to die trying than to not have tried at all.'

'You're sacrificing your own people for nothing,' Idris insisted. 'It's over, all of it. You can't defeat Atlantia and you can't win here because you're outnumbered and outgunned by five to one. All your plays are up,

Salim, yet again. I'm surprised any one of these people is dim enough to follow you to certain death for nothing.'

Salim glanced at his men.

'They know the meaning of loyalty!' he shouted.

Around Salim the pirates began looking at each other, their weapons slowly lowering as they weighed up the odds and realised that following Salim Phaeon had gone from being the best game in town to the worst. One by one, they stood down.

'Stand firm!' Salim almost screamed. 'We have Arcadia!'

'You have nothing,' Idris countered. 'Nothing without us, anyway. We humans, pirates or not, have to learn to start working together or there'll be nobody left at all.'

Salim scowled and raised his pistol to point at Idris.

Instantly, some sixty Marines aimed their rifles back at him, and to Bra'hiv's surprise half of Salim's pirates turned and aimed their weapons at their former leader also. The pirate king glared at his own people, his face twisted with hate.

'You're back-stabbing, slime-ridden scum, every last one of you!' he ranted.

'Charming as ever,' Idris called out. 'Stand down, Salim, or I suspect your own colleagues will shoot you.'

Salim fumed and seemed almost to hop on the spot, but he lowered his pistol and tossed it down onto the ramp. Bra'hiv felt a wave of relief wash over him as the pirates surrounded their former leader and then turned to watch Captain Idris Sansin. The captain cast his gaze over hundreds of former slaves and decided to consolidate his gains.

'You are free, each and every one of you!' he shouted. 'You may go your own way, or you may follow us, but either way it's time to get off this planet!'

A deafening crescendo of cheers burst out from among the crowds of slaves, loud enough to compete with the crashing waves near the cliffs and the buffeting winds that howled endlessly across the barren little world. General Bra'hiv finally lowered his rifle and deactivated the plasma magazine.

Nearby, Evelyn turned as a man with grey hair fought his way through the crowd toward them, and Ishira broke away and rushed toward the man. They collided in a deep embrace, Erin between them, and Evelyn felt a little warmth blossom inside her that briefly veiled the nausea and chills pervading her body.

'That'll be Stefan then, I guess,' Teera said.

'Don't,' Evelyn smiled in response, 'you'll be getting me all emotional.'

Teera raised a questioning eyebrow.

'Speaking of which, I should imagine Commander Ry'ere will be on his way down to you before long.'

'What's that supposed to mean?' Evelyn challenged.

'That your boy will be pining for you.'

'Will you cut that crap out?! He's not *my boy*.'

'Not yet, but it's only a matter of time, right?'

The sound of ion engines cut through the blustering wind, and Teera smiled brightly.

'Ah, that must be him now, racing down in his Raython to sweep you into his arms and…' Evelyn turned to cut Teera off, but then she saw the smile vanish from her friend's face to be replaced with a look of sheer terror.

The entire crowd turned toward the sound of the ion engines, and as Evelyn looked up she saw a large, blocky craft plunge down through the turbulent clouds, its engines glowing and casting plumes of heat down toward the ground as it swooped in and reared up. A boarding ramp beneath the cockpit area lowered even before it had touched down, and Evelyn felt fear creep cold up her spine as she saw figures leap with inhuman agility from the interior of the craft.

'Enemy, front!' Bra'hiv yelled.

Evelyn whirled as she saw dozens of Veng'en spring into action as they landed, plasma rifles cradled in their grip and blades flashing as they charged forward.

'It must be the Veng'en we were following!' Teera yelled. 'They've doubled back!'

And then Evelyn realised that the Veng'en were not alone.

From within the assault craft's interior plunged a black deluge of Hunters, the Legion pouring like metallic black oil to soak the planet's surface in a writhing sea of killer machines.

'Covering fire!' Bra'hiv bellowed, and instinctively he looked up onto the scaffolding above for Qayin's Marines.

To his dismay, he realised that they were gone. Bra'hiv glanced to his right to see the towering soldier fleeing toward the pirate fleet far to his left, his Marines in pursuit.

*

Salim Phaeon's plasma whip lashed out and struck Idris Sansin across the chest as the Veng'en horde plunged from their craft and flooded onto the plain. White pain ripped across Idris's body and he cried out as he stumbled and collapsed onto his back as all around him the crowd of slaves and soldiers scattered in panic.

He heard the pirate king's screams above the din. 'Seal Arcadia! Don't let them aboard!'

Idris rolled over, smelled the stench of burning fabric and looked down to see his uniform singed black and beneath it his skin charred where the whip had struck him. He pushed himself up onto his elbows and turned his head to see a hail of plasma fire zipping back and forth around him as the Marines and slaves opened fire on the charging Veng'en.

'Captain!'

Lieutenant C'rairn dashed to Idris's side and helped him up.

'I'm okay!' the captain insisted. 'Support General Bra'hiv!'

Idris turned to see Salim Phaeon vanish into a thick morass of smoke, several of his lackeys running with him as they boarded Arcadia and raised the ramp behind them.

Pain and rage forced Idris to his feet and he ran low in pursuit of Salim, the roiling smoke provoking tears that ran down his face and blurred his vision as he sought Salim through the smog. Plasma fire crackled and hissed as rounds smacked into the frigate's massive hull and impacted the rapidly rising boarding ramp.

He spotted Salim's brightly coloured coat billowing in the wind as he dashed into the ship's interior. Idris, his chest heaving and pain searing his skin, rested one arm against a scaffolding pillar as he fought for his breath before he dashed forward and jumped up, his hands grasping the edge of the boarding ramp even as gunfire raked the ground behind him.

Idris hauled himself upward, swung his legs desperately to clamber aboard before the ramp closed. He heard the hydraulic jacks whining shut and saw the upper seal rushing toward him. He strained and managed to hook one ankle over the edge and with a supreme effort he hauled himself upward and tumbled inside as the ramp slammed shut with a deep boom that echoed through the ship's corridors.

Idris clung to the deck and waited for a moment in pitch blackness.

Salim's piratical vanguard had vanished into the darkness, the beating of their boots on the deck and a dim flickering of flashlights fading into the distance as Idris peered into the impenetrable blackness of Arcadia's interior, unlit now that the power supply had been cut off. Like all major warships of her age and class she was fitted with a massive central keel that ran from beneath the launch bay all the way to her stern. Service corridors ran alongside and over this central keel, and from them the rest of the entire ship could be accessed if one knew the way.

Idris knew the way, and a few shortcuts alongside them. He also knew that it would be much faster to reach the Arcadia's War Room from her keel than to access the main bridge, which was located atop the hull. Salim, being a pirate and not a Colonial Officer, would likely have no detailed knowledge of Arcadia and as such would simply assume that the bridge was the only point from which the frigate could be controlled.

Idris closed his eyes, trying to let them adjust to the darkness as in his mind he imagined the vast hull before him.

Using his hands, he began feeling his way forward and vanished into the darkness.

★★★

Dean Crawford

XXXV

'Legion!'

The cry went up among the Marines and they threw themselves into firing positions as the Veng'en warriors charged toward them, followed by the rippling sea of nanites as they spilled from the interior of the assault craft and from two more Raiders that burst through the cloud layer far above.

'Enemy high!' Idris shouted.

A barrage of plasma fire blasted out from the Marine lines into the charging Veng'en as Evelyn looked up and saw Hunters falling like veils of black rain from the sky above them, dropped deliberately like lethal little parachutists to disrupt the Marines from within. She looked over her shoulder and saw more deploying far behind Arcadia as more Raiders broke through the cloud layers above.

'They're surrounding us!' Bra'hiv bellowed.

'Get back, under the frigate's bow!' Evelyn yelled at the panicking hordes around her. 'Fall back!'

The crowds of slaves began crying out in horror as they fled beneath the Arcadia's massive hull to escape the coming torrent. Evelyn grabbed Ishira and propelled her with Erin toward cover.

'Get under there and stay in cover!' she bellowed.

Ishira retreated with her daughter and father as the Marines fired upon the charging hordes of Veng'en. Evelyn whirled and aimed at the nearest of the lithe, frighteningly fast Veng'en and fired twice. The first shot was dodged as the creature leaped sideways but her second struck it high in the chest, just beneath the throat. As the plasma round smashed and burned its way into the Veng'en's body clouds of glowing orange embers burst from its eye sockets and mouth as though it were aflame from within.

'That's not possible!' she cried out. 'They're infected!'

The horrific realisation spread through the Marines as they saw the Veng'en close up. Their once-yellow eyes now glowed a dull, soulless red, the surface glinting metallic grey around a mechanical iris. Patches of metallic, powder-like skin merged seamlessly with natural scales as the Infectors within them consumed and replaced their bodies.

'I thought Veng'en were immune?!' Teera shouted above the din of gunfire.

'They were!' Evelyn called back. 'Something's changed!'

The Veng'en's eyes were surrounded by metallic scales, the infection rooted far more deeply there than on other parts of their bodies. Evelyn knew that Veng'en blood was toxic to the Infectors, too acidic for them to survive long enough to take control of their bodies. But if they had found a new vector into Veng'en bodies, perhaps through the eyes or nasal passages, a way to the brain that avoided the bloodstream, then that evolutionary process may have resulted in Ty'ek's crew being overwhelmed and consumed.

Almost immediately Evelyn thought of Kordaz, but she knew the Veng'en warrior had escaped Salim's throne room.

'We can't get aboard!'

Evelyn turned as she saw hundreds of slaves pounding at hatches all across the Arcadia's hull, hatches that had been open moments before but were now firmly closed. She looked up at the ship's gigantic launch bay doors high above and saw them rumbling closed, and from somewhere deep inside the massive hull she heard the sound of enormous ion engines beginning to engage.

'She's preparing to take off!' Teera shouted in alarm.

Evelyn whirled as a screeching sound attracted her attention and a Veng'en warrior loomed before her, his left arm already missing from a plasma blast but his terrifying red eyes aglow with the mindless determination of a machine. Evelyn ducked and rolled to avoid the vicious swipe of the Veng'en's *D'jeck*, the finely honed weapon whispering through the air above her head as she rolled and aimed up at the Veng'en's face and fired.

The plasma shot blasted the Veng'en's head from his neck and sent it spinning through the air in a trail of smoke as the creature's body plunged toward Evelyn. She rolled aside as it thumped down onto the ground, a flood of Infectors spilling from its wounds in a glossy black rush.

'Get away from it!' she yelled at Teera.

The crowd of terrified slaves backed away, the noise from the Marines' plasma rifles nearby deafening as Evelyn clambered to her feet and staggered back from the fallen Veng'en.

The nearby Marines were falling back, not from the charging Veng'en but from the Hunters swarming toward the Arcadia. Above the deafening roar of the frigate's fusion cores and engines powering up were the screams of hundreds of terrified slaves fleeing the onrushing black wave of Hunters and the squeal and hiss of plasma rifles laying down fire against the Veng'en. A double blast thumped the air as two plasma grenades were lobbed into the morass of Hunters, a cloud of them vaporised into glowing embers that spiralled away on the blustering gale.

'We're pinned down!' Evelyn yelled as loud as she could above the cacophony of battle. 'There's nowhere else to run!'

The sea of slaves and Ogrin backed away from the churning Hunters as Evelyn saw General Bra'hiv turn and run from his position, his Marines following suit as their defensive line was over-run by a tsunami of black metal, the sound of a million tiny legs like a waterfall of tiny stones.

'Fall back!' Bra'hiv bellowed, firing as he retreated and hitting a Veng'en square in the chest.

Evelyn saw the warrior fall and then be consumed as the wave of Hunters washed over it like back oil, millions of tiny metallic incisors slicing without thought into flesh, tearing it to pieces. The Veng'en looked as though he were crumbling in a sea of acid, limbs separated and vanishing, bones appearing bright white and pink from within red flesh and then disintegrating into power.

General Bra'hiv dashed to her side, his face flushed with the adrenaline overload of close combat.

'The Atlantia's hack hasn't worked,' he gasped. 'We don't have control of Arcadia and I can't contact Atlantia!'

'They must be under attack by the Veng'en and their signals blocked,' Evelyn replied as Bra'hiv fired at two Veng'en crawling toward them, their legs already torn off by grenade blasts.

'We've got to get out of here,' Bra'hiv agreed. 'There's no other way off this planet except the pirate ships.'

'We need Arcadia!' Evelyn replied.

'We need to survive!' Bra'hiv insisted. 'I'm pulling my troops toward the pirate ships, we'll take what we can!'

Evelyn grasped desperately for a better solution but she knew that the general was right. Even as she admitted it to herself she saw Ishira, Stefan and Erin running toward the parked vessels on the far side of the frigate, where their ship Valiant was waiting. Even as she saw them, she spotted yet more pirate craft lifting off and blasting their way into the turbulent sky.

'All right,' she relented. 'Teera!' Her blue-skinned wingman looked up at her. 'Get to your fighter! You'll do more damage that way!'

Teera whirled and ran for her Raython as Evelyn looked at the Marine's new defensive line and the assault craft still spilling Hunters onto the planet's surface all around them.

'How long?' she asked.

Bra'hiv did not have to ask what she meant.

'Five minutes and they'll have us surrounded, and this will all be over.'

*

'Reaper One break right!'

Andaim heard the command even as his Raython blasted from Atlantia's launch bay. He shoved the control column over to the right and hauled back hard on it as a blaze of bright red plasma shots flashed by his left wing with what felt like scant cubits to spare.

His fighter shot from beneath the Atlantia's bow and straight into a cloud of spiralling, rolling and twisting fighters all trying to get a bead on each other and open fire. Plasma blasts zipped back and forth in a hail of blue and red light as Andaim flew straight through the heart of the dogfight and spotted a stray plasma shot hit a Raython on its left wing and almost tear it completely off.

Andaim blinked, got control of his breathing and almost immediately his instinct for flying took over.

'All Raythons, cease fire immediately!'

'Do *what?!*' came a chorus of replies.

'You're in disarray!' Andaim insisted. 'You're as likely to hit each other as the enemy! Renegades, cease fire and re-group in sector one! Form pairs and re-engage!'

Andaim rolled his Raython over, light from the flaring sun flashing through the cockpit as he slipped into a tight formation behind a Veng'en Scythe fighter and fired once. His port shot hit the Scythe a glancing blow and it wobbled. Andaim kicked in left rudder and fired again. Both shots slammed into the fighter's rear quarter and it burst open like a metallic flower that blossomed a bright ball of orange flame.

Andaim broke off and saw a dozen Raythons stream away from the fight with a handful of Scythes in pursuit, forming pairs once more as they swung around the Atlantia's bow and turned back toward the engagement.

'Now the Reapers to sector one, re-form and re-engage!'

Andaim watched as the Renegades rushed back toward the pursuing Scythes, and in paired formations opened fire. The Scythes were smashed aside as the Raythons burst back into the fight, staying in tightly knit pairs for mutual cover and maximum firepower as they engaged the Veng'en fighters.

Andaim climbed out of the engagement, high above it as he joined the Reapers and selected a lone Raython. He slid into formation alongside it.

'Reaper One, port echelon Reaper Five.'

The pilot looked out of his cockpit over his left shoulder and saw Andaim in position off his wing.

'Roger that, sir!'

'Reaper Flight, engage!'

The squadron wheeled over the top of a loop and plunged back down into the fight, each pair of Raythons veering off in pursuit of a target as Andaim faithfully hung on to Reaper Five's wing as the pilot pulled out of his dive into line astern with a Scythe and opened fire. Andaim kicked in some rudder as Atlantia's hull rushed past at terrific speed beneath them and fired alongside Five.

The four plasma blasts converged on the fleeing Scythe and smashed into it with enough force to blast the craft into five separate pieces amid a flickering fireball that flared light across Atlantia's hull and then vanished as the two Raythons rocketed away from the frigate's stern.

'Whoa, that got 'im!' Five reported gleefully.

'Break left!' Andaim snapped. 'Re-engage!'

'Yessir!'

The two Raythons swept around a hard left turn and raced back into the fray, Andaim this time seeing Scythe fighters spiralling in chaos, all of them damaged or in the process of being shot down as the Raythons began achieving air superiority over their foe.

'Atlantia, this is the CAG! Prepare to launch the Corsair bombers!'

A blast of static interference hissed in Andaim's ears as the frigate's communication sensors struggled to overcome the jamming coming from the Veng'en cruiser.

'Two Corsairs on the cats!' came the response from Mikhain. *'But they'll never reach the surface in time to stop Arcadia from lifting off. Our sensors show that the majority of our people are still on the surface!'*

'I don't want our bombers to attack the surface,' Andaim replied as he watched Reaper Five blast a Scythe fighter into blazing fragments with an explosion that briefly illuminated Andaim's cockpit in an orange glow. 'I want them to hit the Veng'en cruiser and break the jamming!'

'Stand by!'

Andaim followed Reaper Five as they raced beneath the Atlantia's massive hull and came up on the other side. The vast grey bulk of the Veng'en cruiser lay opposite, bathed in the fearsome glow of the dying star.

'Corsairs launched!' Mikhain called. *'Sensors report massive electro-magnetic emissions from the cruiser's mid-section.'*

'Copy that,' Andaim replied. 'Reaper Flight, on me!'

Andaim aimed his Raython at the Veng'en cruiser even as he spotted Raythons breaking away from the fight to join him and the two Corsairs race out of Atlantia's launch bay.

***

XXXVI

'I'm detecting ion exhaust from Arcadia, increasing by the second,' Lael reported from her station aboard Atlantia's bridge. 'She'll lift off within a few minutes.'

Mikhain stood beside the captain's chair, his eyes flicking from one display to another. Atlantia shuddered as salvos from the Veng'en cruiser impacted her massive hull and the deck lights flickered and hummed as power surged through her electrical systems, the ship's shields struggling to absorb the blows.

Two displays showed the scene on the surface, and it wasn't good. Sensors with massive optical resolution showed the Arcadia's form, and the shapes of three Raider assault craft nearby. Flickers of light betrayed the fierce battle on-going between the Veng'en and those on the ground, probably Bra'hiv's Marines, while a dense mass of humanity swarming around the frigate likely denoted the slaves belonging to Salim Phaeon as they tried to board the frigate.

Mikhain turned to the tactical display and saw the Veng'en cruiser manoeuvring to avoid Atlantia's guns while trying to bring her own to bear. Her lumbering size was no match for Atlantia's manoeuverablity at close range, but the cruiser's massive guns were a lethal threat to the frigate. If Mikhain missed a beat or was deceived by a feint on the Veng'en commander's behalf, then a single broadside could smash Atlantia into instant submission and perhaps even complete destruction.

'Helm, two degrees up and five to port,' he snapped. 'Keep those guns at bay.'

'Aye sir.'

Mikhain glanced at a third display, a holographic image of the Raythons engaging the Scythe fighters as they swarmed around the Atlantia's hull. Roughly even in number, the Raythons were now inflicting a terrible toll on the Scythes, wave after wave being blasted as they launched from the Veng'en cruiser.

And then a thought crossed his mind: even despite their combat experience, the Raythons should not be so easily dominating the Veng'en Scythes.

'Communications,' he asked, 'are you receiving any transmissions at all from the cruiser?'

'Nothing sir,' Lael replied. 'No broadcasts, no transponder codes, nothing.'

'What about the Scythes?' he asked.

Lael frowned as she scanned her instruments. 'Nothing that I can see but we're being jammed.'

'I don't want to know what they're saying,' Mikhain urged, 'just whether they're communicating verbally at all?'

Lael spent a moment adjusting her controls and then she looked up again. 'Negative sir, ther are no broadcasts at all between the enemy fighters, coded or not. What does that mean?'

Mikhain listened to the low-volume broadcasts coming from the Raython fighter pilots as they engaged the Scythes, constant calls of warnings, victories, damage reports and new contacts being shared by the pilots in their fast-moving, high intensity environment. He felt his blood run cold as he realised why the Veng'en were attacking them, why they would be engaging in a ferocious battle without speaking a single word to each other.

'They're infected,' he said finally. 'They're under the control of the Legion.'

'That's not possible,' Lael replied. 'I thought that the Veng'en were immune to infection.'

'We must have been wrong,' Mikhain snapped as he whirled to the tactical support officer. 'Enhance the optical sensor arrays, I want maximum resolution right now!'

'Aye sir!'

Mikhain watched as the optical images zoomed in dramatically to the scene on the planet below, to the point where he could pick out individuals running, could see the light from plasma shots zipping between black-fatigued Marines and the scaly brown figures of Veng'en. And there, behind the Veng'en, a roiling black sheet as though a sea of oil was spreading toward Arcadia.

'Zoom out, two per cent,' Mikhain ordered.

The display view widened, and around the docked frigate Mikhain saw a thick ring of black contracting toward Arcadia and the humans trapped beside her.

'Hunters,' Mikhain whispered as he watched the wave of nanites advancing across the compound. He could see that the wave was cutting off the survivors from the ranks of ships parked to the north of their position, pinning them in place around the Arcadia.

'If she launches with those damned pirates aboard, we'll lose the best chance we have of defeating the Veng'en,' he said. 'They might even attack us.'

'We don't know that,' Lael pointed out. 'Likely they'll just run like hell out of the system and jump to super-luminal the first chance they get.'

Mikhain turned away from the screen, his mind racing. There had been no contact from the captain and it was clear that the unexpected Veng'en attack had caused chaos on the planet below. No longer in control of the situation and with the pirates clearly in control of Arcadia, Sansin had exhausted his options. Worse, the Arcadia might not escape the Legion entirely. If even a handful of Infectors managed to get aboard before she launched then she would be a plague ship, lethal to any human vessel she encountered until her entire hull had been swept clean by microwave scanners.

Mikhain looked one last time at the Veng'en cruiser and then at the Arcadia. Salim Phaeon was almost certainly aboard...

'CAG, how long until those sensors are down?'

Andaim's reply came back distorted and broken.

'... *in-bound... heavy fire... stan.. –by...*'

Mikhain turned to the tactical officer, Ensign Scott. 'Power up the starboard batteries for a ground bomnbardment,' he ordered.

Ensign Scott stared back at Mikhain for a long beat. 'The captain said that was a last resort and...'

'That was before the Veng'en attacked us!' Mikhain snapped. 'We're fighting the Legion now and we can't afford to take any chances. Charge the batteries now or I'll find somebody else to do it in your 'stead!'

Ensign Scott turned back to his instruments. 'Aye, cap'ain!'

Mikhain turned back to the image of the Veng'en cruiser, saw the tiny specks of the Raythons racing toward her, and hoped to hell that they got to her before he was forced to destroy Arcadia.

*

Idris Sansin hurried through the pitch-black darkness, one hand running along the surface of a massive heat-exchange pipe that he knew traversed the length of Arcadia's hull. From his memory of the Atlantia he knew that the corridor alongside the pipe ran for a similar length and was unobstructed but for bulkheads spaced at precisely eighty six cubits, roughly a hundred paces for an old man. He smiled at his own imagining of himself in the darkness. Truth was he was only fifty five and probably had a good few years in him yet, but in the mirror the stresses and strains of command had aged him, his hair greyer and his skin more deeply lined that he deserved.

The thump and whine of plasma fire from the battle raging outside the hull faded into the distance as he hurried along, and then found what he was looking for. A bulkhead of different dimensions to the others, bulkier

235

and with double instead of single doors. Built into a crossmember of the ship's architecture, the heavy frames denoted to Idris a position directly beneath the launch bay. Many times in the past, as part of his duties, he and other officers had been required to survey these deep and lonely sections of Atlantia and had been able to hear the roar of the old Phantom fighters as they launched during normal operational cycles just a couple of decks above.

Idris reached up, searching for manual access panels that lined the ceiling. Designed for emergency access from a burning launch bay in the event of fire, they were designed to normally be used by deck crew escaping downward but were equally able to be opened from below. Idris found one, strained against the handles until they began to turn, and then carefully lowered the panel down. He took a few deep breaths and then used the same handle to haul himself up, managed to get a hand up into the access chute and then a boot onto the door handle, and with a final push climbed up into the chute.

Idris took a few more moments to catch his breath and then he hauled the panel closed beneath him and reached out into the darkness above his head. He found the panel to the deck above fairly quickly, off-set from the one he had just used to prevent crew members from jumping down through two decks at a time and injuring themselves. Idris cranked the handle and the hatch opened, a faint glow of light and a cool breeze drifting toward him.

He climbed up and peeked over the edge of the deck to see Arcadia's massive launch bay, the doors wide open. He heard a loud rumble and saw the bay doors beginning to close. Around the bay, lights flickered on as power was engaged somewhere within the ship.

'Damn it.'

Salim was already preparing Arcadia for launch, and time was running out. Idris hauled himself out of the deck panel and left it open as he stood up to survey the bay. And then his breath seemed to clog in his throat.

Idris stared behind him into the depths of the launch bay and saw there two neat rows of Raython fighters, several shuttles and four Corsair bombers. He gasped in amazement, utterly bewildered. All of the craft seemed pristine in condition, barely used, and he wondered again how the hell Salim Phaeon and his mercenary little bunch had been able to overwhelm Arcadia in open combat. He recalled the pirate's boast of how he had defeated Arcadia's captain. There were no signs of combat aboard the ship, and as far as he was aware nobody had laid eyes on the crew.

Over a thousand souls, unaccounted for.

Idris felt certain that they were not among the ranks of Salim's slaves — so many Colonial officers and enlisted men and women would not have buckled so easily. But then, where the hell were they?

A loud, reverberating hum shuddered through Arcadia's hull as though the ship were coming alive beneath his feet, and Idris turned and began running through the launch bay toward the War Room.

*

'Get out there!'

Sergeant Qayin's voice roared above the sound of battle as he crouched down near the Phoenix's boarding ramp and opened fire on the Veng'en plunging toward the mass of panicking slaves packed against Arcadia's hull.

The Marine's of Bravo Company formed up around him, rifles blazing into the Veng'en horde. Dozens of the warriors switched direction and ran with fearsome speed toward the Phoenix, their bodies riddled with the Legion, chunks of metal flashing amid leathery skin.

'Keep them back!' Qayin bellowed. 'Defensive positions!'

The Marines obeyed with fluid and fearless speed, fanning out and covering each other's positions in a staggered semi-circle as they laid down a ferocious field of fire against the Veng'en.

Qayin dropped to one knee, raised his rifle and fired twice into a charging Veng'en, saw the flesh from the creature's massive chest blast apart in a smouldering cloud and drops of molten metal spray like glowing blood from inside as the warrior tumbled to the ground and his comrades ran over his body in their headlong charge.

'Maintain positions!' Qayin roared, firing again. 'Hold the line!'

The big man looked to his left in time to see a lithe, tall man with dark hair dashing toward them and firing as he went. Behind Taron was Yo'Ki with a flashing blade in one hand and a pistol that seemed too big for her in the other. Even as Qayin watched Yo'Ki fired into the face of an attacking Veng'en warrior, blasting his head from his shoulders as she turned sideways and drove the sole of her boot into the dead creature's chest. The Veng'en's headlong charge was arrested in time for the woman to drive the length of her blade deep into another Veng'en's belly and then yank it free along with a torrent of blood.

Taron Forge whirled and fired at the stricken Veng'en, blasting him away from Yo'Ki before the Infectors surging through the creature's body could infect his co-pilot. Together, in perfect and violent harmony, the pair fought their way toward the Phoenix. Taron glanced at Qayin and shouted above the din of combat as he reached the ramp.

'Glad you could make it!'

'We're not out of this yet!' Qayin yelled in reply. 'Pull out the drums!'

Qayin watched as Taron and Yo'Ki retreated up the ramp into the freighter, firing as they went, and then Taron reached down and yanked free a series of thick straps attached to the hull wall. Twenty massive blue drums were instantaneously freed from their mounts and tumbled down the ramp toward Qayin.

Qayin leaped aside and out of the way as the drums rolled out across the barren earth and he shot a dirty look up at Taron.

'Good doing business with you!' the pirate yelled. 'Have a nice day!'

Taron hit a button and the Phoenix's ramp whined as it wound up and closed behind Qayin.

'Son of a bitch!'

Qayin slung his rifle over his shoulder and dashed to the furthest drum, a two-hundred litre sealed unit with a pressure valve and a hose atop the lid. Qayin hauled the drum upright and pulled the hose around as he looked up.

The Veng'en were still coming, sprinting across the fallen bodies of their comrades with frenzied disregard for the hail of plasma fire screeching past and into them. Behind the Veng'en a black sea of Hunters swarmed toward the Marine's position.

'Fall back!' Qayin yelled.

Half of Bravo Company got to their feet and retreated as the other half maintained position and kept firing. A Veng'en broke through and leaped through the air to land on a young soldier. Qayin felt a pinch of regret as he recognised Soltin's face locked in a rictus of pain as thick talons sank into his flesh and savage teeth ripped into the back of his neck. A large, sculptured blade sought to slice the soldier's spine straight out of his body. Qayin heard Soltin's screams of agony even above the battle, but he waited.

The other half of Bravo Company leaped up and dashed back as those who had retreated first took up position around Qayin and covered them. Qayin held his nerve as his soldiers dashed into position even as behind them the Phoenix's engines wound up and the freighter lifted off into the sky.

'Get down!' Qayin yelled.

The Marines crouched down as a searing blast of exhaust washed over them and then smashed into the charging Veng'en. The Phoenix's plasma cannons opened up and hammered the running horde as it departed, blasting Veng'en aside in their dozens and melting huge swathes of the advancing Hunters into smouldering, glowing lakes of molten metal.

'Least you could do, you traitorous bastard!' Qayin yelled as the Phoenix pulled up and accelerated away toward the turbulent skies above.

The black sea of Hunters swarmed in as the last of the Veng'en were cut down, and Bravo Company huddled protectively around Qayin and the drums as his men looked at him expectantly.

'Now what?!' one of them yelled.

Qayin aimed the hose at the Hunters and took a breath.

'Now we hope that the captain's wife is as smart as she thinks she is!'

Qayin yanked the pressure valve open and a blast of red-brown fluid sprayed out toward the Hunters.

***

Dean Crawford

XXXVII

Taron Forge pushed the throttles forward and the Phoenix surged skyward as he pulled back on the control column. Beside him he saw Yo'Ki activate the ship's heavy weapons and lay down a ferocious bombardment onto the Veng'en and the swarming nanites before their ship climbed out of range.

The freighter shuddered and pitched as the turbulent winds battered its hull. Taron guided her upward and the Phoenix punched gamely through a layer of ripped cloud and rocketed toward the heavens.

'Positive climb, landing struts away,' he called. 'That was a close one.'

Yo'Ki was silently performing her take-off checks. He saw her peer at him from the corner of his eye but she said nothing. Instead, she finished her checks and then folded her arms and placed one small boot on the control panel as she stared out of the windscreen at the vast blue sky shimmering with aurora.

Taron watched her for a moment, his hands controlling the Phoenix without conscious thought. Years of working and fighting together had given him the chance to detect Yo'Ki's moods as though by clairvoyance, and he sensed her discord as clearly as if she had slapped him across the face.

'What now?' he uttered, a hint of exasperation in his tone. 'We just got out of there by the skin of our teeth. We're free.'

Yo'Ki said nothing and did not look at him.

'Right,' Taron said, 'because that's not enough for you I suppose? You think that we should be playing hero and picking those losers up, right?'

Silence reigned in the cockpit, only the soft beeping of instruments and the hum of the ship's powerful ion engines giving life to the atmosphere.

'They're not going to survive,' Taron insisted. 'Even if they do get off that rock, they won't make it much further. You heard what their idiot of a captain said: they're travelling *toward* Ethera. I bet they don't make it past the outer core systems before they're zapped, or eaten, or whatever the Word does to people these days.'

The sky outside the Phoenix was already dark, the first stars visible and the veils of light around the star Chiron glowing across the starfields like a veil. The ethereal glow played across Yo'Ki's skin and reflected in her dark eyes. Outside, Taron could see the curvature of Chiron's surface, cloud banks covering swathes of land and aurora shimmering in the upper atmosphere around them.

'They don't have a future like we do,' Taron added for good measure.

Yo'Ki's head slowly turned toward him and she raised an eyebrow.

'What, you don't think we've got a future?' Taron challenged.

Yo'Ki inclined her head toward the starfields now glittering before them.

'Where?' Taron gave voice to her question. 'How the hell should I know? You think there's a better future for humanity on Ethera? For humans?'

Yo'Ki looked away again at the stars and Taron sighed and shook his head.

'They blew it,' he said. 'Humanity destroyed itself with its own ingenuity and people like Idris Sansin can't seem to realise that it's over. They're just committing themselves to the same damned stupidity that got humanity where it is today.'

A warning sensor beeped for attention and Taron accessed the ship's tactical display. A holographic image glowed into life before them on the control console, the Phoenix depicted as a small green dot climbing away from Chiron's surface. Nearby, two more massive ships were in orbit and surrounded by a cloud of smaller fighters. Taron frowned and zoomed in on the two large vessels.

'Atlantia,' he identified it, 'and a Veng'en cruiser.'

Yo'Ki leaned closer to the display and Taron could see the discomfort on her features.

'They're heavily engaged,' Taron said. 'Nothing we can do for them.'

Taron accessed the super-luminal navigation system and began plotting a course. Yo'Ki turned her head to examine him again and he managed to avoid looking at her as he spoke.

'They're doomed and so are we if we join them,' he said. 'They're on their own. This is my ship, I make the rules and I decide what happens. We're not going back and that's final.'

Yo'Ki said nothing.

*

'Cover!'

Qayin ducked as the wave of Hunters swelled before them like a giant black wave, threatening to crash down and consume them as one. The rust-coloured spray soaked them as they rushed in, and Qayin felt the strength go out of his legs as the vast wall of machines filled the field of his vision with impending, horrific death.

'It's not working!'

The Hunters swarmed over the Marines to the sound of horrified screams as the wave of their assault broke and blasted into the soldiers with the weight of tonnes of metallic mass. Soldiers threw their hands over their heads and ducked down in horror and for a moment Qayin saw Ethera in his mind's eye: his mother, somebody he had not thought about in months, years maybe. His father, or what little he remembered of the drunken old man who had often reminded Qayin that he was a mistake that could not be reversed. His life flickered before him like a broken movie reel illuminated only by patches of light, and then even as he stood with the hose in his hand drenching the Hunters with fluid, so they smashed into and around the drum and he felt them hit him with enough force to send him sprawling onto his back.

The machine's metal legs scurried over his body and face, entirely swamping him, and he smelled their metal bodies and hot circuits mixed with the stench of the fluid he had been spraying over them and he realised that it was over. He closed his eyes and waited for the unimaginable pain of his body being consumed by a million tiny pincers and...

He opened his eyes again.

The machines were no longer on his face but were still crawling all over his body. He dared to look down and saw them hungrily scooping the fluid into their mandibles as though gorging themselves. Around Qayin the other Marines, some weeping openly with fear, starting crying instead with relief as they realised that the drums of fluid were working.

'I don't believe it,' one of them gasped.

Qayin looked over at the drum and saw that it was lying on its side and no longer dispensing the fluid.

'Get on your feet!' he bellowed at the Marines. 'Start spraying that stuff wherever you find these little bastards! Draw the Hunters away from our people!'

The Marines bounded upright, brushing the Hunters off of themselves as they began manning the drums and rolling them toward the slaves pinned back against Arcadia. Qayin grabbed his rifle and backed away from the seething, roiling mound of Hunters all squabbling to reach the soil drenched with the fluid.

'Flame-throwers!' Qayin roared.

Two Marines carrying heavy cylinders on their backs and long-barrelled weapons immediately rushed into positon as another Marine sprayed more fluid over the Hunters, the last of them flocking in toward the Devlamine-drenched soil.

'Light 'em up!' Qayin shouted.

The flame-throwers burst into life and in an instant the entire seething mound of Hunters was consumed by a raging fireball of flame and smoke as the fluid ignited. Qayin staggered back and shielded his face from the inferno as he heard a strange shrieking noise, as though the countless machines were screaming in pain. The flames roared and the sound transformed into the whine and crackle of burning electrical circuits.

'Get to Arcadia!' he shouted to the Marines above the rumbling flames. 'Cut the Hunters off before it's too late!'

The Marines formed up, every pair of soldiers labouring to push the drums ahead of them as they rushed toward the Marines of Alpha Company and the hordes of terrified slaves. The Arcadia's massive hull was shuddering now as its huge engines began turning, and Qayin saw chunks of scaffolding tumble from the dizzying heights above to smash into the sodden earth around the panicked hordes in the valley below.

He looked to his left at the vast number of abandoned vessels just waiting to be taken and the boxes of heavy weapons arrayed around them, and then at Arcadia, the desperate slaves and fully-engaged Marines.

'You paid your dues, Qayin,' he murmured to himself. 'Time to leave.'

He turned to grab his rifle from where it lay, and then hesitated as he realised that the weapon had vanished. Qayin turned and saw Kordaz standing with the weapon in his grasp and aiming it directly at Qayin.

***

XXXVIII

'Fall back!'

General Bra'hiv's voice was almost drowned out by the ever-rising roar of the Arcadia's massive engines and the cacophony of plasma blasts crackling through the air.

Evelyn grabbed hold of Teera and they began retreating once more as the Hunters swarmed in toward them, the remaining Veng'en plunging into the Marines with blades flashing in the dawn light. Evelyn noted that the Veng'en assault raiders had now completed their deployment and were sitting with ramps open, presumably awaiting the return of the Veng'en warriors and hordes of infected humans.

The wave of Hunters was frighteningly deep, surging forward as if by momentum alone, broad enough to cut off any escape route to the parked ships and almost reaching the cliff edges to Evelyn's right. The only escape route back toward Arcadia was cut off by the frigate itself - moving past or beneath it as its engines wound up and with the danger of its hull braces collapsing upon take off was virtual suicide. Behind the frigate advanced further waves of Hunters relentlessly closing in on the beleaguered humans.

'There's no way out!' Evelyn shouted.

A Veng'en warrior broke through the Marines and leaped high into the air on its muscular legs before crashing down amid the surging slaves, arms and legs wind-milling as thick talons sliced into densely packed human flesh. Cries of pain and fear rang shrill above the deafening roar of Arcadia's engines and the nearby battle.

Evelyn rushed toward the Veng'en as it bit deeply into the shoulder of a fallen slave. She pressed her pistol against the back of its head and fired, blasted its brain from its skull in a bloody mess that sprayed down onto the injured man beneath it.

The man's eyes stared up at her, poisoned with horror, and Evelyn felt sickened as she saw a splatter of Infectors pouring from the dead Veng'en's mouth and into the slave's bloodied shoulder wound.

Evelyn did not hesitate as she aimed and fired at the man, killing him instantly and frying the Infectors swarming into his body.

'We can't hold them off for long!' Bra'hiv yelled.

Evelyn turned to look toward Qayin's Marines, and her heart skipped a beat as she saw in the distance Bravo Company charging toward them, a pillar of smoke and flame obscuring the parked vessels behind.

'They're on their way!' Evelyn replied as she turned and shot at another Veng'en as it ducked behind a low dune and then propelled itself into the air.

The creature rushed down at her and Evelyn hurled herself to one side as it landed with a dull thud right beside her. She rolled over and aimed up at the Veng'en only for her weapon to be batted aside with a single swipe of its muscular arm that numbed her as the Veng'en plunged down and tried to sink its teeth into her neck.

Evelyn screamed and twisted away from the creature's bite, but she was no match for the Veng'en's power as it leaned in, hot breath and razor sharp teeth brushing her skin.

Suddenly the beast was hauled aside and away from her. Evelyn gasped as she saw a huge Ogrin looming above her, its dull eyes shining with what looked like joy, the Veng'en held aloft in one gigantic hand as with the other the Ogrin tore its head off and hurled the macabre remains far across the barren land.

Evelyn scrambled to her feet as the Ogrin turned and lumbered toward the attacking Veng'en, blithely unaware of the danger to it from the swarming Hunters.

'Cover it!' Evelyn yelled as the Ogrin advanced.

Bra'hiv saw the Ogrin and began firing in support of it as it smashed its way past several Veng'en warriors. Plasma blasts hit it, leaving searing black welts of cauterised flesh smouldering as it moved, but the beast seemed in the grip of some kind of rage as it smashed its way forward.

Evelyn knew that she could do nothing to help the Ogrin, and moments later it plunged into the knee-deep wave of Hunters and smashed them aside with great sweeps of its giant arms. The Hunters were hurled by their thousands into the air like black water, as though the Ogrin were drowning in oil, and then they bit deep.

The Ogrin wailed in pain as the Hunters swarmed over it, consuming it alive. The bulky form of it was enveloped in black machines and as Evelyn watched it lost its shape as it was consumed and torn limb from limb, the deep, thunderous wails of pain lost to the seething symphony of the Legion's advance.

The Hunters flooded past the rapidly collapsing form of the Ogrin and swelled as they reached the Marine's defensive line.

'That's it!' Bra'hiv roared as he got up. 'Full retreat!'

The Marines broke ranks and fled, dashing toward Arcadia and firing as best they could against the handful of Veng'en still rushing at them. Evelyn began running too, and saw Qayin's men pouring down the hillside toward them with huge blue drums rolling before them. Several scrambled to a halt nearby and began waving Bra'hiv's Marines frantically past.

'Keep moving!' Evelyn yelled. 'You're not close enough to torch them!'

The Marines shook their heads and insistently waved Evelyn past. Alpha Company sprinted by in small groups, firing sporadically back at the Hunters as Bravo Company began spraying a thick, oddly-coloured fluid all over the ground nearby.

'What the hell is that?' Evelyn asked.

'Devlamine!' came the reply. 'With a little something extra!'

Evelyn searched for Qayin but she couldn't see him among the Marines. She hurried past and looked up at Arcadia's huge ion engines. It could only be moments before they turned fast enough to fully engage, and then the frigate would lift off.

'The ramps are still sealed!' Evelyn shouted.

'Get everybody as close as we can!' Bra'hiv ordered. 'We either get aboard or this ends here! It's up to the captain and Atlantia now!'

*

'Arcadia's lifting off!' Lael reported as the Atlantia's bridge was rocked by another salvo from the Veng'en cruiser. 'She'll be leaving orbit within minutes!'

Mikhain gripped the rail that surrounded the command platform, his gaze switching from one tactical display to another as he desperately tried to keep track of the situation. Arcadia was about to lift off, and already they were tracking a small armada of pirate craft blasting their way off Chiron IV to leave the system. Bra'hiv's Marines appeared to be pinned against the frigate's hull and surrounded by a sea of Hunters and advancing Veng'en. Commander Ry'ere was fully engaged with the Veng'en cruiser, the jamming from which was blocking communications along with the violent solar wind blasting across the system from the parent star.

If Andaim failed, Atlantia would not be able to take control of Arcadia.

If Sansin was killed, there would be nobody in command of Atlantia.

If Arcadia launched under Salim's command, Atlantia would have lost a valuable piece of Colonial war machinery and would likely find herself having to face battle again to regain her.

If the Veng'en cruiser kept hammering Atlantia with salvos, eventually her shields would fail and she would be destroyed.

'What should we do, captain?'

Lael's voice rang through Mikhain's mind and for an instant there was no sound. Mikhain felt the burden of her question, the heaviest end laden with the word *captain*. Mikhain realised that everybody on the bridge was watching him, waiting for him to respond, to reveal some hidden knowledge or clever tactic that would extricate them all from the dilemma that they were facing.

But there was no clever tactic, nor hidden knowledge.

Mikhain did not know what to do.

Atlantia shuddered as a thunderous blast hammered her hull and the engineering officer's alarmed tones rang out across the bridge.

'Fires through all aft decks! Coolant breach in port engines!'

'The Veng'en cruiser is attempting to cut off our line!' the helmsman bellowed. 'We'll be defenceless if she broadsides us from dead ahead!'

Mikhain blinked sweat from his eyes as he scanned the bridge, seeking some escape from his prison of command.

'Starboard batteries fully charged!' Ensign Scott reported.

Mikhain heard him, and in the desperate heat of the moment he latched on to the only command that he knew he could depend upon.

'Fire all batteries, target the cruiser,' he replied and then turned to the helmsman. 'Then take us out of here.'

'But the Veng'en cruiser?!' the helmsman gasped.

'We can't win the fight!' Mikhain roared as he pointed at the tactical officer. 'Switch all power to our functional engines and take us out of here!'

The helmsman gaped at Mikhain, his features ashen. 'Aye, captain,' he uttered in response.

Mikhain turned and saw the tactical display showing the battle raging on the surface. The captain was down there somewhere, as were many Marines, Evelyn and countless of Salim's slaves.

'Nobody can save everybody,' Mikhain murmured to himself.

A display showing the Veng'en cruiser above them distorted briefly as a targeting reticule appeared along with trajectory and range information. The glowing green digital display flashed suddenly red as the Atlantia's massive guns locked on to the huge Veng'en cruiser.

'Fire at will,' Mikhain snapped. 'Then disengage!'

*

'Watch that crossfire, Five!'

A searing blast of plasma fire ripped across Andaim's field of vision as two of the Veng'en cruiser's cannons fired salvos toward the distant shape of Atlantia, the flickering spheres of red energy zipping past alongside a Raython diving to attack the same pair of guns.

Reaper Five pulled out of its dive and raced across the surface of the cruiser, with its shadow and Andaim's Raython close behind.

'*I can't target the power lines, boss!*' the pilot reported. '*Too much interference!*'

'Where are the Corsairs?' Andaim called.

'*Sector seven low, five thousand cubits!*' came the response from the lead bomber pilot. '*There are too many Scythes for us to risk coming in any closer!*'

Andaim pulled up, his Raython soaring high above the battle between the two capital ships as he pulled over the top and examined the shape of the battle through the top of his canopy from an elevated perspective. He ignored the two Scythe fighters that followed him up, their cannons firing but missing his nimble fighter as he weaved left and right.

Instantly, he saw the Atlantia moving in response to the Veng'en cruiser, which was trying to reach a position where it could fire upon the surface while minimizing the return fire directed at it. But Atlantia was creeping away from the cruiser instead of defending against it.

With a sudden realisation Andaim realised that Atlantia was preparing to disengage.

'Oh no,' Andaim gasped as a mental image of Evelyn leaped into his mind. 'All craft, attack now, point-blank range!'

A chorus of disapproval roared back at Andaim from his pilots as they questioned his order, and he was forced to shout his reply.

'Atlantia's pulling out! Get that jamming down now or we'll lose everything!'

The entire flight of Raythons rolled away from their engagements and accelerated toward the Veng'en cruiser. Andaim saw the specks of the two Corsairs, escorted by four Raythons, change course and race toward the Veng'en ship.

Andaim's Raython roared toward the cruiser, the vast hull filling his vision as he came in under the giant plasma cannon's field of fire and too fast for them to track him and then broke hard right as he opened fire. His cannons pounded the hull before him with bright blasts, but he knew that the cruiser's powerful shields would prevent any serious damage from such small weapons.

He was about to pull away when he spotted movement across the surface of the hull, a mass of twisted, glittering metal around a massive ragged hole in the hull where Atlantia had hit the cruiser square-on with a salvo. The mass of metal looked like a black sea that was reflecting the glowing heavens around them, and for the briefest of moments Andaim's eyes were fixated upon it as he flashed by and rocketed up and away from the cruiser's surface.

His mind processed what he had seen, and suddenly he realised why the Veng'en had attacked them.

'The Legion is aboard,' he murmured to himself.

Andaim searched the battlefield around him, and then his eyes settled upon the immense glowing nebula filling the heavens. His gaze switched to the planet below them, Chiron IV: the perfect place for humans to hide out, and exactly the kind of place the Legion would search for them. Yet it had not come here.

And suddenly Andaim knew why.

***

XXXIX

'Kordaz,' Qayin greeted the Veng'en.

Kordaz remained stationary, his huge muscular bulk blocking Qayin's access to the nearest spacecraft, the heavily armed X-shaped cruiser that Salim Phaeon had used as his command ship.

'Going somewhere, Qayin?' The Veng'en jerked his head backward slightly to indicate the ship behind them. 'I wonder, if I had waited a little longer, whether I'd find that you'd rolled a barrel or two of that Devlamine into one of these ships for future use?'

Qayin glanced up at the ship and then at Kordaz.

'It's tainted goods,' he replied. 'Mixed with flammable fuel as a weapon against...'

'It's filterable,' Kordaz cut him off. 'Just right for selling off to the highest bidder, and you get a ship out of it too. Not a bad plan, especially if you still have a supply of crystals with which to start your supply again.'

Qayin looked over his shoulder at his men now fighting the hordes of the Legion, their flamethrowers glowing in the distance beneath Arcadia's massive hull.

'Too far,' Kordaz told him. 'They'd never get to you in time and I don't suppose they know that you're intending to flee without them anyway.'

Qayin looked back at the Veng'en. 'What the hell would you know about it? I was intending to fly down there and pick them up.'

'Then why didn't you fly down there to drop them off, Qayin? Would've saved some time, not to mention a few lives.'

The Marine's jaw split in a wide grin. 'You know, for a Veng'en you're quite sharp. How about you join me and we get the hell out of this mess together?'

Kordaz flicked the plasma rifle's safety-catch off and the weapon hummed into life.

'How about you get on your knees?'

Qayin's smile faded as he slowly got down onto his knees on the ground, then raised his hands behind his head and into his thick gold and blue locks.

'We can work this out, Kordaz,' he said quickly. 'Ain't no reason to put a round in my head.'

'Who says I'm going to kill you?' Kordaz asked as he approached Qayin's kneeling form. 'Maybe I'll just slice you up a little, then take you back to Atlantia and learn why you sold me out to Salim Phaeon?'

Qayin's eyes narrowed. 'You got sold out?'

Kordaz kept the rifle pointed at Qayin. 'Barely got out with my life.'

'Nobody knew you were here,' Qayin replied. 'First we knew the captain had an ace up his sleeve was when the generators blew.'

'You're dealing, Qayin,' Kordaz said. 'I saw you in the sanctuary. I was right above you when you threatened the civilian and you never knew a thing about it.'

Qayin's shoulders sagged as he realised that he was cornered.

'You seriously give enough of a damn?'

Kordaz leaned closer to Qayin. 'They gave me a home and you're trying to destroy it. What do you think?'

Qayin's arm flashed around and in his bunched fist was a slim, sharp blade that must have been tucked into his locks. Qayin bashed the rifle aside as he shot to his feet and slammed the blade into Kordaz's chest.

The Veng'en shrieked in pain as he leaped backward, the rifle swinging back toward Qayin. Qayin dove forward and grabbed the handle of the blade as Kordaz plunged onto his back and slammed down onto the ground. Qayin landed on top of him and twisted the blade from side to side as he searched for an artery or one of Kordaz's hearts to puncture.

Kordaz's massive arms grabbed Qayin and heaved him aside, the Marine tumbling away and yanking the knife from the Veng'en's chest as he went. Kordaz scrambled to his feet, pain wracking his chest and one hand grasping the wound as Qayin came up onto his feet with the blade held close to his thigh. His tattoos glowed malevolently as he stalked toward Kordaz.

'You should have joined the Mark of Qayin,' the Marine growled. 'Better chance of survival.'

'You'd cut out your own mother's heart if the price was right,' Kordaz hissed back at him. 'I'd rather die.'

'So be it.'

Qayin lunged forward and the blade flashed toward Kordaz's throat. The Veng'en leaped up and to one side, the blade narrowly missing him as he landed with a deep thud. Off balance, Kordaz staggered as he coughed a globule of blood onto the waving grasses beneath them.

Qayin grinned, his head low and his eyes cruel as he stepped in.

Kordaz staggered backward out of range, giving ground to the Marine as his lungs began to pulse painfully with every single breath.

*

Teera ran up the hill through the swathes of smoke as Arcadia's massive engines made the ground tremble beneath her feet. Her chest heaved and her lungs ached as she ran. The Atlantia's level decks were not conducive to exercise of any real merit, and running up the rugged hillside in a gale was virtually impossible.

Teera staggered to the crest of the hillside and rested her hands on her knees as she bowed over at the waist, struggling to fill her lungs with enough air to continue. Behind her, the Marines she had passed with the blue barrels were hosing Hunters down in their millions with flamethrowers, scorching the ground in great swathes of apocalyptic flame and smoke. The whine of the engines and the crackle of gunfire urged her to push on, and through blurry eyes as she looked up she saw a pair of Raythons parked nearby amid spacecraft of various types.

Teera stumbled toward the nearest Raython, her legs numb with fatigue and her throat tight, the wind across the hillside blowing with enough force to almost knock her off her feet. She was almost at the Raython when she heard a shriek that rang on the cold air, and she looked to her left to see a Marine locked in mortal combat with a Veng'en.

*

Qayin stalked closer to Kordaz, the knife light in his grasp, the blade wicked and glinting in the sunlight that flickered between the low-scudding clouds. Kordaz backed away, his chest heaving and blood spilling in copious amounts from the wound. His yellow eyes were pinched with pain, the irises tiny points of black focused entirely on Qayin.

Kordaz backed into the landing strut of the big X-shaped cruiser behind him and Qayin lunged forward and jabbed the blade directly toward Kordaz's throat. The Veng'en's right arm swept across and smashed Qayin's blade aside as Kordaz jerked sideways, grabbed Qayin's collar and smashed him into the landing strut. The Veng'en's immense strength pinned Qayin's chest to the strut, preventing him from bringing the blade to bear as Kordaz leaned in close, all pretence of pain and fear vanished.

'You're the kind of scum that my kind and I used to enjoy slicing to pieces in front of their friends, Qayin.'

Qayin glanced at the Veng'en's chest wound and saw the the blood was already congealing in thick clumps around it, the flesh able to regenerate far faster than that of humans. He looked up at Kordaz in time to see the Veng'en force onto his stoic features something approaching a grin, his fangs bared.

'I should have killed you long ago,' he growled. 'I won't delay any longer, and it will be me leaving aboard this ship.'

Kordaz's fearsome teeth lunged toward Qayin's face and then a terrible heat seared Qayin's neck as a plasma blast smashed into Kordaz. The Veng'en howled in agony as he was hurled aside and the smell of burning flesh scorched Qayin's nose. Qayin whirled to see a Colonial pilot with pale blue skin standing nearby, a plasma pistol held double-handed in her grip and smouldering from the blast.

Qayin looked down and saw Kordaz sprawled upon the damp earth, the flesh of his chest crackling as it burned.

'You okay?' the pilot asked.

Qayin nodded, his heart thumping inside his chest as he turned to the pilot. 'I owe you one,' he said as he pushed away from the landing strut.

'The Veng'en are infected,' the pilot reported. 'The Legion found a way to get to them.'

Qayin nodded and glanced down at Kordaz's body. 'Damn near got me.'

'I've got to go,' the pilot said, and before Qayin could respond she whirled and sprinted away toward two Raythons parked nearby.

Qayin turned as he heard the deafening roar of the Arcadia's engines reach a new height and the huge frigate began to lift off. From his vantage point he could see the massive hull cradles detaching and falling over with deafening crashes as they were impacted by the frigate's thrusters.

Qayin looked down at Kordaz's smouldering body, and then he smiled and threw the doomed Veng'en a mock salute. Qayin whirled and dashed up the cruiser's ramp. As he reached for the switch to close the ramp, he glimpsed the sight of his Marines valiantly fighting off the hordes of Hunters with an apocalyptic blaze of flame and smoke.

Qayin watched them only for a moment longer before he closed the ramp.

***

XL

'Do as I say!' Andaim shouted. 'Maintain orbit!'

Andaim's Raython raced away from the Veng'en cruiser, pursued by a volley of plasma fire that rocketed past his fighter as he weaved left and right to confuse the enemy's aim.

'Negative!' came Mikhain's reply. *'Atlantia cannot withstand much more!'*

'The Veng'en ship is infected!' Andaim yelled. 'Taron was right! The Legion is affected by the star's cosmic rays. It's why they haven't attempted to infect this system before, and how Salim Phaeon's pirates took Arcadia! Some of her crew must have become infected and the rest abandoned her! There was no battle!'

Andaim rolled his Raython over and pulled in toward Atlantia, two squadrons of Raythons following him and forming a protective patrol around the frigate. A cloud of Scythe fighters rocketed in pursuit, plasma shots glowing red as they sought to hit the fleeing Raythons.

'Then how come the Veng'en ship's Legion isn't being fried by the cosmic rays?!' Mikhain asked.

'They're staying inside Chiron IV's magnetic field,' Andaim replied. 'It's allowing them to remain here longer.'

'And what if Arcadia is under Salim's control?!' Mikhain demanded. *'Even if we can escape the Veng'en, if the jamming is broken Salim will be in a position to hack and attack us!'*

'Deal with one damned problem at a time!' Andaim insisted. 'Maintain orbit and protect those on the surface from a Veng'en bombardment!'

'Or we can flee, escape the cruiser and save Atlantia!' Mikhain countered. *'If what you say is true, they can't follow us!'*

'They'll catch up with you eventually once their damage is repaired!' Andaim snapped back. 'We must finish this, now! If we don't give the captain more time and win this battle, the war is over! Atlantia is too far gone to repair her damage, Mikhain!'

Andaim watched as Atlantia was pounded by another broadside from the Veng'en cruiser, and he heard the transmission break up as the immense energy interference threatened to short out Atlantia's entire electrical system. The XO's voice broke through, distorted against crackling static.

'... direct hit ... port nacelle... overloa... weapons down...'

Andaim looked back and forth from the Veng'en cruiser and the stricken Atlantia, fires glowing through her hull like city lights viewed from a distance at night, and he knew that there was no longer any time to defend against the Veng'en cruiser.

Atlantia was already down and out.

'Reaper Flight!' he called. 'Cover me!'

A flurry of affirmatives crossed the communications channel as Andaim rolled his Raython and pulled into a turn that placed the Veng'en cruiser right on his nose. He scanned his instruments and saw that her shields were still at thirty per cent, weak against a frigate like Atlantia, but still far too strong for his own plasma cannons to pierce.

A shower of bright red plasma shots raced up toward him and he banked left and right, rolling hard to confuse the enemy's aim.

Their shields are too strong boss!' one of the other pilots called. *Your weapons won't break through!*'

'I know,' Andaim replied. 'I'm not going to use them. Just keep those Scythes off my back!'

Andaim watched as the huge cruiser grew rapidly in size before him, the plasma shots rocketing past his Raython as he weaved and aimed at a ridge of sensors high on the cruiser's hull. He noted huge gashes where the Atlantia's guns had penetrated the hull, fires and clouds of floating debris spilling from within. Amid the ragged wounds, machines moved, attempting to repair the damage. Countless machines.

Reaper One, pull up!'

Andaim did not reply, instead focusing his every sense on the surface of the Veng'en cruiser. He flew his Raython close to the cruiser's bow and then turned and flew low over her hull, heading toward her stern at maximum velocity. Suddenly the massive ship seemed to leap in size before him, filling his vision as his Raython rocketed toward the sensor array. For a brief instant Andaim saw every tiny detail of the array before him. Hundreds of tiny blisters, each skinned with metal far thinner than the rest of the ship's hull to allow signals both in and out. They ran in a line away from him down the hull, like a runway that no craft could use. His instruments blinked out at the last moment, their circuitry blown by the tremendous electro-magentic radiation blazing from the sensor array, and his communication link switched off.

Andaim let go of his controls and gripped hold of his seat as though doing so might save him from the impact.

*

'Sheilds at eight per cent! We can't hold position any longer!'

256

Mikhain heard Lael's cry and saw the tactical display showing Atlantia's systems at critical overload and the hull breached on four levels.

'If we move, the captain dies and so do the rest of the people down there!' he yelled.

'Arcadia's lifting off!' Ensign Scott shouted above the din of alarms echoing around the ship.

'Maintain a sensor watch on her!' Mikhain ordered. 'Prepare main guns!'

'We can't assault the surface ourselves!' the tactical officer cried. 'We don't have enough power to defend against the Veng'en attack!'

Mikhain's mind screamed for release from the pain of the impossible choice facing him. The chaos, the conflict and the noise swelled in his mind until suddenly everything fell quiet. It was as though he could not hear a thing but for the immense silence humming through his overloaded brain.

In his mind's eye, three simple facts stared at him, beckoned him to make his choice.

We can afford to lose Arcadia.

We can afford to lose the captain, the crew members and the slaves on the surface.

But we cannot afford to lose Atlantia.

We cannot afford to lose Atlantia. He was now her captain, and if they broke orbit the Veng'en cruiser would not be able to give chase. Risk everything in the remote hope that Captain Sansin would succeed in gaining control of Arcadia, or guarantee Atlantia's escape and live to fight another day? The captain had said it himself, *do not risk losing Atlantia.*

Mikhain closed his eyes and thought only for a moment longer. The hell with Commander Ry'ere.

'Helm!' Mikhain yelled. 'Break left, disengage immediately!'

'Aye, cap'n!'

Mikhain whirled to the Ensign Scott. 'Aim all weapons at Arcadia and blow her from the skies if she comes within range!'

Ensign Scott stared blankly at Mikhain, his reply monotone as though spoken by rote.

'Aye, captain.'

Mikhain saw the tactical display switch to focus on the shape of Arcadia as she lifted off from the compound dock far below them on the surface, the pixelated image clear enough to deduce that she was already clear of the ground and moving. Around her, pinned down, were hundreds of human beings.

The helmsman engaged Atlantia's main engines and the frigate surged out from beneath the huge Veng'en cruiser. Almost immediately Lael called out.

'She's charging weapons and targeting the surface captain!'

'Helm, maximum power!'

The helmsman leaned across his console and pushed the throttles wide open.

'Belay that order!' Lael cried out. 'The jamming signal has been broken!'

Mikhain's eyes widened as in the same instant the sounds of the pilots of the Raythons broke through, the radio static clearing.

The Veng'en's sensor array has been destroyed!' one of them yelled. *'Get Arcadia up here now!'*

Mikhain's brain could not comprehend how the fighters and bombers had gotten through, but he did not waste time finding out. He whirled to Lael.

'Hack the ship's systems, now!'

'Signal's already being emitted!' Lael replied. 'Computers are accessing Arcadia's control networks!'

'Helm, reverse course, engage the Veng'en cruiser, full attack!' Mikhain snapped.

'Aye sir!'

'Tactical, open fire as soon as our cannons come to bear!'

'Aye sir!' Ensign Scott replied.

Mikhain clenched his fists as he felt the Atlantia heel over once more, swinging around to broadside the Veng'en ship.

'How long before Arcadia reaches us?' he demanded.

'She's climbing now,' Lael replied. 'Her trajectory will take her into orbit far from our position. Salim must be in control of her, and he's too far out for our signals system to hack the controls!'

Mikhain grasped at his hair. On the surface below, hundreds of innocent lives that he could not abandon. Far away, Arcadia slipping away from them with her massive arsenal of guns. Ahead, he saw the Veng'en cruiser's massive cannons open fire.

'Intercept, now! Maximum power!' he yelled.

The Atlantia surged forward as the shower of massive plasma charges rained down toward the planet below.

'Brace for impact!' Mikhain bellowed as the displays showed the Veng'en broadside rocketing down toward the surface and Atlantia rushing in to intercept them.

The salvo of blasts smashed down across Atlantia's hull and the entire vessel shuddered as the lights flickered erratically and panels were blasted from the bridge walls as circuits overloaded and sprayed showers of sparks across display consoles.

'Hull breach astern!' Lael called. 'Fires through multiple decks, hull integrity at twelve per cent! Another salvo and we're done for!'

Mikhain saw a handful of plasma shots race past Atlantia and rocket down toward the surface below.

'Wait,' Mikhain ordered. 'We can hold on, just a little longer! Helm, maintain position but keep jinking!'

'Aye sir!'

'And keep hitting her with everything we've got left!' Mikhain bellowed. 'We've got to give Captain Sansin more time!'

***

Dean Crawford

XLI

'Take cover!'

Evelyn heard General Bra'hiv's bellowed command even as the shrill din from Arcadia's enormous engines shattered the air around them, the already turbulent winds of Chiron's atmosphere amplified by the gigantic intakes sucking in vast quantities of air.

Evelyn ducked down as the wind howled past her, hundreds of others mirroring her actions. Ahead, she saw clouds of Hunters being sucked up off the ground and whipped upward toward the huge engines.

The massive docking cradles groaned and shrieked as metal under tension was warped by the shifting weight of the huge frigate above them. She tried to aim her pistol straight at the Veng'en warriors advancing from cover to cover on their position, but she could not draw an accurate bead as the gusting winds tugged at her body and arm.

'Where's Teera?!' Ishira cried out.

Evelyn could not reply as the wind buffeted her head, and then she heard the Marines cry out together in unison.

'Fire in the hole!'

A flame-throwing soldier opened up on the liquid drenching the Hunters, the jet of flame licking out and caressing the machines with brutal efficiency. Even though the winds were racing past, the heat was enough to spark the fluid into flame and suddenly the entire wave of Hunters was transformed into a sea of burning machines, heat haze rippling upward from their surface.

'Get down!'

Evelyn threw her hands over her head and crouched down as the flames crackled overhead, the Ogrin around them fleeing in pain as the super-heated air scorched their faces and burned their clothes. The dense, acrid smoke soared upward in billowing veils toward Arcadia's huge engine intakes, thousands of burning Hunters aglow with flame flying up into the air with them as Evelyn squinted against the force of the wind and saw Arcadia's hull lift off its massive cradles and begin to ascend.

'Get flat on the ground!' she cried out around her. 'Lay flat!'

Hundreds of slaves within earshot dropped onto their bellies as Arcadia's main engines engaged and the huge ship eased forward, thousands of atmospheric thrusters blasting jets of vapour at supersonic speed in support of the massive internal anti-gravity gyroscopes that enabled Arcadia to lift off. Evelyn, her eyes squinted against the immense force of the wind, saw clouds of flaming Hunters blasted through the air over their heads like flaming meteors to vanish into the distance.

'We're out of Devlamine fluid!' a Marine shouted in desperation.

Arcadia's thrusters blasted downward into the deep valley of her docking bay and then upwards out of it, clouds of dust and rock spraying up into the sky as she lifted off and thundered away over the cliffs and the ocean. Clouds of debris, vortexes of dust and whorls of burning Hunters swirled through the skies around them as they crouched and watched the frigate escape.

'Enemy front!'

Bra'hiv's cry alerted the Marines as the remaining swathes of Hunters, immune to distraction from their murderous primary goal, surged ever forward as the deafening roar of Arcadia's engines began to fade away. The Marines opened fire again but there was little chance of them holding back the dense sea of machines sweeping toward them.

Evelyn turned and saw more Hunters swarming in across the landscape behind them, running like oil down watercourses and flattening seas of grass as they advanced in their millions.

The Marines switched positions, dashing to encircle the entire crowd of slaves and Ogrin as they began drawing together and away from the advancing machines. The densely packed slaves stood shoulder to shoulder with each other and stared wide eyed as they were encircled by the Hunters. The entire field was littered with the dead bodies of countless Veng'en, their corpses being consumed and torn apart as the Hunters advanced.

'This is it!' Bra'hiv roared.

Evelyn suddenly felt a bizarre sense of calm descend upon her. Faced with certain death and with no possible means of escape, it was as if a terrible burden had been released from her shoulders. Evelyn lowered her pistol, realising that it was useless against the massive army of machines bearing down upon them.

It was over.

'Let's take as many of them down with us as we can!' Bra'hiv yelled.

Evelyn watched as the Marines opened fire as one, and then suddenly a series of massive plasma blasts ripped through the Hunters. Evelyn's eyes widened and she whirled to see a Raython hovering nearby, its engines whining as it fired repeated blasts into the sea of Hunters. Evelyn felt a wave of relief as she recognised Teera's face in the cockpit.

'It's not enough!' Bra'hiv yelled.

Evelyn was about to wave her arms at Teera and try to indicate that she should clear a path for them as best she could when another series of blasts hammered the Hunters around them. The plasma rounds thundered closer and closer as cries of alarm went up from the crowd, explosions rippling toward Evelyn and churning the earth and with it thousands of the nanites.

Evelyn almost ducked as a nearby blast showered the crowd with debris and a ship rushed out of the distance and rocketed overhead, low enough that she felt a rush of wind as it blasted by and pulled up into a steep climb.

The Phoenix rolled over and dove back down, her powerful cannons firing in all directions at the Hunters as it lowered its landing struts and swept in to touch down. Teera's Raython switched position and raked the ground leading to the Phoenix with plasma fire, scorching the soil and blasting Hunters clear.

'Everybody on me!' Bra'hiv yelled. 'Marines to the rearguard!'

Evelyn dashed to Bra'hiv's side as the Marines repositioned again, covering the side of the crowd opposite the landing freighter. The Phoenix touched down on the uneven ground even as her boarding ramp was lowering, and Evelyn glimpsed Taron Forge already there, his pistol drawn as he fired randomly at the nearest clusters of Hunters and waved frantically for them to board his ship.

'Covering fire!' Bra'hiv ordered.

The Marines fired by sections, rifles and flame-throwers blazing as they held the Hunters at bay and withdrew toward the Phoenix. Evelyn fired at anything small, black and metallic, and saw from the corner of her eye Ishira and Stefan with plasma rifles cradled in their grasp and firing a steady stream of blasts to either side of the crowd.

'Get aboard the Phoenix!' Evelyn insisted. 'Go, now!'

The slaves poured past them into the freighter, and Evelyn searched desperately for some sign of Kordaz amid the terrified throng, but she could not see the Veng'en and she could not see Qayin either.

'Where's Qayin?!' she cried out to Bra'hiv.

'We can't stay!' the general replied. 'Get aboard, now! That's an order!'

Evelyn scanned the smouldering masses of Hunters, already being crawled over by their seemingly endless surviving brethren, and then she spotted a narrow course through their metallic corpses toward her own parked Raython high on the hillside.

Evelyn whirled and sprinted away from the Phoenix toward the gap. Bra'hiv's bellowed commands followed her but she did not hear them as she dashed between heaps of metal corpses, glowing red-hot where plasma blasts had hit them and melted them to slag. Thick, acrid grey smoke clogged the air around her as she ran, aching in her lungs as she hit the slope and began climbing toward the parked craft.

The whine of Teera's Raython followed her and she heard plasma blasts strike the ground close behind. She dared to look over her shoulder and saw Hunters streaming in pursuit from all directions. The Phoenix raised her ramp and blasted off into the skies above, packed with surviving slaves and the compound now devoid of humans. She ran harder, her chest heaving as she forged up the hillside and broke free atop the ridge.

Her Raython was still where she had landed, but almost immediately she saw the body sprawled across the ground nearby. Evelyn turned on instinct and sprinted toward it, fear clogging her lungs as she realised that it was Kordaz and that several Hunters were scattered across his body and around him, probably gusted up here when Arcadia took off.

Evelyn screamed as she smashed the machines off his body, stamping on them as they landed and firing her pistol at their damaged bodies until they no longer moved.

She slumped down alongside the Veng'en and looked at the massive wound in his chest. The flesh was blackened and scarred, wisps of blue smoke drifting on the wind. Kordaz's eyes were open but his breathing was shallow and weak.

'Can you hear me?' Evelyn shouted above the wind, checking behind her to ensure they were not about to be overrun by more Hunters.

Kordaz's mouth gaped and he tried to speak, but she could tell that he was too weak. As he stared at her, she saw small black specks drifting behind his eyes and with terrible certainty she knew that Kordaz was infected. She glanced at the dead Hunters around her and recalled that they often carried a small number of Infectors inside them, the better to spread the Legion into other species.

Evelyn tried to drag Kordaz toward her Raython, but his body was far too heavy to move even one cubit. She turned as she heard the Phoenix's engines whine into the distance and Teera's Raython turn to follow the freighter. Below, down the slope, she saw the remaining Hunters swarming toward her as Teera fired a few last blasts down upon them.

Kordaz's powerful hand grabbed Evelyn and pulled her close. Even above the roar of the Raython's engines and plasma cannons, she heard the Veng'en speak with the last of his strength.

'Beware, Qayin.'

Kordaz slumped back onto the ground as his eyes rolled up into their sockets. Evelyn stared at the Veng'en for a long moment, and then a terrific blast smashed into the dock below her. She whirled in shock as the massive plasma barrage hammered into the ground and excavated a huge crater, the debris rocketing upward into the sky as the shockwave hit her and hurled her backwards.

Evelyn tumbled over and slammed into the ground, then struggled to her feet and dashed for her Raython as from the skies above a rain of massive red plasma blasts burst through the clouds and smashed down into the ground.

The shockwaves battered the air about her and rang in her ears as she vaulted into the Raython's cockpit and hit a row of switches concealed beneath the control panel. The fighter's emergency launch sequence initiated, the cockpit closing and shielding her from the deafening noise outside as the controls glowed into life and the engines spun-up under emergency generator power.

Evelyn did not even fasten her harness as she grabbed the control column and throttle and hauled the Raython into the air. She pointed the nose at the sky, away from the shower of giant plasma rounds as she threw the throttles open and the Raython accelerated away from the cliff tops and toward the boiling clouds above.

As she climbed, the Raython shuddered as the shockwaves continued to pound the fighter, the entire pirate compound vaporised behind her in a massive inferno of flame. Evelyn saw towering thunderheads soaring into the skies, the aurora as bright now in daylight as it had been at night, and she knew that any forms of life on Chiron IV were now doomed.

***

Dean Crawford

XLII

Idris Sansin dashed through Arcadia's corridors as he sprinted toward the War Room, his footfalls echoing through the empty ship. He slowed as he reached the heavily fortified chamber that contained the War Room and managed to get his breathing under control as he eased his way around the corner.

The War Room was unguarded, much as he had hoped that it would be. An outsider like Salim Phaeon would have little knowledge of the interior of a Colonial warship, other than the holding cells that he had likely often frequented.

Idris hurried across to the entrance and accessed the control panel set into the wall alongside the double-doors. He entered from memory his security codes, those designed specifically to allow the captain of any Colonial vessel access to another vessel's War Room, and to his delight the double doors hissed open.

Idris stepped inside and came up short as he stared down the barrel of a rifle.

'Greetings, captain.'

Salim Phaeon's little black eyes glared back at Idris, a smile spreading across his evil features as he gestured to the secondary bridge around them where four of his piratical henchmen lounged with pistols all pointed at Idris. 'I knew you would find us here.'

One of the pirates got up lazily and rested the barrel of his pistol against Idris's head.

Idris swallowed. 'How did you know? How did you get in here?'

Salim shrugged as he examined the tips of his fingers. 'It's amazing what you learn when you do business with the son of a famous Colonial Commander.'

Idris briefly closed his eyes. 'Taron.'

'Indeed,' Salim replied. 'Not quite cut from the mold of his father, wouldn't you agree? Taron pushes a hard bargain but I knew that your people would try to take control of Arcadia as soon as we left Chiron. I felt that the access codes to her War Room were a suitable trade for Taron's life.'

'He'd betray you just as easily,' Idris shot back.

'That doesn't seem to be the case here though, does it captain? In fact, I believe that Taron's ship has already left Chiron IV and yours is about to be blown to hell. We disabled the Boarding Protocol from here, and the rest of my men have the main bridge under their control.'

Salim nodded to one of his men and the pirate casually flipped a switch. A display screen flickered into life and showed Atlantia heavily engaged with a massive Veng'en cruiser. Idris could see with barely a moment's glance that his ship was on the verge of being destroyed.

'How long, do you think, captain?' Salim asked. 'Before her hull fractures and she is lost? In that orbit, she'll burn up within a few hours. Such a shame. The only thing preventing your people from using Arcadia to save the day is the Veng'en jamming.'

Salim grinned again and walked to a console before him.

'Would you like to say goodbye?' Salim asked. 'We're linked so that we can get a signal through.'

Idris said nothing as Salim opened a communication link with Atlantia. Another screen flickered into life and there appeared an image of Mikhain, the transmission broken and cluttered as the ship was battered by the Veng'en cruiser. The XO's face was flushed with stress and his forehead beaded with sweat.

'Salim!' Mikhain snapped. 'We need assistance, right now!'

'My my, Mikhain,' Salim purred in response. 'You cry for *my* help?'

'People are dying!' Mikhain snapped. 'You've nothing to lose by helping!'

Salim sighed.

'True,' he agreed, 'but then I have nothing to gain either. I thought that you would like to bid farewell to your captain,' Salim said.

The pirate king waved Idris to join him. Idris walked to stand alongside the fat little man, and saw the dismay in Mikhain's eyes as the XO saw his captain a captive on the only ship that could save them.

Idris lifted his chin, sucked in a breath and managed a smile.

'Disengage from the battle, XO,' he ordered. 'You can't save everybody, so now it's time to save yourselves.'

Mikhain's features were twisted with indecision, a feeling that Idris had come to know well over decades of command.

'There is no easy option, Mikhain,' Idris added, feeling the XO's pain. 'We'll never win every battle.'

'But what about the war?' Mikhain asked.

Idris smiled. 'It's your war now, XO.'

Salim affected an expression of sympathy as he looked at the Executive Officer on the screen. 'Maybe that younger fellow should have remained in command after all? It's been nice knowing you, Mikhain. You probably only have minutes to live, so I'll wish you good luck. Oh, actually, no I won't. May you and your entire crew rot in hell.'

Mikhain's anguish suddenly transformed into a grin that radiated out of the screen at Salim.

'You first,' he hissed.

Salim's podgy features twisted with confusion and then a series of deafening plasma blasts screeched out in the War Room and he whirled to see his henchmen cut down in a blaze of rifle fire.

Idris squinted and flinched as a plasma blast raced past him and smashed into the pirate holding a gun to his head. Idris ducked as the stricken man was flung onto his back on the deck, his back a smouldering mass of cauterised tissue and burning clothes.

Four heavily armed Marines burst into the War Room, their weapons firing controlled bursts that cut one of Salim's men down with brutal efficiency as Lieutenant C'rairn led them from cover to cover, the giant form of Corporal Djimon following him. Idris shielded his eyes against the blasts and then spotted Salim as he fired randomly at the Marines. They ducked down for cover, and Salim dashed past them and vanished into the corridor outside as C'rairn and his men kept firing at the remaining pirates.

Idris scrambled to his feet and ran in pursuit of Slaim, bursting through a cloud of acrid smoke. He hurled himself against the far wall of the corridor as Salim fired at him with a pistol. The blast zipped by Idris with scant inches to spare and scalded the skin on his neck. The captain winced as he hugged the wall of the corridor and peeked out.

Salim was already running, heading for the elevator banks. Idris pushed off the wall and ran in pursuit, the sound of battle within the War Room fading behind him. He could hear Salim's footfalls ahead, but Idris was unarmed and he knew that if he got too close Salim would kill him at the first opportunity.

Idris reached the elevator banks and Salim fired from within one of the elevators. The plasma shot smashed into the wall beside Idris's face and he ducked aside as white-hot plasma sprayed past him in glowing globules. The elevator door hissed shut and Idris leaped out to see the elevator's deck indicators climbing.

Salim only had one play left, and that was to seal the bridge and get Arcadia as far away from Chiron as he could before attempting to regain control of the ship. Idris knew that even if the pirate managed to do so it would be useless – an Atlantia Class frigate required a minimum crew of a hundred people and Salim was aboard with barely a dozen men, half of whom were likely already dead. Most likely, Salim would set a course for other hidden lairs in order to swell his numbers aboard Arcadia with more slaves and the pirates that controlled them. Aboard a ship as large and powerful as Arcadia, Salim would become the undisputed king of all pirates, able to wander and plunder at will.

Idris knew that he could wait for C'rairn and the other Marines to back him up, but he also knew that Atlantia was in critical condition and that every second counted. He also knew that Salim would not fail to wait for him at the bridge deck and blast him should he take an elevator up.

Idris thought for a moment and then he began unzipping his uniform.

*

'Fires on decks twelve through nineteen!'

Lael's voice cried out above the din of battle as Atlantia was pounded by another broadside from the Veng'en cruiser.

'We're losing power to the cannons!' Ensign Scott yelled. 'Plasma lines are ruptured aft of the launch bay!'

'Divert all power to remaining shields!' Mikhain snapped.

The tactical officer scrambled to re-route the power from the weapons to the shields as Mikhain turned to the tactical display and watched the huge form of the Veng'en cruiser loom into position, ever closer to the Atlantia's battered hull.

'They're charging main guns,' Ensign Scott said, no longer shouting as a tone of resignation poisoned his words. 'One more salvo and we'll lose everything, captain.'

Mikhain glanced at the screen showing the surface and then at the Veng'en cruiser. Lael's voice reached him as though from afar.

'There's nothing more that we can do, captain,' she said.

'Where is Arcadia?' Mikhain asked.

'Four thousand cubits, quadrant four, elevation minus three,' Lael replied. 'She's leaving orbit!'

'Are there any remaining people on the surface?!'

'None that we can detect, captain,' Lael reported. 'But our sensors are out of action.'

Mikhain gripped the rail surrounding the command platform and sucked in a deep lung full of air that spilled from his body laden with the regret and dismay that poisoned his innards.

'Helm,' he ordered. 'Full power, take us out!'

'Aye, cap'ain!'

Atlantia surged as her engines engaged and she accelerated away from the Veng'en cruiser even as the massive vessel's starboard batteries opened up with a brilliant crescendo of bright red plasma charges. The salvo of shots rocketed toward Atlantia and plunged past her stern as she accelerated out of their way.

Mikhain watched as the lethal barrage plunged down and vanished into tiny red twinkles of light racing down toward the compound far below, and felt as though his humanity were plunging down toward unknown depths with them.

His first command action, and he had failed.

'Captain?'

Ensign Scott's voice reached Mikhain as though from a great distance as the din of battle vanished to be replaced with a deep silence upon the bridge. The only sound was the tinkling of scorched circuitry and the distant wail of alarms echoing through the huge frigate.

'Yes?' Mikhain asked vacantly.

'Orders, sir?'

Mikhain stared blanky at the tactical display and then he focused on Arcadia as she climbed away from the planet's surface toward orbit. Salim would be aboard her, the frigate the perfect escape vessel if Mikhain could take control of her. If not, he had another idea.

'Target Arcadia,' he hissed with sudden rage. 'Hit her with everything we have left.'

'She's battle-ready,' the tactical officer replied. 'We're in no better shape to engage her than we are to turn back and...'

'Hit her, now!' Mikhain yelled. 'Maximum combat speed, a full broadside as we pass!'

Nobody on the bridge moved.

'Why, captain?' Lael asked. 'What purpose would that achieve?'

Mikhain clenched his fist by his sides as he replied.

'I want the Veng'en to attack her instead of us,' he hissed in reply. 'They'll pursue us, will they not?'

He gestured to the image of the compound on Chiron's surface, the image flaring with blinding flashes of light as the Veng'en broadside ploughed into it and churned the earth into an unrecognisable, burning field of destruction.

'They have destroyed the human presence on the surface and now they'll seek to finish us off,' he went on. 'Let's give them Salim instead and make good our escape, shall we?'

The helmsman smiled. 'Aye, captain.'

'Wait,' Lael said.

Mikhain turned as the communications officer scanned her instruments and flipped several switches.

'Her frequencies are open,' she announced. 'We can hail her.'

Mikhain ground his teeth in his skull. 'Salim will not negotiate with us, we know that. I want him dead.'

'So do I, captain,' Lael said. 'But let's make sure we've tried everything before we attack her. Arcadia could finish the Veng'en cruiser off, if she can be turned.'

Mikhain felt his anger rising but somehow he managed to contain it.

'Do it,' he said, 'open a channel to her bridge.'

***

XLIII

Salim Phaeon burst out onto the bridge deck as soon as the elevator doors opened, his chest heaving with the exertion of his flight from the War Room. He paced back from the elevator banks and saw that another elevator was making its way up to the bridge deck.

'Salim?'

The pirate king turned to see two of his men standing at the entrance to the bridge.

'Sansin is aboard with his damned Marines,' Salim hissed. 'Get us out of here and prepare to seal the bridge. Sansin's coming up! Get your weapons!'

The two men whirled and dashed back inside the bridge as Salim turned and aimed his pistol at the elevator doors, watching the deck numbers rise. He smiled grimly to himself as he waited.

'Foolish old man,' he sniggered to himself.

The two pirates returned and aimed their rifles at the elevator door.

The elevator whined as it reached the bridge deck and then the doors hissed open and Salim fired without hesitation into the interior. His two henchmen fired at the same moment, the three plasma blasts smashing into the back of the elevator in a cloud of blue smoke and a deafening crash amplified by the elevator's confined space.

Salim waited, his pistol still aimed at the elevator as the smoke cleared in thick whorls that glowed beneath the white ceiling lights.

The elevator was empty.

'Where the hell is he?' asked one of Salim's companions.

'He's behind you,' came a voice that sent a shudder of fear down Salim's spine.

Salim spun around but the man to his left inadvertently blocked him from aiming his pistol as two plasma blasts crackled out. Salim screamed and hurled himself behind the body of his henchmen as the two blasts hit the pirates, their weapons spinning from their grasp as they were hit.

Salim rolled awkwardly along the deck and scrambled for the safety of the bridge as he saw Idris Sansin floating in mid-air above the deck stairwell, his fatigues devoid of their iron-filled gravity plating, a pistol in his grasp as he fired twice.

Salim screamed as a shot narrowly missed the back of his legs and he hauled himself inside the bridge. He turned and saw Idris rocketing through mid-air across the deck outside the bridge. Salim reached up and hit the emergency close switch for the bridge and the doors hissed into motion, but before they closed Idris flew through the gap. Salim desperately raised his pistol as Idris kicked off the closing bridge doors and plunged down toward him.

Idris whirled in mid-air and forced Salim's pistol aside as he crashed down and smashed his head into the fat man's oily nose. Salim's nasal bridge collapsed with a dull crunch as he staggered backward into a control panel, one fat hand searching for the wicked curved blade at his belt.

Idris rushed forward as Salim yanked the blade free and screamed as he charged, his free hand desperately wiping tears from his eyes. Idris kicked off a control panel and hurled himself to one side to avoid the blade and Salim faltered, off-balance and half-blinded as Idris grabbed his wrist and lifted the blade up between them. The action pulled Idris down toward the deck and he put his feet down and found his balance.

Idris heaved one leg up and drove his knee deep into Salim's belly. The pirate's eyes bulged and his breath burst from his lungs with a deep rasping noise. Idris drove upward with both legs and forced Salim's knife arm up as the fat man doubled over in pain.

Salim flipped sideways and slammed backwards into a control panel, one hand still gripping the blade. Idris pinned Salim against the panel as he leaned his full weight into Salim's arm and bent it backwards over the panel.

Salim screamed and the blade fell from his grasp and hovered above the console as Idris jerked back from the pirate and then drove the sole of his boot into the fat man's face with a scream of rage. Salim's jaw collapsed under the blow and his eyes rolled up into their sockets as Idris grabbed the blade and then braced himself against the fat man's body and pressed the tip of the weapon against Salim's chest.

The pirate regained his focus and looked up at Idris, and the slimy smile spread across his face again as he bared his bloodied teeth and kept the grin there despite the obvious pain it caused him.

'You won't kill me,' he hissed, his breath rattling in his ruined nose. 'You're a Colonial, through and through. You know that I deserve a fair trial, it's what your government would have wanted.'

Idris held the blade at Salim's bulbous chest for a long moment.

'As you keep reminding me, Salim,' he growled, 'there is no Colonial government any more and nobody to witness what happens to you.'

Salim's eyes widened and he opened his mouth to protest, but Idris leaned his weight in behind the blade and it sank to the hilt into Salim's chest. The pirate king's mouth gaped wide and a strangled cry of agony pierced the air as the blade sliced through his heart and hit the metal surface of the control panel behind him.

Idris pushed back and away from Salim and watched as the cruel tyrant's life blood leaked away inside him and the mischievous, nasty glimmer of life slipped away from his eyes. The fat man slumped onto the deck, the hilt of his blade still poking from his chest.

Idris hovered in mid-air above Salim's bloodied form and wiped the sweat from his face. He was staring down at the dead pirate when he heard a voice call him.

'Captain?'

Idris turned and saw that a display screen was showing Mikhain and the Atlantia's bridge. He belatedly realised that Atlantia must have established contact with Arcadia and linked in, and that the entire bridge has just witnessed what he had done.

'Mikhain,' Idris gasped, both elated and shocked at the same time. 'Status report?' he demanded, to cover his discomfort.

'We're all out,' Mikhain replied. 'The Veng'en are pursuing us. We couldn't save those on the surface.'

'You did all you could, I have no doubt,' Idris said, his expression pinched with regret. 'And now, we have another vessel.'

A thunder of approaching boots alerted Idris and he aimed his plasma pistol out of the bridge as he turned. Lieutenant C'rairn, Corporal Djimon and two more Marines stepped fully inside and turned to seal the doors behind them. Idris grinned and lowered the pistol.

'About time, Lieutenant,' he greeted the officer. 'Are her hacking frequencies open?'

'She's ours,' the Marine replied as he looked over his shoulder. 'Time to finish this, sir.'

'Not us,' Idris breathed as he looked up at Mikhain. 'XO, would you care to take control of this ship and use it as you see fit?'

Mikhain's face almost burst with delight as he whirled to Lael.

'Access her computers and bring her here, right now!'

Idris smiled as he heard Lael's voice reply to Mikhain without hesitation.

'Aye, captain!'

Even before Idris could formulate further commands, Arcadia turned under Atlantia's control and a new voice could be heard breaking across the Atlantia's bridge. Evelyn's radio call sounded like music after the hellish roar of battle and death.

'Atlantia, this is Reaper Two, all craft away and all survivors aboard. Repeat, all craft away from the compound and climbing for orbit!'

Idris heard the cheer go up across Atlantia's bridge and saw Mikhain's shoulders slump as what looked like an eternity of stress drained from his shoulders.

*

'Reaper Flight, on me!'

Evelyn's Raython was in tight formation with the Phoenix as the surprisingly fast freighter rocketed out of Chiron's orbit, Teera's Raython on the far side of the ship. Evelyn broke away from the Phoenix as it turned for the safety of deep space and away from the brightly illuminated hull of the giant Veng'en cruiser looming before them.

'Roger that,' came Teera's reply. *'All fighters inbound.'*

Evelyn saw Teera form up on her wing, and ahead she saw the bright specks of eight Raythons swarming toward her.

'There's Arcadia!' Teera announced.

Evelyn had already seen the frigate moving toward Atlantia, the latter glowing with multiple fires and trailing debris that sparkled like diamond chips in the vast halo of sunlight filling the heavens as she rocketed toward the fight.

A cloud of Scythes swarmed toward them, wings flashing in the light as they pursued the Raythons.

'Enemy inbound,' Evelyn announced. 'Maintain course, we'll catch them as they pass.'

'Roger that, three!'

The six Raythons flashed past overhead as Evelyn opened fire on the incoming Scythes, the enemy fighters unprepared for the unexpected attack. Teera's cannons blasted into the tightly packed formation and several fighters exploded or banked away with their engines aflame as Evelyn sped between them toward the Veng'en cruiser.

'Reaper Flight, re-engage!' she commanded, and looked over her shoulder to see the fighters sweep into tight turns to engage the pursuing Scythes.

'This is Arcadia,' a voice called across the communications channel. *'Repeat, this is Arcadia, engaging now!'*

As Atlantia limped away from the Veng'en cruiser, the brilliant flare of the sunlight consuming her, so Arcadia took her place and bore down upon the damaged cruiser at attack speed, the two vessels closing head on. Evelyn saw the frigate break away to the left and then her starboard batteries opened up on the Veng'en cruiser's bow as it tried to match the manoeuver, a shower of blue-white plasma rounds hammering the cruiser's damaged hull as bright explosions flared and rocked the ship.

Evelyn flew overhead the vast hull as Arcadia battered her, lights across the Veng'en vessel flickering out as Atlantia reversed her course and let rip with any cannons that were still serviceable. The two frigates passed slowly on opposite sides of the Veng'en cruiser, each battering her with a crippling series of salvos. Evelyn heard cheers across the communications channel as the cruiser's hull was ripped open and an enormous blast split through the plating at her stern as the two frigates flew clear.

Evelyn squinted and looked away, one hand whipping up to shield her eyes as the cruiser's fusion cores erupted like dying stars. A supernova blast radiated outward and vaporised the entire rear-quarter of the cruiser in a brilliant halo of flame and radiation.

The Raython's wings rocked as the shockwave hit Evelyn and she fought for control, still hearing the cries of delight as the enemy vessel was torn apart by internal explosions. The cruiser's bow dipped toward Chiron IV, her stern trailing debris and glowing tendrils of plasma from her shattered engines as the gravity of the planet below began to pull her down.

'Reaper Flight, disengage,' Evelyn called. 'We'll mop up the survivors one by one!'

She watched as the Scythe fighters all suddenly ceased to engage the enemy, their command source gone as the Veng'en cruiser lost power and the last remaining lights flickered out around her bridge.

'Commander Ry'ere, report in,' Evelyn called as she watched the huge vessel slowly plunge toward a terminal descent into Chiron's atmosphere.

The radio calls and cheers gradually fell silent as Evelyn awaited a reply.

'Commander Ry'ere, report,' she repeated.

Moments later, the voice of Mikhain broke through.

'Commander Ry'ere was lost in the battle,' he said. *'We have detected no distress beacon from him. I'm sorry.'*

Evelyn stared momentarily into deep space, as though if she did not process what she had heard it would somehow cease to be true. Her voice when she replied was choked.

'How?'

'He charged the Veng'en cruiser and took out their sensor array, breaking the jamming,' Mikhain replied. *'His weapons could not have broken through their shields, so we believe that he performed a controlled impact into the array.'*

A deep silence enveloped the radio frequency as Evelyn and many others heard of what the CAG had done.

'You're sure he didn't get out?' Evelyn asked.

'We have detected no emergency distress beacon,' Mikhain repeated.

Evelyn looked briefly at the star radiating its massive clouds of cosmic rays and stellar debris, and then down at the aurora soaring through Chiron's atmosphere.

'Reaper Flight, Renegade Flight,' she called, 'all Raython's, visual search pattern. Make it fast!'

'It's no use,' Mikhain insisted, *'the debris field is too large and all of it will burn up within the hour.'*

'He didn't give up on me,' Evelyn snapped back as she recalled Andaim's search for her in the aftermath of the battle in the asteroid field months before. 'I'm not about to give up on him.'

'You'll never locate him before he hits the atmosphere,' Mikhain cautioned her.

Evelyn did not respond as she flew through the debris field of the Veng'en cruiser, the massive vessel now rolling slowly out of control and tilting ever more steeply toward Chiron IV. Clouds of sparkling metal fragments glittered around her amid massive torn chunks of hull plating as Evelyn slowed down, searching for any sign of a distress beacon on her instruments.

'The interference from the star is too strong,' Teera called out to her. *'I'm not seeing any signals from inside the debris field.'*

Evelyn looked behind her, at where the Veng'en cruiser had been and then at the faint debris trail that extended off around the planet, marking the cruiser's course as it had pursued Atlantia.

'Damn it,' she cursed, 'we're looking in the wrong place.' Evelyn threw her throttles forward and turned the Raython out of the debris field as she accelerated alongside the trail of metal fragments. 'He'd have hit her way back here,' she explained, 'if he ejected before impact, he'd be floating about somewhere before the cruiser started trailing debris.'

Evelyn guided the Raython alongside the debris trail and started to slow down again.

'Atlantia, send me the coordinates of Commander Ry'ere's last known position when he hit the cruiser, and include the cruiser's position too.'

'Stand by,' came a voice that Evelyn did not recognise but assumed was the current tactical officer aboard the frigate. *'Sending now.'*

Evelyn looked down and saw a tiny speck appear on her holographic tactical display alongside that of the Veng'en cruiser, off to starboard and below her. She turned toward the signal, and then as she passed through it she looked again at the image.

Evelyn figured that Andaim would have probably flown down the length of the cruiser's spine in order to maximize the damage he could cause upon impact with the solar array. He would have ejected just before impact and likely continued on a similar trajectory, possibly having rolled his Raython beforehand to angle his ejection slightly away from the cruiser to avoid hitting the hull.

She turned a practiced eye toward Chiron IV. In such a low orbit, and having ejected at such high velocity, the tiny thrusters on the Raython's ejection capsule would have been unable to slow him down enough to avoid being pulled in by the planet's gravity, and although the jamming had been broken the solar interference might have been powerful enough to shield his capsule's distress beacon from view.

Evelyn let her eye trace a natural arc, the most likely course Andaim would have been forced to take as he struggled to reduce his rate of descent toward the planet's atmosphere.

Evelyn threw her throttles open again even as the other squadron craft reached her and she raced down toward the planet's atmosphere. She could see small items of debris hitting the atmosphere below and lighting up as they were super-heated by atmospheric friction. She forced herself to keep an eye on her scanners instead, trusting in her instruments as she descended.

A blip sounded in her cockpit and a signal flared on her SAD, the sound a harsh, distorted beep transmitted once per second that demanded her attention, the signal bright red.

'Contact!' she yelped. 'I've got him! Repeat, I've found him!'

As Evelyn slowed, she saw the tumbling cockpit capsule of the Raython ahead of her. As it rotated slowly and the sunlight pierced its gloomy interior, she saw Andaim's face peering out. Slowly, without fuss, Andaim raised his right hand and with his left finger he tapped his wrist-com and raised an eyebrow.

Evelyn stifled a grin and transmitted again.

'He's alive,' she reported. 'Better send a shuttle before he gets too warm.'

***

XLIV

'You're a lucky girl.'

Meyanna Sansin ran a scanner over a sample of Evelyn's blood as she sat in Atlantia's sick bay. Around her on the ward's many beds were injured Marines, pilots, liberated slaves of all races and even a couple of pirates who had been caught up in the rush to escape Chiron IV and found themselves in with the fleeing slaves.

Meyanna kept her voice down as they spoke, despite the rush and bustle around them as nurses and orderlies struggled to keep up with the flow of patients flooding into the bay.

'I guess,' she replied. 'I didn't know what I was getting into.'

'Yes you did,' Meyanna whispered harshly. 'You just went to the wrong damned supplier.'

Evelyn knew that Qayin had not joined the exodus from Chiron IV, and that several Marines from Bravo Company had also not been present when the company had been mustered after the battle. What nobody knew for sure was whether they had all died on the surface or that some fled the battle in the confusion.

'I didn't think I could fly without the drug,' Evelyn whispered, partly in shame and partly because she still believed it to be true.

'That's an illusion caused by the medicine I gave you months ago,' Meyanna shot back. 'Now you believe that you need it to perform, that you're useless without it, and that's given you a confidence problem.' Meyanna removed her surgical gloves and tossed them into a secure waste bin. 'You think you're out of your depth when in my opinion you're in your element.'

'What's that supposed to mean?'

'That you're a natural born leader and a hell of a pilot,' Meyanna explained, 'but because you're a woman you're not prone to arrogance. You can't see how good you are at what you do. Men can, and then can't realise when they screw up.'

Evelyn sighed. 'I screwed up.'

'You made a bad decision, from which you must learn,' Meyanna corrected her.

'The captain's going to murder me for this,' Evelyn sulked.

Meyanna smiled to herself as she replied. 'Your time on the surface away from Devlamine has cleared the drug from your system. It didn't show up on the test, hence there's nothing for me to record.'

Evelyn stared wide-eyed at Meyanna, but then her heart sank. 'When will the withdrawal symptoms start?'

'They won't, because it looks like Qayin, for all his faults, had your back,' Meyanna explained. 'You could only have escaped from addiction with such mild symptoms if he supplied you with a diluted form of the drug.'

Evelyn frowned. 'He watered it down?'

'In a manner of speaking,' Meyanna confirmed. 'You should be experiencing massive withdrawal symptoms right now, but you're virtually clear. That means he only gave you enough to make you feel better about yourself, like a placebo with an extra kick to it. Clever guy.'

Evelyn sighed. 'Qayin. He's gone, isn't he?'

Meyanna nodded. 'As is Kordaz. Taron Forge made it out though, right?'

'Yeah,' Evelyn agreed. 'But who knows how long he'll stick around for?'

Meyanna seemed to sense a melancholy in Evelyn's response and was about to speak when another voice burst in.

'Who cares? You've got us!'

Evelyn turned and saw Teera stride in, her pale blue skin a strange hue under the sick bay lighting. Behind her walked Ishira, Erin and Stefan, and behind them the stocky, grumpy looking Caneerian that Evelyn had learned was named Dantin.

Teera flung her arms around Evelyn and hauled her to her feet. 'How you doin'?'

'I'll live,' Evelyn replied as she glanced at Meyanna, 'just a routine check up.'

'Ishira got her ship back,' Teera said as she released Evelyn and jabbed a thumb in Ishira's direction.

'And not a scratch on her,' Ishira said.

Of the forty eight stolen craft that lifted off from the surface of Chiron IV, twenty nine had made it to orbit and landed aboard either Atlantia or Arcadia after the Veng'en cruiser had plummeted to a fiery doom in the planet's atmosphere, taking its compliment of the Legion with it. Along with the destruction, the Legion would also have lost its new and unique ability to infect Veng'en.

'We owe you a great deal,' Stefan said, his metal prosthetic arm wrapped protectively around his daughter's shoulders. 'Your people turned up and didn't abandon us, and you stood by my family when I couldn't be there.'

'They're not my people,' Evelyn said, 'we're all in this together. I'm glad you all made it out of there.'

'Good to be back in deep space,' Ishira said.

'I'll miss the fresh air,' Dantin muttered.

Erin rolled her eyes and jabbed the stocky miner in the belly as Evelyn picked up her flight jacket and slipped it on.

'We're due for de-brief in ten,' Teera informed her. 'Best get moving.'

Evelyn nodded and glanced again at Meyanna. 'Thanks, doc'.'

Meyanan waved her away with a smile and Evelyn walked with Teera through the ship toward the briefing rooms. They passed a series of large windows looking out over the Chiron system. Evelyn saw the brilliant halo of the dying parent star and Chiron IV itself, a small disc silhouetted against the vibrant panorama of glowing stellar gases and starfields. The view was spectacular in itself, but what made her stop and stare was the shape of Arcadia, the frigate softly illuminated by the distant stellar glow as she cruised alongside Atlantia.

'Pretty special, huh?' Teera said. 'Been too long since we've seen something like this.'

Evelyn nodded, a tingle of excitement rippling down her spine as she realised that in taking on Salim Phaeon's pirates they had effectively doubled their strength. But the losses once again had been great.

'We got any idea what happened to Qayin yet?' Evelyn asked.

'Nope,' Teera replied. 'But he was alive when I last saw him up by the pirate's ships and shot one of those damned Veng'en off his back.'

Evelyn grabbed Teera's arm.

'A Veng'en, up by the slave ships?' she asked. 'You shot him?'

'He was fighting with Qayin,' Teera shrugged. 'Got him a great shot, right in the chest.'

Evelyn felt her guts turn over inside of her but she forced a smile onto her features, not willing to reveal to Teera who she in fact had killed.

'Good shooting,' she managed to say. 'And Qayin, he just vanished after that?'

'I didn't see,' Teera shrugged, 'I was too busy trying to make it to my Raython, but he was right alongside Salim's spacecraft could easily have made it aboard and escaped during the confusion. Can't say I blame the guy, really. He didn't exactly have patriotic Colonial blood running thick in his veins, did he?'

Evelyn did not reply as she led the way into the briefing room, where Atlantia's compliment of pilots were already seated. Before them stood Andaim, Mikhain and Captain Sansin. As Evelyn took a seat with Teera, Andaim stood forward and spoke loudly enough to be heard throughout the room.

'Ladies and gentlemen, I don't think that I need to elaborate on what we achieved yesterday,' he said. 'Our fleet is now doubled in size, and I'm happy to report that Arcadia is equipped with two full squadrons of Raythons and four more Corsair bombers.'

A cheer went up in the briefing room, the CAG smiling broadly and waving them all down as spoke.

'We've got a long way to go, but we're stronger now than we've ever been.' Andaim's gaze lingered on Evelyn for a moment, and Teera nudged her friend as Andaim went on. 'Arcadia is very much under-manned, but with Atlantia so full I'm confident we can provide manpower to both vessels as well as providing better living conditions for more of us. Arcadia was retired to life as a prison ship much the same as Atlantia, and is also equipped with a sanctuary in her hull for accommodation purposes. She's also in better shape right now, so we'll be using her for spare parts to repair some of the damage to Atlantia's hull.' Andaim's smile faded slightly. 'Despite our gains, we also lost four good pilots and their Raythons, along with twelve Marines and our Veng'en friend, Kordaz. This was a hard-won victory, so let's not forget the price we have had to pay for it.'

A silence descended on the room for a moment, and then Andaim went on.

'You also almost got rid of me too, but I'm afraid Reaper One scuppered your chances of a peaceful life and found me before I got fried.'

Heads turned to look at Evelyn, who managed to keep a straight face as she replied. 'My apologies folks, I'll try harder next time.'

A ripple of chuckles filled the room. The CAG smiled at Evelyn and stood back as the captain took centre stage.

'I can't add much to what Commander Ry'ere has said regarding both the heroism and the sacrifice displayed by you all,' he began. 'What started as a routine supply mission became a crisis and was almost the end of us, but once again we pulled through. As ever there was a high price to pay, but our renewed strength represents another victory for us over the Legion and another pace on the journey home.'

The captain broke his gaze from the crowd of pilots for a moment before continuing.

'We have now ascertained that during the engagement we lost Sergeant Qayin, not to enemy action but to cowardice.' A rush of whispers gusted across the room and Evelyn felt her guts clench. 'Analysis of data shows that Sergeant Qayin abandoned his post and his men to steal a freighter and escape Chiron IV. The ship he took was last seen jumping to super-luminal shortly after the battle began. In contrast the Veng'en warrior Kordaz, whom we took under our wing and who was often subject to fear and resentment from our compliment, undertook a dangerous mission to Chiron's surface under my command and blew the generators protecting Salim Phaeon's compound. I regret to inform you all that Kordaz died during the bombardment after being attacked by Qayin, a courageous Veng'en who learned to see human beings for what we truly are.'

Teera looked at Evelyn, the young pilot's features twisted with dismay as she learned that she had been responsible for killing Kordaz. Evelyn shook her head briefly to indicate that Teera should remain silent as the captain went on.

'Corporal Djimon of Alpha Company, who had been suspicious of Sergeant Qayin's motives for some time, undertook a personal mission to monitor Qayin's movements aboard ship, and has confirmed that it was almost certainly Qayin who was responsible for informing Salim of my identity as captain of Atlantia and of Kordaz's presence on the surface. Qayin's holopass was used to access Atlantia's War Room and send a signal to Salim Phaeon's compound alerting him to the attack. Given Qayin's notorious history of crime this doesn't surprise me in the least, despite the fact that he often fought ferociously on our behalf.'

The silence returned for a long beat.

'It has become clear,' the captain went on, 'that the Legion has now overcome Veng'en immunity to infection. The ship we were following was presumably clean before it encountered the Sylph all those months ago, and somehow the infection made it aboard the cruiser and then evolved to infect their crew. I am hoping that this adaption has died along with the Veng'en cruiser that harboured it, but we can only assume that, sooner or later, our current immunity will also be overcome by the Legion's infectors. We now have a weapon that can be used against them en masse – their chemical affiliation with Devlamine, the drug with which they first entered the human population, and which seems to override their programming somewhat like an addiction in itself. But their ability to evolve at high speed is something that we must all learn to guard against. No species, anywhere, can be considered immune to the Word or its Legion.'

The captain hesitated, and looked at them all.

'We very nearly were destroyed today, but once again we have come through. I hope that this affirms in all of your minds, as it does mine, that we are stronger together and always will be. Dismissed.'

***

Dean Crawford

XLV

Evelyn walked out onto Atlantia's landing bay and watched as a squadron of Raythons were prepared for launch. The captain had ordered the transfer of most of the fighters and bombers to Arcadia to allow repair work to continue on Atlantia's battered hull. Technicians swarmed over the fighters, refuelling and repairing, but for once her eyes were not drawn to the sleek Raythons but to the angular shape of a freighter parked at the rear of the bay.

Evelyn slowed as she saw Taron Forge and his fearsome sidekick, Yo'Ki, busily loading barrels aboard the Phoenix.

'Couldn't stay away from us, huh?' she asked.

Taron looked up, his shaggy brown hair almost covering his eyes.

'Not for long,' he replied with a tight smile.

Evelyn glanced at the barrels and saw that they were filled with water, fuel and other supplies essential for travel in deep space. 'You're leaving,' she realised.

'Damned right,' Taron replied. 'Almost got my ship vaporised getting off that damned rock. It's not something I intend to be doing again real soon.'

Evelyn managed to stifle a smile at Taron's forced selfishness.

'You saved hundreds of lives,' she said. 'People are looking up to you as a hero.'

Taron grunted an unintelligible reply and refused to look at her, focusing instead on lifting barrels onto a pallet that was being used to hoist them up into the Phoenix's hold four at a time. Evelyn helped him to push the pallet upward and peered up into the hold to see Yo'Ki working to secure the barrels inside.

'You have anything to do with Taron's heroic change of heart?' she called up.

Yo'Ki's exotic dark eyes flashed her a glance, but behind the hostility a wry smile touched her sculptured lips before she turned away.

'There are worse places to be, you know?' Evelyn said to Taron as she stepped down off the loading ramp.

Taron laughed, genuine humour melting his grimace. 'Sure. You all stand for everything I don't believe in and your crew has stolen my consciousness veil. I'm real glad to be here.'

Evelyn shrugged. 'Oh well, so long captain, have a good trip.'

Evelyn turned away and strode out across the landing bay. She made six paces before Taron called after her. She managed to bludgeon the smile that spread upon her features back into place and then turned, confronting the smuggler with a demure expression and a raised eyebrow.

'You're not one of them,' Taron said. 'You're more like me.'

'Is that so?' Evelyn almost laughed.

'You're brave, forthright and you know what you want,' Taron said.

Evelyn faltered, suddenly feeling exposed as though Taron could see right through her. The smuggler looked her up and down appraisingly.

'You should definitely come with me,' he said. 'We'd make a good team.'

'Really?' Evelyn asked flatly. 'I doubt that.'

'Then why'd you come down here?' Taron challenged, that grin still on his face. 'Couldn't stay away?'

Evelyn chuckled in disbelief. 'Wow, Taron, you've really got your mojo in overdrive, don't you? I came here because I want you to stay, because I think you'd be good for us.'

Taron leaned against one of the Phoenix's landing struts and watched her for a moment.

'Why bother?' he asked. 'We're all dead in the long run, so why worry about all of this?'

He gestured casually to the Atlantia around them, and his laconic grin was suddenly annoying to Evelyn.

'It's fatalism like that that will destroy us,' she replied. 'We're stronger together.'

Taron rolled his eyes. 'Ugh, I can almost hear my dear old dad.'

Evelyn clenched her fists by her sides as she walked up to Taron, her face barely inches from his as she spoke.

'I saw your dad,' she whispered. 'I was one of the last people to see him alive, or what was left of him.'

Taron's casual mirth slipped away and his eyes turned hard. 'I hope you hard-duked the son of a bitch for me.'

Evelyn shook her head slowly, a bitter smile curling from her lips.

'If you'd seen what had become of your father, of what the Legion did to him, you'd be leading every charge at every battle we'll ever fight.'

Taron stared at Evelyn long and hard and then he shook his head. 'I'd walk away, because you can't change the past.'

Taron turned his back to Evelyn and strode back toward his ship.

'No, but you can change the future,' Evelyn said.

She turned and walked away, but this time Taron did not call after her.

'He's not one of us.'

Evelyn came up short as she realised that Andaim was standing nearby and had watched the entire exchange.

'He's as human as we are,' she said defensively.

'That's up for debate,' Andaim shrugged, and then he smiled. 'I guess I owe you one.'

'We're even,' Evelyn replied. 'You had my back, I've got yours.'

'Which is what makes us different from him,' Andaim said as he gestured at Taron Forge. 'He's only interested in himself.'

'He came back,' Evelyn pointed out. 'We could never have got everybody off of Chiron IV before the bombardment if it were not for him.'

'He's got a conscience, good for him. I don't think it often gets ahead of his pragmatism though.'

Evelyn peered at Andaim. 'Why are you so keen to put him down?'

'Why are you so keen to big him up?'

'We need every pair of hands we can find, right?'

'What we need,' Andaim said as he moved closer to her, 'are people who are willing to fight for *each other*, not for themselves.' The CAG was looking down at Evelyn and she realised with some panic that she could not avoid his gaze as he went on. 'Loners have no future in this cosmos now.'

Two passes in one day was too much even for her. Evelyn draped a thin veil of amusement over her nerves. 'Is that your idea of a proposition?'

Andaim's eyes quivered in their sockets as his nerves overcame his bravado. 'It's…. It's a fact.'

Evelyn felt a wash of relief drench her soul as she realised that the CAG was not about to bare his soul in front of a hundred technicians and a smuggler on the landing bay. Mischief ran through her mind as she realised that Taron was watching them with interest. She reached up on tip-toe and kissed Andaim briefly on the lips.

'Thanks for being there,' she said.

Evelyn walked past the CAG and strode with far more confidence than she felt toward the bay exit, and she felt sure that she could sense the eyes of both men watching her as she left.

*

'So, can we use it?'

Mikhain, Bra'hiv and Captain Sansin stood in Meyanna Sansin's laboratory as they looked down at the shimmering veil recovered from Taron Forge. Sealed in an air-tight cylinder, the veil seemed partially transparent and constructed of something between a liquid and a gas, like plasma but even more ephemeral.

'It's impossible to handle physically,' Meyanna explained. 'It can only be deployed by machinery, but so far it is effective on all biological species tested. It can render them unconscious for as long as required. I don't know how useful it would be in battle though. It seems extremely delicate otherwise.'

Mikhain looked at the captain. 'What are you thinking?'

Idris inhaled a deep breath and expelled it as he put his hands on his hips.

'We don't know anything about this technology or who created it,' he said, 'and neither does the Word. There could be technologies out there beyond the Icari Line that could render the Legion useless or even dead. We've just proven it possible with Devlamine.'

'There's also the small matter of crossing the Icari Line,' Mikhain pointed out. 'It's there for a reason: we don't know what lurks beyond it.'

'We know what lurks *within* it,' Idris replied, 'and it's what we're trying to defeat. Even though we've doubled our strength we're still no match for the Word. It has control of the entire Colonial Fleet and we'll be annihilated the moment we try to enter the Etherean system.'

'You're advocating a change of plan?' Bra'hiv said. 'Most of the crew believe we're heading home to take on the Word.'

'We are,' Idris said. 'But we may be well served by taking on a diversion and seeking new allies and weapons to aid us in the fight.'

A silence descended as they digested the possibilities of such a course of action.

'What's out there beyond the Line may be more dangerous than what we're leaving behind,' Mikhain reminded him. 'Most ships that have crossed the Line have never been seen again.'

'But some have,' Idris insisted. 'Salim Phaeon spent half of his career beyond the reach of Colonial forces. All we need is a suitable guide.'

'But who would know where to go and how to...' Mikhain winced. 'Oh no, surely not *him*?'

Idris smiled but said nothing.

'We spent weeks tailing a Veng'en cruiser and it nearly destroyed us,' Bra'hiv pointed out, keeping his voice reasonable. 'Now you want to follow a man who despises us and stands against everything we're trying to build?'

They turned as Evelyn tapped on the glass wall of the laboratory and Meyanna hit a switch to let her in. Evelyn walked inside the laboratory and up to Captain Sansin as she shook her head.

'He didn't buy it,' she said. 'He's leaving at the first opportunity.'

'Taron Forge is his own man,' Idris replied.

'We should convince him to stay somehow,' Evelyn protested. 'He's a good pilot and somewhere inside of him there's a good man, I can see it.'

'That's no good to us if Taron cannot see it himself,' Idris pointed out.

'We should let him go,' Bra'hiv agreed. 'The man's a menace, just like Qayin was.'

'Qayin was misguided,' Evelyn shot back, 'so is Taron, but that doesn't make them our enemies.'

'It does when they start betraying our own people,' Bra'hiv snapped.

'Hang on to every soul, isn't that what you've been saying captain?' Evelyn challenged.

Idris sighed.

'Yes, but not every soul can be saved,' he replied and looked at Mikhain. 'Allow Captain Forge to depart as soon as he wishes.'

'Aye, cap'ain,' Mikhain replied and walked toward the exit.

'Then report to the bridge,' Idris added. 'We'll talk there.'

Mikhain nodded, curiosity swimming behind his eyes, and then departed.

'Taron will not be easy to track,' Bra'hiv warned as the XO left the laboratory. 'He's used to evading Colonial ships and will no doubt want to disappear as fast as he can.'

Idris nodded as he looked at Evelyn. 'You planted the tracker?'

'It's in place, attached to their stores,' Evelyn nodded. 'It'll be packed deep inside the Phoenix's holds by now.'

'You bugged him?' Bra'hiv stammered in surprise. 'How the hell did you manage that?'

Idris looked at Evelyn and smiled. 'You have the most remarkable ability to get under the skin of men and make them drop their guard, Evelyn.'

Evelyn shrugged but said nothing.

'Aren't you forgetting something?' Meyanna asked the captain. 'We have an extra thousand souls with us now. If we're about to go galavanting into uncharted space, don't you think they should have their say?'

'I don't know what they could offer,' Idris replied. 'They don't know what's out there any more than we do.'

'All the more reason,' Meyanna insisted, 'to allow them to speak. Mikhain organised their vote for a new spokesperson, somebody to replace our lost councillors.'

Idris sighed and rubbed his temples. 'And you think that will placate them, remove some of the issues we've been having?'

'It'll be a damned good start,' Meyanna replied. 'These may be military vessels but the majority of the people aboard are civilians and that's never going to change. You need to accept that and start engaging with the populace before they reject you entirely.'

'I doubt that any mutiny will occur for a while now,' Evelyn said. 'Word travels fast aboard ship and they're already talking about how the captain killed Salim Phaeon with his own hands. There are about a thousand slaves who'll gladly follow you to hell and back right now.'

Idris smiled briefly at Evelyn, but he put his hands behind his back and nodded to his wife.

'Very well,' he said finally. 'Count the damned vote, and I'll announce to the people who will speak for them.'

***

XLVI

'Salim is dead, and so is Qayin.'

Mikhain's whisper was harsh as he walked and the big Marine alongside him nodded with satisfaction.

'We are better and stronger without them,' Djimon said as he walked.

'I see you got your rank back,' Mikhain observed, noting the Sergeant's flash on Djimon's shoulder.

'Reinstated after Qayin's betrayal of his men,' Djimon confirmed. 'Captain Sansin suspected Qayin of dealing Devlamine from the start, and pulled me out of the cells to be deployed with Lieutenant C'rairn as his escort. General Bra'hiv has now handed full control of Bravo Company to Lieutenant C'rairn, while I support the general at Alpha Company.'

Mikhain walked slower as he approached the bridge.

'We lost Kordaz,' he said.

'That was to be expected,' Djimon replied without concern. 'All Veng'en deserve nothing but death, it's the only language they understand. With Salim now also dead there is nobody to know what happened.'

'Except you,' Mikhain pointed out.

Djimon's broad jaw fractured with a thin smile. 'Your secret is safe with me,' he replied. 'Mutually assured destruction, I think we can call it. Agreed?'

Mikhain frowned.

'The captain suspects something. He knows that Kordaz was betrayed, and only believes Qayin's involvement because of one pilot's witness testimony and the fact that you obtained Qayin's holopass. If Qayin is not dead...'

'He's gone either way,' Djimon insisted. 'He's not going to come back and even if he did nobody would believe him, not even his own men whom he also left behind. Qayin is history and so is Kordaz. We must focus on now.'

Mikhain stopped outside the bridge and turned to face Djimon. 'The captain's killing of Salim Phaeon has won him a new league of devoted followers. They all think he's a damned hero for killing Salim.'

'He is, in a way,' Djimon replied. 'But one act does not a great man make. All you have to do is maintain support among the military staff and win them over one man and one woman at a time.'

'And if he knows?' Mikhain snapped. 'If he knows what we have done?'

'Then we must deal with it one act at a time,' Djimon insisted. 'But if you try to hang me out to dry in there, I swear I'll bring you down with me.'

'What makes you think the captain will listen to you?'

'I'm the only one who knows exactly how you set Qayin up and betrayed the captain,' Djimon replied.

'That isn't enough,' Mikhain smirked. 'You'd face maroon protocol before the day was out.'

'Not if I can prove it,' Djimon sneered back.

Mikhain opened his mouth to protest but Djimon hit the button beside the bridge doors and backed away as the access request was granted and the doors slid open.

Mikhain turned and faced the door as he struggled to compose himself. Djimon watched him walk inside and then turned and marched back the way he had come. From the pocket of his fatigues he retrieved a small, portable recording device. He looked down at it as he walked, and accessed two saved files that he watched.

The sergeant smiled as he relived Mikhain betraying Kordaz to Salim Phaeon in the War Room, and their conversation of moments before. Sergeant Djimon slipped the device back into his pocket and kept walking.

*

'XO on the bridge!'

Captain Idris Sansin did not look up at Mikhain as he stood to attention before the command platform. Mikhain watched as Idris finished reading a report and then set it down before him.

'How long have we known each other, Mikhain?'

'Twenty six years,' Mikhain replied, 'give or take.'

Idris nodded, his expression sombre as he finally made eye contact. 'Long enough, I think, to know when something is amiss.'

Mikhain swallowed as apprehension flushed like ice water through his veins. 'I'd say so.'

Idris stood up and moved to stand before it, confronting Mikhain. The XO tensed slightly, uncertain of what to expect. The bridge around them had fallen silent, all eyes watching the two men.

'We have a traitor aboard, Mikhain.'

Mikhain nodded without thinking. 'Qayin,' he replied, 'but he's gone.'

'No,' Idris said as he walked past Mikhain and folded his hands behind his back. 'Qayin was a criminal and frankly a fool, but he possessed a twisted sort of loyalty beneath the bravado. This wasn't the sort of thing he would have done.'

'What wasn't?' Mikhain asked.

'Betrayal,' Idris replied. 'Qayin knew that Kordaz had risked his life for us more than once. What happened was cold-blooded treachery, an act of vengeance of some kind, and I need to know who did it.'

Mikhain frowned.

'Captain, with all due respect Qayin was seen fighting to the death with Kordaz, and would have been killed if one of our pilots had not intervened.'

'Teera Milan,' Idris identified the pilot. 'That's very true, and it was she who confirmed Qayin's abandonment of his men, and us, in battle. What bothers me is the fact that Kordaz was betrayed before Qayin ever got to the surface and that nobody told Qayin that Kordaz was down there. He wasn't in the loop.'

Mikhain held his nerve.

'Somebody else must have passed the information on,' he suggested. 'Maybe Taron Forge or one of Qayin's lackeys? There were witnesses to the launch of the shuttle that carried Kordaz to the surface.'

'No,' Idris shook his head. 'Nothing quite fits when you think about it. I think that somebody else aboard Atlantia betrayed Kordaz and they may have had the best intentions when they did so, but they condemned a brave warrior to death. I want to know who did it, Mikhain, and I want to know that you're going to help me.'

Mikhain lifted his chin. 'Of course, captain.'

'Good,' Idris said. 'Now, tell me why you were so against Andaim Ry'ere commanding Atlantia?'

Mikhain swallowed thickly, acutely aware of the command crew listening in.

'I didn't know at the time that your promotion of the commander was designed as a deception,' he explained.

'No. But that's not what I asked, is it?'

Mikhain sucked in a lungful of air. 'I felt that he was too young and inexperienced for a full command, captain, and that the choice may have endangered the crew and compliment.'

'And that you should have been chosen in his 'stead,' Idris added.

'Somebody more experienced in command, captain,' Mikhain replied. 'Not necessarily me.'

Idris moved to stand before the XO.

'Mikhain, in the last twenty four hours you have done nothing but question my every command. You have played Devil's advocate on numerous occasions, have opposed many of my ideas and orders and have frequently spent far too much time fraternising with junior officers in an attempt to curry favour at a grass roots level.'

Mikhain opened his mouth to protest but Idris forestalled him with an open palm as he went on.

'You have directly attempted to undermine my command on the bridge in front of fellow officers, and have flagrantly disobeyed my orders on numerous occasions when you have seen fit to do so. You represent the most powerful force working against my command and thus a danger to the continued team-work of our personnel both on the bridge and within the wider service aboard this ship.'

Mikhain felt his eyes sting and he tried to speak, but the captain's stern gaze silenced him.

'You leave me absolutely no choice, Mikhain,' Idris said finally, 'but to permanently remove you from your position aboard Atlantia.'

Mikhain felt as though his guts had dropped several decks below him. Tears welled in his eyes and his legs felt as though they had turned to rubber, but somehow he realised that he had only himself to blame. He could not bring himself to admit to the captain what he had truly done, but nor could he deny that this was a suitable and just punishment. From somewhere within he excavated sufficient courage to maintain his bearing and lift his chin, his voice sounding weak in his own ears as he replied.

'I understand, captain,' he rasped.

'Good,' Idris replied with finality. 'I didn't want to have another argument here on Atlantia's bridge. I would be relieved if you would do me the honour of handing over your Executive Officer's shoulder insignia and leave this bridge immediately.'

Mikhain's chest felt hollow. He reached up to his shoulders and removed his insignia, and then handed them over to the captain. Idris snatched them briskly away and tossed them across the bridge as though they were nothing more than trash. Mikhain stood in shameful silence, the eyes of the entire command crew burning into him.

The captain reached out and patted Mikhain on the shoulder with a sympathetic smile.

'Dismissed,' he said. 'You are to report immediately when you reach Arcadia's bridge.'

Mikhain worked his jaw and managed to dredge his voice back. 'What will my duties be?'

Idris grinned and rolled his eyes as he nodded toward Mikhain's shoulder.

Mikhain looked down, and through blurred eyes he saw a Captain's insignia now adorning his shoulder, emblazoned with Arcadia's logo. He almost lost his balance as his head snapped back to stare at Idris and his jaw gaped open.

'You should see your face,' Idris smiled. 'You looked like you've been slapped. Congratulations, captain. Your new command awaits.'

A burst of applause crashed through the bridge and Mikhain staggered to one side and gripped the rail as relief flooded through him. He looked at Idris and shook his head, his jaw aching as a smile spread wide across it.

'Damned old fool, you nearly gave me a heart attack.'

Idris clapped him on the shoulder again.

'Good, you'll get a lot more moments like that now you're in command, Mikhain. Be ready for them.' Idris gripped his shoulder tightly. 'You held Atlantia in position and protected everybody on the surface from a Veng'en bombardment for almost an hour, Mikhain. You never wavered and you've never been afraid to question my judgement. I know that you have my back, just as the Admiralty had ours back in the day. We'll have yours here.'

Mikhain worked to dislodge the tight knot of shame that suddenly clogged his throat.

'Aye, cap'ain.'

Idris stood back and snapped off a quick salute. 'Now get the hell off my bridge and get back to work.'

Mikhain smiled broadly and returned the salute, then turned and marched off the bridge to the applause around him. Moments later he was gone, and Commander Andaim moved alongside Idris.

'You sure he's ready for this?' Andaim asked. 'Sit-rep shows he was almost overcome during the battle.'

'Almost,' Idris said, 'but not quite, and I can't command both ships. Mikhain's the most qualified for the job and he was obviously keen to gain command of Atlantia. This is the best I can do to keep him onside.'

'You think he's a threat of some kind?'

Idris turned to Andaim and spoke softly so that nobody else on the bridge could hear.

'When I was on Arcadia's bridge with Salim, the pirate addressed Mikhain by his name,' Idris confided. 'Yet Mikhain never revealed himself on our bridge nor was his name spoken in Salim's presence in this entire engagement.' Idris's eyes bored into Andaim's. 'How could he have known the XO's name?'

Andaim's features cracked like thin ice. 'You should have him arrested immediately,' he hissed.

'No,' Idris insisted, and sighed softly. 'These are difficult times Andaim, and they're testing us all. Mikhain may have sought control of Atlantia, but he also fought to protect her and all of us too. He's conflicted, but we cannot do without him.'

'You could have given Arcadia's command to somebody else!' Andaim snapped.

'Or I could extend the opportunity to win Mikhain's loyalty back while removing the motivation which drove his betrayal, his jealousy and desire for command. That's why I've got you here,' he said. 'You'll command the Raythons aboard Arcadia and report back to me.'

'This is a dangerous game,' Andaim replied. 'If Mikhain goes AWOL with Arcadia…'

'Keep an eye on how the new captain goes about his duties and if he gets out of hand we'll have ample warning. And keep an eye on those damned Marines of Bravo Company too.'

'You're sending *them* over there? I thought you'd send Alpha and keep some loyal blood aboard Arcadia.'

'I wanted to,' Idris replied, 'but I also want Mikhain's hand weakened a little. I don't want him becoming a Fleet Commander, just a captain.'

'Divide and conquer,' Andaim said.

'Indeed,' Idris replied. 'Now, get over there with your pilots and leave Atlantia to me. While repairs are under way we'll be vulnerable, so I want a full fighter escort and patrol sweep in action until we're ready to depart.'

'Aye, cap'ain,' Andaim replied, and walked away.

***

XLVII

The Arcadia's sanctuary was filled with over two thousand souls, Atlantia controlled via the Arcadia's bridge as the remains of humanity gathered together in one place for the first time since the apocalypse that had enveloped Ethera and the populated core systems.

'Been a long time since I've seen this many people in one place,' Teera noted.

Evelyn nodded, looking at the sea of civilians behind them, punctuated by the occasional looming bulk of an Ogrin.

She was seated along with the pilots of Reaper Squadron at the front of a raised dais situated in the heart of a tree-lined valley. It was deceptively easy to believe that the horrors of the past three years were all just the remnants of a particularly bad dream and that in fact they were all seated on Ethera on a warm summer afternoon.

Nearby sat the pilots of the Renegade Squadron, along with the entire compliment of Marines under the command of General Bra'hiv. The military contingent was arrayed before their civilian charges, and in front of them stood Captain Idris Sansin and Captain Mikhain. Sansin's voice echoed out over the crowd as he spoke into a microphone, his words amplified by speakers arrayed around them.

'Ladies, gentlemen,' Sansin began, 'Ogrin, Hybrid and Denesian, welcome. You are slaves no longer, and will be welcome to share with us the freedom of our ships.'

A clatter of applause and a few cheers went up from the gathered civilians as they learned officially that they were no longer subject to piratical tyranny. Evelyn watched them as the captain spoke, but found herself wondering about Commander Andaim and Taron Forge. The CAG was not present, leading a patrol to protect the two frigates, and Taron was already long gone, having blasted off as soon as he was cleared to leave.

'By now you will all have learned of the major events that have occurred recently aboard Atlantia, and her engagements against the Legion and other species it has infected,' Idris went on. 'Our mission is, somehow, to build our strength and take back the worlds that belong to us, to crush the brutal machine that has taken so many innocent lives and ensure that it never, ever happens again.'

Idris looked them over silently before continuing.

'We have formulated the opinion, based on the experiences of others who have travelled before us, that our best means of defeating the Word is to obtain technologies that it cannot defend against. To do this we must locate and learn to deploy devices that we have never before encountered, and to find them we have no choice but to travel to places that no human being has ever seen.' Idris paused. 'We must travel beyond the Icari Line into uncharted space and endeavour to find a way to defeat the Word.'

A rush of whispers and gasps of astonishment broke out among the crowd and a number of voices cried out.

'You just saved our lives and now you want to get us all killed?'

'Nobody knows what's beyond the Icari Line!'

'They put it there for a reason!'

'Nobody has ever come back from there alive!'

Idris raised his hands for calm and let the speakers amplify his voice, keeping his tone level.

'We know all of this,' he said, 'and as such we cannot compel you all to follow us. I have been convinced by my fellow officers that as passengers aboard Atlantia and Arcadia, you have a say in what happens to us. If we go into battle, then by your presence here you go with us, and now that need has been addressed. You all have received the chance to vote on a new councillor, a voice through whom you may speak and voice your concerns. I understand that the results of the ballot have been counted. Captain?'

Mikhain stood up, and Evelyn noted a soft but notable ripple of applause from some quarters of the audience for the former XO as he stood and held aloft an envelope.

'Almost a thousand votes from Atlantia's civilian contingent,' he said, 'each cast for a selected number of candidates. The military and command were blocked from voting, allowing the civilian contingent an unhindered choice of candidates and anonymity in your votes.'

Mikhain ripped open the envelope and retrieved a small slip of paper. Evelyn saw his eyes widen as he looked at it, and then he glanced over his shoulder.

'The candidate chosen to represent the people of this fleet,' he said, 'is Doctor Meyanna Sansin.'

More applause burst out among the civilians as Meyanna got to her feet and smiled brightly, although clearly surprised at being the first choice, and Teera leaned in.

'Not surprised, she's been treating people ever since we left Chiron. She's probably the most popular person aboard Atlantia.'

'And the captain's wife,' Evelyn pointed out. 'There are going to be some unhappy voters out there.'

As if on cue, a ripple of moans and shouted accusations of vote-rigging tainted the scene. Idris Sansin stepped up to the microphone.

'Believe me,' he said, 'if this vote had been rigged, I'd have rigged it to have anybody other than my wife as councillor. I never get my own way when she's around, *ever*.'

A ripple of laughter swept across the gathered civilians and drowned out the complaints with ease as Meyanna approached the microphone to speak softly but clearly.

'Thank you, everybody, I really wasn't expecting this. I'll do my best to accommodate the new role alongside my work in the hospital and speak for you when you need me to.' She glanced at her husband. 'And he's right, I do always get my way.'

More chuckles, and Teera shrugged.

'I don't know, I think this could work out really well.'

Evelyn glanced at Mikhain, who was clapping along with everybody else but wearing a thin smile that looked anything but earnest.

'Yeah,' she replied. 'But for who?'

Captain Sansin returned to the microphone.

'As of now, and for forty eight hours, Atlantia and Arcadia are officially stood-down but for a skeleton crew and fighter patrols. We have a long way to go ahead of us, so enjoy this moment of peace while you can. Dismissed.'

More cheers went up, the captain skilfully winning the majority of the audience to his side as he stepped down and the military contingent got up from their seats.

'Well, whatever happens it's going to be new for all of us,' Teera said cheerfully. 'Let's just hope that there's something friendly beyond the Icari Line.'

Evelyn managed a smile in response, but somehow she felt certain that whatever lay in the vast expanses of uncharted space ahead of them was likely to be anything but friendly.

*

The wind.

It gusted and whirled, tugged and buffeted across the lonely, smouldering plain. Above the roiling pillars of thick oily smoke that puffed from weakly fluttering flames, clouds scudded across a sky awash with glowing watercolour streaks of radiation that bathed the surface in a rippling light as though the air itself were aflame.

He opened his eyes.

The sky looked different, a haze of flickering, monochromatic light. The atmosphere, he realised. The dying star's raging geo-magnetic storms had broken through and were bathing the planet in microwaves of countless frequencies.

Kordaz heaved in a lungful of air and his colour vision sharpened to reveal the glorious shades bathing the heavens above. He lay for what felt like aeons, just staring upward and unaware of his body. Slowly, fragments of awareness reconnected themselves like forgotten dreams and he sensed pain in his chest and limbs, a dull, throbbing ache that was not at all unpleasant. The pain of healing surged through his synapses and he breathed deeply again before, entirely on impulse, he sat upright as chunks of broken soil fell from his body.

Around him the pirate's compound was a smouldering wasteland of churned earth and soil, burning fragments of ships, bodies and weapons twisting pillars of smoke up into the sky around him. Flames licked at the edges of shattered spacecraft hulls as he turned his head left and right to survey the scene.

Soil fell from his head and shoulders as he moved, and he looked down to see amid the dust and grit tiny machines fluttering from his body to be snatched away on the breeze like ash.

Kordaz froze as his memory leaped back to him and he grasped at his chest, then looked down. A clump of long-dead infectors fell away, draining from his grip like black sand between his fingers as he looked down at his chest and saw that the charred cavity where he had been shot was now filled with a metallic sheen, the surface strangely smooth and silvery. He tentatively touched it with one finger and felt it, cold and yet fluid, a metal and yet as flexible as flesh.

Kordaz looked down and saw patches of the metal wherever his body had been injured: lesions sealed, abrasions re-surfaced. Both horrified and amazed, he reached up to his eyes and felt them, sensed beneath his fingertips the metal obscuring his face.

Dead infectors tumbled away like iron filings, and he realised that all around him were Hunters, not burned like those attacked by the Marines but simply devoid of life as though short-circuited. Kordaz looked up to the heavens burning with aurora, and he made the connection. The solar flares had wiped out the attacking hordes before they had been able to infect his mind, but not before they had repaired the damage to his body.

Kordaz slowly got to his feet and stood amid the smouldering wasteland and then he looked up once more to the heavens as images of Qayin and the pilot who had shot him flared as brightly as the dying star in his mind.

Betrayal. Anger pulsed through his heart like fire, rage setting his nerve endings aflame. Fuelled by the pain surging through his wounds Kordaz opened his mouth and screamed up at the sky as he searched for any sign of Atlantia.

His deafening roar faded away, snatched by uncaring winds and cast into the distance. It was answered by the lonely howls of beasts that even now were converging on the smell of carrion, the countless burning corpses around him like a beacon for carnivores for countless cubits downwind.

Kordaz searched the smoky gloom around him and there in the distance he saw a small number of abandoned spacecraft that had partially escaped the bombardment. Freighters, a couple of aged interceptors, some old Colonial prospecting craft, all of them leaning at odd angles from collapsed undercarriage and with hulls scorched by the plasma blasts that had levelled the compound.

Kordaz set off toward them and spent several minutes examining them one by one before he selected the craft in best condition. He looked about and saw amid the debris fuel canisters, food packages, water tanks and countless abandoned weapons and plasma magazines strewn across the fields.

Kordaz, revenge poisoning both of his hearts, began gathering the supplies he would need to give chase to Atlantia and settle a score with a humanity he now hated once again with all of his fearsome passion.

**

ABOUT THE AUTHOR

Dean Crawford is the author of the internationally published series of thrillers featuring *Ethan Warner*, a former United States Marine now employed by a government agency tasked with investigating unusual scientific phenomena. The novels have been *Sunday Times* paperback bestsellers and have gained the interest of major Hollywood production studios. He is also the enthusiastic author of many independently published Science Fiction novels.

REVIEWS

All authors love to hear from their readers. If you enjoyed my work, please do let me know by leaving a review on Amazon. Taking a few moments to review our works lets us authors know about our audience and what you want to read, and ultimately gives you better value for money and better books.

Printed in Great Britain
by Amazon